THE VORPAL BLADE

COLIN FORBES

THE VORPAL BLADE

POCKET
BOOKS

LONDON · SYDNEY · NEW YORK · TOKYO · SINGAPORE · TORONTO

First published in Great Britain by Simon & Schuster UK Ltd, 2001
This edition first published by Pocket Books, 2002
An imprint of Simon & Schuster UK Ltd
A Viacom Company

5 7 9 10 8 6

Simon & Schuster UK Ltd
Africa House
64–78 Kingsway
London WC2B 6AH

www.simonsays.co.uk

Simon & Schuster Australia
Sydney

A CIP catalogue record for this book is available
from the British Library

Typeset by Palimpsest Book Production Limited,
Polmont, Stirlingshire
Printed and bound in Great Britain by
Cox & Wyman Ltd, Reading, Berkshire

Author's Note

All the characters portrayed are creatures of the author's imagination and bear no relationship to any living person.

The same principle of pure invention applies to all residences, villages and apartments in both the USA and Europe. Also to companies.

Prologue

'How do you know the body was Adam Holgate's – if the head was missing?' Tweed asked.

It was a misty night in London. December was being ushered in with normal weather. Tweed sat beside Chief Superintendent Roy Buchanan, who drove the unmarked police Volvo expertly through the almost deserted streets. The windscreen wipers went *whip-whap*, keeping the view clear. Seated in the back, Paula Grey, Tweed's trusted assistant, wanted to ask questions but kept quiet.

'Simple,' Buchanan replied. 'I unzipped the body bag wide enough to feel inside his jacket. He was carrying his security pass with photo for ACTIL, the huge organization he worked for after he walked out on you.'

'Holgate didn't take much vital information from us,' Paula commented. 'He never entered our building in Park Crescent. Howard at least had sufficient sense to post him inside the Communications section further along the Crescent.'

'Bray, where the body was discovered, is close to the Thames,' Tweed remarked. 'What the devil was Holgate doing out in such a remote spot? Dragged out of the river, I gather. Is that right?'

'Not exactly. The corpse had been swept into a shallow creek. Chap walking his dog found him, used his mobile to call the Yard.'

'And you arranged for it to be sent to Professor Saafeld's

place in Holland Park. Presumably because he is the most distinguished pathologist we have.'

'I did.' Buchanan's voice was grim. 'It was a particularly brutal murder and I wanted the best man to do the autopsy. I phoned you, picked you up on my way. Holgate was yours once.'

'Doesn't make sense,' remarked Bob Newman, international correspondent, who sat beside Paula. 'Removing the head suggests an attempt to delay identification. Yet the killer leaves the security pass inside his pocket.'

'No sense at all,' Buchanan agreed. 'This one worries me.'

He glanced at Tweed, who was a man of uncertain age and medium height, sturdily built inside his dark overcoat. His thick hair was dark, his face clean-shaven, with a strong nose on which he perched his horn-rim glasses. Couldn't tell anything from his expression and you could pass him in the street without noticing him, a trait which he found helpful in his capacity as Deputy Director of the SIS.

Buchanan was taller, lean and lanky, and in his forties. He sported a trim moustache and a stern look which disconcerted his many subordinates. In Tweed's shrewd opinion he was the most competent policeman in the country. The two men trusted each other completely.

'Nearly there,' Buchanan remarked. 'Holland Park is a nice area with some good houses.' He swung off into a side road, pulled up in front of an entrance with tall wrought-iron gates. The mansion was concealed behind dark evergreen trees and shrubs bordering the short drive. Tweed jumped out and went to the speakphone, a metal grille let into one of the stone pillars, and pressed a button.

'Tweed here with Roy Buchanan.'

'About time,' a gruff voice replied as the gates swung open. On either side new eight-foot-high railings spanned a low wall. London these days had become a jungle of crime and its inhabitants had installed every form of protection – glare lights which illuminated as soon as you approached a doorway, strong grilles over lower windows, the most sophisticated burglar alarms. It was as though the great city was under siege. Which in a way it was.

They walked up the drive, Buchanan's long legs striding ahead of them. Saafeld's home and workplace was a handsome square house built of stone and three storeys high. Tweed noticed the basement windows had been bricked up since his last visit. What have we come to? he thought as one of the double doors opened when the glare light came on, almost blinding Paula, who shielded her eyes.

'Come inside,' growled Saafeld. 'Don't just stand there.'

He's in a bad mood, Paula thought. Never known him to be like this before. Saafeld was a short, powerfully built man in his late fifties. His hair was turning white but his complexion was ruddy, his movements swift. They entered a large hall with a wood-block floor and various doors leading off it.

Saafeld's expression became amiable as he greeted Paula with a hug. He held her at length. Five feet six tall, she had long well-coiffured dark hair which touched her shoulders, well-shaped bone structure, a chin which hinted at stubbornness. Her blue eyes missed nothing, and when she smiled many men would do anything for her. Slim, with a good figure, she wore a dark two-piece suit and a silk scarf round her long neck. Releasing her, Saafeld turned and glared from under bushy eyes at the men.

'For God's sake, you won't believe it. I've been raided. Come into the morgue . . .'

Crossing the hall he produced a code card and descended stone steps to a heavy door, in which he inserted the card. They walked into a small room protected by armoured glass from floor to ceiling. Once inside, Saafeld closed the outer door, inserted his card into another slot, and they followed him into a large room below ground. The morgue.

Paula's nostrils were immediately assailed by a familiar odour. Formalin. Used for preserving specimens and bodies. Along one wall were rows of large metal drawers where the bodies were stored. A large metal-topped table in the middle of the room was empty. Above it hung cameras suspended from telescopic arms. Saafeld pointed at the empty table.

'The body was there when they came and took it away – the body from Bray,' he rasped.

'Who took it away?' Tweed asked quietly.

'A delegation led by your friend, Tweed, Mr Nathan Bloody Morgan of Special Branch.'

'On what authority?' Tweed asked, still quietly.

'He had an official document from the local Chief Constable authorizing the body's immediate return to Maidenhead. On top of that,' he fumed, 'there was a brief letter from the Home Secretary confirming the order. I had to let them walk off with the body immediately. I said they came with a delegation: Nathan Morgan had arrived with a team of paramedics, an ambulance, plus two thuggish Special Branch officers to back him up. It's outrageous.'

'It's also sinister. Why is the government involved? The whole operation reeks of a cover-up. Had you time to start the autopsy?'

'No. I had examined the body for fibres and other debris. I omitted to tell Morgan about this. He was aggressive in checking whether I had taken any photographs.' Saafeld smiled grimly. 'I told him no, although I have two sets of colour prints. Then I shouted at him, told him to get the hell out of my house, that I was going to complain, nail his hide to the wall. He didn't like that. Tried to take back the documents but I refused to let him have them.'

'You had finished the photography?'

'Yes. Luckily my assistants had gone home so I took the

photos myself. No witnesses. Here they are, with a set you can take with you, but keep them out of sight.'

Tweed began pacing round the spacious room, thinking. Saafeld unlocked a drawer, took out a large cardboard-backed envelope. Paula held out her hand. 'May I?'

Saafeld hesitated. 'They're pretty grisly.'

She smiled. 'If I faint you can catch me, but I don't think I'll give you the pleasure,' she teased.

First she put on the latex gloves he handed her to avoid her fingerprints appearing on them. Then, very carefully, she extracted the colour prints, arranged them on the metal table top. Newman moved close to her shoulder and sucked in his breath.

Holgate's headless body had been laid out on a white plastic sheet covering the table, arms and hands stretched close to his sides. He was still clothed in a crumpled blue suit and Paula realized why. Saafeld had wanted the first photos taken to avoid the risk of disturbing the top of the body.

Above the collar and tie protruded the thick stump of most of his neck. Surprisingly the flesh was hardly ragged where the body had been decapitated, coated with brownish-coloured dried blood. His head had been cut off just below the chin, she surmised.

She examined the other colour prints. Saafeld had taken pictures from every angle. Looking at the first print she had felt slightly queasy: she had known Holgate as a distant acquaintance. Bending forward she swallowed to avoid the others detecting her reaction. She was aware that Buchanan was standing close to her.

'Like a glass of water?' he whispered.

She shook her head, went back to the first print she had looked at. It was the most detailed version. She frowned, stood up straight, still staring at the print.

'Come to any conclusions?' Tweed asked Saafeld.

'Yes. I'm sure a knife wasn't the killing instrument.

Sawing through the neck would have left the stump very ragged – to say nothing of what a job it would have been. I suspect an axe was used, an axe with a very sharp blade. The severing just below the chin is so clean. The killer must have been very strong to decapitate with one blow, which I think is what was done. I turned over the body before replacing it on its back. There was a stream of coagulated blood, which suggested to me the killer's first act was to strike the victim hard on the back of the head with the blunt end of the axe. I also believe the killer is right-handed, but that's an assumption.'

'Professor.' Paula turned to face him. 'Would you mind if I examined this print under a strong magnifying glass?'

Saafeld didn't ask her why. He led her to another table where a large instrument with a small gunlike projection holding a lens was perched. Close to it was an adjustable secretary's chair. As Paula sat down, peered through the eyepiece and adjusted the chair's height, Saafeld placed a metal plate on a rack behind and below the eyepiece. Then he positioned the print on top of the plate.

'That will hold the print stable,' he explained. 'That small wheel to the right adjusts the magnification. It is very sensitive.'

Having said that he walked back to where the others waited, a gesture which Paula appreciated. It was more difficult to concentrate with someone hovering over you. The wheel controlling the magnification *was* sensitive – so much so she removed the latex glove from one hand to operate it.

She turned the wheel very slowly forwards, then back a bit. The section of truncated neck the lens was aimed at suddenly jumped out at her with startling clarity. She studied what she saw, to be sure. Then she swivelled the chair round to face the others.

'Professor, I'm sure the axe has a notch in the blade.

6

Triangular with the apex deepest in the neck, widest at the edge. I expect you've already observed it.'

'I haven't.'

Saafeld walked rapidly towards her. She slipped off the stool, being careful not to move the wheel. Saafeld took her place, put on a pair of gold-rimmed glasses, peered in the eyepiece. Taking off the glasses, he stood up, stared at Paula and then Tweed.

'I've told you before, Tweed, Paula is very smart. I'd take her on my staff any time she got tired of working for a slavedriver. There is a notch . . .'

Newman looked through the magnifier next, then Tweed and finally Buchanan, who had to adjust the seat to allow for his extra height. He spent at least one minute gazing at what he saw, then stood up slowly from the stool, ran a finger across his trim moustache. It was a mannerism Paula had oberved before when a fresh development occurred in a case.

'This is very important,' he began. 'If we ever find the murder weapon, that notch will identify it. I'm surprised the killer hasn't noticed it.'

'Probably has,' Paula said. 'Doesn't care.'

'We ought to get moving,' Buchanan said, checking his watch.

Saafeld, wearing latex gloves, had unlocked the drawer again. He fished out two cardboard-backed envelopes. In one he placed the colour print they had been examining. In another he inserted the duplicate. He handed one envelope to Tweed.

'Expect you'd like this,' he said gruffly. He gave the other envelope to Buchanan. 'This might help as you pursue your investigation.'

'Thank you. It may turn out to be invaluable . . .'

'Want to take you somewhere,' Buchanan said as he drove the car away from Holland Park. 'Take a couple of hours.'

'Where to?' Tweed asked.

'Bray. Where the body was discovered. May be our last chance now this Chief Constable has grabbed the case. We won't be expected this evening.'

'Then now is the time to go,' Tweed agreed.

No one spoke until they had left the suburbs behind, were passing through Windsor. It was no longer raining, the sky had cleared and by the faint light of a new moon Paula saw the massive silhouette of Windsor Castle. Soon they were in open country, the road bordered by flat fields and black leafless trees like skeletons.

'Will we see anything in the dark?' Paula wondered aloud.

'I have four powerful torches. Tweed, open the glove compartment. One for each of us.'

Paula tested hers by shining it on the floor. She glanced out of the window, saw more sullen fields, more naked trees.

'One thing I can't understand,' she called out. 'Saafeld said the killer's first move is to hit his victim on the back of the head with the blunt end of the axe. I think his theory holds water. But then how on earth is he able to cut off the head so neatly with one blow? The body would have to be on its back, the neck resting on some kind of execution block.'

'I'd thought of that myself,' Tweed agreed. 'It's a puzzle.'

Buchanan had just swung off to the right away from the main road and down a narrow lane. 'We're approaching Bray,' he informed them.

'How close is it to the river?' Tweed enquired.

'About a mile. Bray is the last genuine village before you approach London. The rest of the old villages higher up the river have been wiped out by so-called developers. And this is Bray.'

In his headlights Paula saw fine old large houses built

8

long ago. The road curved back and forth. All the houses were close to the road. Lights shone behind curtained windows but no sign of any people.

'When we're almost through Bray we turn off to the river, to the scene of the crime,' Buchanan continued his commentary.

'I haven't seen any shops,' Paula remarked.

'Because there aren't any. The last one closed down ages ago. The locals drive to Maidenhead to shop at supermarkets. Sign of the times.'

He turned right again down an even narrower lane lined with hedges. The surface became rough and Bray was a distant memory. More fields on both sides, the grass long. When he stopped the car, parking it on the verge, Paula was struck by the sudden silence. She stepped out. The silence was eerie, punctuated only by the occasional drip of water off trees and a vague sound of the gushing river.

'I'll lead the way,' Buchanan told them as he locked the car and switched on his torch.

He had advanced some way into the field when a uniformed policeman appeared. Behind him crime scene tape had been strung round a large area, supported by small branches dug into the soggy ground. Paula was glad she'd put on knee-length boots before leaving Park Crescent.

'Can't come here,' snapped the policeman rudely. 'Police.'

'Yes, we can,' Buchanan barked back. 'I'm from the Yard and I've arranged for the body to be transported to a pathologist. Look at this folder.'

He was holding the folder close to the policeman, shining his torch on it. The policeman reached out to take it but Buchanan kept a firm grip.

'Nobody said you was comin' out,' the policeman objected.

'Get out of my way – and lift that tape so my assistants can get through. I'm short of time. Move it, man.'

The dull-faced policeman lifted the tape and they followed Buchanan who was striding out as the sound of the river became louder. The river was in full flood. Hands inside the pockets of his old Gannex raincoat, Tweed joined Paula and Buchanan at the river's edge.

'Who discovered the body?' he asked again.

'Chap called Weatherspoon taking his dog for a walk. He lives in Bray and is retired. I've checked him out and am sure he's had nothing to do with the crime.'

'Exactly where was the body discovered?' asked Paula as she crouched near the edge.

'In that shallow side stream to your right. Trouble is it could have been thrown in somewhere upstream, Heaven knows how far.'

'Mind if I try an experiment?' Paula suggested, standing up.

'Go ahead,' Buchanan said with a cynical smile.

Paula looked round. The ground was littered with portions of tree trunks, possibly cut for firewood. She walked a short distance upriver, selected a sizeable trunk, lifted it to test its weight, decided she could just cope with it. Not as heavy as Holgate's body but close enough. Heaving it up with both hands protected with motoring gloves, she carried it chest high and made it to the river's edge. Now for the tough part. She took a deep breath, hoisted it higher, hurled it as far out into the river as she could.

It landed in the river about six feet from the bank. The powerful current took hold of it, swept it further out, rushed it downstream out of sight. It had passed the shallow creek without going anywhere near it.

Sweat dripped down her back and her arms ached as she walked back to where Buchanan and Tweed stood staring.

'Someone shouted at me,' she said.

'I called out, "For God's sake don't fall in,"' Buchanan said, glaring at her.

10

'Excuse me –' she rubbed her gloves together, ridding them of bark from the tree trunk – 'but I think you're wrong in assuming the body was dropped in upstream. It must have been deposited from the bank straight into the side stream, where it would be found sooner or later. That tree trunk I threw in was pretty damned heavy – almost as heavy as the headless body, yet it never went anywhere near the stream.'

'She's right, you know,' commented Tweed.

'So the murder could have been committed somewhere near here,' Buchanan said thoughtfully. 'But where?'

'I'll be back in a minute,' Paula told them.

She trudged off, lifted the police tape which defined the area of the police search. She continued beyond it, sweeping her torch slowly over the field. More sawn hunks of trees were scattered over the grass, some peeking up like alien spacecraft just landed from Mars. Several minutes later her torch illuminated something different: a circle of flattened grass which looked as though it had been stamped down. In the middle of the circle was a weird branch with two arms projecting outwards. The arms were joined at the base by a smooth section of wood about half a foot wide which had been stripped of bark.

She approached it slowly, frequently beaming her torch on the ground she would tread on next. More grass flattened slightly. She stepped into the circle, her torch aimed point-blank at the smooth section joining the two arms. Recently stripped of its back, it should have been white but it was stained a dark brown, the colour of dried blood.

'I've found the execution block,' she said quietly.

They had hurried over to her when she beckoned. Buchanan and Tweed crouched down to examine the smooth base. Newman was taking pictures with his camera.

11

'Damn it,' said Buchanan, 'there's a narrow wedge in the wood where the axe ended up after the blow that severed Holgate's neck. And there's blood behind the base and this side of it, traces on the grass.'

'And,' Paula continued, 'the width of the base would comfortably fit the neck of poor Holgate. A makeshift execution block, but it did the trick.'

'So what happened to the head?' Buchanan asked, looking up at her. 'Thrown into the river, I expect.'

'Maybe,' Paula said, 'but maybe not. I'm getting a pretty horrific feeling about this murder.'

'We'll have to seal off this whole area,' Buchanan said, standing up.

'And I wonder who lives in that big house over there,' Paula said, pointing.

Less than a quarter of a mile away, downriver, was the only small hill for miles around. Perched on top of it, just visible in the moonlight, was a large ancient two-storey mansion, Tudor-style. No sign of life as they all gazed at it.

'There was a light in a side window a moment ago,' Paula told them.

'No light there now,' Buchanan said dismissively. 'It must have been your imagination. The place is empty – I visited it when I was here earlier. Wrought-iron gates were padlocked. I scrambled over a wall, went to the front door, rang the bell time and again. No one at home. Walked all round it. Blinds closed over all the windows. Had an unoccupied feel.' He turned round, clapped both hands to his mouth, shouted at the top of his voice.

'Guard, get over here as fast as you can. Come on – that's an order.'

The dull-faced policeman Buchanan had encountered when they first arrived began running towards them. Then he fell, sprawling face first in the grass. Paula knew why – her boots were smeared with mud and she'd had to walk carefully when she had begun her exploration. The policeman scrambled to his feet as Buchanan yelled at him to move faster. He saluted when he arrived and faced Buchanan, his uniform covered with mud.

'I want this whole area, five yards from here, cordoned off with crime scene tape. Got any on you?'

'A whole reel. Sergeant gave it to me when he left. Said he had enough stuff to cart around. And I'm due off duty. My relief has just arrived.'

'You stay on duty until the job of cordoning off this area is completed. You'll have your relief to help you,' Buchanan told him abruptly. He repeated his instruction. 'Tweed, we can't do any more here in the dark. Let's get back to London.'

They were moving off when Buchanan noticed Paula had stayed behind. She was staring at the grim-looking house on the hill.

'What are you doing?' Buchanan called out.

'I'm *sure* I saw a light in that side window.'

'You're exhausted – and no wonder. Back to the car with us.'

'Who does that house belong to?' she asked as she joined them.

'A company called ACTIL. I asked the same question in Bray when I was here earlier. Actually owned by the billionaire who created ACTIL. A man called Roman Arbogast.'

'ACTIL,' Tweed repeated. 'The conglomerate Holgate worked for after he'd walked out on us. Curious.'

1

The following morning Tweed sat behind his desk in his
large office on the first floor at Park Crescent. The windows which faced him along the opposite wall overlooked
Regent's Park in the distance. This was the real HQ of the
Secret Intelligence Service. The hideous modern building
on the bank of the Thames was a 'front' – mostly occupied
by administrative staff. The action was controlled from
Park Crescent.

Paula, seated at her own desk in a corner facing Tweed,
suppressed a yawn as Newman walked in. She called out
to Tweed.

'How do you like your new desk – or perhaps I should
say old, as it's an antique?'

With the financial support of the rest of the staff she had
bought the desk in the Portobello Road. It was Georgian
and had a green leather top. She had even had new locks
put on the drawers.

'I think I'm getting used to it.' Tweed smiled. 'I may
even get to like it.'

'You'd better,' chimed in Monica, his secretary of many
years, who wore her grey hair in a bun tied at the back. 'It
cost a pretty penny.' She ducked down behind her word
processor, feeling she'd said the wrong thing.

'And I'm very grateful to all of you,' Tweed assured her.

'Get any sleep after what you went through yesterday?'
Newman asked Paula.

She looked at him. In his forties, five feet nine tall, well-built with an impressive head to match his body, he had fair hair but was clean-shaven with a jaw that discouraged louts coming anywhere near him. The most famous international foreign correspondent in the world before Tweed persuaded him to join the SIS, he had proved to be a great asset to the unit.

'Not a lot of sleep,' Paula admitted. 'Which surprised me. When I got back to my flat I threw off my clothes and dived into the shower. It soothed away the aches and pains, I flopped into bed and fell fast asleep. Then I had the most horrible nightmare, which is unusual for me.'

'What kind of nightmare?' Tweed asked.

'It was night, I was near a river, watching the back of a black-coated figure. It was stooped over Holgate, sawing off his neck with a chainsaw. I woke up screaming, "Stop it, stop it." Then I realized it was a bad dream. Checked the time. 3 a.m. I remember thinking a chainsaw couldn't have been used. The neck would have been so ragged. No sleep after that. One of those things.'

'I had Roy Buchanan on the phone just before you came in,' Tweed told Paula. 'He congratulated you on your brilliant work last night. Said he'd take you on to his personal staff any day.'

'That's two job offers I've had in less than twenty-four hours,' Paula replied, pushing a curl of her black hair behind her ear. 'I'll have to think about them,' she teased.

'Let me know when you decide which one, then I can start looking for a replacement,' Tweed teased her back.

He had no more intention of letting her go than he had of resigning his position as Deputy Director. She just seemed to get better and better.

'Buchanan also told me,' he went on, 'that he phoned the local Chief Constable at three in the morning. He wasn't very popular but he told Colonel Crow, the Chief

Constable, that he'd better send out another team of men to patrol the two taped areas and search thoroughly round the so-called execution block area. Crow ended the conversation by warning Roy that it was no longer his case and to keep off the grass. Roy told him his team would have to walk all over the grass to check for clues, then slammed down the phone. He was quite right to warn Crow, a pompous idiot I met once. The type who bullies his subordinates, then creeps and grovels to people who can help to hoist him higher up the ladder.'

Besides desks, the room was furnished with a mushroom-coloured wall-to-wall carpet and three armchairs for visitors. Newman was settled in his favourite armchair, taking in what was being said while he read a copy of the *International Herald Tribune*. He looked up.

'Odd, this copy is a fortnight old – I pile them up, then go through them when I have time, in date sequence. A fortnight ago there was a similar murder at some nowhere place called Pinedale, south of Portland in Maine. A headless corpse inside a body bag was washed up on the cliffs during a storm. Victim a caretaker called Foley. Head never discovered.'

'Very unlikely there's a connection,' Tweed told him. 'Maine is three thousand miles or so across the Atlantic.'

'There are such things as aircraft services.'

'Oh, and did you know the Vice-President of the US of A arrived in this country two days ago?'

'Yuck,' Paula commented, 'we can do without someone like Russell Straub. I've seen him yacking away on the TV. Thinks he's the cat's whiskers.'

'They think Straub is likely to succeed the present President in the White House,' Newman informed her. 'He's already making campaign noises.'

'Well, I wouldn't vote for him,' Paula said savagely as the phone rang.

17

Monica answered it, frowned, carried on a brief conversation. Then she put a hand over the phone and gazed at Tweed.

'You're not going to believe this.'

'Try me.'

'George has had a fierce argument with someone who has just arrived.' She paused. 'Nathan Morgan, Head of Special Branch. Morgan arrived with two of his thugs, demanded to see you, was coming up with the thugs. George forced the two thugs to go into the waiting room, locked the door on them. He's still holding Morgan in the hall.'

'I see. Ask George to escort Mr Morgan up here.'

Newman stood up. He walked to the door, opened it and stood half in the way. Morgan arrived, tried to push Newman out of the way. Newman smiled as he slowly stood to one side.

'Easy does it,' he said amiably.

Their visitor stormed into the room. Wearing a smart trench coat with wide lapels, which gave him a military appearance, he marched up to Tweed's desk. Heavily built, he had a large squarish head, black hair, thick black eyebrows, a pugilist's nose, a thin-lipped mouth and a prominent jaw. A brute, Paula thought to herself.

'Your gangster downstairs has imprisoned two of my men in a room, locked the door on them,' he roared.

'Well, if you want to talk to me we don't need them to be present,' Tweed said quietly. 'And it's normal to phone for an appointment before calling on me.'

'You were out at Bray late last night. The policeman who was going to relieve the man already there recognized you.'

'I thought he seemed familiar,' Tweed remarked.

'You don't deny invading territory, a crime scene under the control of a local police force?'

18

'One of my staff with me was able to detect how and where the victim was beheaded. Something the local force had overlooked. Do sit down. You're not looking very comfortable, standing there like a waxwork in Madame Tussaud's.'

'This whole matter is confidential,' Morgan snapped. 'We can't discuss it with all these people hanging around.'

'Then let me introduce you. The lady sitting in the corner is Miss Paula Grey, my chief assistant. Incidentally she is also the person who solved the problem of how Holgate was murdered.'

Morgan turned, saw Paula for the first time. His whole manner changed. He walked over to her desk, smirking as he held out his ham-fist of a hand.

'What an attractive assistant. Something to keep you warm on cold nights.'

Paula stared straight at him. As she did so she used one hand to open a drawer. She took out a bottle of Dettol, placed it on her desk close to him, her eyes still meeting his.

'There's some Dettol to wash your mouth out with.'

Morgan was speechless. He opened his mouth, closed it without saying anything. Then he swung round, pointed a stubby finger at Newman.

'I recognize you. Robert Newman, news reporter.' He made the last two words sound like something out of a sewer. Newman, his expression bleak, stared straight back without saying anything. It was Tweed who spoke.

'Mr Newman has been fully vetted, trained at our place in the country, has completed the SAS course, which few do. He's worked with me for years.' His voice rose. 'For God's sake stop making a fool of yourself. Sit down or leave.'

The vicious expression receded from Morgan's face. He looked round as though not sure what to do next, then sat in one of the armchairs.

19

'Why have you wasted your time – and mine – coming here?' Tweed demanded.

Tweed sat upright, hands clasped together on the desk. He was gazing at Morgan, his eyes hard. Paula was waiting for an explosion. Normally so calm and watchful, there were times when Tweed could explode and the results were devastating. Morgan reached inside his jacket pocket, wrestling to find it under his trench coat. At that moment the door opened and Marler walked in.

Five feet seven tall, Marler was slim, in his late thirties, always impeccably dressed. He was wearing a stylish pale-grey suit, crisp white shirt, a Valentino tie. Among his many talents he was the deadliest marksman with a rifle in Western Europe. He walked quietly across close to Paula's desk, took up his usual stance, leaning against a wall. His trim hair was corn-coloured and he was clean-shaven. He took a long cigarette out of a gold case, lit it. Morgan turned, stared at him.

'Another one. Who is this?'

'Marler,' Tweed called out, 'meet Nathan Morgan, newly appointed Head of Special Branch. He has just gatecrashed his way into our sanctum.'

'I hear he does that,' Marler remarked in his upper-crust voice. 'New boy.'

Morgan again opened his mouth, then closed it without responding. He was still struggling with his jacket pocket, clearly embarrassed by his performance. Everyone waited in silence. Then he produced an envelope, took out a sheet of paper stamped with Home Secretary at the top.

'It has been decided,' Morgan began in what he imagined was an official tone, 'to create a system of close collaboration between the Special Branch and the Secret Service. We shall be appointing an observer to stay on the premises here, so you will need to give him office space and all communication facilities.'

He handed the letter to Tweed, who read it quickly.

Then he opened a drawer, dropped the letter inside, looked across at Paula.

'That's for the shredder along with the other junk.'

'The shredder!' Morgan was outraged. His expression became ugly. 'You can't do that with—'

'On whose authority was this absurd idea thought up?'

'Whose authority?' Morgan's rage was growing. 'You have just read the letter from the Home Secretary.'

Tweed stood up slowly, placed his hands inside his trouser pockets. He walked slowly round his desk and there was something menacing in his movements. Disturbed, Morgan jumped up out of his chair so he was standing when Tweed reached him. There was a hard edge to Tweed's voice when he spoke, only inches away from his visitor.

'There will be no observer, so-called, infiltrated into this building. Apart from anything else the question of security arises. Also, you do not seem to realize I answer only to the PM—'

'I did ask for Mr Howard when I arrived—'

'Don't interrupt me again. What I have just said also applies to Howard. Then again your organization comes under the control of New Scotland Yard. In case you did not know that—'

'There's going to be a restructuring . . .'

'I did tell you not to interrupt me. I did not work well with your predecessor, a man called Bate. Rather like you. Thought *finesse* was a French pastry. Before him Special Branch was run by Pardoe, a man I respected and collaborated with from time to time. I cannot possibly work with someone like you.' His voice rose. 'So, Mr Nathan Morgan, please leave the premises at once. You will be escorted downstairs by Mr Newman.'

Tweed returned to his chair behind his desk. Newman stood up, opened the door, smiling broadly.

'This is the way out, Nathan.'

21

Morgan was trying to straighten up his trench coat as he walked towards Newman. At the open doorway he turned to fire a parting shot.

'You'd better realize the investigation into the murder out at Bray has absolutely nothing to do with you.'

'Goodbye,' said Tweed, studying a file without looking up.

'Paula,' he said, closing the file when the two men had left, 'I have an appointment in an hour to meet Roman Arbogast at ACTIL headquarters in the City. He kindly agreed to see me since Adam Holgate was once on my staff. Newman will drive us there and I'd like you to come with me.'

'Well, that should be a change from listening to that piece of rubbish you just threw out. I gather you are still investigating the case, but you look worried.'

'After Colonel Crow's extraordinary action – snatching away the body from Saafeld – and Nathan Morgan's boorish intervention, I sense the government is anxious that Holgate's brutal killing is never solved. Which happens to coincide with the unexpected arrival of the American Vice-President, Russell Straub.'

'Surely there can't be a connection?'

2

'This traffic is like a logjam, and it's wet,' Newman grumbled.

'We're nearly there,' Paula called out from the rear seat. 'Tweed, you're going to be stunned when you see the ACTIL building. It's the tallest in London – taller than the buildings in Canary Wharf. And it's built like a giant cylinder. You don't come down into this part of the City, do you? Thought not.'

'I don't like these stone and cement canyons that hem you in. Lord knows how people work here.'

'It would have been quicker to walk,' Newman grumbled again.

They were inching their way forward. Beyond the pavements the solid walls of office buildings sheered up. Like a cement jungle, Tweed thought, seated beside Newman. Paula tapped him on the shoulder.

'There it is. They call it the Cone. They say Arbogast himself drew up the plans, imported workers from Germany to get it up in record time.'

Tweed stared at the immense cylinder perched where the street forked, a round colossus so high he couldn't see the top. There were people everywhere, hurrying along under umbrellas. More cones, an army of them as pedestrians hustled along. No wonder the word 'stress' had travelled across from America.

'There's a big limo pulled up outside the entrance. Most helpful,' Newman grumbled again.

Paula peered forward. A figure in a camel-hair coat had emerged from the building, stood at the top of the steps leading up to it. Slim, with dark hair, he was waving his arms about while several men in grey suits stood behind him, by his side, on the steps below.

'That's the Vice-President,' Paula called out. 'Russell Straub in person. Always waving his arms about. He's come out of the ACTIL building.'

'What does ACTIL stand for, if anything?' Tweed asked.

'A is for Armaments,' Paula began. 'C is for Chemicals. T is for Technology. I for Intelligence. L for Leisure.'

'Intelligence is what Holgate was involved with. Interesting. Leisure – don't understand that.'

'He has a vast network of travel agents, including some in Russia.'

'Armaments sounds sinister,' Newman remarked, tapping his fingers on the wheel. They were stationary.

'When the Vice-President's limo gets moving it should help clear the jam,' Paula predicted.

As she spoke Straub ran agilely down the steps, leapt into the rear of the limo, where a grey-suited man stood holding open the door, closing it swiftly as soon as Straub was inside. Several bodyguards climbed into the car. Newman was watching them through field glasses.

'Those bodyguards are carrying guns. I can see the bulges under their armpits. Bet they didn't get permission. A police escort too.'

In front of the limo a police patrol car was edging its way forward. In front of it uniformed policemen were waving people out of the way, holding up traffic to give the limo a clear run. It disappeared round one of the corners at the base of the Cone.

'You're sure that was Straub?' Tweed asked.

'It was,' Newman assured him. 'I've also seen him on TV and caught a good glimpse of Mastermind in my glasses.'

'I take it that was sarcasm,' Paula suggested.

'It most certainly was. Chap has the personality of a peacock. Wouldn't trust him an inch. Something not so nice behind the perpetual smile when cameramen are about.'

As the traffic got moving Newman manoeuvred his Mercedes, pulled up by the kerb in front of the ACTIL building. Paula and Tweed jumped out as a uniformed doorman ran to Newman, asked him to drive a few yards further on.

'That woman across the road, watching this building,' Paula said. 'She's so small and still. In her sixties, I'd say, and the pale green coat and dark green fur hat suit her.'

'We get every type visiting London,' Tweed replied impatiently, then he turned round and gazed up. 'Oh, my God. It's a giant.'

He was staring at the endless pink wall which rose above him like the side of a mountain, a round mountain. At its distant summit wisps of cloud drifted, floated away to reveal its huge cone-shaped top, bronze-coloured. He had never seen anything like it, even in New York.

'Stunning, isn't it,' Paula replied.

Newman had handed the keys to the doorman, asked him to park the car until they got back. Tweed and Paula mounted the wide stone steps to an outsize revolving door. Paula nudged Tweed to go first. The door revolved slowly, then stopped when Paula went forward to step in. Beyond her Tweed's glass-walled compartment continued moving and he stepped into the vast reception hall. Paula waved her hands in a gesture of surprise. A voice spoke from somewhere.

'You may enter now, madam.'

The door revolved again and she stepped inside. Behind

25

her Newman, who had caught on to the trick, stood with his arms folded. He looked up at the speakphone grille above the door.

'Don't forget me. I've got the money.'

'You may now enter, sir,' the voice replied as Paula waited inside the hall.

Newman waved at the camera beamed at him above the speakphone. 'Thanks a lot, old boy . . .'

Inside he gaped at the spaciousness of the reception hall, its walls solid marble, the floor also marble. Tweed and Paula were walking over to the huge reception desk behind which an attractive red-headed girl smiled. Before she could speak a tall muscular man wearing an Armani suit appeared out of nowhere. He snapped at the receptionist.

'I'll deal with this, Clara.'

Below his brown hair he had a face hewn out of stone. In his thirties, he was clean-shaven with a long sharp nose, hostile eyes, a thin-lipped mouth, a prominent chin. Paula doubted whether he even knew how to smile. His expression said: *Don't mess with me.*

'Mr Tweed?' he demanded. His rough accent was Midlands.

Tweed nodded, completely unintimidated.

'And you're Miss Grey.' He turned. 'Easy to recognize you. Robert Newman, foreign correspondent. I've read some of your articles in the past. They're dangerous.'

'They're meant to be . . .'

'And you have a gun under your left armpit. Leave that with the receptionist.'

'As the Americans would say,' Newman replied amiably, 'I can see you're packing a piece yourself.'

'I'm Broden. Chief of Security.'

Newman went over to Clara, who had been listening gleefully. It was the first time she had heard Broden talked down. As Newman took out his Smith & Wesson, removed the bullets, she ushered him behind her desk where she had

26

opened a metal drawer, one of many, using a master key and a second one. He placed his weaponry inside, closed the drawer, she turned both keys, handed him his own.

'We are waiting,' Broden called out.

'With a system like this Mr Arbogast should allow five minutes extra on his appointments,' Newman told him.

'He does. This lift. Used only by the Chairman.'

'Park your stomach outside,' Broden told them without a trace of humour before he closed the doors. 'The lift moves up like a rocket.'

Paula grabbed hold of one of the gold railings lining three sides of the luxurious lift. It did indeed shoot up like a rocket. Paula watched the numbers alongside one of the doors. A hundred and five floors. Lordy. The numbers flicked past so quickly it reached 105 before she realized it.

Their destination was beyond a door facing the lift, a door which Broden unlocked, using the same computer card he had inserted in the hall to open the doors. They entered a large room occupied by four men behind desks, working IBM Selectric typewriters. No word processors, no sign of the Internet. At the far end Broden opened a heavy oak door, stood to one side.

'That will be all, Broden. You may leave now,' a strange throaty voice rumbled.

Newman glanced at the security chief. Was it possible his expression was even icier? Not wanted on the voyage.

Paula almost gasped as she entered. The room, with circular walls and windows, floor to ceiling, was more like a drawing room. A deep grey wall-to-wall carpet across which were scattered plush armchairs and couches. In the spaces between windows hung gilt-framed landscapes. At the far end was a massive Regency desk and behind that, seated in a comfortable-looking carver chair, was a man.

He was tall and plump with a very ugly head, the face plump: in his sixties, she guessed, but it was the face which

27

she gazed at. Ice-blue eyes were half-hidden by pouches of flesh, his short nose was wide and below it thick lips twisted sideways. Below them he had a massive jowl and his expensive suit was rumpled. His right eye twitched several times as he stood slowly, waved a fat hand with short stubby fingers.

'Welcome to my humble abode. Certain members of my family will join us. One is the key member of my staff who may one day take my place. Do sit down.' He padded round his desk to shake hands. Paula was surprised at how tall Roman Arbogast was. His shoulders were very broad and she was aware of a sense of power. No arrogance but an aura of immense determination.

He remained standing when they had seated themselves, close to them, bulky arms folded. His head was twisted slightly to one side as he looked down.

'Now, Mr Tweed, you are one of the few people I respect. You are a very dangerous man. I pay you a compliment. Why have you come to see me?'

'Adam Holgate was a member of my staff before he came here. I owe him my interest in finding out who killed him with such savagery. When I know why I shall know who.'

'What would everyone like to drink?' Arbogast swivelled his head to include all his guests in the invitation.

'Nothing for me, thank you,' said Paula.

'The brilliant lady who is a natural detective. Who makes the police look like the fools they are.'

'What do you base that on?' she asked quickly.

'On information received. Any success I may have had in this world of idiots is based on my ability to know what is – or has been – happening, happened.'

His voice, although quiet and throaty, carried a long way. Still standing, he switched his attention as Tweed spoke.

'What exactly was Holgate's job here?'

'Security. I didn't like him but Broden thought he was good. He was also nosy, very inquisitive.'

'In what way?' Paula asked with a smile.

'He searched through files which were nothing to do with his duties. He would hover outside open doors to listen to conversations which did not concern him. He may have found out too much. A reason why he was executed.'

'Executed?' Paula was shocked.

The door into the spacious room opened and two women walked in, one behind the other. Newman stared at the first woman – he couldn't help it.

'This is Marienetta,' Arbogast announced. 'My niece.'

She walked in with long elegant strides. She was in her early thirties, Paula thought as she studied the stunning beauty. Tall and slim, Marienetta had golden hair trimmed to just below her ears, an exceptionally well-shaped bone structure, a nose which expressed driving power, strange lips, the upper one thin, the lower full, the mouth wide. But it was the eyes which hypnotized Paula. Greenish, the irises were clear of the lids, which gave them an extraordinary penetration.

The slightly stern look disappeared into a warm smile as she advanced on Paula, slim hand held out. She held on to Paula's hand for longer than usual.

'Your grip suggests a strong character, Miss Grey. I have heard a lot about you. I was hoping we would meet and I am not disappointed.'

'I'm Bob Newman.' Like Tweed he was standing up.

'The foreign correspondent. Pushy, aren't you? Mr Tweed,' she went on, again holding out her hand. 'I am happy to meet such a distinguished man.' Her tone was sincere. 'You are one of those rare people who hide a strong intellect behind a passive manner. I sense inside you a volcano of energy.'

'I'm still here, in case everyone has forgotten,' a voice spoke up irritably.

'My daughter, Sophie,' introduced Arbogast.

Sophie was also tall and slim but her hair was dark, thick, her nose snub and her forehead high. Her grey eyes were cold, the features sharp, almost aggressive. Paula had the immediate impression she had always come as number two compared with the niece. Not because Marienetta dominated her but the niece's appearance and personality would always cast a shadow over the daughter. She gave Sophie a friendly smile as Arbogast introduced his guests.

'I saw you the moment you came into the room,' Paula assured Sophie. 'Come and sit next to me.'

'Makes a change to be invited,' Sophie commented as she sat down.

'We are all going to be friends, Sophie,' Marienetta said with a smile.

She was wearing a close-fitting green dress with a gold belt round her slim waist and a pair of medium-heeled green shoes. Sophie wore a beige woollen jumper with a high neck, a pale grey pleated skirt and red high-heeled shoes. The contrast between the two women was strident, and there was no doubt who had first-rate dress sense.

'I'm going to smoke,' Sophie said, making a statement.

Paula saw Arbogast open his mouth, caught Marienetta's frown at her uncle. Arbogast closed his mouth without saying anything.

'Go ahead,' Marienetta said, 'provided I have one too, please. Thanks.'

'What,' Sophie demanded, 'were you talking about when I came in and then shut up?'

Arbogast sat behind his desk, his eyes gazing at Sophie. She dropped her glance as he spoke, took a quick puff.

'We were talking about murder,' Arbogast told her bluntly.

'Nice topic,' Sophie snapped, took a deep puff. 'That means you've been gossiping about poor Adam.'

'We have been discussing the case with Mr Tweed.'

'Adam isn't just a case. He's a human being,' protested his daughter. 'Or was.' She frowned. 'I wonder what he felt like when someone cut off his neck.' She spoke as though it was an interesting subject. 'Must feel strange when your head is rolling away.'

'I doubt,' Marienetta said gently, 'if you feel anything.'

'Tweed,' Arbogast broke in, 'you came here to ask me for my impression of Holgate – Adam, that is – and I think I've told you all I can.' He opened a drawer as his guests stood up to leave. 'It's Sophie's birthday this evening so we're celebrating it at a nice restaurant, the Tree Creeper.' He stood up holding three printed and engraved cards, gave one to each of his guests. 'I would be most honoured if you would join us. And I am sure Sophie would be pleased.'

'So long as Paula is coming.' She squeezed her hand. 'I'm going to make a speech.'

'You may find it interesting,' Arbogast went on, staring at Tweed, his eye twitching. 'One of the guests will be Sophie's friend Black Jack Diamond.'

They had left the spacious office when Marienetta slipped her arm inside Tweed's. She gazed at him, smiling.

'That wasn't much fun. I insist you come and look at my studio – cubbyhole would be a better word. That's where I enjoy myself when I can get away from acting as Administrator.'

'Administrator?' Tweed queried.

'That's my vague title here. Uncle wanted me to keep an eye on things and I told him I didn't want a title which

31

restricted my powers over some of the senior personnel. Administrator could mean anything. So I can roam wherever I want to check up. Including Security.' She laughed. 'You may not be surprised to know I'm not Broden's favourite person.'

Paula glanced back as they entered the special lift. Newman was walking with Sophie, talking, grinning, joking. As far as Paula could make out Sophie had her head down and was not saying a word.

Marienetta pressed the button for level 103, twirling the computer card she'd used to open the doors. Paula turned to her as she made the comment. 'Your uncle doesn't seem to have taken to new modern equipment like computers. In the room you go through to reach your uncle his staff were using the old IBM Selectrics. No sign of the Internet.'

'You're right,' Marienetta agreed and chuckled as they stepped out on to level 103. 'He knows how easy it is for rival companies to employ top hackers to break into a computer system. As for the Internet, forget it. Actually I do agree with him. Here we are, my cubbyhole.'

'But you use computer cards instead of keys,' Paula pointed out as Marienetta used a different card to open a door.

'He agreed to those – so did I – providing the cards are changed every evening. Which they are. Enter. Don't expect too much.'

They walked into a spacious room with shag carpet, a luminous blue which gave a feeling of warmth. It was divided into two sections with a panelled partition excluding one half. The walls were rounded and Paula realized they were still at the summit of the Cone. More comfortable armchairs and antique tables were scattered about. Marienetta headed for the closed door in the panelled wall, taking out another computer card from her gold handbag slung over the shoulder.

'Inside here,' she announced in a tone of mock gravity, 'is my Holy of Holies. Few visitors see it. I ban all bores.'

'I want a drink,' Sophie called out rudely.

She was pursing her lips, using one hand to stroke her hair. She stood stock-still.

'You can have a glass of water,' Marienetta said, picking up a glass by a water cooler. 'No alcohol here.'

'Don't want water. I'm going to my office. Open the bloody door.'

'Do watch your mouth when we have visitors,' Marienetta said gently, going back to open the outer door.

Newman said something about how he hoped they'd meet later. Sophie brushed past him without a glance in his direction.

'She's in a mood,' Marienetta said amiably after relocking the door. 'But she's a genius with security and inventing new weapons.'

'Weapons?' asked Tweed.

'She can tell you how Marlborough fought the battle of Ramillies and the function of the hydrogen bomb. Science is her real flair. Now, let me show you.'

The room beyond the panelling was a surprise. A white tiled floor, work tables with half-finished sculptures, modern, large bowls of plaster, a variety of tools. Beyond was an easel with an unframed portrait of Roman Arbogast. Very lifelike. A palette with squelches of paint, a large ceramic pot crammed with long-handled paint brushes.

'Is this your work?' asked Paula as Marienetta donned a long white coat smeared with paint.

'It's where I'm really at home.'

She picked up a hammer and tapped hard at the shoulder of a sculpture in stone of a sprawling man half-sitting up. The whole arm broke off, Marienetta shrugged, slammed down the hammer on the metal table top.

'That's ruined it,' she said. 'Have to start again.'

Tweed had walked over to a mantelpiece, where a

33

small maquette – or miniature sculpture – rested. He picked it up carefully, admired it, turned round to address Marienetta.

'This is your creation?'

'You have an artistic eye, Mr Tweed. Unfortunately it is not mine. Roman lent it to me for inspiration. It is a genuine Henry Moore maquette, cost a fortune at auction.'

Tweed was carefully returning the precious maquette to its place on the mantelpiece while Paula wandered over to the easel with the unframed portrait of Arbogast. 'You paint too,' she said to Marienetta who had followed her.

'I daub, but it clears my head of other problems.'

'It really is a marvellous likeness. You've got him perfectly.'

'Turn it over. There's another painting on the other side.'

Paula gingerly took hold of the top of the picture. It was painted on board, not canvas. She swivelled the picture round and perched it back on the easel with the second painting showing. She stepped back a pace, shocked.

It was another painting of Roman, a horrific version of Marienetta's uncle. The face was distorted, the mouth open, exposing small sharp teeth, the lips twisted far to one side. The expression was of incredibly murderous rage, the jowls large and twisted the opposite way to the lips. The flesh was bloated, the head unbalanced, one vicious eye lower than the other. She had the impression the head might leap out at her, the teeth tearing her face. She felt her heart beating faster. The picture was terrifying.

'He was in a bad mood when I painted that,' Marienetta said calmly as she reversed the board back to show the lifelike version.

'Must have been something he'd eaten,' Newman said standing at Paula's shoulder.

Marienetta chuckled, then began laughing and couldn't

34

stop. Taking out a silk handkerchief she placed it over her mouth, turned to Newman.

'Bob, I love your sense of humour. That was really funny.'

Paula glanced beyond Newman. Tweed was standing perfectly still. He had the grimmest expression Paula had ever seen.

3

Marienetta accompanied them down in the special lift. As they walked out she paused to have a word with a uniformed guard. Tweed was walking with Paula to the exit while Newman collected his revolver and bullets from the desk when Broden appeared. Earlier he had worn a grey business suit but now he was clad in a rough-haired sports jacket and corduroy trousers tucked inside knee-length leather boots. The gamekeeper, Paula thought.

'Hope you enjoyed your session with Cat's Eye,' he barked.

'Cat's Eye?' Paula queried.

'That's what the staff call Marienetta behind her back. Jasper has gone to fetch your car, Newman.'

'I don't think you realize how your voice carries,' said Marienetta as she joined them, giving Broden a radiant smile. 'Now could you please go outside and make sure the coast is clear for Mr Tweed and his party to leave?'

Broden tightened his lips, strode off. A minute later he beckoned. They went through the same business of passing through the revolving door one by one. Broden was on the pavement when, on the top step, Paula gripped Tweed's arm.

'That strange lady is still waiting across the street.'

'Strange lady?' His thoughts were miles away.

'The one who is so small and still. Wearing a pale green coat and a dark green fur hat.'

'As I said before, you get all kinds of visitors coming to London.'

'Which woman is that?' demanded Broden who had run back up the steps. 'Oh, I see her. She was here when you arrived?'

'I'm not sure,' Paula said quickly. 'Let her be.'

'Jasper,' Broden called out to the doorman, 'check out Fur Hat standing across the street, why she's hanging round here for for so long.'

Broden disappeared inside the building as Tweed walked down the steps, got inside the front passenger seat. Paula gazed across the street but then Newman was driving off.

'I hope Jasper doesn't spot her camera,' she remarked.

'Camera?' Tweed asked, turning round.

'Yes, she had a small camera in her hands, rather like mine. She used it when we arrived and again as we left.'

'She's not committing an offence,' Tweed replied. 'Now what did you think of the Arbogasts?'

'They're a very unusual family. I thought I sensed an aura of hatred in Roman's office.'

'Sophie,' Newman commented, 'doesn't feel they take enough notice of her. I rather liked her. She's got brains behind that rather quiet front she assumes.'

'Marienetta was nice to her.'

'Neither of you have noticed the absence of something,' Tweed said. 'Roman never said a word about the visit of the American Vice-President. And I'm sure it was Roman he went to see. Who else in the building would he want to talk to? And what is the link between Roman and Russell Straub?'

'Can't imagine Roman controls many votes in an election in the States,' Newman replied. 'And votes are the only thing politicians are interested in. Probably all about nothing.'

'Maybe,' said Tweed.

*   *   *

38

Their car was stationary. Ahead as far as the eye could see was a solid block of cars, bumper to bumper. The stone buildings hemming them in on either side were grimy. The pavements were crammed with pedestrians. Lunchtime. Men and women shoved their way along. In doorways stood girls eating greasy food out of greasy paper bags.

Paula pulled a face. 'I don't see any nutrition anywhere.'

She closed her window. A heavy overcast hung low over the city. The 'air' in the street was a mix of petrol and diesel fumes, pressed down by the overcast.

'London is turning into a mob hell,' she remarked.

'Talking about hell,' said Newman, 'what did you think of Marienetta's second painting of Roman? Made him look like an ogre.'

'A monster,' retorted Paula.

'Like many painters,' Tweed explained, 'she's influenced by famous artists. In her case Picasso. And in sculpture by Henry Moore.'

'Picasso's worst effort was never as brutal as the one she painted of Roman,' Paula commented.

The traffic had started to move. Soon they were turning into Park Crescent. A man was sitting on the steps leading into their building. Newman groaned.

'Him I can do without. That's Sam Snyder, chief crime reporter on the *Daily Nation*. His name should be spelt Snide. He's good, I'll grant him that, but ruthless where people's feelings are concerned. Don't let him inside.'

Tweed got out first, was about to hurry up the steps when he was accosted. The reporter had stood up, spoke rapidly.

'Mr Tweed. Thought you might like to know I have a splash story in tomorrow's paper. About the first one in the state of Maine. I'm just back from America. Murder.'

What he'd said stopped Tweed. He paused before pressing the bell, stared straight at thre reporter.

'Which murder?'

'The caretaker who was beheaded at a dot on the map called Pinedale, south of Portland. Head missing there too. Like Holgate.'

'And you want to talk to me about it? Come upstairs.' He pressed the bell.

As they followed the two men to Tweed's office Paula looked at Newman. He raised his eyes to Heaven as much as to say, 'Tweed's blown it.' She poked a finger into his arm and whispered.

'Keep quiet. Tweed usually knows what he's doing . . .'

Inside the office Monica sat behind her desk, hammering away at her word processor. Tweed ushered his visitor into an armchair, sat behind his desk.

'I'm Sam Snyder . . .'

'I know. I'm afraid I haven't much time. You talk, I will listen.'

'My story also mentions that the Vice-President has a wreck of a mansion just outside Pinedale.'

'He's going to love that,' Tweed commented. 'And he has just arrived in London.'

'I simply report the facts. I thought it was interesting. Russell Straub arrives here three days ago. Now Holgate's beheaded body is discovered out near Bray.'

'You're linking the three events in your story?'

Snyder smiled. He was a strange impressive figure. He had a hawk-like face, long and cadaverous. His nose reminded Paula of the prow of an ice-breaker; his eyes were dark and very still. His well-educated voice was commanding and he sat erect in the armchair. His age was difficult to guess. Forty? Fifty? Sixty? Later Paula asked Newman and he told her Snyder seemed ageless, always had. Despite disliking his arrogance Newman admitted he was a formidable force.

'Link those three events, Mr Tweed?' Snyder again gave his peculiar smile. 'Of course not. The facts merely appear in different sections of my story.'

'So why did you fly to America?'

'I read a long account in the *New York Times* a few days ago. This was before Holgate's murder. I was struck by an item reporting that the pathologist – or medical examiner as they call them over there – was brought up from Boston. Why not the local man in Portland? I was over there twenty-four hours, flew straight back. Yesterday a member of the FBI detachment at the American Embassy phoned me. That decided me. I wrote the story.'

'What did the FBI man ask you?'

'I didn't take the call. The pathologist from Boston was a Dr Ramsey. Quite a reputation.'

'What made you suspicious of this business? Something you found out apart from the medical examiner coming from Boston?'

'Outside Pinedale there is a nursing home, really a lunatic asylumn. Hank Foley, the decapitated caretaker, worked there. The asylum was burnt to the ground a few hours after Hank Foley was murdered. Fortunately there were no patients left inside the building. It was the sort of place where very rich people parked an unwanted relative – unwanted because of a mental condition. It was run by a married couple, the Bryans. They have disappeared and no one seems to know where they have gone.'

'Intriguing,' commented Tweed.

'Now, sir, I have been open with you. So what did you discover last night when you travelled to Bray with Chief Superintendent Buchanan?'

'You pick up some strange rumours, Mr Snyder.'

The phone rang, Monica answered it, listened, gestured for Tweed to take it. He lifted the phone, pushed his chair nearer to the wall. Snyder stood up, ignored Newman, wandered over to the wall near Paula's desk to study a

41

framed print on the wall. She had been staring at his clothes. He wore a rough jacket with trousers to match. At his throat a cravat was tied which had a design of foxes capering about. He was clad more like a countryman than a London reporter.

'I like this very much. It's a Turner print. Did you choose it?' He smiled warmly, his manner now pleasant.

'As a matter of fact, I did.'

'You have excellent taste. It's Perugia, isn't it? Thought so. What an atmospheric genius Turner was. The fortress town perched up suggests massive strength. I congratulate you.'

'Thank you.'

Tweed had taken his brief call as Snyder returned to his armchair. He had been surprised when the throaty voice spoke. Roman Arbogast.

'Tweed, I do hope you will attend Sophie's birthday party with your two friends. Other also distinguished people will be there.'

'We will be glad to come . . .'

The phone went dead. Roman was not a man to waste time on what he'd regard as pointless conversation.

'What is your opinion of the horrific Holgate murder?' enquired Snyder.

'I don't think I've formed one.'

'You're as tough as granite,' Snyder observed in his normal arrogant manner. 'I think I'd better go. I've received an unusual invitation to a birthday party – for Sophie, the daughter of Roman Arbogast. Expect he wants a write-up.'

Tweed fiddled with his pen. 'I've heard a rumour that one of the guests may be Russell Straub. Thought I'd warn you.'

'The paper with my story won't be on the streets until tomorrow.'

'The early editions will be available at midnight,' Tweed

reminded him. 'Straub is the sort of man who likes a team of aides with him wherever he goes, I suspect. One of those aides may hear of your article and drive over to get a copy.'

'Well, if Straub is going to be there so am I.' He paused. 'I suppose you know that when you arrived back here you had been followed? The men inside the car had Special Branch written all over them.'

'Nice to be protected,' replied Tweed, concealing his surprise at this news.

'Something very funny is going on.' Snyder stood up. 'When I was in Maine I noticed I had to penetrate a blanket of silence. People were very nervous about talking. Keep well, all of you. I'll be in touch, Tweed . . .'

And with that brief farewell Snyder said he could find his own way out and left. No one spoke for a few minutes. Paula broke the silence, glaring at Newman.

'You never said a word to him,' she snapped.

'Didn't have a word to say. Neither did he to me.'

'He was our guest. A polite greeting would have done no harm. Where are your manners? The fact that you don't like him is irrelevant,' she went on, working herself up. 'And he was very nice with me during our brief exchange of conversation.'

'Hope you enjoyed it,' Newman rapped back ironically.

'You're impossible,' she retorted.

The phone rang, Monica answered it, looked at Tweed. 'We've got Chief Superintendent Buchanan on the line for you.'

'Hello, Roy,' Tweed opened. 'How is life with you?'

'Pretty grim. I've been taken off the Holgate murder case, told that no one on my team is to go anywhere near it. And guess where the order comes from? The Commissioner himself. Said it was strictly a matter for the local force in Berkshire. He was pretty rough about it – as though he'd received word from on high. Are you staying with it?'

'After what you've just told me I most certainly am. What is going on, Roy?'

'For some reason they're putting a cordon round the Holgate murder. Who are they? No idea. But they're pretty high up – someone had obviously twisted the Commissioner's arm. Someone very powerful. I'll contact you if I learn more. If you want to call me, use my home number. Got to go . . .'

Tweed told the others what Buchanan had said. Paula was furious. 'Buchanan is the best detective they've got.'

'Which is probably why they – the mysterious *they* – have put him in quarantine. And while I remember it, I won't have you two fighting each other. Clear?'

'Sorry,' said Paula.

'Ditto,' added Newman. 'What did you think of Snyder? He had obviously hoped you'd let slip some information he could use. Silly chap.'

'But how could he have known about our visit to Bray?' Paula wondered.

'He has so many informants,' Newman explained. 'Some in the police force. Plus a depthless access to expenses. Two hundred quid offered and one of those policemen we encountered would spill his guts. The world has changed a lot.'

Tweed brought up another point. 'What did you think of Sam Snyder, Paula? I know what you think, Bob.'

'I think he's very shrewd,' she began, 'the sort of man who never gives up once he suspects he's on to a really big story. I think he'll continue with his investigation.'

'He did say several things which interested me,' Tweed said thoughtfully, staring out of the window. 'A very weird picture is building up in my mind.'

'Which you won't reveal to us yet,' Paula complained. She stood up, peered out of the window through the thick net curtains. 'A car followed us from the ACTIL building, a brown Volvo with one man behind the wheel. It's still out there.'

'Probably Special Branch,' Newman remarked. 'Is Harry Butler on the premises?'

'Yes, he is,' Monica replied.

'Could you call him? Ask him to go out and persuade that driver it's time he moved on.'

'Knowing Harry, I wouldn't like to be that driver,' Paula commented.

Harry Butler was only five feet five tall but his body was burly, his shoulders wide. His face rarely revealed any expression, but no mugger ever approached him. Wearing a heavy windcheater, the material worn and shabby, his powerful legs were covered in equally shabby jeans and his feet were encased in heavy boots.

He left the building by a back entrance, coming up on the parked Volvo very silently. He could see the squat driver through the rear window, holding a pair of field glasses aimed at Tweed's windows.

'Right, matey,' he said to himself. Walking round to the driver's side as it began to get dark he tapped on the window. The squat man lowered his glasses, glared with piggy eyes at Butler, who continued tapping. The driver lowered the window. Butler immediately leaned both brawny arms on the window so it couldn't be closed again. His large right hand was closed in a fist.

'What the friggin' 'ell do you want?' the driver snarled.

'This is a nice area,' Harry said cordially. 'Not one for voyeurs. Expect you've been salivatin' while you spy on some poor girl takin' a shower. Go back to the East End to the hole you crawled out of. Shove off.'

The driver reached down to his side, pressed the button to shut the window. The pressure of Harry's strong arms held it open. The driver gave up, glared at Harry.

'Get your flamin' arms off my window.'

'I'm not a patient man.' Butler opened his fist, revealed he was holding a small canister, the nozzle aimed at the driver's face, his thumb close to the release button. 'See this? It's Mace. I press the button and you get an eyeful, two eyefuls. Last guy I used it on couldn't see for over a week. Very painful.'

'That's illegal.'

The driver's voice was less aggressive as he stared at the small canister. Butler smiled pleasantly.

'It would be your word against mine. You'd be screamin' in agony. So be sensible. Key's in the ignition. All you have to do is turn it, shove off.'

'I'll remember your face,' snapped the driver.

'Do that. Just hope you don't meet me in a dark alley. Now, on your way, sonny . . .'

The driver suddenly grabbed the ignition key, turned it quickly, released the brake, rammed his foot down on the accelerator, aiming to hit Butler with the side of his car as he shot forward. Which is what Butler had expected so he had already nipped round the rear of the Volvo, standing on the pavement.

The car rocketed to the other end of the Crescent, scraped the side of a Mercedes, both cars stopped. Butler could see them shaking their fists as he returned to the building.

'Terrible drivers on the roads these days,' he said to himself.

'That brown Volvo has gone, collided with another car,' Paula reported, sitting down at her desk.

'Of course it has,' Newman replied. 'Harry Butler has his little ways. Incidentally, I was aware it was following us from ACTIL. Saw it in my rear-view mirror. Didn't think it was worth mentioning.'

'Bob,' Tweed addressed Newman, 'Roman Arbogast mentioned as we were leaving that one of the guests tonight is a Black Jack Diamond, a friend of Sophie's. I've heard the name but know little about him.'

'There's a story. Can't say I admire Sophie's taste in men friends. He's good-looking, a professional womanizer, and he used to be a big-time gambler at blackjack. Hence his nickname. Used to play at Templeton's, the swish club in Mayfair. Skilled. Won huge sums. One night the club had to send out to their bank for more money – he'd cleaned them out. Came in an armoured car. He cleaned up that lot. Became so rich he bid for Templeton's, bought the place. Stopped gambling immediately. Now he runs the club. Athletic type. Diamond is his Christian name. Hence Black Jack Diamond.'

'I shouldn't have thought Roman Arbogast approves,' Paula remarked. 'What's his surname?'

'Arbogast. He's a cousin. As for Roman's approval, I doubt he has much choice. Sophie struck me as strong-willed, does what she likes . . .'

'I've never met this Black Jack Diamond,' Paula said with a thoughtful look.

'And you don't want to,' Newman warned. 'He's dangerous. A typical rich man's son, thinks the world's his oyster. His uncle, Alfred, Roman's father, went into the munitions business. Roman bought him out when he wanted a life of leisure. Hence the A for armaments in ACTIL. The plant is in America.'

'Whereabouts in the States?' asked Tweed.

'Boston.'

4

'Ladies and gentlemen, the Vice-President of the United States, the Honourable Russell Straub.'

All eyes at the array of round tables in the Tree Creeper's spacious first-floor room turned to gaze at the door. His bodyguards, two tough-looking men in grey suits, stood aside at the doorway, and Russell Straub, clad in a dinner jacket, walked swiftly into view, both arms raised as thunderous clapping broke out. He stood there, keeping his arms raised as applause continued.

'Milking the audience for every second he can,' whispered Newman, seated next to Paula.

'Shsh!' she admonished him. 'And that's not the way to clap.'

Newman had both hands lifted and was patting his fingers together with a bored look. Straub still stood at the top of the steps leading down to the tables, a broad grin on his thin face. More applause.

'He paints that grin on his face so it will last,' Newman whispered again.

'You're impossible,' Paula responded, smiling.

Straub was a tall lean figure with dark hair brushed well back over his head, thin dark eyebrows, glowing eyes, a long sharp nose, a mean mouth and a stubborn chin. As he descended the steps he spread his arms wide as though to enclose the crowded room in a warm embrace.

'He's going to kiss us all next,' Newman commented.

'Keep your voice down and shut up,' Paula snapped.

'Difficult to do both at the same time.'

As he was escorted to his table at the head of the room Straub first toured it, shaking the hand of each guest as nearly everyone stood up. The sole exception was Roman Arbogast, who simply twisted round in his chair to accept the hand clasp. Straub bent down, said something to him, Arbogast merely nodded. Then at long last he sat down, with Sophie on his right. He handed her a parcel he took from a bodyguard, a present wrapped in the Stars and Stripes.

'Very subtle,' Newman said.

'I couldn't agree more,' added Paula's companion on her left. She had been taken aback when she first saw the name card in front of the tall handsome man next to her. Black Jack Diamond. 'Should have been the Union Jack,' he continued, 'but what can you expect from an ignorant politician.'

'Hear, hear,' called out Marienetta seated opposite, chuckling. 'I see Chicken Maryland is on the menu. Let's hope it's fresh, coming all that way.' She chuckled again, joined by Newman and Black Jack.

'Won't have been in the fridge more than six months,' Black Jack responded. 'The Americans are very proud of their giant fridges. That's where they store politicians who have got beyond it – their version of Madame Tussaud's.'

Newman was drinking wine and nearly choked when he heard Black Jack's comment. Paula was feeling embarrassed, penned between two such rednecks – as she described them to herself. Marienetta had sensed her reaction and when the man on her right apologized for slipping away, saying he felt unwell, she beckoned to Paula, tapping the empty chair beside her.

They had finished two courses and in long intervals guests walked through between folded back doors into another room where there was dancing. The band was playing a quick foxtrot. Paula stood up to join Marienetta, and Black Jack stood up at the same moment, clasping her by the arm.

'Please do me the honour,' he suggested. 'It would give me great pleasure to dance with such an attractive and clever woman.'

Paula hesitated for a second. She was wearing a black knee-length dress and her shoulders were bare. Unfortunately Marienetta was clad in a jet-black dress with full sleeves and a high collar. She decided she couldn't refuse but she had noticed Black Jack had consumed a great quantity of wine. As they stepped onto the dance floor he took hold of her, one hand on her bare shoulder, the other wrapped round her waist. He pulled her close to his body.

As they moved round the dance floor she studied him. He had the figure of a male model, but his craggy face did not fit in with that impression. He had thick fair hair, long at the back, a well-shaped forehead, a prominent nose below oddly large eyes which seemed depthless. His lips were thick and she thought they could be cruel. His hand caressed her bare shoulder with growing enthusiasm. She smiled.

'I hope you don't mind but I have sensitive skin and your hand is gripping it tightly.'

He relaxed the hand immediately, moved his face close to hers. 'Later on I'll remember that, be gentle as a lamb.'

'Later on?'

'Thish place ish becoming a bore,' he replied, slurring his words slightly. 'There's a rear exit over there. Come and have a memorable evening with me at my little flat in Eaton Square.'

'I don't think so. I like it here.'

'Tell you a shecret. I've been offered ten thousand poundsh to knock out a man called Tweed. He'sh your boss. Right? You're some kind of a secretary to him.'

51

'You could say that. What's this joke about knocking out Tweed?'

'He'sh getting in the way of some important people. He won't be able to walk for three months when I've had a few wordsh with him. Be a pal, point him out to me when we go back into the beanfeasht.'

Paula had drunk only one glass of wine and she was shaking inside. Her alert brain spun round. How to handle this crazy situation? Did he mean it? She saw the odd eyes gazing into hers, assessing her reaction.

'I'll do what I can,' she said.

Shortly afterwards they returned to the restaurant. She glanced back and saw a young blonde, clad more as though she was going to bed than attending a dinner, had trapped Black Jack in a conversation. Paula hurried back to her table. No one except Newman saw her skilfully scoop up his name card, concealing it in her hand. He leaned towards her.

'Something up?' he asked quietly.

Amid the clinking of glasses and the loud babble of voices as inhibitions melted no one could hear them. She bent close to his ear.

'Black Jack told me he'd been paid ten thousand to rough Tweed up savagely. I don't think he recognizes Tweed. I'm going to point you out.'

'Do that. I'll handle the situation.'

Tweed, she had seen earlier, was seated at the top table next to Arbogast. He was drinking coffee when she stooped close to him, whispering.

'When you leave here it's vital you have Newman by your side. A matter of safety.'

Arbogast, who had been talking to a beautiful woman on his left, turned in his seat. He reached across Tweed, holding out his paw to Paula, who took it. He squeezed her warmly, smiling as he spoke to her. 'If you ever get tired of spending time with this modern Einstein, give me a call, then come over so we can chat. I meet so few attractive ladies who have a powerful intellect.'

'I might take you up on that.' She smiled again and left, then slipped back.

The Vice-President had leaned over the table. His cold eyes were fixed on Tweed as he spoke. Everyone else listened to what the great man was going to say.

'You are Tweed, I understand,' Straub rumbled. 'So what is your role in life?'

'If you know my name . . .' Tweed paused, leaning forward. His voice was harsh. '. . . then obviously you know my role in life. So what is the point in asking the question?'

His voice was loud, almost ferocious. Paula was startled – she had rarely heard him speak in this aggressive manner. For a fleeting second she saw a vicious expression flash across the Vice-President's face, then the politician took over.

'Ladies and gentlemen, we have a lion present, one with teeth. Well, I've met such people all my life and I've yet to encounter one who disturbs me.' He raised his glass. 'I wish to propose another toast to the beautiful Sophie on her thirtieth birthday. Bless you, my dear . . .'

Paula returned to her table, this time occupying the empty seat Marienetta had earlier offered her. Roman's niece had a soft voice so she could chat to Paula without anyone hearing what she was saying.

'Your boss scored a bull's-eye there. I've seen Straub a lot on television and normally nothing throws him.'

'He asked for it.'

'He certainly did. Oh my, Sophie is going to get up and make a speech. And she's been drinking heavily. Keep your fingers crossed. She came back from the States a few days ago and I think she's still jet-lagged – on top of the drink.'

'Do you also visit America?'

53

'Only now and again. Sophie flies over far more. We've got a company over there. Here we go . . .'

Sophie was standing up close to a large tree creeper planted in a huge green tub. She waved her half-full glass back and forth, as though anointing her audience. A hush fell on the room. Sophie began speaking.

'I want to thank you all . . . I want to thank you. I want to thank you . . .'

'Needle's got stuck,' Marienetta whispered.

'To thank you for the most wonderful birthday party I'm ever going to ecksp . . . ecks . . .'

'Experience,' whispered Tweed, leaning across the table.

'. . . ever going to experience.' She raised her glass. 'Three cheers for Tweed. And above all I'm so honoured to have the Vice-President, the next President of the United States of America, as the most honoured guest I could hope for. I'll be opening my presents later but thank you all for being so generous. Bless you all.'

As she sagged back in her chair thunderous applause broke out, continued for two minutes. Marienetta leaned close to Paula, so close she could just smell very expensive perfume.

'Tweed saved her, got her going again. It should have been Straub who came to her aid. He's smirking now, the bastard.'

'Like me,' Paula commented, 'you have very acute hearing. I just caught what Tweed said to her.'

'An ear specialist once told me I would hear a ping-pong ball dropped into the sea. It's a family trait. Mind if I smoke? Would you like one?'

'Yes, please. One of my rare pleasures.' When Marienetta had lit her cigarette with a jewelled lighter Paula asked her question. 'I hope you don't mind my mentioning it tonight, but have you any idea what Holgate could have been doing out at a remote spot like Bray after dark?'

'No. Uncle has pondered that and not come up with

54

even a theory. Adam wasn't popular with the staff but I found him charming.'

'Someone told me you have a large old house near the river where it happened.'

'Abbey Grange. Roman hardly ever uses it. He bought it for private conferences, then decided he didn't like the place. I've only been there once and I didn't like it either.'

'You have someone to look after it?'

'Not now.' Marienetta shook her head. 'We've had a series of housekeepers and one by one they've left. At the moment there isn't one. The house is empty.'

Then who was in that room with the light on at the side of the house, Paula asked herself, on the night of the murder?

Straub, accompanied by his bodyguards, had left and the party was breaking up. Earlier, Paula had loitered near the doorway leading to the dance floor. When Black Jack appeared she began walking, pointing to Newman's back.

Tweed, who had been talking to Arbogast, was among the last to leave. Newman walked by his side and Paula watched as Black Jack put on his coat and followed them. Outside the night was chilly, inclined to sprinkle with rain. Newman stood by himself, but still not far from where Tweed waited for a taxi to appear.

Paula stood outside the entrance as Black Jack lit a cigarette. It was the ideal moment for the ex-gambler to launch his attack. To her surprise he waited until she walked out and approached her.

'Come and have a drink with me. We could go to Marino's off Piccadilly.'

'Thank you, but I'm too tired to go anywhere except home.'

'Another evening? Tomorrow? Day after? Come on.' He took hold of her arm.

'Don't think the lady's interested,' Newman said, walking close to them.

'Ah, the celebrated foreign correspondent,' he sneered. 'I really am pleased to meet you.'

Tweed moved close. 'She really has had a day of it. So why not go home by yourself?'

'I thought Paula might like to hear something I happen to know about Adam Holgate. Something no one else knows. It hasn't appeared in this long article by Sam Snyder in the *Daily Nation*.' He pulled a folded copy out of his trench-coat pocket, opened it up, showed the front page to Tweed. The headline blazed in huge letters.

SECOND HEADLESS BODY FOUND
AT BRAY
US Vice-President Visits London

Black Jack's manner was cordial and he'd shown no sign of attacking anyone. Tweed took the paper handed to him, quickly read some of the long article below. He looked at Black Jack.

'How did you get hold of this copy?'

'One of the guests at the back of the room wanted a breath of fresh air. He told me he'd seen this pack of papers strung up outside a closed newsagent's. It's tomorrow's paper – or rather today's now. Well after midnight.'

'You said you knew something about Holgate.' Tweed gazed at him. 'You were joking, of course.'

'Never been more serious in my life.' He had minutes ago taken his hand off her arm as he turned to Paula. 'The offer still stands. Take you out for a drink and I'll spill the beans. Interesting beans – in view of what has happened to the poor devil.' He was amiable without being persistent. 'Give me your phone number and I'll call you.'

Behind Black Jack's back Tweed nodded at Paula. She hesitated, then produced a card from her evening

56

bag. It was printed with the cover name for the SIS, the General & Cumbria Assurance Company. Plus the phone number for Monica's second telephone for outside calls.

'Make it seven o'clock the day after tomorrow,' Paula decided. 'At Marino's.'

'Give you a buzz,' he said, and walked off into the drizzle with long strides.

Newman had hailed a cab and they all piled inside. Tweed gave the driver the address of Park Crescent and then closed the glass panel so he couldn't hear what they were saying. He had seen the expression on Paula's face. She had perched on the folding seat facing him.

'What the hell do you think you're playing at?' she began. 'All right, just before he pushed off Black Jack was the soul of good manners, but you didn't see him when we were dancing together.'

'No, I didn't,' Tweed admitted quietly.

'He was drunk, behaving like an animal. Now you ask me to go and have a drink with him on my own in a bar. His story about knowing something about Adam Holgate is probably just that. A story, a fairytale.'

'I'm inclined to agree,' said Newman. 'He's the biggest liar in town. Then there was that tripe about someone offering him ten thousand to rough up Tweed. He said that to get your attention. Comes outside and he's as nice as pie.'

'My turn?' Tweed enquired quietly. 'I was watching him when he said he knew something about Holgate. I am supposed to be good at spotting when someone is lying. I don't think he was. He might just have information of a vital nature. He's the sort of chap who gets around. Paula, if you don't like the idea we'll drop it. You don't take any calls from him.'

The cab driver was aware a row was going on. Newman saw his eyes in the rear-view mirror, glared at him. The driver looked away. Paula had quietened down, was staring at Tweed thoughtfully.

'I suppose I could come with her to Marino's,' Newman suggested.

'Won't work,' said Paula. 'He wants a girl he can have a drink with. Then – and only then – he might talk.'

'Both of you think about it,' Tweed suggested. 'And I've just realized I stupidly gave the driver Park Crescent as our destination. Our first stopping point is Paula's flat in Fulham.' As he reached forward to slide back the glass to speak to the driver Paula's mobile phone buzzed.

He waited while she answered it. Her conversation was short. She put away the mobile, looked at Tweed. 'You gave the right address. That was Monica asking us to go to the office. Something has happened but she wouldn't say what – not over a mobile phone.'

Newman sighed, grinned wrily. 'Sounds like another crisis. Something tells me this is going to be a long night.'

'Professor Saafeld called,' Monica told Tweed the moment he entered his office with the others at his heels. 'Asked you to contact him no matter what time of night it was.'

'Get him on the line,' Tweed said as Paula took his coat.

'Tweed here,' he began as he heard Saafeld's deep voice.

'You know I occasionally attend a conference of pathologists in America?'

'Yes.'

'I take the *International Herald Tribune*. It has a long article in one issue on the murder at Pinedale in Maine . . .'

'I know. Newman was talking about it this morning. I've read it.'

'Then you may have noticed the autopsy on the victim,

a man called Hank Foley, was carried about by a top medical examiner brought up from Boston. Dr Ramsey. We happen to be chums. All this goes back a few days ago. I called Ramsey and we compared notes. The upshot is he's sent me copies of the photos he took, plus X-rays. They came by Fed-Ex this evening. In return I've sent Ramsey copies of my photographs.'

'So?'

'I wouldn't be adamant. I didn't do the autopsy on Hank Foley. But, having studied all Ramsey sent me, compared his photos with mine, I'm pretty sure an axe was used to behead him. One very strong slicing blow just beneath the chin, and at the same angle.'

'But is that conclusive?' Tweed persisted.

'The razor-sharp blade used has a notch in it – same shape, same place as the blade used on Holgate. Have you a strong magnifier?'

'Yes. One very like the one we peered through at your place. In Boffinland downstairs in the basement.'

'Would you like me to Fed-Ex Ramsey's material to you?'

'Yes, please. And thank you for calling me . . .'

Once again the phone went dead. No wasted words from Professor Saafeld. Tweed put down the phone, told Newman and Paula what Saafeld had said, was doing.

'Another random serial killer?' Newman snorted. 'One at the edge of the Thames, the other thousands of miles away across the Atlantic? It seems damned unlikely.'

'Not a random serial killer,' Tweed contradicted. 'I am getting a feeling these murders are linked. That the victims had to be silenced at all costs because they knew some great secret.'

5

Tweed arrived back at his office at seven o'clock that evening. He found not only Monica waiting but also Paula and Newman. On his desk was a huge magnifying instrument and a package from Fed-Ex.

'I resisted the temptation to open it,' Paula said.

'I hope you didn't carry that magnifier up from the basement. It weighs a ton.'

'I got Freddie to bring it up. You know he's as strong as an elephant. He wants to look at the photos himself. Not that he has a clue as to what they are.'

'You can open up the package. I can tell you're dying to.'

He sat at his desk while she struggled with the package, using a pair of scissors and her nimble fingers. A strong carboard box eventually appeared and she prised off the lid. Typically Saafeld had enclosed the photos inside plastic envelopes with even stronger protection for the X-rays. Tweed selected the best pictures of the necks of Foley and Holgate and the result was grisly. Then he asked Monica to summon Freddie up from the basement.

He arrived very quickly, a heavily built man over six feet tall with a dour expression which never changed. Tweed gave him two photos, one of Foley which was on better paper than the one of Holgate from Saafeld.

'Freddie, this is top secret. No gossiping about any of this down in the underworld.'

'Never tell them anything.'

'You know how to fix the plate so we can study these two photos side by side.'

Freddie inserted a large plate in a holder below a lens. He carefully placed the two photos in position, looking through another lens to adjust them. Then he stood back.

'What do you think, Freddie?' Tweed asked. 'You may have noticed the stumps of the necks are very cleanly cut, but on one, at least, there's a ragged patch. As though the blade which did the job had a notch in it.'

'I suggest, Mr Tweed, you look for yourself.'

Tweed peered through the lens. He took several minutes studying what he saw. Then he straightened up, turned to Paula. 'Your turn now.'

'Ugh!' was her first reaction. But she continued gazing through the lens. Her nerves were rattling inside but she forced herself to continue her examination. When she stood up she nodded at Tweed while Newman, with a sceptical expression, peered through the lens.

'Freddie,' Tweed said suddenly, 'your opinion, please.'

'A perfect match. This candidate –' he pointed at the photo of Foley's stump – 'had a thinner neck. Even so the blade has to be an axe. And whoever wielded it has to have plenty of strength. Especially to create such a neat cut.'

For Freddie this was a long speech. Tweed thanked him and he left the room. What he had seen and heard was kept inside his head as though he had locked it in a safe. Newman stood up.

'I do see what you mean,' he conceded.

'Bravo for you,' Paula snapped.

They spent the next half-hour examining the X-ray films sent from Boston. Paula had fetched up a special lamp from the basement, with which the strength of the light could be adjusted. The X-rays further confirmed the presence of a notch in the missing axe. Paula had carefully repacked everything inside the outer box when the phone rang.

'It's Chief Superintendent Buchanan again,' Monica reported.

'What can I do for you, Roy?'

'It's what I can do for you. Hope you don't mind, but since I've been pushed firmly out of the picture I'm passing on to you tips I'd normally handle myself.'

'I'm listening.'

'I've been talking to a remarkable woman who helped me locate a murderer once. She sensed it was someone I hadn't even considered – and she was right. A Mrs Elena Brucan. I'll spell that . . .'

'Sounds foreign,' Tweed commented as he wrote down the name.

'She's from Romania and was standing outside the ACTIL building for a long time yesterday. She sensed something wrong.'

'She's a spiritualist?' Tweed asked without enthusiasm.

'No, she isn't. Never attended – or held – a seance in her life. She's very sensitive to people. No harm in seeing her. Can I give her your address, using Cumbria & General Assurance, of course?'

'She's in London?'

'Yes. Rented a flat not far from where I live. Would you say, eleven tomorrow morning – today – be all right for you?'

'Yes, it would.'

'And I've someone else I've used unofficially I could send to you.'

'Tell me,' said Tweed, keeping the exasperation out of his voice.

'Dr Abraham Seale, the well-known profiler. He helped me with another case. Located a top drug baron I'd thought was a respectable stockbroker. Three o'clock tomorrow afternoon any good?'

'Agreed. And thank you, Roy, for trying to help. You're at home?'

'Yes. If I called from the Yard there's a good chance my call would be monitored.'

'What? I'm beginning to find this incredible considering who you are.'

'Oh, there's more.' Buchanan chuckled without any hint of humour. 'Came home to my flat and noticed there were small scratches on both Banham locks on the front door. Alerted me, so I checked this phone I'm calling on. Someone had inserted a bug, no larger than a pinhead, glued in. Took it out before I called you. A friendly visit from Special Branch, I'm sure. I "flashed" the rest of the place and found it clean.'

'This is iniquitous. Shouldn't you inform the Commissioner?'

'What would be the good? The Home Secretary, the man he'd approach if he agreed, which I doubt, is the evil genius behind the net they've drawn round me. Probably round you too. Sorry to bother you so late – or early.'

'Again, Roy, my grateful thanks for your help.'

'Watch your back. Sleep well. I hope . . .'

Tweed put down the phone, told Newman and Paula about the two people who would be coming to see him. Newman exploded.

'Oh God! That's all we need. A spiritualist woman and a profiler. You don't like them.'

'No,' said Tweed, 'I'm not happy about so-called profilers. They tell you the murderer is between the ages of twenty-five and forty, that it's a male and a white man who probably has a menial job. All of which gets me nowhere.'

'I once attended a lecture by Dr Abraham Seale,' Paula commented. 'I went in a sceptical frame of mind but found he impressed me. He's shrewd and sensible, even if a bit odd.'

64

'Can't wait,' snapped Newman.

Tweed went on to tell them about Buchanan's experience in his flat. Paula looked stunned. Newman detonated again.

'They're turning Britain into a police state. But it isn't the police who are doing it. I have the stench of Special Branch in my nostrils.'

Marler walked in as he said this, still dressed in his smart outfit. He never seems to sleep, Tweed thought as Marler leaned against a wall close to Paula, lit one of his long cigarettes.

'You could be right, Bob,' he remarked in his clipped tone. 'I've been roaming round contacting my informants. They won't talk for any amount of money. Not that Bob's Special Branch friends know my people, except for one. He told the thug in the grey suit who approached him to get stuffed. A cockney, of course. Same chap told me the news has been spread on the grapevine that anyone who opens his mouth will go behind bars for possession of drugs.'

'All of which,' Tweed observed, 'confirms my suspicion that someone very high up is involved – at the very least concerned – about the Holgate murder. Now, we have a lot to do tomorrow.'

'And I have my evening appointment for drinks at Marino's with Black Jack tomorrow,' Paula reminded him.

'Not on your own?' asked Marler.

'Just little me.'

'I'll come with you,' Marler said. 'By which I mean I'll be there discreetly, watching. Black Jack is known to subject women to cruelty, both mental and physical.'

Tweed caught her expression. Outright disapproval. She rightly regarded herself as a senior officer, capable of taking care of herself. She did not want a babysitter.

'Thank you, Marler, for the suggestion,' Tweed told

65

him. 'But I think Paula would sooner go on her own. Monica, you're leaving with us.'

'I feel fresh, have a ton to get through.'

'It will be there when you come in after a good night's sleep. That is an order.'

Paula had stood up, was peering out into the night between two curtains she had pulled a fraction apart. She closed the curtains, turned round.

'Thought you might like to know there's a man behind the wheel of a big grey Ford. He was gazing over here through a pair of field glasses.'

Newman jumped up, clapped his hands. 'Feel like a bit of exercise, so we can shift him before we all leave. You go out the back way, I'll use the front door.'

Back inside her bedroom in her flat Paula fell into a deep sleep. She had another nightmare. Roman Arbogast was advancing towards her, his face twisted into a hideous mask like the second picture Marienetta had painted.

She was backing away from him but stayed in the same place. She felt for her .32 Browning in the special pocket inside her handbag looped over her shoulder, realized the weapon wasn't there. He was elevating the axe in his right hand when she woke up, screaming, her body covered in perspiration. She checked the time by her illuminated wristwatch. 3 a.m. She got up.

'Hell and damnation, I had a shower before going to bed. Now I need another . . .'

Tweed didn't try to sleep. Leaning against the pillows, arms behind his head, he checked over facts. No theories. Stick to the facts. He felt he was returning to his long ago role of Chief of Homicide at Scotland Yard. The two horrific beheadings – Hank Foley's in Maine and Adam

66

Holgate's near Bray – had been committed with the same weapon, probably an axe. The photographs and X-rays Saafeld had sent him proved that. So logically the same killer had wielded the axe.

The Arbogasts were a strange family. Roman seemed stable but tough. Sophie did not seem to have inherited his stability. She was subject to mood swings. Sometimes a sullen aggressiveness, then the buoyant vitality she had shown at the birthday party.

Marienetta. Brilliant, with Roman's brains. Sophisticated. Different interests – painting, sculpture, administering the giant ACTIL. He had the impression she was taking to Paula, that the friendship was reciprocated. Funny if a woman solved this complex mystery.

Black Jack Diamond. Where did he fit in? A rich man's son, often the black sheep in a family. But he'd struck out on his own. An unbalanced man where women were concerned – was this an important factor? Yet the two victims so far had both been men.

A random serial killer on the loose? Tweed rejected the idea out of court. All his instincts told him there was a link between the two murders. On the surface that seemed implausible. A caretaker in Maine, a security expert in London. He clung to his insistence that there was a link.

Russell Straub. The vicious look he'd given Tweed when confronted across the table at the party. A dangerous man to cross. Of course! Tweed sat up straighter. The Vice-President was *frightened* of something, someone. What? Who? Why?

Broden. He didn't know enough about him. Broden kept his thoughts mostly to himself. What was his history before he took on the big job at ACTIL? I must find that out, he said to himself. More than once, years ago, he'd found that it was the character who submerged himself who should be investigated. Sometimes with surprising results.

Sam Snyder. A difficult man to read. As a reporter a wily fox. But when he'd gone over to look at the Turner painting on the wall at the office he'd treated Paula with a gentlemanly courtesy. His hawk-like visage had melted into an expression of kindness, his voice had softened. In a brief minute he had become a different personality. Men and women are so complex, Tweed thought.

Now who had he missed out in his review of the characters involved in the unfolding grim drama? He couldn't think who it was as he sank into a deep undisturbed slumber.

As he descended the steps into the street, slippery and wet, the next day, his new neighbour, an attractive and intelligent widow called Mrs Champion, came out of her doorway. She looked across and gave him a warm smile.

'Isn't it a pity, Mr Tweed, that we never get time to have a chat. About the world situation or something a little less ponderous. Now I'm rushing off to my work.'

'Yes, it is a pity. Perhaps one evening . . .'

He stopped speaking as a free taxi came along and he hailed it for her. She thanked him with another warm smile, got inside, closed the door. He stood, watching the cab retreating swiftly. He'd been on the verge of inviting her out to dinner, then he saw another taxi coming, hailed it, jumped inside, asked the driver to take him to Park Crescent. He'd suddenly remembered he had two unknown people coming to visit him, the thoughts he'd had in bed before falling asleep. Mrs Champion became only a forgotten encounter.

'More trouble,' Newman announced as he walked into his office.

'Thanks a lot,' said Tweed, as Monica helped him off with his coat. He sat at his desk, glanced at Paula seated behind her desk. 'What is it, then?' he asked.

'We've had Professor Saafeld on the line. I took the call. He's fuming. A car was parked just beyond his house all night. One man behind the wheel. He stormed out in the morning to ask the driver what the hell he was up to. When he threatened to call the police the driver reluctantly produced a folder identifying himself as an officer of Special Branch. Then he drove off.'

'They really are closing a net round all of us,' Tweed replied with an expression of satisfaction. 'They keep giving themselves away. Something very big is worrying the government. Sleep well, Paula?'

She hesitated, then gave a brief version of the nightmare which had woken her up. She said the trouble was that her mind was too active at the moment.

'It was that ghastly painting in Marienetta's studio which triggered that off. It really was quite horrible. Something else I thought off while I was taking my second shower. That episode when Sophie made her speech—'

'Half-seas over,' Newman interjected.

'No,' said Paula. 'That's the point. I had a good view of her and she drank almost nothing. Except water.'

'Come off it,' Newman protested. 'She was drinking glass after glass.'

'She appeared to be,' Paula insisted. 'But when no one at her table was looking she emptied nearly all the wine into that huge tub beside her – the one with the tree creeper in it. She's clever. Then she pretends to be tiddly when she makes her speech. Why?'

'You tell me.'

'All through the dinner she chatted but her cold grey eyes were sweeping the room methodically, checking up on who was there.'

'Gives us rather a different view of Sophie,' Tweed said thoughtfully. 'I was near her and didn't spot her trickery.'

The phone rang. Monica listened, called out to Tweed. 'A Mrs Brucan is waiting downstairs to see you.'

69

'She was coming at eleven o'clock.'

'It is eleven o'clock,' Paula told him. 'You arrived late.'

'I should have realized. Mrs Champion, my new neighbour, was leaving at the same time. She goes off at ten thirty to her fashion design business.'

'Tweed,' Paula said, studying a pen she was twirling between her fingers, 'she's that rather beautiful widow who waved at us when we were getting a meal one evening. I thought so. You really should ask her out.'

'Mrs Bruchan is the first on the agenda today.'

'The lady downstairs who can see into the future,' Newman mocked.

Marler walked in as he spoke, wearing a new grey suit with a tiny check pattern, crisp white shirt, Chanel tie. He made his remark to Newman as he walked across to lean against the wall close to Paula, taking out a cigarette.

'If she can see into the future maybe she can tell me next week's lottery numbers.'

'She'll be a waste of time,' Newman replied, disgusted.

'Suspend judgement until we've seen her,' Tweed advised. 'Wheel her up, Monica.' All eyes turned to the door when Monica had left, wondering what apparition would arrive.

Paula suppressed a gasp as Elena Brucan walked in. She was the lady she had seen across the road, watching the ACTIL building. Their visitor was small, probably no more than five feet tall, in her late fifties or early sixties. She was still clad in her pale green overcoat, her green fur hat. But it was her face which intrigued Tweed. A hint of the Slav in her well-moulded cheekbones despite a full face. Under thick dark eyebrows she had large observant almost black eyes above a strong nose, a wide mouth and a chin expressing character. Her smile was glowing and

70

warm and she moved nimbly. There was something about her presence which created a hush in the room.

Tweed, standing up with Newman, introduced her to Paula who was again surprised, this time by the firmness of her grip.

'And this is Marler.'

She walked closer to him, felt his suit. 'This is the first time it's ever been worn.'

'True enough.'

'You're a man of great kindness.'

Behind their backs Newman stared at the ceiling in sheer disbelief. Paula on the other hand agreed with Elena. Marler, she knew, had helped many people in trouble, but by stealth. He never wanted anyone else to know.

'Over there,' Marler said, indicating Newman, 'is a gangster.'

Newman was clad in blue jeans, an open-necked shirt and a jacket he'd hastily put on before their visitor appeared. Elena went over to shake his hand, still smiling. She shook her head over her shoulder at Marler.

'He could cope with gangsters. He's a formidable character. But he's very human, a man of great honesty. I would trust him with my life.'

'Do sit down,' Tweed urged her when she had shaken hands with Monica. He was anxious to hear if she had anything important to say. 'And please don't attempt to analyse my personality. I'd find it embarrassing in front of my staff. Now, Chief Superintendent Buchanan said you might have something to tell us.'

'Many won't believe this but I was born with a gift for assessing people. Thank you, my dear,' she said to Monica who had handed her a cup of coffee. 'Early yesterday morning, probably before anyone arrived at the ACTIL building – I saw one individual arrive and unlock the doors – I felt I should wait there.'

'Why?'

71

'I don't know. I was just out for an early morning walk. I suppose I was caught by its strange shape, like an enormous drum with a cone perched on the top.'

Tweed was undergoing a strange experience. Elena sat facing him, her glowing eyes never leaving his. He felt she was able to see right inside him. He held her gaze as he continued his gentle interrogation of this nice woman.

'You saw the staff arrive?'

'Yes. Sometimes in a group, sometimes individually. I do recall a very tall lady, very smartly dressed and beautiful, who moved quickly, very upright.'

Marienetta, Tweed thought.

'But there were so many people going in there.'

'Excuse me,' Paula called out, 'you were taking pictures of some of them with your camera.'

'Quite right, Miss Grey,' Elena agreed, turning round. 'But I took pictures of *all* of them.'

'Including the Vice-President of America?' Tweed suggested.

'Oh, yes. I took several of him, both coming and going. I have all the developed prints in my handbag. I'll give them to you before I leave. It was while you were there that an unpleasant guard came over and told me to leave. He didn't know about my small camera hidden between my fur gloves.'

'How did you react?' Tweed asked with a smile.

'I told him this was Great Britain, that visitors were permitted to stand in the street providing they were not committing a crime. So what crime was he going to charge me with?'

She's gutsy, Paula said to herself.

'That confused him,' Elena continued, 'so he went back to the building and I stayed where I was.'

'You come from Romania, I understand,' Tweed mentioned.

'Yes. I was there for a short time under Ceauşescu's evil

72

dictatorship. I had met him just before he seized power. He took an instant dislike to me. And he worried me. As soon as he became dictator he sent secret police to where I was living. I saw them coming, slipped out down a back staircase into a maze of alleys. I hid with friends and then escaped from Bucharest to Paris and on to here.'

'This is what Buchanan wanted you to tell me?'

'No. Watching all those people go inside the ACTIL building I sensed great evil very strongly.'

'One particular individual?' Tweed asked casually.

'I don't know. I have copies of the photos I'm giving you. I want to study them. Then maybe, sooner or later, I'll know.' She leaned forward, spoke intensely. 'The sensation of terrible evil was so strong my hands shook.' She turned to Paula and the smile returned. 'Luckily I was not using my camera when this happened.'

'You sound so sure,' Paula told her.

'I was absolutely certain,' she said vehemently. 'Now I have wasted enough of your time.' She took a large envelope out of her embroidered handbag, placed it on the desk. 'There are the photos.'

'I don't think you have wasted my time at all,' Tweed assured her as Elena stood up to leave. 'We shall carefully study the photos you so kindly have given us. And maybe sometime you would join me for tea at Brown's.'

'Oh, yes please, and thank you. I love their tea – the best in the world.'

'I'll escort you to the front door.'

'Again, thank you. Oh, inside the envelope is a card with my address and phone number. I live not far from Roy Buchanan . . .'

6

'Paula, Bob, tomorrow you're flying with me to Maine,'
Tweed announced, returning from seeing off Mrs Brucan.

'Maine?'

Paula could hardly believe she'd heard correctly what he
had said. Out of the blue they were on the move. Tweed
had done this before – suddenly taken off – but never so
dramatically.

'This is terrific,' she said almost wildly. 'Why?'

'I thought a lot last night before I eventually fell asleep.
Woke up this morning, took the decision. Why? Because
I want to see where that caretaker, Hank Foley, was
murdered. I want to see the area, to ask questions about
that asylum, nursing home – whatever. When I was at the
Yard I was notorious for wanting to see everything in a case
for myself. But I should warn you both it will be tricky,
dangerous even.'

'Why?' Newman asked this time.

'Because we're flying into the unknown. From my flat
I did call my old friend Cord Dillon of the CIA . . .'

'He's still Deputy Director?' Paula wanted to know.

'He is. He's taking a chance too. We're flying into
no-man's land with no authority. Cord gave me a contact
in Portland. The Chief of Police. But I'm sure there are
people over there who won't want me poking my nose in.
I'll just have to bluff my way through.'

'We fly to Portland?' Newman asked.

'No. Can't do that. I called Monica, who as usual was here before either of you. She's planned the only possible route, called me back. We fly United to Boston, arrive after dark. About a six- or six-and-a-half-hour flight. At Boston we can link up with a commuter flight from Boston to Portland. We'll hire a car there, drive down to Pinedale, then back to Portland, catch another commuter flight to Boston, linking up with the flight home. Doubt if we'll be there twenty-four hours.'

'I've got to pack,' Paula decided.

'It will be cold,' Tweed warned. 'Cord said freezing.'

'I expected that. Damn! I've got that drinks session with Black Jack Diamond this evening. I'll fit it all in. Tweed, it's time you sat down,' Paula suggested. 'You've been pacing ever since you saw off Mrs Brucan.'

'And the tickets for your trip are on the way,' Monica informed him.

'And don't forget you've got this meeting with Dr Abraham Seale this afternoon at three,' Paula reminded him as he settled behind his desk.

'I know. Now, what did you think of Elena, Bob?'

Tweed looked at Marler, still leaning against the wall, and prepared himself for Newman's outburst. Marler winked.

'I thought she was a very nice lady,' Newman began, 'but she shook me with what she said. She left behind her a strange atmosphere in here.'

'She sure did,' Marler agreed. 'Can still sense her presence, as though she's still here.'

'I feel the same as Bob and Marler,' Paula said. 'Exactly the same.'

'Then let's look at the photos she left us,' Tweed decided.

Tweed opened the envelope, spread across his desk so many photos it was covered. Armed like Tweed with

76

magnifying glasses, Paula and Newman hauled their chairs over. Marler stood behind them.

'Lord knows how many films she used up,' Tweed commented.

'These look interesting,' Paula said, selecting a batch of prints while Tweed shuffled others around. She swept her magnifying glass over a crowd of people entering the Cone. Stopping suddenly, she leaned further forward, nudged Tweed.

'Here she is. Marienetta. Running up the steps. Ready to sort out anyone who isn't doing what she considers a perfect job. Broden is waiting for her in front of that beastly revolving door. They've fixed the door, I suspect, so at that moment it revolves all the time.'

'They'd never get everyone in until lunchtime otherwise,' Tweed said leaning over. 'Even from the back she really is a beautiful woman.'

'Lots more to check out,' she said selecting another print. 'Oh, here is the Saviour of the World. The very honourable Russell Straub. Even arriving he has to perform his act.'

'What's that?' Tweed asked looking again.

Straub had been caught standing at the top of the steps, facing the street. Both arms were raised high to acknowledge a crowd which had gathered below. Beside him stood a man, presumably a bodyguard, lean, energetic looking and grinning from ear to ear. Paula pointed at him.

'Rather like the look of him. Wonder who he is? A lot of character.'

'I wouldn't trust Straub as far as I could throw the Cone,' commented Marler.

'Join the club,' agreed Newman, peering through the glass as Paula shifted it so each man could see clearly.

'Here's Sophie, looking sullen and grim,' Paula reported, checking another print. 'I'm having tea with Marienetta today at six this evening, or just before when it's quiet.'

'How did that come about?' Tweed asked. 'You're due to have drinks with Black Jack at seven.'

'It's only a short walk from Brown's to Marino's. I'll fit them both in. Marienetta suggested we get together during the dinner.'

'You two seem to get on well,' Tweed remarked.

'I think she feels comfortable with me. Because Roman thought Security was the key department at ACTIL, Marienetta worked as a detective for Medford's before being taken on the staff.'

'Medford's?' Tweed was impressed. 'They're the top private investigation agency in London. And they're very choosy who they take on.'

'Marienetta could talk and smooch her way into almost any job in this fair city . . .'

The checking of Elena's photos went on. Marler had found a magnifying glass and was himself checking. There was silence for a while until Tweed suddenly spoke.

'What is this? What was he doing there? Sam Snyder going into the building.'

'Let me see.' Newman checked the print. 'Yes, it's him. I wonder who he was going to see? Doubt if it would be Roman Arbogast. He never gives interviews.'

'Something even stranger,' Tweed said, spreading out five prints. 'He's the only person she photographed five times. On arrival in the street, going up the steps, turning round halfway up, pausing before the door, going in. Snyder. Five times. Why?'

7

Dr Abraham Seale was late for his appointment and made no apology when Monica ushered him into the office. Paula took an instant dislike to him and he hardly seemed the same man whose lecture she had once attended.

Very tall and slim, he wore a frock coat, dark black. At his neck, below a prominent Adam's apple, protruded the ends of a stiff white Victorian collar. His long face was craggy, his eyes cold, his hair dark and thick like his eyebrows. He carried in his right hand a thick black cane with a silver head shaped like a serpent.

He sat in an armchair, facing Tweed, sat erect as a flagpole. It was impossible to guess his age and his voice was high-pitched, his manner condescending. Grasping the head of his cane in both large strong hands, he swept his gaze round the room swiftly, turned back to Tweed.

'I haven't much spare time. I'm a busy man but Buchanan insisted I came to see you. I presume you are Tweed.'

'I am.'

'That's a splendid cane you have,' Newman remarked, and held out his hand.

Reluctantly Dr Seale extended the came, keeping a firm grip on it. Newman reached out to examine the strange head. The cane was jerked away.

'The head is pure silver. I wouldn't like it smeared.'

'What can you do for us – or what can we do for you?'
Tweed enquired.

'Listen with both your ears. I understand you are
involved in the murder of the caretaker Hank Foley, in
Pinedale. Also in the similar murder of Adam Holgate at
Bray. The most significant factor in both cases is that the
heads are missing.'

'Foley's could have been thrown into the sea, Holgate's
into the River Thames,' interjected Paula.

'Nonsense,' snapped Seale. 'If that had been the case
the corpses would have been disposed of in the same
way. They were not. Another significant factor. We are
dealing with a murderer who is abnormal. Then there is
the question of gender. Quite abnormal,' he repeated in
his emphatic way.

'Then he should be easy to spot,' Tweed suggested.

'On the contrary. Most of the time it may well appear to
be quite normal. It is not generally realized that we are all
abnormal in some way. We do something and think: Why
did I do that? A tinge of abnormality. There are degrees.
When we have someone who decapitates people we have
reached the ultimate. But don't imagine you can't have
dinner with it without realizing what horrors lie beneath
the surface.'

'Not a pleasant thought,' commented Tweed.

'It is, I am quite sure, very sly and cunning. An expert
at mingling with fairly normal people so they have no
inkling of what they are dealing with. Bundy, who raped
and killed so many girls in the States, was able to do so
because when he approached his victims he appeared so
normal. The murder method is intriguing,' he went on as
though discussing the merits of a meal. 'It has perfected
an admirable technique – the neat slicing of the head off
the neck just below the chin so the head is preserved in
perfect condition. Concentrate on that and one day you
may identify it. Or you may not.'

'Any more tips?' Tweed enquired, his eyes half-closed as he fiddled with his pen.

'Tips!' Seale was outraged. 'My dear sir, years of study of many specimens have gone into every word I utter. You have to exert your brain, imagine you are it. How would you go about exercising this brilliant technique?' He switched his gaze to Paula. 'Are you acquainted with the Wychwood Library?'

'Yes,' replied Paula staring straight at the dark eyes. 'But you have to be a member.'

'I am a member,' Tweed said quietly.

'Then,' said Seale, still gazing at Paula, 'use Tweed's card to borrow a copy of *A History of Executions* by Jonathan Wylie. Study the volume.' His gaze was stern. 'It may help you to understand it – how it operates. There is a factor no one has mentioned. I leave you to discover what it is.'

'It would help Miss Grey if she knew what she was looking for in the book,' Tweed suggested.

'No, it wouldn't,' Seale snapped again. 'She must find out for herself what Wylie's marvellous book tells her. And that man leaning against the wall over there,' he said referring to Marler, 'adopts that stance for a good reason.'

'What reason?' Tweed asked, not in the least put out by his strange visitor's appalling arrogance.

'He is a combat man. Sitting down would put him at a great disadvantage, if attacked. Standing up he is in a much stronger position to deal with any situation that arises.'

Seale stood up, stroked his cane, his gaze swept once more round the room. He turned to the door, not looking at Tweed.

'That is all I have to say. I have now done my duty by Roy Buchanan. Goodbye . . .'

*   *   *

81

'That is a character and a half,' Tweed mused when they were on their own.

'Like something out of Charles Dickens,' Newman commented. 'Doesn't belong to this age at all. Stuffed shirt.'

'I did found something he said very interesting,' Tweed replied.

'From now on I'm going to refer to this homicidal maniac as "it",' announced Paula. 'I think the word will help us to track it down.'

'Why?' Newman prodded her sceptically.

'Because the murderer is inhuman but will look human. Seale confirmed that. Referring to the killer as "it" will remind us of that fact, keep us on our guard.'

'I think Paula is right. A good idea,' agreed Tweed.

'He was right about one thing,' Marler interjected. 'I do lean against walls so my back is guarded. Shrewd of him to make that observation.'

'He's a crackpot,' Newman snapped. 'I wonder how he makes a living? That weird outfit he was wearing was new, must have cost a pretty penny.'

'I've just remembered,' Tweed remarked. 'Seale even goes to the States on lecture tours. I'm sure he rakes in the dollars. Dressed like that he'll be a raging success with his American audiences.'

'He believes in self-protection. That cane he wouldn't let me touch is, I'm sure, a formidable swordstick.'

'Swordstick?' Marler interjected again. 'Could you slice a head cleanly off a body with something like that?'

'It's a thought,' said Tweed. 'Seale is the sort of character you see once in a lifetime.'

'Don't agree,' said Newman. 'He was at Sophie's birthday party in full evening dress. At one of the tables near the back.'

'Don't miss much, do you?' commented Paula.

'Sam Snyder was also at that party,' Newman told her. 'He was also sitting at a table near the back.'

'Sam Snyder,' Tweed repeated, gazing out of the window. 'I still wonder why Elena took five pictures of Snyder but of no one else.'

8

Paula, armed with Tweed's library card, walked rapidly down Harley Street. Seale's late arrival had thrown out her whole schedule. She had looked for a taxi but, of course, when she really needed a cab there wasn't one anywhere. She had a very long walk to reach the Wychwood Library off St James Square. The weather was cold and she had slipped on a coat before leaving Park Crescent. The sky was pewter grey. So cheerful.

As she hurried along she found herself gazing at the people she passed. She thought, you look normal, but are you? Seale's personality had impressed itself on her mind. Eventually she crossed Piccadilly where people crammed the pavements. They all began to look abnormal to her. *Stop it!* she told herself.

Her first encounter with the receptionist, a middle-aged woman who kept sliding her glasses back up her nose, was not promising. Pale-faced and unsmiling the woman studied the card Paula had given her dubiously, then slowly gazed at her.

'You're a woman,' she began. 'This card is for a man.'

How damned observant of you, Paula fumed inwardly. Was this going to take for ever? She disliked this type of woman, who reminded her of a civil servant. She felt in her bag, found a General & Cumbria Assurance card, the cover name for the SIS.

'Call that phone number and Mr Tweed will confirm who I am. His personal assistant.'

'Line's engaged,' the dreary woman informed her after calling the number. 'If you'd like to sit over there I'll try again when I can.'

No good telling the old trout she was in a hurry. That would only slow her down even more. Paula sat on the couch, facing the desk from the far wall, placed her briefcase beside her. And I haven't got a book to pass the time, she thought. Not my day. Checking her watch she decided she'd have time to go to a deli for a little sustenance. Not too much. The tea at Brown's was a major event. I should have plenty of time to get to the hotel, she decided. I *have* to be there on time – she had summed up Marienetta as a tigress for punctuality – but I won't have time to change for drinks with Black Jack. I don't care. Why should I fuss about a man like that?

An old gentleman with grey hair had entered the hall. He stopped by the desk and began to engage the receptionist in a long conversation. So no quick second attempt to phone Tweed. Someone was walking down the upper steps on his way out. Dr Seale, erect as a martinet. The receptionist said 'Excuse me,' to the grey-haired man and stood up.

'I hope you found what you needed, Dr Seale.'

Nice to be royalty here, Paula thought. Seale took not a blind bit of notice of the receptionist. Instead he swivelled to his right, bowed, took the seat next to Paula on the side away from her briefcase. She felt stunned. He placed a hand on hers, squeezed it gently.

'How very gratifying to find someone who not only listens to me but acts swiftly on my suggestion.'

'Which is exactly what I am doing. Do you travel much, Dr Seale?'

'A great deal, my dear. I have recently returned from the United States.'

'Which part?'

86

'New England. The weather was disgusting. Icicles were hanging from the gutters of their wooden houses. And they think they do things better than anyone else. I ask you. They don't seem to have heard of brick. But they are a warm friendly people.'

His severe expression had again softened. He smiled as he gazed at her. What a weird mix you are, she was thinking. Normal and abnormal? He wished her luck and stood up to go. The receptionist was again on her feet, calling out to him. He walked out without a word or a glance in her direction.

At long last the grey-haired man stopped talking, wandered up the steps into the library. Paula was marching grimly back to the desk as the receptionist picked up the phone. This time she got straight through. More twittering from the middle-aged woman, a request for a description of Paula. A voice at the other end, Tweed's, rose loudly.

'For God's sake, woman, I'm a member. Give Miss Grey the go-ahead . . .'

Paula was walking up the steps before the receptionist had time to speak to her. She began her arduous search for Jonathan Wylie's tome, *A History of Executions*. No attendants were to be seen to help her. She began with the huge section on Domestic History, which was not arranged in alphabetical order. No luck. By pure chance she eventually found the volume in Medieval Agriculture. Someone had put it back in the wrong place.

She ran back down the steps, saw with relief no customer was standing in front of the receptionist. She placed her card and the precious volume on the desk.

'I am in a hurry now,' she said pleasantly.

A blank stare. 'We have a very meticulous record system.'

A large leather-bound ledger was opened. The receptionist explained as she slowly wielded a pen. Everything had to be noted. Name, address of the borrower, membership number, date, title, author and the book's number. Paula stood very still, her stomach quietly rumbling with hunger. She'd have given anything for a drink of water. The pen kept on scrawling at a snail's pace. After what seemed hours the receptionist handed Paula the volume.

'You do understand,' she said in her toneless voice, 'you have to take great care of the book. You see, it is our only—'

Paula snapped. 'You saw me place the bloody thing inside my briefcase!'

She stormed out and it was dark. She made her way to Piccadilly, walked into a sandwich bar, ordered two toasted teacakes and a cup of tea. Had to leave space for the coming orgy at Brown's. Before her hands became greasy she took out the volume, glanced quickly through it. Full of ancient text which she felt she'd be able to decipher – and a lot of the most horrific drawings illustrating what they did to people in those days. Including the execution of Charles I. She slipped it back into the briefcase as tea arrived.

By hurrying after her modest meal she reached Brown's at 5.45 p.m. No sign of Marienetta. She'd beaten her to it. A quick trip to the ladies' to tidy up, then back up to the lobby. A minute later, at 5.55 p.m., Marienetta walked in, wearing a smart blue two-piece business suit, a white blouse buttoned to the collar and a pair of Ferragamo shoes.

'Why don't we collaborate on investigating this brutal murder of Adam Holgate?' Marienetta asked Paula in her direct manner.

They were seated in the second lounge, where you could smoke after six. Marienetta had already lit up after offering a cigarette to Paula, which she declined. No one was near them so they could really talk.

'Might be a good idea if we exchanged some information,' Paula said cautiously.

'Right, me first. I didn't like him. I didn't trust him. Broden thought he was a jewel, but Adam had a way of getting round people. Even a brute like Broden.'

'What caused your mistrust?'

'Mind if I eat and talk at the same time?' Marienetta suggested as the cakestand, a four-decker, was laid in front of them. 'Bad manners, I know, but I haven't eaten since breakfast. Why? I found out Adam was poking his nose into departments that had nothing to do with him. Once I caught him photographing some highly personal records. He slipped the camera into his pocket when he realized I was close. I challenged him and he turned so aggressive – a tactic. Swore it was a tobacco tin I'd seen. He did smoke a pipe. I didn't make an issue of it because at that moment Broden walked in, but I ordered the guard on the door to search him when he left. That happens at times. The clever so-and-so hadn't got the camera on him – probably hidden it in a locked drawer. But I'm damned sure he had the film in his socks or somewhere.'

'So you think he was a spy?'

Marienetta gave a ravishing smile. 'Not for you, I hope.'

'Certainly not. When he worked for us Tweed banished him to Communications in a building further down the Crescent.' She felt she had to contribute something. 'Howard, our Director, hired him while Tweed was away.'

Marienetta smiled again. 'He'd never have got past Tweed. I met Howard at a party. A nice man but without a tenth of Tweed's brains.'

'He's very good at smoothing down high-ranking civil servants, very at home in Whitehall.'

'Where again they haven't a tenth of Tweed's brains. We exist, even prosper, in spite of our lousy government. I once talked to a Foreign Office diplomat about Laos. He hadn't a clue where Laos was.' Marienetta spoke very fast, chuckled a lot.

'Why do you think Holgate was roaming around near Abbey Grange, Roman's country house near Bray?' Paula asked.

'No goddamn idea. Roman decided he'd blundered, buying that old pile to entertain businessmen from abroad. It's empty. I tell him he should sell the place, take what he can get for it. He says he will. In due course when he's not so busy. What do the autopsy records on Holgate show?'

'No idea. Colonel Crow won't let us see them.'

'Colonel Crow. A pompous pig. Crawls to anyone who can do him some good. Met him once. He complimented me on what I was wearing. I'd just thrown on an old rag. Is Tweed still investigating the Holgate murder?' she asked quickly.

Watch it, Paula warned herself. 'He does have a lot of other problems to attend to,' she replied.

Marienetta smiled cynically. 'I can see why you are the key member of Tweed's staff. Long ago, like met like.'

'Where did Holgate live?'

'In some dump somewhere in Pimlico. Since he took it over the value has soared. He was boasting to me about it. Adam loved money. I spotted that when I interviewed him for the post in security at ACTIL. Broden overruled my doubts and anyway the job was for his department.'

'You said at the party you flew to America now and again. When was your last trip?'

'A few weeks ago,' Marienetta said tersely.

'And you also said Sophie flies over there. When was she last there?'

'A few weeks ago. We didn't fly together. Sophie would think I was keeping an eye on her.'

'And where did you fly to a few weeks ago?'

'Boston.'

90

*　　*　　*

Leaving Marienetta, who was calling a cab, Paula had to walk rapidly once more to Marino's. Due to meet Black Jack Diamond at 7 p.m., she knew she could just make it if she kept moving. Her legs were beginning to ache.

Entering the dimly lit street leading through to Piccadilly, she paused just beyond an alley to smooth down her jacket under her coat. The single street lamp cast her shadow in front of her. Suddenly she realized there was a second shadow, very still, tall, wearing a hat, behind her.

The hat, a man's, was wide-brimmed, possibly Spanish. She froze. The street was otherwise deserted. Then she recalled hearing a car stop by the kerb near the entrance to the side street. Shadow was now tailing her on foot. An ominous development. Whoever had followed her had been caught out by her suddenly stopping to tidy herself. Now Shadow's sinister outline was motionless, almost alongside her own shadow. He was very close to Paula. Her throat was dry with fear.

Then her brain accelerated. She was carrying the briefcase in her left hand, her handbag looped over her right shoulder. With one sudden movement her right hand dipped inside her handbag, gripped the .32 Browning in its special pocket. Her left hand propped the briefcase against the wall, she was swinging round, the Browning gripped in both hands.

Shadow had disappeared. Down inside the narrow alley. The only way it could have vanished so quickly. *Don't peer round a corner.* She heard in her mind the warning words of Sarge, the man who had trained her at the mansion in Surrey with its acres of grounds.

With her finger resting lightly on the trigger, she jumped forward, faced down the alley. Nothing. She had half

91

expected this. A short way into the murky alley it turned a corner, blotting out what lay beyond. She wasn't going down there.

She walked back, picked up the briefcase, walked back swiftly to the main street. Just beyond the entrance a brilliant red MG was parked. Brand new. Realizing she was going to be late for her appointment, she walked back into the side street, the Browning still in her hand, concealed under her coat. She walked quickly past the alley. Damn! She hadn't noticed the licence number of the red MG. Too late now.

As she entered Marino's the Browning was back inside its special pocket. The hat-check girl took her coat but Paula kept the briefcase. The absurd ordeal of obtaining the volume inside it made her decide to hang on to it come hell or high water.

Marino's was a large square room with a long bar against the left wall. The only occupant was Black Jack, seated at a table by the bar with a drink in front of him. December and the weather, which was getting colder still, would stop people from coming out.

Black Jack stood up in the aisle, arms held out to embrace her. She evaded him, smiling, slipping into the banquette opposite where he had been sitting. He waved his arms in a futile gesture to express his disappointment at her stand-offishness, sat down facing her.

'I thought you weren't coming,' he said with a broad smile.

'I got held up. Gave you time to have a few drinks.'

He held up his glass, which was half full. Scotch, she guessed. 'This, Paula, is my first drink. What is yours?'

'A glass of Chardonnay, please.'

The barman heard her and a glass was in front of her in no time. She raised it, clinked glasses with him. Do relax, she told herself. You want him to talk. He might just have valuable information. And he's very sober.

'You're investigating the murder of the late Mr Holgate,' he began, making it a statement.

'What on earth leads you to that conclusion?'

'Your reputation. You never give up. Like Tweed.'

'Only when we have started,' she evaded.

'Excuse me a moment,' he said looking towards the door.

He ran, and because he left the door open she saw what happened outside. He grabbed hold of Nathan Morgan by the collar of his astrakhan coat. He pushed him against the wall, twisting the collar.

'What the hell are you doing, Nathan, spying on me?'

'Lemme go,' Morgan croaked. 'Have you arrested . . .'

'Make a great headline in the press,' Black Jack shouted. 'Gestapo operating in Britain. Paris will love it. So get well away from here. Now! Don't want to see your ugly mug ever again . . .'

Paula turned round. Beyond the net-curtained windows she could see Morgan tugging at his collar, feeling his throat as he stumbled off. Black Jack was calm when he sat again in his seat.

'Special Branch do have a lot of power,' she warned.

'So does the press abroad. The Americans would lap it up. Your Bob Newman could set Whitehall alight. Now, where were we?'

'You were going to tell me something important about Adam Holgate.'

'He was getting a pile of money from somewhere. Far more than could come from his ACTIL salary.'

'How do you know that?' she asked.

'He'd roll into Templeton's, my gambling house in Mayfair. He'd buy chips worth five hundred pounds or more. Play with the lot. Win a bit, then lose the lot. He was an addict when it came to gambling. A few nights

93

later he'd turn up with more cash, buy the chips, play the lot, lose the lot. The source of his funds must have dried up. One night he came in and asked me for a loan. I turned him down. He looked grim, said he'd get it from somewhere. That was the night before he lost his head. Excuse me – rather nasty pun.'

'I see.' Paula sipped her drink. 'Any idea what the source was?'

'None at all.' He gave her the wide grin which knocked over most women. 'Occurred to me he could be blackmailing someone. If so, maybe that's why he ended up the way he did.'

'Did you like him?'

'I did not. He could be nasty. When he lost he started using foul language. I had to tick him off, warn him that if he did that again he wouldn't be allowed into the club.'

'Anything else you can tell me about him?' she pressed.

'Nope.' He grinned again. 'When we've finished our drinks it's time you had a little relaxation. Have dinner with me at Santorini's. They have a terrace projecting out over the Thames. I'm known there. We'll get a great table.'

'I can't. I have another date,' she lied.

The grin vanished as though wiped off his face with a cloth. He finished his drink, looked around the place. He was thinking what his next move would be, she guessed.

'I'll drive you back to Park Crescent,' he decided, standing up. 'My car's parked outside.'

'That's very kind of you,' she said, thinking quickly. Car parked outside?

They walked out, turned left, went past the alley where the Shadow had vanished earlier. Entering the main street he walked over to a parked red MG which had a ticket on it. He was opening the door for her when she flagged down a cab coming down the street.

'Thank you for the drink,' she called out. 'I've changed my mind. A cab will get me there quickly.'

94

'Ladies have this habit,' he called back in a sneering tone. 'Change their minds like the cue ball on a snooker table.'

As the taxi proceeded at speed with very little traffic in the way she thought hard. Vaguely she recalled other cars parked further up the street, any one of which could have been the one she'd heard. Could Shadow have been Diamond? He might have nipped across the street, hidden in another alley, then sidled swiftly into Marino's? Seemed unlikely, but not impossible. Then there was Nathan Morgan. Was he tall enough to have thrown that sinister shadow she'd seen? She wasn't sure. It was unsettling.

9

The huge United Airlines Boeing was well out over the Atlantic. Flying first class, Tweed with Paula and Newman were comfortable and their flight was half empty, so they could talk without risk of being overheard.

Knowing Tweed's dislike of flying, Paula had insisted he took a Dramamine pill in the departure lounge. It was dark outside and Paula rarely looked through the window by her side. This, she decided, was a good chance to report what had happened the day before.

'I collected that volume Dr Seale suggested. It's with me. The funny thing was that while I was waiting for ever to get into the library who should walk down the steps? You won't guess. Dr Abraham Seale. He chatted with me for a short time. Was very nice.'

'He couldn't have been,' Newman remarked, speaking across Tweed. They were sharing a spacious three-seater.

'During tea with Marienetta,' she went on, 'she suggested we collaborate on investigating Holgate's murder. As you know she is a trained detective.'

'I should watch that,' Tweed warned.

'She's a very clever woman,' Newman remarked.

'I should still watch it. What about Black Jack Diamond?'

She told him everything that had happened, had been said, since she'd left Brown's. Tweed looked perturbed when she told him about Shadow.

'You must be very careful while we're engaged on this case. All of us must be. The killer is ruthless and cunning.'

'Case?' queried Paula. 'Anybody would think you were back at the Yard.'

'In a way I am, in my thinking. Surprising the way all that experience comes flooding back. I can do without DNA and all the rest of it. If you just listen to people they'll tell you what they're really like without realizing what they are doing. It's called egotism. And we may already have met the killer.'

'You have a suspect?' Paula probed.

'No. It's far too early.'

A following wind landed them ahead of schedule. Even so it was a rush to find and board the commuter flight which would take them north to Portland.

Earlier Tweed had warned them both to leave all the talking to him. Paula had queried the wisdom of travelling under their own names. Tweed had told her this was a very tricky expedition they were undertaking, that if their stealthy trip to Pinedale was discovered later it would be safer if they had travelled using their real passports.

As the commuter aircraft took off from Boston, Paula peered out into the night. Below them the city was a galaxy of lights and a few ships on the Charles River showed up at their bows and sterns. Otherwise the Charles was a huge black snake making its way inland.

It took them less than an hour to fly to Portland. The further north they went the more plantations of evergreens Paula saw spreading out below, their green nearer to black in the moonlight. Then they were descending with white surf bordering the coast to her right. Several fishing vessels were moored in the harbour.

'Who are we contacting?' she asked.

'My CIA friend, Cord Dillon, told me over the phone we should reach the Chief of Police, Andersen, as soon as we left the airport here. Bumpity-bump. We're down.'

Andersen led them out of the headquarters building into the night. To escort them the short distance to the waiting police car he had thrown on a shabby old fur coat. Paula understood why. As in Boston, the air was raw, a biting cold which froze her face, but it seemed even worse in Portland.

No one had known anything about the hire car Monica had ordered. Andersen had said it didn't matter – he'd a police car and driver who could take them down to Pinedale but they would have to find transport to bring them back.

'I guess you folks chose the wrong time of the year to come over here,' he commented. 'And the forecast is for a big storm to come in from the Atlantic.'

'Seems very quiet,' Paula replied, 'here in town.'

'Folks are battening down for the storm.'

Andersen was a businesslike giant, well over six feet tall. He had expected their arrival, had wasted no time taking them out to the car where a driver sat behind the wheel. Very few people were about and those who were hustled along the pavements, well muffled up.

The car waiting for them was a battered old Ford. Across the front of the roof was the transparent box with red and blue lights lit up. An aerial which had seen better days projected at a slanting angle. Andersen made quick introductions.

'Driver is Sam. He'll take you there. Then that's it.'

'Thank you, Chief Andersen,' said Tweed.

'Sam has to get back here fast. A team is checking out a big robbery. It needs Sam to kick their asses to keep them moving.' He glanced at Paula. 'Excuse me, Ma'am.'

Tweed sat with the driver while Paula and Newman occupied the back. Then they were moving. Soon out of Portland, Sam pressed his foot down, his headlights gleaming on the blacktop ahead of them, now passing through open country.

Paula started out excited. This was an adventure. Like Newman she had let Tweed do the talking when they passed through Customs in Boston.

'Business or pleasure?' the impassive officer had asked.

'Business,' Tweed had replied.

'Profession?'

'Security adviser.'

Nothing more. Tweed had thought what a tremendous contrast to entering New York. He'd endured an hour-long trudge as a crocodile of passengers slowly reached freedom. Surly questions before he hurried to find a cab.

The blacktop stretched out of sight before them while Sam sat hunched behind his wheel, saying nothing to Tweed, not giving him a glance. Then they entered the forests. Walls of fir trees so high Paula could not see their tops hemmed them in on both sides. Her sense of adventure evaporated. She began to feel claustrophobic. The blacktop climbed crests so you couldn't see what lay on the other side until the car popped over the top, descended the far side. No other traffic. Occasionally there was a break in the wall of firs where she had a glimpse of a logging track vanishing round a curve. Didn't anyone live in this eerie wilderness? she wondered. Then they passed a large gap in the forest on her side. In the open space she saw a red barn, the colour gleaming in a shaft of moonlight. It must have been recently painted. Someone did live somewhere.

The weather was changing. A fleet of low dark clouds sailed in from the sea. Sam glanced up, made no comment. He had a face which reminded her of a squirrel, a police cap rammed down over his forehead. She wanted to ask 'How much further?' but remembered what Tweed had said, so kept her mouth shut.

Sam was slowing down, the fir trees were thinning out. He suddenly swung off the highway up a track of granite chippings. Space opened out. Perched on a small hill was a two-storey clapboard building badly in need of fresh paint. A railed porch ran along the front and several wooden rails had collapsed. Shingles had been blown off the roof. Behind smeared windows, beyond the top of wooden steps leading up to the porch, lights glowed on the lower floor. Somebody isn't bothered much about appearances, Paula said to herself. The car stopped several yards away from the flight of rickety steps between the wooden rails. Sam suddenly became voluble.

'Deputy Parrish is inside there,' he said in a distinct accent. 'Doubt you'll find him very cooperative. Sea is over there behind the police headquarters. Hear that wind?'

Paula became aware of a strange swishing sound. Looking back to the edge of the forest she saw the huge trees swaying slowly. It was a disturbing sight.

'Storm's close,' Sam continued. 'A buster's comin',' they say. One helluva a murder took place near here recently. The killer chopped off the head, dumped the corpse damn near into the ocean. Head's still missin'.' He made a funny sound which Paula realized was a chuckle. 'Why'd he want the head? Maybe collects them. Gotta get back now. Andersen is tough but fair.' He waited while they got out, leaned his head out of the window. 'Jed, Parrish's helper, might drive you back to Portland.'

'That's so hopeful,' Paula said to herself as biting cold entered her lungs.

The wind was rising more dangerously while Sam waited for them to reach the foot of the steps. Paula wondered why he was waiting. Suddenly Sam gunned his engine, swung the car round in a mad swerve of a hundred and eighty degrees. Chippings were hurled everywhere and Paula realized why he had waited – for them to be far enough away. With mixed feelings she watched his red tail-lights vanish back along the highway. She had a depressing feeling of isolation.

'Let's get on with it,' said Tweed briskly, full of energy. 'The rail's shaky,' he warned as he mounted the steps to the porch. Reaching a large door he turned the handle and bounced inside. Paula wondered how he managed it.

Beyond the door was a large room with a wooden board floor. Behind an ancient desk near the far wall a man in his fifties sagged in a large wicker chair, his booted feet resting on top of an old desk. Untidy brown hair covered his large head, streaks plastered to his forehead. He had small piggy eyes above a fleshy nose and below that a hard mouth and jowls. He was fat and his old soiled red check shirt was rolled up to his elbows, exposing ham-like flesh; his gut protruded well beyond a leather belt low down on his stomach. His full-cheeked face was red as a setting sun. Tweed guessed the source of the redness was the bottle of beer held in his right hand. He upended the bottle and swallowed several times.

'Deputy Parrish?' Tweed asked as Paula and Newman hurried in behind him, closing the door.

A wave of heat had met them tinged with a stench of beer. Parrish hammered the empty bottle hard down on the desk, stirred so now they could see his gun belt with a holster and a revolver protruding from it. Paula felt faint with the sudden change from icy cold to stuffy heat. Taking off a glove, she dug her nails into the palm of the hand. The pain helped.

'Yeah, I'm Parrish. The law round 'ere. The only law it's got. You Tweed?'

'Yes.' He introduced his companions. Parrish ignored Newman, was leering at Paula. Tweed started to move forward and Parrish spoke again.

'On your way over 'ere you might put another log in the

stove. Keep the lady's legs warm, although she's keeping me warm.'

'I'll do the fire,' another voice suggested. Tweed was picking up two logs, walking over to place them in the open stove, which was roaring. Humour the old brigand – but only so far.

Paula was smiling at the much younger man who had offered to help. His grey check shirt and blue denims were spotless. He looked physically strong, had thick corn-coloured hair, good features and a nice smile. Parrish burped, then growled at the younger man.

'She's not for you, Jed. You'd have to get past Tweed and the tough guy he's brought with him.'

'If you don't mind, Mr Parrish,' Paula snapped, 'I would like to sit down until I get used to the heat in here.'

'Of course!' Parrish dragged three wicker chairs from the side of the room, placed them in front of his desk. He waved a stubby-fingered hand with dirt under the nails for her to sit down. 'Jed,' he called out as she sat down, 'we're forgettin' our manners.'

He placed a hand on her arm, bending over her so she had a stronger aquaintance with beer fumes. 'There, are we comfortable now?'

She grasped his hand, removed it from her arm. Parrish was obviously surprised at the strength she displayed. Tweed, seated, had had enough. He leaned towards the Deputy who had returned to his own chair.

'You were here when Hank Foley's body was found?'

'You might say I oversaw the operation.'

'How was he found? I presume you know that since the murder happened within your jurisdiction. I need data.'

'Well, in that case, maybe you ought to have a nice chat with Jed over there. Later on. He found the corpse. Didn't find the head though, did you, Jed? Sure you didn't drop

103

it when you'se was 'elpin' the Portland team to use ropes to haul it up?'

'You know perfectly well I didn't,' replied Jed with an edge to his voice. 'And it wasn't a joking business.'

'Then take 'em out, show 'em where you found Mr Missing 'Ead.'

'Is your investigation into the crime proceeding?' Tweed demanded. 'If so, how far have you got? I need details.'

'Takes time,' Parrish mumbled as Paula glanced round the room, noticing the contrast between Jed's desk in a corner, with an old Remington typewriter, and neatly arranged piles of reports, and the mess Parrish had created. His desk was covered with papers scattered at all angles, the marks of the bottom of beer bottles staining them. Stacks of files, almost toppling, were shoved against the walls.

Tweed stood up. He'd decided they would get nowhere with Mr Parrish. He wasn't doing a thing about the Foley case.

'I'd like Jed to take us immediately to where he discovered the corpse. We're short of time.'

'I can drive you there now,' Jed said, on his feet as he put on a windbreaker, zipped it up. 'Be there in five minutes at the outside.'

'Then let's go,' said Tweed.

Parrish stumbled to his feet, followed them as Jed walked quickly outside. He led them down the steps and headed for the back of the house. The icy cold stabbed into them like a knife. Parrish stood in the open doorway, called after them.

'You're gonna have a mighty long walk back to Portland.' As he turned back into the house he held a fresh bottle of beer by the neck. At the top of his voice he laughed, almost choking.

'My car's round the back,' Jed explained. 'Anything you want to know you just ask.' The storm wind battered them as they turned a corner. Jed ran back, took Paula by the arm. 'You were nearly blown over there. You'll get used to it.'

10

Jed's car was a battered Chrysler parked behind the house. He turned the heater up full blast, stood outside as Tweed sat in the front passenger seat while Paula was in the rear with Newman. The warmth was building up as he called out before slamming the rear door shut.

'Back in a minute. Got to collect something.'

Paula watched him run to open a door at the back of the house, reached inside to pick something up. He returned carrying a suitcase, which he dumped in the boot before he jumped in behind the wheel.

'Going somewhere?' Paula enquired.

'You bet!' The car was already moving, heading back to the main highway. 'All my things. I've had a bellyful of that Parrish. Andersen in Portland has secretly offered me a much better job, plus more money. The real appeal is I'll be working under Andersen, a real right guy.'

He had reached the highway. He turned left, away from Portland in the direction of distant Boston. He turned round to look at Paula, grinning. 'I can start enjoying my work now. And I'll drive you folks back to Portland. But only when you've seen everything you need to.'

'Does Parrish know?' Paula asked mischievously.

'Hasn't a clue. I'll phone him from Portland to give him the good news.'

The landscape had changed as they sped along the

blacktop. On both sides the ground opened out across stretches of crusted clods of earth where fields had been ploughed. Ahead were more trees but the forest had been thinned out. Jed was whistling to himself.

'Where is Pinedale?' Tweed asked.

'This is it.'

Glory, Paula thought. Here and there, well spaced out, were small miserable clapboard houses with lights behind the closed curtains. People live here all their lives, she was thinking. Londoners who take cheap package deal trips to Italy, to the Caribbean, have no idea what the rest of the world is really like.

'See that burnt-out building near the edge of the highway in the distance?' Jed asked Tweed.

'Yes.'

'That was the asylum – nursing home, they called it – where people parked their unwanted relatives who were mental kooks. Sometimes patients went in for treatment and came out again. You needed a load of dollars to get in there. Privacy was absolute.'

He suddenly swung off the highway along a track, climbing. Paula was aware of a booming sound as the track veered closer to the burnt-out ruin. The storm was hammering against the windscreen. Tweed peered across Jed to his left.

'How far is the asylum from the point where you discovered Hank Foley's body?'

'No distance at all. I found traces suggesting the body had been dragged from the asylum to the coast. Streaky patches of blood. All gone now. We've had heavy rain and no one believed me.'

'How did you come to find the corpse?'

'I was patrolling the edge of the coast in case some ship was heading for the rocks. It was stormy that night. I'd have called the Coastguard in Portland. Parrish of course didn't give a s– –t. Excuse me, ma'am.'

108

'I'm familiar with the word,' she assured him. 'What is that booming sound?'

'Huge waves coming in and smashing against the cliffs. So here we are.' He stopped the engine. 'Don't get out yet, folks. When you do, watch yourselves. The cliff drops straight down. The wind's off the ocean, which helps, but you can get blown flat like when you hit a pin in a bowling alley. You guys can manage but,' he went on turning to look at Paula, 'mind if I hold your arm?'

'I'd welcome the protection,' she replied, meeting his eyes in the rear-view mirror, smiling.

Taking Jed's advice, they got out of the car on the right-hand side, away from the ocean. Paula first buttoned up the collar at her neck before climbing out. Leaving the car, the wind hit them like a moving wall. They bent their heads as Jed clung on to Paula, and suddenly they were at the brink.

Monster waves rolled in as though determined to over-whelm America. They slammed against the cliffs below and spume splashed their faces. The noise was deafening. Still holding on to Paula, Jed pointed down, yelled to Tweed.

'Body was crammed in that huge crevice.'

'Was the storm worse than this when you discovered Foley's corpse?' Tweed shouted.

'No. This one is the biggest we've 'ad this year.'

Tweed had noticed the biggest waves were breaking a good twenty feet below the chasm-like crevice tucked into the cliff. So if the corpse had been thrown into the sea, how had it ever been hurled back, when the ocean didn't reach anywhere near the crevice? He shouted his observation at Jed.

'Never thought of that,' the American replied after staring down for a while.

'I'd like to explore over there,' Paula yelled, pointing down the scrubby slope towards the wrecked asylum. 'I

109

can manage on my own, but thanks for looking after me.'

Then she was off, taking out of her large bag a powerful torch, which she switched on. It was a dreadful night. The howl of the wind, the thudding of the sea against the cliffs. As she moved her booted feet carefully, descending the slope towards the asylum, she was visualizing what direct route she'd have used dragging a body from the wrecked nursing home to the cliff. Except she doubted the place had been burnt down by then.

She was close to the ruin when she found what she was looking for. Earlier she had entered an area of tall grass but here the ground was exposed, as though handfuls of grass had been torn up. Imprinted in the ground was an oblong shape.

'What is it?' Tweed had followed her. They were sheltered from the wind at this spot.

'The place where the execution block was placed. Foley was beheaded here.'

'Keep that idea to yourself.'

'Information, not an idea.'

She took out her small camera, which took perfect pictures without a flash. She clicked the button five times, slipped the camera back into her handbag just before Newman arrived with Jed. Tweed turned to the American. Earlier he had told him when their commuter flight left for Boston, a flight which hopefully linked up with a plane to Heathrow.

'Jed, have we time to look at that nursing home, or what is left of it?'

'Sure. I'll ram the pedal down on our way back. Take you straight to the airport. We'll go back to the car first. Not far.'

It was a short drive to the burnt-out building. As soon as Jed had parked, Paula jumped out and pushed open the wrought-iron gate, which was still standing. She

110

approached the blackened ruin slowly. Brick walls still reared up. So Dr Abraham Seale was wrong when he'd said the Americans didn't know about brick. Had he been here? Now why do I wonder that? she asked herself.

'Where would I hide it?' she asked aloud.

'Hide what?' Tweed asked.

She didn't reply as she was now imagining she was an arsonist. Behind the building was a dense area of evergreen shrubs.

With her gloved hand she picked up a long charred stick, began poking round inside the shrubbery. Tweed had also found something to root around with. Unlike Paula, he plunged deep into the shrubbery, sweeping his thick stick back and forth deep down. There was a *clang!* as it hit something metallic. He stooped down, holding the stick in place with one hand while with the other he felt down the stick. When he straightened up he was holding a large red metal container by the handle.

'This what you're looking for?' He turned to call out to Jed. 'Can you identify this?' He shook it. 'Empty. Any idea what it contained?'

'Gas,' said Jed. 'Highly inflammable.'

'And if,' Tweed continued, 'the full contents were spread over the bottom floor of the house what would be the result when it was ignited?'

'An inferno. And the asylum had a cellar with windows low down. The records were kept there.'

'What sort of records?'

'Detailed records of the patients who were staying here – or had stayed here.'

Paula had crept towards a standing wall cautiously. She peered round the end. Jed was right. There was a spacious cellar with small arched windows which would enable anyone inside to peer outside.

'I was looking for something like that,' Paula commented. 'Someone was anxious those records were destroyed. The cellar is knee-deep in burnt debris.' She opened her glove and showed Jed a fragment of paper curled at its edges. 'Any idea what this is?'

'A bit of the bottom of a medical record,' he said, examining it by the light of her flashlight. 'I can just make out Bryan's signature. Millie, the asylum's cleaning woman, showed me one of these – although she shouldn't have done.'

'What kind of medical record? And who is Bryan?'

'A confidential summary of a patient's problems, why they were admitted, treatment, name –' Jed was staring at the sky, trying to remember what he'd seen when secretly he'd been shown one of the documents – 'address, sex, age . . .' He grinned. 'And who was paying the enormous bill. As for Bryan, that was Dr Bryan, who ran the place with his wife and a staff. Since the fire the Bryans have disappeared. They couldn't be located and we gave up the search.'

'Were there casualties? Patients? Staff?' Paula asked.

'No. A few days before the fire all the patients were sent elsewhere. Staff were all laid off with a bonus. They've scattered all over the country. One, I know, went to Ohio.'

'Curious,' Tweed remarked. 'The timing.'

'The rumour was the Bryans had made their pile and left. They were going to sell the place – but after the fire . . .' Jed waved his hands in a gesture of resignation.

Tweed persisted. 'Is there no member of the staff left in Pinedale?'

'There's Millie. Lives just down the highway. A two-minute drive.'

'Have we time for you to take us to see her? I'd like to ask her a few questions.'

'Sure. Fat Boy Parrish would bust his gut. He's declared the case closed. Maybe money changed hands. Let's move.'

*   *   *

112

They drove down the highway a short distance beyond the ruined asylum. There were more trees, and inland it was hilly, small rolling slopes climbing up to forest. Jed stopped outside a small clapboard house on their right near the highway. Two storeys high, several shutters drawn over windows hung at bizarre angles, presumably supported only by the top hinges. There was no porch, only a wooden rail with a gap leading to the front door. There were lights on behind the windows.

'Millie's in,' Jed remarked. 'But then she would be. Doesn't go out after dark since the murder. Best if I let her know I'm here.'

He knocked twice, loudly, on the wooden door, then called out, 'It's Jed, Millie. Jed.'

They waited in the bitter cold while Paula stared round at the wilderness. Once again she wondered how people lived here all their lives. They heard two locks turning, the removal of a chain. The door was opened a crack and Jed spoke again, then he shoved his face closer and the door opened wide.

They walked straight into a living room, out of the Arctic into overpowering heat from a stove crackling cheerfully. Millie attended to relocking, putting the chain back into position. Paula noticed a shotgun on a sideboard. Millie was taking no chances.

Millie was quite small, in her late thirties, and her brown hair was neat, well-brushed. She wore a spotless white dress rather like a nurse's and peered curiously at her visitors.

'These are Brits,' Jed explained, 'sent down from Portland by Andersen.'

Tweed was grateful for his phrasing. It gave them an air of authority. Standing against one wall was a huge new-looking TV, turned off. On a table stood a set of fine cut glasses and four bottles of expensive Scotch. Their hostess was sharp-featured but had kind eyes. Paula noticed there

113

wasn't a speck of dust on the furniture surfaces, despite their cheapness. Jed made introductions. Millie ushered them to sit in sturdy wooden chairs, settled herself into an ancient armchair close to the whiskey on the table, picked up a glass and sipped from it.

'Your friends can be trusted,' she told Jed. 'I've checked them out.'

'Saw you doing it,' Newman told her with a broad grin.

'We haven't much time,' Tweed began quietly. 'We have to get back to Portland. I'm investigating that horrible murder. Hank Foley.'

'Thank 'Eaven someone is doin' that. They tried to cover it up. I feel guilty. They bribed me to keep my mouth shut.' She pointed at the TV. 'That arrived with the bottles of whiskey. Don't normally drink but it's a comfort after what 'appened.'

'I can understand that,' interjected Paula with a smile. 'I drink a glass of wine when I'm rattled.'

'Who is they?' Tweed asked. 'Who gave you the presents?'

'Bribes,' she snapped. 'No idea where the stuff came from. Delivered by a truck with no note. They keep well 'idden.'

'Did you notice anything strange at the nursing home while you worked there?'

'They 'ad six to ten patients. No room for more. And that included the prison room.'

'*Prison room?*' Tweed queried.

'The one only Dr Bryan could enter. 'Eavy door with two locks, special windows with extra bars. A Mr Mannix was kept in there. Never saw 'im. Bryan even took 'is food in. Told us all the patient was dangerous. Once saw inside the prison room when it was empty. Furnished like a top 'otel in Boston, it was.' Now she had started Millie was voluble. Paula guessed she was glad of someone to talk to.

'Whoever was payin' for 'im must have 'ad a fortune. The last patient to leave on the night of the fire. The others went days earlier.'

'How do you know he was Mr Mannix?' Tweed asked.

'He 'ad his name on the outside of that prison door. I only saw 'is back when he left to get into the limo. A queer business. Wore a black coat and was tall. On 'is 'ead he wore a funny wide-brim 'at. Couldn't see 'is face.'

'The hat,' Paula interjected again, concealing her excitement. 'Was it a Spanish hat? Sorry, you probably don't know what I mean.'

'I do,' Millie told her. 'On a rare trip into Portland I saw a man with same kinda 'at. Bumped into Jed, asked 'im who this queer-looking guy was. He said Spanish.'

'That's right,' Jed confirmed. 'He was behaving suspiciously so I questioned him. Turned out he was a tourist. Guy called Rodriguez. He was OK. Not the same guy Millie saw leavin' the asylum. He was short and fat, not tall. Rodriguez, I mean.'

Paula's mind had flashed back to the night in London when a second shadow had appeared behind hers. Shadow had worn a wide-brimmed Spanish-style hat. Millie was talking again.

'Like I said, Mr Mannix was the last patient to leave. I was down in the cellar where the records were stored. Hank Foley was in the far section of the cellar with a locked door. Somewhere he shouldn't 'ave been. Didn't know I was there. Don't know 'ow he got a key, but 'e always was a snoop. I kept quiet by a window at the front, squeezed in an alcove. Hank was pullin' out a patient's file. It must 'ave been one of the new patients. I cleaned in there once and noticed the dates. New ones were in this cabinet nearest the door, which was where Hank was.'

'What happened next?' Tweed enquired while she sipped

115

more whiskey. She spoke without a slur, as though quite sober.

'Peerin' through the window I saw Mr Mannix leavin' and get inside the limo, which drove off towards Boston. But that wasn't the end of it. A minute or two later limo returns, rear door opens. I didn't like it. I left the cellar real quiet, got my coat, slipped out of the back door and walked 'ome.'

'Did you see Mannix's face then?' Tweed probed.

'Didn't wait to. I was frightened. Something queer was goin' to 'appen. Felt it in my bones. A couple of hours later I saw the flames when the asylum started to burn.'

'Where was Dr Bryan while all this was going on?'

'Dr Bryan and his wife 'ad driven off towards Boston about two hours before what I've just told you 'appened. In the cellar.'

'Leaving you and Foley to clean up the place? He must have been in a hurry to get away. And it's odd that Mannix, a dangerous patient, was left to depart on his own.'

'I didn't like it.' Millie looked frightened. 'Thought it was queer.'

Jed stood up. 'We'd better get going if you're to reach Portland in time.'

They thanked Millie for all her help. She had obviously hoped they'd stay longer. Outside the arctic atmosphere hit them badly after their time in the warmth. Jed spoke to Tweed as they headed for the car.

'Something I should have told you earlier. When I went in the back way to collect my bag from headquarters I heard Parrish on the phone in the office. He was phoning Washington. I heard him swearing at the operator. "Three or four more hours to get through? Bloody ridiculous." Slammed down the phone and I came out, closing the back door quietly. He'd be phonin' his brother, who has done better than 'im. Brother is with the Justice Department.'

Paula glanced at Tweed. His expression had become

116

grim. Would they get clear in time? Before climbing inside the car she pointed across the highway to a large mansion perched on top of a hill, Mock-Tudor-style with wooden beams crisscrossing the gables. A long drive led up to it and there were no lights visible.

'Who does that place belong to?' she asked.

'Someone I don't like. Thinks he's Lord God Almighty. The Vice-President, Russell Straub.'

11

The United Airlines Boeing was flying them further and further east through the night, was close to the mid-point over the Atlantic from Boston to Heathrow.

Jed had driven like the wind to Portland airport where they were in time to catch the vital commuter transfer to Boston. It had still been a rush at Boston to board the transatlantic flight. Now, in first class, they occupied another three-seater: Paula by the window, Tweed in the middle, Newman by the aisle. Their section was two-thirds empty. No one was talking. Tweed's grim mood seemed to have silenced Newman.

Paula was relaxed, glad to feel they had 'escaped'. She liked America but winter-set Maine's atmosphere had disturbed her, especially outside Portland. Maybe it was the grim event which had taken place there – she could see it so vividly in her imagination now they had visited the area. She glanced at Tweed, who appeared to be asleep, but she knew he wasn't, sensed his grim mood reflected in his expression. What was wrong?

A few minutes later the copilot emerged. He approached them and instantly Tweed was alert.

'Mr Tweed?'

'Yes, I am. What can I do to help you?'

Tweed's mood had changed instantly. He was smiling as he looked up at the copilot bending forward, more than smiling he was positively cordial.

'We have a problem, sir.'

'Tell me about it. Maybe I can help.'

'We've received a garbled radio message from Washington. It appears to say that if a Mr Tweed is aboard, the plane must turn round immediately and return to Boston. Could be from the Justice Department. There's a lot of interference over the air but that's the best we could make of the signal.'

'And you're not sure what course of action to take?'

'Frankly, that's the situation. We have a heavy load. Economy is packed full. In twenty minutes we shall be more than half way to Heathrow. The captain isn't happy about turning back.'

'Maybe it would help if I told you I'd been to the States on a mission.' Tweed produced his SIS folder, handed it to the copilot. 'And,' he went on, 'before leaving Britain I was talking to Russell Straub.'

'The Vice-President? Oh, I see.'

'I have a further suggestion as your captain is disinclined to go all the way back. Wait for half an hour, then send your reply. Say the message received was garbled, not understood.'

'I think the captain will like that idea.' The copilot had caught on to Tweed's strategem. 'By the time we get a reply we'll be well beyond the halfway mark, heading for Heathrow. He won't turn back then. Thank you, sir. I'll mention the Vice-President to the captain.'

'That was very quick of you,' said Newman when the copilot had vanished. He checked his watch. 'Let's see if it works.'

'It was positively brilliant,' commented Paula. 'That bit about talking to Russell Straub.'

'Rather a short exchange of words,' Tweed remarked, 'but no one can accuse me later of telling a lie.'

Three-quarters of an hour later Newman nudged Tweed, who again appeared to be sleeping. His eyes opened instantly.

'We're well over halfway there and the pilot hasn't turned back. It worked.'

'And I can bet where that call originated,' Paula said. 'Jed told us he'd heard Fat Boy Parrish calling his brother in the Justice Department. Reporting our presence nosing round Pinedale, I'm sure.'

'I think you're right,' Tweed agreed. 'They have given themselves away again. Why would they be so bothered, so high up, about the murder of Hank Foley? Enormous power is very worried about this case. About the murder of a caretaker. I ask you. I can almost hear the wires humming between Washington and the American Embassy in London. Russell Straub is probably staying there, in Grosvenor Square.'

'And Mr Straub,' Paula reminded him, 'has a large mansion very close to where that asylum stood.'

'I doubt if he was involved in burning down the place, but its proximity could be significant in another way.'

'I forgot to tell you,' Paula remembered. 'When Jed hustled me to the flight at Portland airport I asked him if they knew where the fire had started. He told me an expert with the fire team told him it originated in the cellar.'

'Where the patients' records were kept,' Newman recalled.

'What did you think of Millie's strange story?' Paula pressed.

Tweed was summoning the steward who had served them their excellent dinner earlier. The man came running.

'Have you, please, a pad I could write a radio message on?' Tweed requested.

It arrived in no time. Tweed began writing carefully in block letters. When he'd completed his message he folded it, summoned the steward again, his hand holding a large tip as well as the folded message.

'Could you please send this urgent message now to the address I've written in London.'

'Certainly, sir. And thank you very much.'

'What was that about?' Paula enquired.

'To cover the possibility that a hostile reception committee may be waiting for us when we reach Heathrow . . .'

'Your party is first off the flight, sir,' the steward informed Tweed.

The huge machine had made a perfect landing. The steward led them to the exit. They received curious and sometimes indignant stares from the other passengers. As soon as they stepped out Chief Inspector Buchanan, lean and lanky in his damp overcoat, met them. Behind him stood Jim Corcoran, Chief of Security and a friend of Tweed's.

'Got your message,' Buchanan said tersely as they walked up the sloping ramp. 'There are some unpleasant people waiting for you. Passports here.'

An official accepted the passports, glanced at them quickly, returned them and disappeared. Holding on to Tweed's arm Buchanan continued his explanation.

'We've squared Customs. We bypass them. Have a profitable trip? Good. State of siege here as far as you're concerned. Howard is repelling an army of bureaucrats. Has an appointment to see the PM within the next few days.'

'I've had bureaucrats up to here,' stormed Tweed. 'Any of them get in my way and I'll steamroller the swine.'

Paula was startled. She had rarely witnessed Tweed exhibit such rage. She gripped her briefcase, containing the book from Wychwood Library, tighter. They followed a complex and strange route along deserted corridors and suddenly walked out into a cold drizzling night.

'Here's my car,' said Buchanan. 'Jump in quick.'

Newman and Paula occupied the back while Tweed sat next to Buchanan, who was behind the wheel. He had just started off slowly when a man rushed into the road, held up both arms. Nathan Morgan in a dark overcoat. Buchanan was compelled to slow, stop.

'I'll deal with him,' Newman called out before Buchanan could move. 'You may be up against a clash of authority.'

'Nathan, how nice of you to come and—'

Newman was still speaking when he trod with all his well-built weight on Nathan Morgan's right foot. Nathan yelled in agony, bent over, trying to speak but making only a choking sound. A man jumped out of a car parked on the far side, ran across.

'You one of his?' Newman demanded.

'What happened?' the man asked. 'Yes, I'm on Mr Morgan's staff.'

'He bumped into me while I was still walking. You'd best help him into the airport, find somewhere you can sit him down. Get a move on, you're holding up traffic.'

The aide had his arm round Morgan's shoulder as he helped his chief, who was now limping badly, towards the interior concourse. Newman was already back inside the car.

As they drove closer to Park Crescent through the traffic Paula found she was hankering for the mysterious atmosphere of the forests of Maine. She'd forgotten what a hell London could be as pedestrians in the dark pushed past people huddled under umbrellas.

As he parked at the kerb of the Crescent Buchanan said he wouldn't come in. He had two days' work waiting on his desk. Tweed thanked him for his response to the message he'd sent from the aircraft over the Atlantic.

'Any time . . .' Buchanan drove off.

Entering Tweed's first-floor office they found not only Monica behind her desk; Howard, the Director, was seated in an armchair in his normal posture, one leg looped over the arm. He was smoking a cigar, a new habit.

Howard was six feet tall, had the plump pink face and the large body of a man who patronized gourmet restaurants.

123

Clad in a new grey tailor-made suit, he sported an Hermès tie, handmade shoes. He stood, hugged Paula, and she caught the whiff of his aftershave, which was not to her taste. She thought him pompous with his upper-crust voice and manners. But in times of crisis he had surprised her with the full backing he gave Tweed.

'I've been repelling boarders, kept them off the battlements,' he informed Tweed, who had taken off his coat, seated himself behind his desk.

'What kind of boarders?' Tweed enquired.

'Special Branch idiots – and the Home Secretary.'

'He has no authority over us,' Tweed pointed out.

'I told him that in more diplomatic language. I took my time, knowing how impatient he is. Kept him on the phone for ten minutes while I droned on and on. Saying the same thing in a dozen different ways. Wore him down. Conversation ended when he slammed the phone down on me.'

'Good. I don't like him. Sneaky little man.'

'How did your trip to Pinedale go?'

Tersely, but fully, Tweed gave him a complete picture of their experience in Maine. He quoted what Parrish, Jed and Millie had said. Howard's expression became grave as the story unrolled.

'Strange that the Vice-President has a home so close to the murder scene . . .'

He never finished. The phone had rung. Monica called out to Howard that there was an urgent call on his line. He left quickly. Paula sat up straight, staring straight at Tweed.

'Now maybe you'll answer my question.'

'Which one? You ask so many,' Tweed responded with a smile.

'The one I asked you on the return flight. What do you think of Millie, the cleaning lady at the asylum?'

'Close your eyes mentally. She gave invaluable information.' Paula had closed her eyes physically, seeing the sequence in all its horror described by Tweed. 'The mysterious patient, Mr Mannix, returned in the limo, came back to the asylum. Fortunately Millie had run for it by slipping out of the back door, or she might have lost her own head. It, as you suggested we call the killer, surprises Hank Foley rifling the records cabinet, maybe with *its* record in his hand. It smashes Foley over the back of the head with the blunt end of the axe it's carrying. The body is dragged out and across the slope where Jed found faint traces of blood. It places the execution block where you found that oblong imprint, places Foley on his back, his neck fitting into the block. It uses the blade of the axe to sever the head from the body in one blow. It then hauls the headless corpse to the edge of the cliff, drops it down into the crevasse. I noticed the house and road were concealed from both those points, so the driver of the limo sees nothing. On its way back to the limo it collects the head, drops it inside some kind of container, returns to the limo, is driven away.'

'The head could have been thrown into the sea,' Newman suggested.

'Could have, but I don't think so, the way my mind is working.'

'That was horrible.' Paula had opened her eyes. 'I saw it all happening the way you described it.'

'In Maine,' Tweed went on, 'the corpse was carefully dropped into the crevasse, where it would be found. At Bray, Holgate's headless corpse was dropped into a shallow stream, where again it would be found. The *modus operandi* is exactly the same in both cases.'

There was a grim silence in the office for several minutes. Monica had stopped typing, her face ashen.

'Still doesn't make sense,' Paula protested eventually. 'According to Professor Saafeld the same axe was used in both murders. No one would dare transport that by air – thinking of passing through security.'

'There's a way of pursuing that,' Tweed decided. He asked Monica to try and get Roman Arbogast on the line.

'Tweed here,' he said when the throaty voice answered. 'I'm wondering whether anyone has approached you recently about the Adam Holgate case.'

'I've ordered Broden to take any such enquiries. Do you wish to speak to him?'

'No, thank you. Sorry to bother you.'

'I'd like to meet and talk to you, Tweed. Give me another call when you can.'

The call was once more ended when Arbogast slammed down the phone. Tweed heaved a sigh of relief. 'Changed my mind at the last moment. Wrong approach. Get me Jim Corcoran on the line please, Monica . . .

'Jim. Do you know of any way that Roman Arbogast could fly the Atlantic in complete privacy?'

'Certainly do. He keeps a big Gulfstream parked here in a secluded area. All one of his passengers has to do is to bring me their passport before departure. No Customs check. Then they fly off.'

'That's a very unusual concession.'

'Between you and me there's a reason. Arbogast has coughed up a huge sum towards the expense of building a fifth runway. So we help him.'

'You said passengers. Plural. Any names? As you know, I'm conducting a murder inquiry, a pretty grim one. Roy probably told you on the quiet.'

'He did. Names? Have to search my memory. Sophie, his daughter – Roman's. Marienetta, his niece. Black Jack Diamond, the gambler. A Dr Abraham Seale. Oh, and Sam Snyder, the crime reporter.'

'You have an amazing memory. Any dates of when they did fly?'

'Sorry. I just check the names, recall them. They always carry a note for me, signed Roman A.'

'Are these recent flights?'

'Very. Within the past two or three weeks. Which is why I remember the names. That Gulfstream has been off the ground a lot.'

'Any one destination?'

'Always Boston.'

12

'Hello,' said Tweed on the phone.

'That's Tweed, isn't it? Recognize your voice.'

Marienetta. He recognized her distinctive way of speaking.

'Yes, it is, Marienetta. Is there a problem?'

'A whale of one. Could I ask you to come over here quickly? It's a gym. Charlie's Physical. It's in a basement. In King Street, Covent Garden. Stand facing the Strand and it's on the right. A war's started.'

'I'll be over right away. Do I come alone or bring Paula – and maybe Newman?'

'*Bring the cavalry!*'

'On my way . . .'

As he put on his coat he told Newman and Paula, suggested they came with him. Newman drove them in his car, zigzagging round the back streets and driving far more slowly down King Street. It was Paula who spotted the gym.

'Two buildings down,' she called out. 'The white board over the basement windows. And that car's pulling out. You can grab his slot.'

Leaving Newman to shove coins in the meter, Tweed led the way down an iron staircase, followed by Paula. Beyond a door they emerged into a large well-equipped gymnasium. Marienetta was standing, arms folded, in a leotard, close to Sophie cycling like mad on a machine.

Black Jack Diamond was a distance away, lifting weights while he watched the two women.

'Peace reigns,' Tweed called out amiably.

'It bloody well doesn't!' shouted Sophie.

She stopped cycling, ran over and picked up some barbells. She paused for a moment, breathing heavily. Tweed noticed that Sophie, also clad in a leotard, was as tall as Marienetta but heavier. She screamed the words, glaring with venom at Marienetta.

'You always do this, you bloody thief.' She looked at Tweed. 'Black Jack and I are going to get married. Marienetta hears, starts working her wiles on him. She's done it with other boy friends I thought I had in the past.' Her voice was rising ferociously. 'This time she's not getting away with it. I'll kill her . . .'

She rushed towards Marienetta, the barbells held to strike. Black Jack was suddenly behind her, one arm round her slim waist, the other grasping the barbells. She struggled, but he held her close to him. This went on for maybe half a minute before Sophie slumped. He removed the barbells as she sat on the floor. Suddenly, with Black Jack well clear of her, she jumped up, screaming again, her face convulsed.

'No one can have a man except you. So you take them all off me. Because you're nothing but a bloody whore!'

Marienetta snapped. She walked slowly forward. Her right hand moved like a whip. She gave Sophie a powerful slap with her hand on the right-hand side of the face. Sophie staggered sideways. Tweed moved forward with the speed that had surprised Paula in the past. He held one arm over Marienetta's chest, the other over Sophie's. His voice was biting, harsh.

'Stop this nonsense or I'll call the police. Roman will love the newspaper headlines. With pictures.'

It was the power of his voice as much as his words which defused the situation, although Paula noted that

Marienetta was now perfectly calm, her expression neutral.

Fortunately there was no one else in the gym. Sophie backed away. She turned to call out. 'Jack, get your clothes on while I do the same. Then let's get the hell out of this place . . .'

'Could you wait for me, please,' Marienetta called out quietly to Tweed. 'I'm a quick dresser.'

'Take your time. No hurry,' he assured her.

'You handled that well,' Paula said as the three of them left stood in the empty gym, waiting for Marienetta to reappear. 'Did you see the look on Sophie's face? It was murderous.'

'Well,' Newman commented, 'she did threaten to kill.'

'I got the impression Marienetta wanted to talk to you on her own,' Paula told Tweed. 'With just the two of you together she may talk more frankly.'

'You could be right,' Tweed agreed.

'So Bob and I are late for an urgent appointment. We'll see you back in the office . . .'

Only a minute after they had gone Marienetta walked towards Tweed, dressed in a smart grey two-piece business suit. She frowned.

'I haven't chased your friends away, I hope.'

'They had to rush to another appointment. They give you their warm regards. Where shall we go?'

'That was tactful of them.' She smiled. 'I doubt if they did have another appointment. There's a coffee shop just down the street . . .'

It was a smart place with black marble tables, comfortable leather chairs, an arched ceiling decorated with vivid paintings of a forest. The decoration took Tweed back to the atmosphere near Pinedale. Marienetta was unusually quiet until the coffee had been served. Tweed realized Marienetta was keeping quiet until the waitress vanished. The only other customer was a well-dressed old lady sitting at a table a good way off in the back.

'Coffee's not bad,' said Tweed.

'I want to thank you for answering my distress call so quickly,' Marienetta began. 'You, Mr Tweed, were the only person I could think of who would quieten her. And you did, most ably. She was working herself up into a major fit. The doctor prescribed Valium but of course she forgets to take it.'

'How long has she suffered from these outbursts?' asked Tweed.

'Ever since early childhood. I can usually soothe her down but, as you saw, there are times when she goes volcanic. And I'm worried about this crazy idea of hers to marry Jack. My uncle is livid, but as she's thirty, five years younger than me, he can't stop her.'

'Has she always been jealous of you?' Tweed wondered. 'It's usually the youngest who gets all the attention.'

'I know.' She paused, drank coffee. 'It's embarrassing to explain. But Uncle – Roman – soon decided my intellect was more powerful than hers. I'm quoting him, so don't think I'm egotistical. As to Black Jack, she's quite capable of throwing him over suddenly. She's done that with two other men she proposed marrying. When they didn't agree with her over something, she kicked them out.'

'Didn't you say she was in charge of armaments at ACTIL?' he recalled. 'Explosives. Is that a good idea?'

'I was just going to tell you the other side of Sophie. At science she's brilliant. Broden has a watching brief over that department, so she's not on her own.'

'Can't imagine she likes Broden. A rough type.'

'Oddly enough they get on well together. I did think of calling Broden when the crisis built up but his solution could have been to slam a fist into Black Jack.'

'Diamond can look after himself.'

'I thought of that. I decided you were by far the one man who could handle it quietly but decisively.' She smiled. 'And I was right.' It was a ravishing smile without a hint of flirtation. 'Maybe the two of us could have dinner somewhere nice one evening. I prefer more mature men – anyone younger is so macho these days. Have only one thought in mind where a woman is concerned.'

'The way of the world ever since the Stone Age, I suppose. Yes, it would be interesting to have dinner together – when I get clear of a pile of work.'

'Forget the pile,' she coaxed. 'I get the impression you work like a Trojan. It would do you good to have a relaxing evening. To the devil with Park Crescent.'

'Don't say a word,' Tweed warned.

A familiar figure had appeared, stalking through the entrance with a self-satisfied look on his hawklike features. He was heading for their table.

Sam Snyder.

Snyder looked even more bony-faced, his prominent nose even larger than Tweed remembered from their encounter in Park Crescent, his manner more aggressive, his dark eyes even more penetrating. Without being invited he sat on an empty chair at their table. The waitress appeared.

'I'll have what they're having,' he said brusquely.

'Which hole did you crawl out of?' snapped Tweed.

'You haven't introduced me to your lovebird,' he said to Tweed, grinning unpleasantly.

'We have met before,' said Marienetta, her voice cold as she used a silk handkerchief to remove an imaginary spot from her dress without a glance in his direction.

'You want to watch your language – and your manners,' Tweed responded, his expression grim.

'The hole I crawled out of was Charlie's Physical, the gym across the street. Don't think you saw me. I was sitting up in the gallery.'

'Hunched well down out of sight,' Tweed said contemptuously.

133

'Quite a show I witnessed. Darling Sophie attacked Marienetta.' He took out a notebook. '"I'll kill her" were the exact words she used, I believe. I do a gossip column as well as major news stories,' he went on, putting away the notebook. 'Make a great item for the column, don't you think?'

Out of the corner of his eye Tweed saw Marienetta tense. He knew she wanted to administer one of her powerful slaps to Snyder's grinning face. Instead she kept her control, gazed up at the ceiling. Tweed leaned forward until he was inches from the predatory nose. His voice was quiet, a clear whisper.

'I'm going to make you a promise, Sam. You know Bob Newman has reluctantly helped you in the past when a "D" notice was clamped on a topic by the government. He has shown you how to write the article and evade the notice. You print anything in that gossip column and he becomes your enemy – a deadly enemy. On top of that you're making yourself a name in New York, up to a point. Newman will write a satirical piece about you for the *New York Times*. You'll be the joke of the city, a joke passed round all the parties there. It will finish you in the States.'

Different expressions crossed the hawklike face, none of them confident. Snyder started to lift his coffee cup and it trembled so much he had to put it down without drinking.

'I guess you thought I meant it,' he said eventually. 'I guess you took it seriously. I didn't. Sorry about the lovebirds remark. It was tasteless. Unfounded. Guess I'd better push off after I've paid for my coffee.'

'I will pay for the coffee.'

Tweed's tone was as grim as his expression. Snyder stood up, was uncertain how to leave. He decided it was best not to say anything more. He was careful not to look at Marienetta as he left, went out into the street.

'I didn't know you could be so tough,' Marienetta commented when they were on their own. 'Your voice sounded like the crack of doom. Even though so quiet. You really do protect a woman. I'm so grateful.'

'Don't be.'

He had just uttered the words when Marienetta's mobile rang. She spoke very quietly, listened, spoke again, put it away.

'That was Roman. He would like to see you in his office as soon as you can manage it.'

'Did he say why?'

'Yes, I was coming to that. He says there's a crisis.'

'I'm becoming an expert on them. Now would be as good a time as any to go and see him, if you think that would suit him.'

'I'm sure it would. He sounded grim – but not as grim as you can be. He also said if you could bring Paula it might be a good idea.'

'Really? Do me a favour – I don't use mobiles – phone Paula at Park Crescent, explain the position to her, please . . .'

While Marienetta was on the phone Tweed paid the bill, then gazed into space. His brain was moving at high power. Black Jack Diamond, Sophie and Snyder. It all fitted into a pattern he couldn't get hold of. And who had Snyder followed to take him to the gym where the real 'lovebirds' were exercising? Behind these domestic developments loomed the brutal murders of Hank Foley and Adam Holgate.

'Paula said she was coming to ACTIL like a rocket. Bob Newman has insisted on escorting her, but said he'd wait in the lobby. Ready to move? You look miles away.'

'I was just wondering where Russell Straub is, what he's up to. You're right. We'd better start out.'

They had to waste time searching for an empty taxi. Then the journey to the City was a traffic-jammed crawl.

135

Tweed had closed the windows to keep out petrol fumes. There was a faint purple haze above them, the accumulation of the fumes.

They reached the ACTIL building eventually, to find Paula waiting on the entrance steps. She gave them a mocking wave.

'What kept you?'

'Where's Newman?' Tweed wanted to know.

'He got the doorman to park his car. He's sitting behind the net curtains of that café over there. Hadn't we better get a move on?'

'Paula,' Marienetta mocked her back, 'one of these days I'm going to take you on a two-hour taxi ride through central London. Then you'll know what we've just experienced.'

'Yes, Marienetta,' snarled Roman Arbogast as she followed Paula and Tweed into his office, 'you might as well sit in on this.'

'If you don't want me here all you have to do is say so.'

Marienetta had spoken amiably. She stood erect with her hands on her hips. Roman glared, waved his hand for her to sit down as though resigning himself to the inevitable.

Not in a good mood, Paula thought as, with Tweed, she sat in one of the armchairs placed before his desk. Roman, lighted cigar in one hand, stood, padding back and forth which reminded Paula of Tweed, although his step was firmer.

'Has Marienetta told you,' Roman began fiercely, 'that my stupid daughter, Sophie, has lost her head . . .'

'Not like Adam Holgate, I hope,' Marienetta said. 'Oh, I am sorry, that really was in the worst of taste. I do apologize.'

'Maybe,' Roman told her, in deceptively soft tones, 'you could make an effort and keep your trap shut.' He turned to Tweed and Paula. 'Sophie is determined to marry that ruffian Black Jack Diamond. I know what he wants, a portion of the ACTIL shares held in a private company. I'll outmanoeuvre that clever dick.'

'Can you tell us how you'll manage that?' Tweed wondered aloud. 'Sophie is very headstrong.'

'She's also greedy for lots of money, like all my relatives. There's a very good-looking American in London. George Barrymore. A multimillionaire. He rather fancies Sophie. I'm going to manipulate matters so they meet at a party, after someone has told Sophie how very rich he is. She'll salivate at the prospect of capturing him. Then she'll drop Black Jack like a hot brick.'

'I suppose,' Tweed suggested carefully, 'it's not possible that Black Jack's game is to hope you will buy him off? A spot of blackmail?'

'*Of course it is!*' Roman thundered. His face twisted into a savage grimace. Paula was taken aback. He reminded her of the horrific portrait Marienetta had painted. 'But he doesn't know me,' he roared on. 'I would resort to any method to stop him succeeding. Any method available on the face of the earth!'

'Now calm down, Uncle,' Marienetta said quietly. 'Your strength has always been to stay cool.'

Her words, spoken as she stared straight at him, had an astonishing effect. His face semed to dissolve, to resume a quiet expression. *Normal and abnormal.* Shaken, Paula recalled the words Dr Seale had used.

Roman sagged his large body slowly into the chair behind his desk. His right eye was twitching as he stared at Tweed. He raised a fat hand. He spoke softly.

'The real reason I asked you here was to enquire whether you are still investigating the murders.'

'Murders?' Tweed enquired.

'I should have said murder – the murder of Adam Holgate.'

'May I ask the reason for that question?'

'You may. Early this morning, soon after I had arrived, Nathan Morgan of Special Branch tried to storm his way in to see me. He had to be physically restrained by the forceful Broden. He was almost thrown out of the building.'

'I see.' Tweed paused. 'Among other problems concerning me I still retain an interest in that case.'

'You have a suspect?'

Hands clasped tightly on his desk, Roman's strange head was twisted to the right, watching Tweed.

'No, I have not. It is far too early to get the hang of all the people involved.'

'You will let me know if you focus on one individual?'

'I will do all I can.' Tweed stood up. 'Now you are a busy man and we've taken up a lot of your time. Let us keep in touch . . .'

Marienetta accompanied them through the first office into the hall. She pressed the button of the special lift after inserting her computer card, then turned to Tweed.

'If you don't mind, I will leave you here. I want to go back and make sure he really has quietened down. It's Sophie who is worrying him. And thank you so much for all your help with this and that . . .'

When they reached the ground floor after the bomblike drop, Broden was waiting to escort them to the door. He had fixed it so it revolved continuously. Newman emerged from the café and stood on their side of the pavement waiting for his car.

A strange figure was seated halfway down the steps, crouching over a board supporting a sheet of cartridge paper partly covered with a complex diagram. Dr Abraham Seale looked up. He was still dressed in his Dickensian attire.

'Good morning, Mr Tweed. I was originally going inside

138

to ask Mr Arbogast something. Then I decided it would be unwise. I am preparing a family tree of the Arbogasts. I study genealogy in my spare time. The Arbogasts originally were the Arbogastinis. Most intriguing.'

'From Italy?'

'Exactly.' He rolled up the chart, tucked it with the supporting board under his arm. 'Perhaps a dangerous place to indulge in such activity. I will leave. Goodbye, Paula . . .'

'The Arbogasts are a strange family,' Paula commented.

'I wonder why he thought it dangerous to be here,' Tweed mused.

13

'I'm feeling jittery,' Paula said. 'That's not like me.'

They had arrived back in Tweed's office at Park Crescent after a quick lunch. With Monica at her word processor, Paula and Tweed were the only ones in the room. Newman had gone off with Marler 'to frighten some informants', as Marler had put it, hoping to pick up information about Holgate's murder.

'Jittery?' Tweed repeated. 'I'm not surprised. You always have been hypersensitive where people are concerned. And we've just witnessed one tense drama in that gym, another when Roman Arbogast detonated.'

'I don't think it's either of those things. Doesn't matter.' She waved a dismissive hand, wishing she'd kept quiet.

Like Paula, Tweed's desk was littered with piles of files, many from Howard and which needed decisions taken. Between them, they had enough paperwork to last them two days. Tweed sighed, got down to the work. He found he was absorbed by returning to his old role as detective.

'Half these agents abroad are sending in data to justify their existence,' he grumbled. 'Which is why Howard has dumped this lot on us. He prefers chatting with Whitehall mandarins over drinks at his club.'

'If we had to go away suddenly,' Paula reminded him, 'then Howard would take over and really apply himself. You do know that.'

'Stop nagging . . .'

141

Tweed paused in mid-sentence as Monica answered the phone. He waved a warning finger at her.

'I'm out. Don't care if it's the Palace.'

'Are you sure?' Monica pressed him. 'It's Mrs Elena Brucan downstairs. She is apparently worried.'

'You must see her,' Paula prodded. 'She's such a pleasant lady.'

Tweed, who was a speed-reader, shifted six files he had dealt with, initialled, into a tidy pile. He glared at Paula without any anger.

'Sometimes I wonder who is running this unit. All right, I'll see her. But no one else afterwards . . .'

Paula opened the door for their visitor. Elena Brucan was again wearing the pale green overcoat, the green fur hat. She took Paula's hand, squeezed it warmly, entered as Tweed stood up, smiled, ushered her towards an armchair. The Romanian lady looked back at Paula.

'It's really you I've come about.'

Monica rushed out to make her coffee. And that, grumbled Tweed to himself, will prolong the interview. He sat down and again smiled at his guest.

'Now what can we do for you?'

'I was outside the ACTIL building again when you left late this morning. I caught a cab to follow you but you stopped to have lunch, so I waited, then caught another cab. I *do* hope you don't mind my behaving like this.'

'Of course not. I'm sure you have your reasons. The ACTIL building seems to fascinate you.'

'They're all in there – whoever is connected with Holgate's murder – and probably that other man who was murdered in Maine. Which is why you flew there, I expect.'

Tweed was taken aback, completely baffled. He glanced over at Paula, now seated at her desk. She was grinning. He could have waved his fist at her. He switched his gaze to Elena's glowing eyes. Again he found them hypnotic.

142

He waited while Monica served coffee, decided he needed some himself.

'The remarkable thing, Mrs Brucan,' he began, 'is none of us, including myself, saw you either this morning outside ACTIL or earlier at Heathrow. Yet you have a distinctive, distinguished appearance.'

'Thank you for the compliment.' Paula felt sure she had blushed. She drank more coffee. 'I told you a bit of my earlier adventures. How the Romanian dictator, Ceauşescu disliked me, so he sent the secret police – brutal people – to arrest me. That experience made me skilled at remaining invisible. It does when it is a matter of life of death. At Heathrow I was in a crowd when I heard you asking the check-in lady about the flight to Boston. Then I'm an avid reader of the newspapers, including the American ones. They reported the murder in Maine in detail. So similar to the murder of poor Adam Holgate. It was very simple, really.'

Simple? Tweed thought. If I'd met this woman years ago when I was at the Yard I'd have hired her. She's uncanny. Paula was studying a file, still smiling to herself.

'When you came in you said something about Paula,' Tweed reminded his guest.

'Miss Grey, I sense, is in danger. Great danger. I would suggest she is guarded everywhere she goes.'

Tweed again glanced at Paula. The smile had disappeared. The idea that she should be guarded certainly did not appeal to her.

'Could you be a bit more specific?' Tweed suggested. 'Who is menacing her?'

'I'm sorry. I have no idea of where the danger comes from. But danger there is.'

'I'll bear it in mind and thank you.' He paused. 'We have studied the photos you kindly gave us. Why, in one case only, that of Sam Snyder, did you take his picture no less than five times?'

'My camera.' She gave him a wide glowing smile. 'I was convinced it wasn't working properly, so I kept taking photos of the same man.'

The first fib. Tweed didn't believe her. She was concealing something. Maybe because she was not yet sure of her grounds. Taking hold of her embroidered bag, she stood up.

'I can see how much work you have on your desk. I hope that I haven't wasted too much of your time.'

'As I said before, you have not wasted a moment.'

'And you will come and see me sometime? You have my address, my phone number.'

'We shall meet again,' responded Tweed warmly. He meant it.

Their guest thanked Monica for the coffee, told her it was the best she had ever tasted. Paula escorted her down to the front door.

'She's done it again,' commented Monica. 'She's gone but her presence is still here.'

'It's very strange. She really is the most extraordinary lady.'

Paula returned with Newman and Marler in tow. Marler took up his stance by the wall, near Paula. He lit a long cigarette as Newman flopped into an armchair.

'How did it go?' Tweed asked. 'You both look flaked out.'

'We've interrogated a lot of snitches,' Marler reported. 'I kept out of the way while Bob was talking to one of his and he followed the same procedure.'

'And the result?' Tweed demanded impatiently.

'Zilch. Zero. Nothing,' Marler said grimly. 'We walked into a wall of silence. Several took to the hills. I have never known anything like it. I did get a hint from one man that Special Branch have been hyper-active – spreading the word in the underworld that anyone who talks will find himself up on a drugs charge, for possession of heroin.'

'The damned fools are giving themselves away all along the line,' commented Tweed. 'It has to be a very big secret the government is worried about to issue such orders. It will take me two more days to get through Howard's junk. Then I will decide what to do to blast the thing wide open. I just hope I get no more visitors while I get on with it.'

Tweed, with Paula's help, worked steadily. They had cleared up everything at the end of two days. But there was one more visitor.

In addition to Newman, Paula and Marler, Tweed had summoned two more key members of his staff for a meeting on the evening of the second day. Harry Butler walked in, followed by Pete Nield. The contrast between the two men was striking but they had often worked together as partners, each trusting the other totally in situations which turned hairy.

Harry Butler was five feet five tall, his body bulky, his approach to a problem aggressive. In his thirties, he had a round head like a cannonball, which was a deadly weapon if he butted an opponent with it. He wore shabby jeans, a windcheater which had seen better days. In the East End he had often passed as a local.

Pete Nield, of a similar age, was a complete contrast. Good-looking, he had a neat moustache and wore a smart blue suit, a new blue shirt and a powder-blue tie. Popular with the ladies, and always smartly dressed, he nevertheless had not quite the flair for clothes possessed by Marler. Five feet eight tall, his slim build had several times encouraged a thug to think he was easy meat. The thug had always ended up painfully sprawled on the ground.

'Now strategy in this strange case,' Tweed began. 'We are peering into a fog . . .'

It was the signal for the phone to ring. Tweed swore under his breath. Monica was asking George, the guard downstairs, several questions before she looked at Tweed.

'An American, Ed Danvers, is wanting to see you. Won't say why. Says it's top secret.'

'Tell him to go away.'

'He also said he's FBI. Showed George his badge.'

Tweed sat very still. Paula could almost hear the wheels of his brain moving at top speed as he considered this highly unexpected development. He looked round at everyone, standing, seated in the room.

'You all stay where you are. This FBI man is on his own?' he asked Monica. She nodded. 'Most unusual. They nearly always travel in pairs. Ask him to come up.'

Paula stared at the door. She knew what to expect. A dour-faced man in a grey suit. The uniform. Instead a tall man wearing a sand-coloured suit which matched his thick tidy hair, walked in. Thirty-something, Paula thought he was good-looking. A good forehead, grey eyes beneath sandy eyebrows, a strong nose and mouth, his smooth face was creased in a gentle smile.

'Please sit down, Mr Danvers,' Tweed invited him, his tone neutral.

'Hi, everyone.' The smile took in everyone. He had a raincoat folded over his arm and Monica relieved him of it. He sat down in an armchair, his movements lithe, gazed across the desk.

'Mr Tweed, I assume?'

'You assume correctly. Just over from the the States?'

'No, sirree. I'm with the FBI detachment permanently stationed at our Embassy. Been here six months so far.'

'I thought you were probably attached to the Vice-President's staff.'

'I have shown him round your unique city, but not any more.'

'Why not?'

'Mr Straub flew to Europe two days ago.'

'Whereabouts in Europe?' Tweed asked swiftly.

'No idea. He didn't say. So I didn't ask.'

'Of course not,' Tweed said cynically.

'I really have no idea where he flew to.' Danvers leant forward to say this emphatically. He had caught the scepticism in Tweed's voice. 'He is his own man.'

'You know nothing about Europe, then?' Tweed continued brusquely.

'Actually, sir, I've travelled a lot in Europe. A great continent.'

'In that case he should have taken you with him. I doubt he's ever been there before.'

'He hasn't.'

'Most curious. Why have you come to see me?'

'It's rather confidential.' He looked round at the crowded room.

'Every single person in my office has worked with me for a long time. They are trusted – highly trusted – professionals. If you have anything to say you say it now or I shall be obliged to ask you to leave.'

'They said you were tough . . .'

'Who did?'

'Folks at the Embassy. Only one man knows I've come here to see you.'

'And that is?'

'The Ambassador.' He continued when Tweed just stared at him. 'Could we relax, sir?' Danvers leaned forward again. 'The Ambassador is very concerned about your sneak trip to Maine.'

'*Sneak?* What the devil do you mean? If I have visited Maine it would have been under my own name. The word verges on insulting.'

'I'm sorry, sir. I really am. The word was the Ambassador's. I personally would never have used the word. I am truly sorry.'

Because she liked the look of Danvers Paula was feeling sympathetic towards him. Tweed was being relentless,

147

firing questions like bullets. But it had been stupid to use the word 'sneak'.

'Now we've sorted that out,' Tweed resumed in a genial mood, 'what is it the Ambassador hoped you'd be able to tell him?'

'That you weren't involved in investigating the murder of Hank Foley, the caretaker brutally murdered in Pinedale.'

'How could I be involved?' Tweed smiled. 'Pinedale is in Maine? So how does this Ambassador think I can investigate something which happened over two thousand miles away when I'm sitting in London?'

'It does stretch the imagination.' Danvers glanced across at Paula and he was smiling. 'And it's not like the Ambassador to pry into British organizations,' he remarked, staring across the desk.

'Russell Straub has taken bodyguards with him on his trip to the Continent?' Tweed enquired casually.

'No.' Danvers paused. 'Well, you've brought the subject up. He's travelled alone. Despite the protests of our security people. He's trawling the Continent to get acquainted with the key people over there.'

'The beginning of his campaign to be the next President?'

'Some people might say that. Thank you for your time, sir. I think it's time I took my departure.'

'Paula,' Tweed called out, 'maybe you'd escort our guest to the front door . . .'

Marler winked at Newman who was grinning, then laughing so much he had to take out his handkerchief.

'Do share the joke,' Tweed suggested.

'You spotted Paula likes our American visitor – and Mr Danvers was not averse to her charms. You manipulated that, in the hope Danvers will sooner or later provide her with valuable information about the inner workings of the American Embassy.'

148

Paula returned before Tweed could reply. She closed the door, stood in front of his desk, her arms folded. Her expression was not friendly.

'Ed – Danvers – asked me to go out and have a drink with him sometime.'

'Well . . .' Tweed was looking down at a file on his desk. 'He is well-mannered, has a pleasant personality, is likeable.'

'I'm the bait,' she snapped. 'You hope I'll extract information from him about what goes on inside their Embassy.' She was furious. 'You're a cunning old fox.'

'I object to the word old,' Tweed said mildly.

'I'm right. Damn it! Tell me to my face. Am I right?'

He looked up, stared straight at her. 'You hit the bull's-eye.' His voice was serious. 'You don't ever have to meet Danvers for drinks if you don't want to. But his visit told us a lot. The Ambassador doesn't normally pry into a British organization. So he was asked to. By whom? I've no doubt the instigator of Danvers's visit came from the Vice-President pressuring the Ambassador before he flew to Europe. And why has Russell Straub flown to the Continent alone? Not just to show the flag. If that was the reason he could have taken a dozen bodyguards with him.'

'I'm sorry I blew my top,' Paula replied, then went to her desk. 'But I'm feeling sort of jittery from two days ago. It's silly, but I wish I could pinpoint what triggered it off.'

'Don't worry about it,' Tweed told her gently. 'We did have a lot of people and incidents of an unpleasant nature crammed into those two days.'

He sighed as the phone rang again. Monica answered it, then called across urgently to Tweed.

'Chief Inspector Arthur Beck of the Swiss Federal Police wants to talk to you. He sounded very serious and in a great rush. I think something has happened.'

149

14

'A third headless body has been found, at Montreux.'

Tweed had spent several minutes on the phone with his old friend Arthur Beck. He had asked the occasional question, which Paula had attempted without success to fit into a conversation. Now she was stunned by what Tweed had announced. Everyone in the office was silent. Paula was the first to break the heavy silence.

'In Switzerland now. First in Maine, then out at Bray. And now Switzerland. The geographical span is enormous. Whose body is it?'

'No identification yet. Beck was talking quickly so I only got a fragmented picture. I gather the body was found at the edge of the lake. Something about a pick-boat.'

'Could it have been *pic-bot*?' suggested Paula, who was fluent in French.

'Yes, it did sound like that.'

'Then I saw it once when I was in Montreux. It's like a large barge without a deck. It has sloping sides descending to the base. Two men were using it to claw out of the lake debris which had floated in. Branches of trees, leaves, all kinds of rubbish. They had tools like huge rakes to haul it aboard.'

'So the serial murderer is operating on different continents,' Newman commented.

'I'm sure,' Tweed said grimly, 'this is not the work of a random serial killer. There is a link between the victims.

151

And until the corpse is identified it may have nothing to do with Maine and Bray. Beck keeps up with worldwide crime, mentioned both Maine and Bray. He wants us to fly out today.' He looked at Monica. 'Could we catch a flight to Geneva this evening? Beck said he'd have a limo meet us, drive us to Montreux.'

'Yes you could.' Monica carried timetables in her head. 'But I'd have to get cracking now. So would you – packing. How many people?'

'Everyone in this room. The complete team. Travelling under their real names.' He looked round his office. 'It may be cold so pack warm clothes.'

'It's freezing,' Paula said. 'Winter has started early out there. Snow has fallen on the peaks. Very early indeed.'

'My case is packed, the one for emergencies such as this.' He gestured towards a large corner cupboard. 'What about yours, Paula?'

'Ready. In the same cupboard. So is yours, isn't it, Bob?'

'My skiing clothes are in my case, also in that cupboard, so I'll be OK.'

'I won't,' interjected Marler. 'I'll have to dash home. I wonder how long we've got?'

He waited while Monica continued to talk like a machine-gun to the girl at Heathrow. When she had completed her long conversation she held up one thumb, looked at Tweed.

'You're booked on an evening flight. All of you. Hadn't I better phone Beck to give him flight data if he's sending transport to meet you at Geneva?'

'That's the next thing to do.' He walked to her desk, gave her a slip of paper with Beck's number. 'How long have we?'

'Three hours to be back here and ready to go. I'll book cabs. Taking cars and parking at Heathrow in Long Stay will hold you up.'

'Three hours?' Marler repeated. 'I'm off.'

There was a flurry of people leaving to go and fetch warm clothing. Tweed said he was popping up to see Howard to keep him in the picture and vanished. Only Paula and Newman were left in the office with Monica, who was already calling Beck. Paula suddenly realized she no longer felt jittery. The prospect of action had rejuvenated her. She unlocked a drawer, took out Wylie's *A History of Executions*, packed it carefully in her briefcase. Bedtime reading, she said to herself. I don't think.

'Lord,' she said aloud. 'I have to phone Marienetta.'

'What for?' Newman asked.

'We were going to fix a date for dinner. I must tell her I'm not going to be available for a while.'

Newman shrugged. She was talking on the phone while he read the latest issue of the *Herald Tribune*. Not a word in it about the murder of Hank Foley. Tweed returned as Paula put down the phone and spoke.

'That's strange.'

'What is?' Tweed asked, heading for the cupboard to check his suitcase.

'I phoned Marienetta and her secretary said she had gone abroad a couple of days ago. So has Sophie. They never travel together, the secretary informed me after I prodded, suggesting I'd better speak to Mr Arbogast. Then the girl told me Mr Arbogast also was out of the country. They all left independently a couple of days ago.'

'Which,' Tweed remarked from behind his desk, 'was the same time Russell Straub disappeared into the wild blue yonder. A coincidence? I wonder.'

'Had you better phone Mrs Brucan to tell her you have to go off somewhere?' Paula suggested. 'It might save her a wasted journey – she doesn't seem to be able to keep away from here.'

'I suppose I'd better.'

Tweed looked up the number he had written down in

his notebook. Picking up the phone, he called the number, waited. Thinking maybe he had misdialled, he tried again. He listened for a while, then gave it up.

'No reply. Just the ringing tone. All these people disappearing. It's like a massacre by absence. Howard is fully informed, will take over while I'm away. He was very shocked by my news. I told him it might be anyone.'

'Anyone?' queried Paula.

'The third headless corpse found in Montreux.'

'Let's hope to Heaven it's no one we know.'

15

The flight to Geneva was little more than an hour. This time they sat near the pilot's cabin. Again Paula was in a three-seater but she occupied the middle seat with Tweed by the window and Newman by the aisle. The plane was half-empty so they were able to talk with no risk of being overheard. Several rows behind them Butler sat with Nield. At the rear Marler sat alone. He liked to be able to keep an eye on everyone aboard.

Outside it was dark as Paula delved into her briefcase and brought out her cherished book. Slips of paper protruded where she had marked several pages. She glanced at Newman.

'This is pretty grisly. Hope you've got a strong stomach.'

'I'll be happy with this,' he replied, raising his glass of Scotch. 'Do your worst.'

'They were very methodical with their executions,' she began. 'Here's phase one – a condemned man mounting to the top of the scaffold, arms tied together.'

Tweed peered over to look at the picture drawn in what he suspected was charcoal. On the platform the executioner waited, a big tall brute with his head covered with a woollen helmet with eye-holes. Grim. In his right hand he held a long-handled axe. The victim was then laid on his back, his neck placed carefully on a wide curved block. The executioner raised the axe above his head.

The next drawing showed it descending. Then the blade slashed through the neck, the head rolled back, dropped onto a large piece of sacking. Black blood pooled down on all sides from the ragged stump of what remained of the neck.

'Good job it wasn't in colour,' Newman commented.

The executioner lifted the severed head by its hair to display it to the crowd below. It was then dropped into the sacking. The executioner gathered up the sack, wrapping it round the head, dropping it into a cart below.

'Now that is important,' Paula said.

'I guess it was important to the poor devil who had his head chopped off,' Newman remarked.

Paula nudged him hard in the ribs. 'Be serious. This is very serious.'

'What is?' Tweed asked.

She had turned back a page which showed the sack spread out behind the block, in front of the executioner standing waiting with his axe.

'The sacking,' Paula emphasized. 'The heads were missing from Hank Foley and Adam Holgate. I think *it* used sacking placed behind a makeshift execution block – then the head rolled free and fell on the sacking. That would give it something to carry away the head and put it inside some kind of container.'

'I'll have another Scotch,' Newman called out, summoning the steward.

Paula closed the book until the drink had been served and the steward had gone.

'So what kind of container would hold a human head?' asked Newman.

'I think Paula is right,' Tweed decided. 'We should have thought of that before now. I did once see a human head preserved in formalin after an autopsy. Stored in a huge laboratory glass with a glass lid on top. If I'm right what would it put a large laboratory glass in, to carry it away?'

156

'One of those wheeled suitcases people cart around these days when they're travelling,' she said.

'Must have been a lot of blood dripping from a head,' Newman pointed out.

'So it holds up the head by the hair until only dribbles of blood are dropping,' Paula explained.

'We really *should* have thought of that,' said Tweed. 'At Pinedale we should have searched further. There must have been an area where the ground had been soaked with blood. And at Bray.'

'Any more delicacies?' Newman enquired.

'There's the guillotine where you see the same system.' She turned to another marked page. 'You see, again behind the execution block there's sacking waiting to receive the head.'

'Look at the neck's stump,' Newman said. 'Now turn back to the earlier example of a portrait.'

She found the page immediately. Newman stared at the hideous drawing. He pointed.

'See? The neck stump again is ragged. Whereas Foley and Holgate had their necks severed neatly just below the chin. No raggedness.'

'It must have practised on something inert,' Tweed reflected. 'Maybe a dummy.'

'I'm not at all sure it would be a dummy,' Paula objected.

'What then?' Tweed asked.

'I don't know. I'll have to think about the problem. And we're descending.'

She wrapped up the book, placed it carefully back inside her briefcase. Then, to clear her mind of what they had been studying, she gazed out of the window.

The night was now cloud-free. As the descent continued she looked down on the Jura mountains rising up behind the vast pale blue smoothness which was Lake Geneva, or Lac Leman. There was snow on the peaks and the scene was one of great beauty as their machine swung out over the lake, like a giant flat plate, motionless in the moonlight. Then they were landing, wheels bumping gently on the tarmac.

Walking out onto the concourse at Cointrin Airport, Geneva, Tweed and Paula were surprised and pleased to see Arthur Beck, Chief of Federal Police, waiting for them. Behind him several uniformed police formed a protective circle. Beck ran forward, hugged Paula, shook hands with Tweed and Newman, led them to two waiting limos.

Beck was tall, fortyish, lean with greying hair and a trim moustache. His head was long with a well-shaped forehead, a Roman nose, a determined mouth and jaw. Tweed regarded his friend as the most efficient and energetic policeman on the Continent.

Beck was carrying Paula's suitcase although she had insisted on hanging on to her briefcase. The cold was icy but this was the sort of weather Tweed thrived on. Very quickly both Tweed and Paula were seated in luxurious seats in the middle section of the limo, behind the driver who had two policemen alongside him. Newman and Marler occupied the row behind them while Nield and Butler travelled together in a second limo. They were gliding beyond the station, heading east, when Beck, seated beside Tweed, spoke.

'I have negative news for you, I fear. After bringing you out here at such short notice.'

'You've lost the body?'

'Only temporarily, I'm sure. It was alongside the *pic-bot* when a storm blew in suddenly off the lake. So the body was washed further out. Not to worry – the storm is due to end tonight and then the body will be washed in again.'

'Was there time to get any idea of its appearance?'

'Only that it was headless. It was sealed inside a body

158

bag – or body pouch, as the Americans call them. The bag was zipped up. One of the crew of two men reached down, unzipped the bag, saw what was inside, had an attack of sickness, the fool, so he let it go.'

'It wouldn't be a pleasant sight,' Paula said quietly.

'The other crew-member was made of sterner stuff. He moved fast, took one Polaroid photo, leaned over the side and zipped the bag shut just before it was swept away. I have the Polaroid.'

He glanced uncertainly at Paula. She knew exactly what his reaction was.

'Don't worry,' she assured him. 'I've seen headless bodies in Maine and out at Bray. I won't faint,' she said smiling.

'Here it is, then.'

He produced the colour print out of a transparent envelope taken from inside a leather case. He gave it to Paula while Newman leant over from behind them. Earlier, before saying a word, Beck had slid the glass partition shut so the driver and his companions could hear nothing.

'It's a good photo, even taken looking down on the stump of the neck,' Newman commented.

Paula stared at it closely by the overhead light Beck had switched on. She turned it slowly this way and that to try and see something which would identify the body. It was hopeless. Just a nerve-racking mass of dried blood.

'I can't even see whether the cut is a neat slice or ragged. That's important.'

'Why?' asked Beck.

Tweed explained to him what they had discovered in both the Foley and Holgate beheadings: the clean way the blade had cut and the position and shape of the notch in the blade.

'I'll tell Dr Zeitzler. He's the pathologist I called to Montreux from Zürich. I persuaded him to stay on until we get our hands on the corpse.'

159

'Why is this Dr Zeitzler from Zürich?' Paula wondered. 'I would have thought a pathologist from Berne, the capital, would be called.'

'Ah!' Beck chuckled. 'I insist on using the absolute tops in every sphere of my operations. The best pathologist by far in the whole of Switzerland is Dr Zeitzler. Very dominant but he knows what he's talking about. Like him, you will spend the night at Le Montreux Palace. You and Paula have suites.'

'That's very generous,' said Paula. 'I remember Le Montreux Palace. It's by far the best hotel in the city.'

'I've booked Newman into an attic,' Beck remarked casually.

'Thanks a lot,' Newman growled from behind them.

'Just joking,' said Beck, so fluent in English. 'You do have a very nice room waiting for you . . .'

While they were talking the limo had made good progress along the wide autoroute leading to Montreux at the far end of Switzerland's largest lake. Paula looked out of the window on her side, revelling in the undulating crests of the Jura, tipped with the white of snow. Stretching across to the highway she saw in the moonlight the neat grids of the vineyards which would start to flourish later. Here and there neat little villages of stone were laid out in organized rectangles. Each had an onion-domed spire of a tiny church. So Swiss. So peaceful.

She looked the other way beyond Tweed and Beck, towards where she knew the lake stretched. In the distance, on the French side of the lake, grim mountain crags reared up. Sheets of rain like long slanted needles close together suddenly appeared, sweeping towards them. Beck pointed in their direction.

'We shall soon pass Ouchy, where the autoroute is close to the lake,' he remarked. 'The storm is building up at this end of Lac Leman. The forecast is for it to go away in the early morning. Then we hope the body will return to us.'

160

Paula felt sleepy. She moved so her head was on the rest. So comfortable. The limo purring quietly along on the superb highway. She fell fast asleep.

She was woken up by Tweed gently shaking her arm. Blinking, she sat up straight, aware of two things. The limo was slowing, then stopping. Her right hand still clasped the briefcase with the precious book on her lap.

'We have arrived in Montreux,' Tweed told her as the limo stopped.

She peered up out of the window. A yellow-gold colossus of a hotel which seemed to stretch along the Grand-Rue forever loomed above her. Many rooms had balconies but no one was using them tonight as the rain sheeted down. Smartly uniformed servants appeared holding huge umbrellas, opened their doors. Huddling under the umbrellas, Tweed and Paula hurried inside followed by Beck and the rest of their team.

At the reception area they produced their passports while Beck stood a distance away. The receptionist welcomed them warmly as he noted down details.

'You're not full at this time of the year, I imagine,' remarked Tweed.

'No, sir. But you have just missed being with us at the same time as another honoured guest.'

'Who was that?'

'The Vice-President of the United States.'

16

'Can't be helped,' Tweed said to the receptionist. 'I was talking to Russell Straub in London barely a week ago.'

Paula had trouble stifling a chuckle. Tweed certainly extracted mileage from the brief confrontation he'd had with the Vice-President at Sophie's birthday party.

'Really, sir,' the receptionist commented, impressed. 'He left here about an hour ago. After dark.'

'By train, I expect?'

'Oh no, sir. He drove himself off in a big Ford.'

'On his way to Berne, I suppose,' Tweed replied, choosing the first city which came into his head.

'I've really no idea where he was going. He was out of the hotel a lot, kept very much to himself.'

'We'd better get up to our rooms. Dinner is still being served?'

'Yes, indeed, it is.'

Paula was taken one way to her suite while Tweed, accompanied by Beck, was taken in another direction. His suite was spacious, had a balcony overlooking the lake. He turned to Beck after paying the porters.

'Can we see from this balcony where the body was discovered first?'

'If you don't mind risking getting a bit wet, although I see they have lowered the blind.' He led the way outside and pointed. 'You can hardly see it from here because of the evergreeens. It was down there by the *quai*.'

163

'So now we can only hope,' Tweed said, going inside.

'I have sent out a large patrol boat with a huge scoop to see if they can find it. I'll be leaving now.' He picked up a hotel pad, scribbled down a number. 'I shall be at this number all night. It's the police HQ not far from the *quai*.'

After a quick wash Tweed went in search of Paula's suite. On the way he bumped into Newman on the same quest. The hotel was huge but eventually they found the room. Tweed knocked on the door.

'Who is it?' Paula called out cautiously.

'Tweed here.'

She unlocked the door and they walked into a suite on the scale of Tweed's. Paula had already changed for dinner into a sleeveless midnight-blue dress and a high collar. Tweed walked round, peered out of the window.

'This is pretty isolated,' he remarked.

'That's what I thought,' Paula agreed. 'If either of you needs me, knock four times on the door, pause briefly, then knock once. Repeat the code if I don't respond. After dinner I think I'm going to fall into a deep slumber. But now I am *ravenous* . . .'

Reaching the entrance to the restaurant Tweed paused, told the head waiter he'd like a moment to look round. Paula peered round him while Newman shuffled his feet impatiently. She let out a gasp.

'Oh, my God. I don't believe it.'

'What is it now?' Newman asked.

'Look at that table over there by the window, half hidden. Marienetta with Sophie. *And* with Black Jack Diamond. What the devil's happening?'

'Why don't you go over and see them?' Tweed suggested. 'Bob and I will grab a table over there, well away from them. I suggest you chat to Marienetta. You get on well with her.'

Paula made her way between the tables. She was only

164

halfway there when Marienetta, wearing a strapless dress, spotted her, jumped up from her chair. She hugged Paula the moment she reached their table.

'Now I will have someone interesting to talk to. I'm so glad to see you.'

'What the devil are you doing in this part of the world?' Black Jack, lolling in his seat, called out.

'I might ask you the same question,' Paula rapped back.

'She's following us,' Sophie said unpleasantly.

'Since I'd no idea you were even in Switzerland that would have been a difficult achievement,' Paula replied amiably.

'They've been having another row,' Marienetta said, taking Paula by the arm. 'Let's go over by ourselves to the bar. I feel like a Cointreau.'

And I feel like food, Paula thought, but she allowed herself to be parked at the bar. She asked for a *small* glass of Chardonnay. Marienetta ordered her Cointreau, enthusiastically admired Paula's outfit.

'What *are* you doing here?' Paula enquired.

'Uncle has a very advanced plastics plant at Vevey just down the lake towards Ouchy. He came over unannounced to check progress. Expected me to come with him because he knows I'm better at administration. Sophie's baby, really. She is the scientist.'

'Roman is staying here?'

'He was. He drove off somewhere by himself a couple of hours ago. Don't ask me where to. He's so secretive. An early business experience gave almost a mania for secrecy. I saw police cars rushing down to the lake front before dinner.'

'What was that about?' Paula wondered.

'No idea. Before we left London, Roman introduced Sophie to the American millionaire he'd chosen to get her away from Black Jack. Apparently he was taking Sophie

165

out for lunch in a cab. They arrived at the restaurant, the American found he had no English money, tried to borrow the fare from Sophie. That did it. She turfed him out, told the cabbie to take her back to ACTIL.'

'Doesn't take a lot to upset her, does it?'

'Not if she's in a mood. She found out we were flying out here and decided to fly out on her own, that is with Black Jack.'

'Why?'

'To pay back Uncle for trying to palm her off on the American. The slightest little thing can set her off. Uncle was livid when he saw Black Jack out here – refused to eat with them.'

'When did you all come out here?' Paula asked casually between munching pretzels. Anything to keep the demon hunger at bay.

'May I ask why you're out here with the formidable Tweed and the tough guy, Robert Newman?'

'We're heavily involved in these horrific murder cases. A third victim – another headless corpse – has been found floating in the lake. Still out there somewhere.'

'Oh, my God! That explains the flurry of police cars.' She paused. 'Whose body is this one?'

'We don't know. Hope you don't mind my mentioning it but I haven't eaten for weeks.'

'Oh Lord! You should have spoken earlier. Back to the table right now. You poor thing.'

Strange, Paula thought as they headed for the table, how everyone came out here two days ago. The Arbogast family and the Vice-President. Tweed would never believe that was a coincidence. Especially with a third murder.

17

Paula was consuming pasta avidly when Sophie took her over, speaking so sensibly and knowledgeably Paula could hardly credit it was the same woman. Sophie the scientist.

'We've got a plastics factory down the road which was my idea. I've invented – and patented – a new technique for plastic. It's going to make my father another fortune.'

'Tell me about it,' Paula said between mouthfuls.

'It's stronger and much more flexible than any existing form of plastic. I spent months working on the theory but now it's in production—'

'Let Paula eat her meal,' Marienetta interrupted. 'She is starving.'

'So,' Sophie continued, ignoring the hint, 'you can warm it then mould it into any shape you like with your hands. A lot of airlines have placed contracts. The flexibility can be adjusted – by hand or machine – to any strength or shape simply by moulding it, and when it's cool it keeps its form, solid as a rock. I read chemistry and physics at Durham University and came out with a double First.'

'Really?' Paula stopped eating and gazed into Sophie's intense eyes. She was impressed. The lady had a first-rate brain, something she had missed. 'Your father must be very admiring of your achievement.'

'Oh, I suppose he is.' Her expression had darkened. 'He goes to Vevey with Marienetta and they pore over the money side. Marienetta flies over without telling me so she

167

can organize the administration. I invented the damned stuff and I'm not even a director. Both of them are.'

'Yes,' Black Jack interjected with a sneering smile, 'but you're a scientist. A balance sheet is hieroglyphics to your limited intellect.'

'Paula,' Sophie said quietly, picking up a fork, 'may I have a taste of your pasta?'

'Go ahead,' Paula urged her. 'There's far too much for me.'

Sophie piled her fork full of pasta, suddenly turned to her left and emptied the contents into Black Jack's lap.

'That's a messy way to eat,' a new voice commented nastily. Sam Snyder had appeared out of nowhere.

The hawk-faced reporter stood close to Diamond as he waved a hand at the other diners round the table. He was wearing a dinner jacket and looked very different from when he had walked in to the coffee shop in faraway London's King Street.

'Good evening, ladies.'

Black Jack stood up, stumbled, knocked over his chair. He glared at Snyder savagely. His left fist clenched and he snarled: 'I'm going to put you in hospital, you dirty little tyke.'

Here we go, Paula said to herself. Black Jack was going to beat up the reporter badly. His left fist moved back to give extra violence to the blow. It slammed forward, Snyder moved so swiftly Paula hardly saw what happened. Black Jack's left arm was gripped in an arm-lock, twisted round, turning its owner with it. Paula was surprised by Snyder's strength.

'Ouch!' yelled Black Jack. 'You're breaking my arm.'

'Breaking it yourself, mate, by moving. So just you keep quite still or you will be the one in hospital.'

For several moments both men stood motionless, like

figures in a tableau. Other diners stared. Paula was struck by the grim look on the reporter's face. It occurred to her that Snyder was more than capable of carrying out his threat.

'Now, going to keep quiet, mate?' Snyder asked. 'If you are I can let you go. You do need to clean yourself up.'

'Release me,' Jack croaked. 'I'm heading for the bathroom.'

Snyder let go, Jack stood up slowly, his right hand clutching his left arm. Still slowly, he began to walk away. Then he paused, turned round and addressed the table.

'See you, folks,' he said in a parting attempt to express bravado. He brushed aside a waiter who had rushed forward with a napkin to help clean him up. Then he was gone.

'Sorry about that,' Snyder remarked. 'Seeing as there's an empty chair here I might as well sit in it. If that's OK by you.'

He didn't wait for an answer, seating himself in the chair vacated by Black Jack. The waiter placed a fresh glass before him. Marienetta poured red wine for him, clasped her hands together, the points of her fingers steepled under her chin, staring at him.

'What brings you to Montreux?' Paula asked him.

'I followed Sophie and Black Jack, travelled in the rear of the same plane they took to Geneva. Then hired a taxi to follow the car waiting for them. Simple as that.'

'I don't think you've really answered my question,' Paula persisted.

'Murder brought me here.' Snyder tried the wine, looked at Marienetta. 'Thank you, this is excellent. Most kind of you.'

'Murder?' Paula was puzzled. 'You couldn't have heard of any murder in Montreux. It hadn't happened when you caught the flight at Heathrow two days ago.'

'True. It hadn't. I was referring to the murder of Adam Holgate at Bray. The Arbogasts have a mansion out there.

169

Abbey Grange. Now the Arbogasts are here and out on that lake another body is floating. So my hunch was right. My hunches are often on target.'

'I don't like your implication,' Marienetta said, her tone chilly.

'No implication, Marienetta.' Snyder gave her a smile, so warm and pleasant it surprised Paula. There was another side to this reporter. 'No implication at all,' Snyder continued. 'But I think a member of the Arbogast circle may have vital information without realizing it.'

Smooth too, Paula decided. Clever with using words.

'What so-called vital information?' Marienetta asked in the same cold voice.

'Well, in London at the Cone building Mr Roman Arbogast agreed to see me. Then I saw you and the result was a total negative. As though there's something important to hide. It ended up with your calling Broden to throw me out.' Snyder turned to Paula. 'Did you know Broden is here? At this moment he's sitting at the bar, watching us in the mirror behind it.'

'No, I didn't know he was here,' Paula replied. 'But that is the business of the Arbogasts.'

'Paula.' Marienetta leaned forward. 'Broden is here as a bodyguard. For Uncle. He flew to Switzerland with him.'

'But someone told me Roman left the hotel a few hours ago in his car, driving himself and on his own.'

'You're quite right. Uncle heard about the headless body in the lake and left Broden behind to look after us – Sophie and myself. He was worried.'

'So Broden has been here two days,' Paula remarked.

'That's right.'

'One thing I wanted to check,' Snyder said, looking at Marienetta. 'What exactly were Adam Holgate's duties at ACTIL? And did he snoop around at all?'

'Try minding your own business.' Marienetta's tone was freezing now.

'I can tell you,' piped up Sophie, annoyed at being left out of the conversation. 'Adam never stopped snooping. He was careful to wait until Broden was out of the way . . .'

'*Sophie*,' warned Marienetta.

A mistake, Paula said to herself, it will only egg Sophie on, and it did.

'I think Adam had made duplicate keys of cabinets containing top secret files. He probably learned that trick when he was working for you,' she said, looking at Paula. 'Once I caught him using a camera to photograph certain documents. Don't know what they were.'

'Intriguing,' commented Snyder.

'I think we should have coffee in the lounge,' suggested Marienetta, standing up, 'then the waiters can clear the table. Do take the bottle with you, Mr Snyder. I have heard reporters are partial to alcohol to stimulate their wild imaginations . . .'

Paula walked over to join Tweed and Newman, who were drinking coffee. She told Tweed everything that had been said, quoting dialogue from memory. Like Marienetta and Sophie, Snyder had left the dining room. Tweed lit one of his rare cigarettes, leaning back in his chair as he listened to Paula.

'That's it,' she said eventually. 'You've got the lot.'

'It was well worthwhile suggesting you joined them,' Tweed said thoughtfully. 'That bit about Holgate photographing documents could be significant.'

'Broden is now watching us in that mirror,' Newman observed. 'There's something not right about the Arbogast set-up. Interesting that Sophie is much brighter than we'd thought.'

'That plastics factory could be a key factor,' Tweed remarked dreamily.

'In what way?' Paula asked.

'Time we moved,' he replied. 'Paula, I want you to help me play a trick on the receptionist, to divert his attention after I've asked him something.'

'I suppose I'll think something up.'

The receptionist was behind his counter when they strolled into the hall. Beyond the entrance doors a car had pulled up and new visitors were getting out. Tweed hurried to the desk.

'Excuse me,' he began, 'but when I registered I think I made a mistake with my address. Could I correct it, please.'

The receptionist opened the register, pushed it towards Tweed as guests began to enter. Paula asked the receptionist if she could have a train timetable. The receptionist gave her one and then was occupied with the new arrivals. Tweed's eyes scanned the whole page, starting with the top. Then he took out a pen and wrote again the same address over the one he had written earlier.

He went over to where Newman was chatting to Paula. He kept his voice low.

'Bob, that locksmith who came up from the mansion in Surrey taught you how to open doors. Could you manage a door here upstairs? You've seen your own door.'

'I guess I could. Why?'

'I saw in the hotel register someone arrived here two days ago. A Mr Mannix. Remember the name of the patient in the asylum near Pinedale? The mysterious one, in the prison room as Millie called it.'

'Mannix. It couldn't be the same one, could it?' wondered Paula.

The corridor on the third floor was deserted. Newman took very little time operating the instrument he always carried since his training session with the locksmith. Before unlocking the door he pressed the bell three times. No reaction.

Paula whispered to Tweed. 'I think Bob should stay outside. Then he can warn us if the chambermaid turns up. Three presses of the bell means trouble.'

'I heard that,' said Newman. 'I'll stand guard. In you go.'

Tweed went first, followed by Paula. If there was someone in the room he planned to say, 'The door was open. I know a Mr Mannix and thought you were him.'

Tweed explored the living area while Paula checked the bedroom. The sheets had been turned down on the bed and two wrapped chocolates were perched on the pillow. She started opening closets, found they were occupied by men's clothes. When she opened the next one she gave a little cry of fear. Tweed was alongside her in a flash.

'What is it?'

'Look in here. A long black coat and that wide-brimmed hat. It's just like the second shadow which stood behind me in that side street off Piccadilly at night. I told you. When I swung round the figure throwing the shadow had gone, probably down inside a dark alley.'

'Mr Mannix is tall and all his clothes seem new. Suggests he has a pile of money. I checked the bathroom, found a hairbrush but not a single hair in it. Something very odd here. Two empty brand-new suitcases parked in the living room.'

'Let's get out of here. We've seen what we can and it's creepy . . .'

Outside Newman closed the door, which automatically locked, and Paula made a suggestion.

'This is close to my suite. Wait while I rush along and check something.'

After a short absence she came running back. She spoke quietly.

'Just as I suspected. My bed isn't turned down yet. I don't think Mannix has slept in that bed.'

'We'll go down and have a word with the receptionist . . .'

Tweed approached the desk and now the night receptionist had taken over. Tweed stared at him as he explained what was bothering him.

'I have a friend, a Mr Mannix, staying here. I wanted to take him to the bar. He doesn't ever seem to be in.'

'No, sir, he does not. We have talked about it. Since I booked him in two nights ago no one has seen him. Not even in the restaurant.'

'Maybe I've got the wrong Mr Mannix. Could you describe him?'

'When he booked in we were very busy.' The receptionist frowned. 'I seem to recall a tall man in a long dark overcoat. He wore an unusual hat. A very wide brim and the brim was well pulled down. He also wore large dark glasses.'

'Doesn't matter,' Tweed said as though it wasn't important. 'Nabokov, the man who wrote *Lolita*, stayed here for fifteen years, the last years of his life.'

'*Sixteen* years,' the receptionist corrected him.

'Probably before your time,' Newman remarked wickedly as he moved away.

'He didn't like that,' Paula whispered. 'He can't be a day over thirty and Nabokov died in 1977.'

'I know. Maybe we ought to get to bed.'

'I'm dropping,' said Paula. 'If anything happens you'll wake me with the code – four knocks, a pause, then one knock.' She was thinking as they walked down the hall. 'I suppose the mysterious Mr Mannix couldn't be the body in the lake? Weird thought.'

Paula forced herself to have a shower, then flopped into bed. She fell fast asleep within minutes. She was confident she would enjoy the deepest sleep she'd experienced for a while. The nightmare invaded her mind suddenly.

She was by herself, searching the grassy ground close to the asylum at Pinedale. It was very quiet and clouds of mist floated towards her. She was looking for a lot of blood, where the head of Foley must have been held up by his hair. The asylum still existed, a vague shape as the mist swirled round it. Where were Tweed and Newman? She had no idea.

She heard a sound like the slow padding of heavy feet coming towards her. Her right hand dived into her looped handbag. Then she remembered, with a spasm of fear, they had brought no weapons with them to Maine. She did not have her .32 Browning. She looked round for a weapon, a heavy branch. Nothing. She turned in the direction of the approaching padding footsteps.

A shadowy figure moved in the mist. Something tall and wearing a long black coat. It wore a wide-brimmed hat pulled down so she could not see the face – only a white blur. She tried to run but her legs wouldn't move, felt like they were made of lead.

The figure advanced closer, the long black coat swinging with its motion. Then she saw it more clearly and her throat choked up. There was still no wind but the hat was blown off, exposing the head. She wanted to scream but couldn't make a sound. Below where the hat had been was a horrific face, twisted in a grimace of hate, one eye twitching. The face of Roman Arbogast as Marienetta had painted it 'when he was in a rage'.

In his right hand he held a long-handled axe. He was lifting the axe as he came very close. Her feet were glued to the ground. He elevated the axe, the blunt end in front. He was going to smash her skull before he decapitated her. She screamed. Someone was hammering somewhere. She woke up, covered in perspiration. Her mind blurred, she threw back the bedclothes, hobbled to the door in her pyjamas. Her trembling fingers unlocked it. Tweed was outside clad in a dressing gown.

'You screamed,' he began. 'What happened? Are you all right?'

'I'm OK. I had a nightmare. I think it was triggered off by seeing those clothes in the Mannix room.'

'You're sure you're all right now? Drink a lot of water.'

'I will. Why are you here?'

'Just heard from Beck. They have the body. The patrol boat scooped it up on its huge shovel, then dropped it close to the *pic-bot*. Is that how you say it?'

'Your French is perfect. I need ten minutes.'

'So do I.'

She had another quick shower. Her pyjamas were soaking-wet. The shower woke her up and she was alert. She was ready when Tweed, half-dressed, returned with Newman. She let them in, hauled on her trousers and jacket. She'd checked the time. 7 a.m. It was dark outside and would be very cold.

Newman asked her, 'Recovered from the nightmare yet?'

'Completely. I'll tell you about it later. I'm ready.'

'Bring a torch,' Tweed advised.

'And my little camera,' she added.

There was no one about inside the hotel as they approached the exit. Newman had reconnoitred the route after dressing swiftly and throwing on his overcoat, then returned to the hotel. He led the way. The early morning air chilled her face as they crossed the Grand-Rue and descended a steep flight of steps to the promenade and the lakeside. On their way down the flight of steps Paula saw autumn leaves plastered to a stone wall. Some were orange, some blood-red. It had been quiet in the hotel

176

but the atmosphere changed as they came close to the police tape.

Crowds jammed the promenade, men and women in dressing gowns and scarves with overcoats pulled over them. Over them TV lights glared above huge cameras. The bush telegraph had brought out the media in swarms. Three uniformed police barred their way, shaking their heads, pushing towards them with gloved hands. Beck appeared.

'Let these three people through,' he ordered in French.

The sightseeing crowd was silent. Paula heard the swish of small waves breaking against the front. The storm had gone away. Tweed noted that Beck was well organized.

Further along the *quai* a large truck carrying a hoist was backed to the edge. The hoist was lowering a stretcher. The body, Paula realized, had to be floating alongside the *pic-bot*. The strange vessel was as she remembered it, like a long metal barge with slanting sides sloping down to its capacious flat bottom. Its two crew-members were seated at one end, smoking. Their tools rested on the base – a long-handled rake for hauling in debris, a long-handled scoop for lifting the debris into the *pic-bot*.

'They thought they could help,' Beck explained. 'They can't, as you see now.'

The large stretcher hovered just above the lake's surface. Two divers were starting to lift a gleaming body bag into the stretcher.

'Now don't rush it,' a high-pitched voice shouted in French. 'Do not disturb the body bag in any way. *Slowly!* Treat it as though it were alive. You *do* hear me.'

A short plump man wearing a raincoat buttoned to his neck was responsible for shouting the orders. He couldn't keep still as he paced, never taking his eyes off what was being lifted and placed in the stretcher.

'That's Dr Zeitzler, the pathologist from Zürich,' Beck

explained. 'He's very fussy that nothing should be disturbed until he's conducted his autopsy. He's right, of course.'

The stretcher now contained the rubberized body bag. The hoist lifted it very slowly, swung it away from the lake, carefully lowered it on to the promenade near an ambulance backed to the kerb.

'It might just be someone we know,' Paula said quietly. 'If you want an immediate identification.'

'The three of you come with me,' Beck said, grasping Paula by the arm.

'Dr Zeitzler,' Beck said in English and a commanding voice, 'we have someone here who might be able to identify the body. And I need identification at the earliest possible moment to pursue my investigation.'

'I am only prepared to open the bag a few inches,' Zeitzler replied in English. 'She'll probably faint anyway if the corpse is indeed headless.'

'No, I won't,' Paula snapped back.

The pathologist put latex gloves on. While he was doing this he walked all round the body bag. Then, giving her a grim look, he bent down, very slowly and carefully taking hold of the zip, pulled it gently down several inches.

A very powerful TV light perched on a truck was suddenly switched on, illuminating the scene. Beck cupped both hands and shouted an order in French. 'Put that bloody light out now or I'll have it put out.'

The glare remained. Beck whispered some instructions to a policeman who held a carbine. The officer raised his carbine, took very careful aim, fired once. The glare light was shattered. There was the faint sound of tinkling glass.

'They don't muck about here,' Tweed commented to Paula. 'I wish we had their police in Britain. The crime rate would plummet.'

Paula steeled herself. The body was headless. Then she saw the once stiffened, now limp, points of an old-fashioned collar. She gave a gasp. She put a hand to her throat so she would speak clearly.

'That is – was – Dr Abraham Seale, the well-known criminologist. We met him in London.'

18

'I urgently need a safe phone,' Tweed said.

'Come with me to the police station,' Beck suggested.
'I have to go there myself. It's only a short walk.'

The ambulance carrying Dr Abraham Seale to Zurich
had left. Dr Zeitzler travelled with the corpse, clearly
anxious to watch over it until he had performed his
autopsy.

Beck led the way followed by Tweed, Paula and Newman.
Water dripped from the profusion of trees. Paula remembered Montreux as a lush oasis of peace. Not this time.
Tweed was telling Beck all he knew about Seale as they
hurried uphill. Once inside the police station Beck gave
them a room on their own with a phone. Tweed sat down,
pressed the number for Park Crescent.

'Monica, I'm going to speak quickly. At the moment we
are in Montreux. Your favourite hobby is tracing family
trees, I know . . .'

'Yes, it is. I spent a lot of time tracing my own family
roots. Took me all over the world. Then I found we were
descended from a notorious pirate, right-hand man to Sir
Henry Morgan. I gave up then – not sure what I might
find if I persisted.'

'The Arbogast family. I want you to trace their family
tree if you can.'

'I can. I kept all my contacts when I was checking my
own origins.'

'Thank Heaven. I think this is very important. Arbogasts originated in Italy. I can tell you that much. Their name then was Arbogastini. Shall I spell it?'

'No, I've got it. And one of my contacts is in Rome. She is an expert on documentation. I'll start there.'

'You know anyone in the States? You do. One of the family emigrated to America, I heard. Could be several generations ago. I think his name was Vicenzo – may have changed it to Vincent. How long will it take you? A week? I understand. When it's ready send it to me by courier. I'll keep you in touch with my movements . . .'

Paula had been sitting, listening, watching. She was fascinated by the change in Tweed's personality. It had become positively electric.

'You sounded so determined, almost excited,' she commented when he had ended the call.

'We may have had a big break. *May* have. You remember we last saw Abraham Seale sitting on the steps of the ACTIL building? He was working on a family tree. He remarked it could be dangerous. Why? What had he stumbled on? Whatever it was may have led to his murder.'

Beck walked in, stern and businesslike. 'I've traced where Seale was staying. Got lucky with my second shot. Tried the Montreux Palace first. No good. Then the Eurotel, a big modern place further along the Grand-Rue, perched on the edge of the lake. He arrived there two days ago and spent a lot of time away from the hotel.'

'Two days again,' Paula mused. 'Everyone arrived here two days ago. It must mean something.'

'I've sent men to the Eurotel,' Beck continued. 'They'll search his room, bring his things back here. We may find something.'

'You may not, Arthur.' Tweed stood up. 'Thanks for the use of your phone. I think we'll get back to our hotel. I'm sure Paula is gasping for breakfast.'

182

'So is Newman,' said Newman. 'Breakfast, coffee and some water.'

'I'll be leaving for Zürich,' Beck told them. 'Zeitzler should have his autopsy report by tomorrow. What about you?'

'I'll come if I can. That autopsy report will be very important. Can I use your phone again? I want to call Professor Saafeld, the pathologist who autopsied the body of Adam Holgate. He has films and photographs. Also he's received films and photos of the body of Hank Foley, found in Maine, because he knows the medical examiner in Boston. If you give me your address at that police headquarters in Zürich I'll have them sent to you by courier . . .'

As they were leaving Beck ran after them. 'One detail before I leave for Zürich. You may see two men in white coats examining the promenade. Zeitzler left them behind in the hope they'd find traces of blood – and where Seale was executed. Here's my card in case you want to question them. I've scribbled a note on the back.'

'Can you hold out a bit longer?' Tweed asked Paula. 'Then we can check on what the white coats have discovered. If anything.'

'If I must.'

As they descended to the promenade the dawn sun was rising, a hazy blur in the mist. The lake was calm, a smooth stretch of grey water disappearing towards the French shore on the far side. It was very quiet now the crowds had dispersed. When shown Beck's card a policeman lifted the tape for them.

Paula thought how beautiful – and tragic – it was. Along the promenade there were trees and shrubs, the gentle sound of the lake lapping against the wall. It was like heaven but hell had intruded. They found the two white coats walking slowly, using powerful torches to examine the promenade's surface, pausing to check the area. Tweed showed them Beck's card, asked them in French, 'Have you found any blood?'

'Only by the *pic-bot*. It must have taken great strength to insert the corpse inside the rubberized body bag.'

'And to chop off the head,' Newman added.

'Do you mind?' Paula snapped, ravening with hunger.

Her last glimpse of the lake was the pinkish glow of the sun colouring the mist. It was like a dream, like a Monet painting, a radiance of colour. Then she remembered her dream, the nightmare she had experienced. So when they entered the hall she received a shock. The tall figure of Roman Arbogast, wearing a smart black suit, stood as though waiting for them, hands clasped behind his back.

'I thought you had left Montreux,' Tweed said.

'Oh, but I did.' Roman was at his most amiable, gave a twisted smile. 'I have been visiting my plastics factory at Vevey.' He glanced round. 'Sophie wouldn't like that. She thinks it is her factory. I found she has a room there – no windows, and with two locks on a strong door. She is the only one allowed inside it. She has her quirks. Maybe you would like to join us after breakfast for a spectacular trip.'

'Where to?'

'By train to the summit of Rochers de Naye. Six thousand feet up. It has a fantastic view of the lake below.'

'Yes, we would,' Tweed decided. 'Thank you for inviting us.'

His decision had been influenced by his conviction that Paula was in a state of semi-shock. First the nightmare, then the discovery of Professor Seale. The trip would take her mind off what she had experienced.

In the dining room Paula, sitting with Tweed and Newman, had invited Marler, Butler and Nield to join them. They had been rather left out of what had been going on. She consumed two eggs and bacon, four croissants and three cups of coffee. Then she felt alive, alert and ready for anything. Tweed noticed the colour had returned to her face and she was having a lively conversation with Marler, Butler and Nield.

'Although out of sight,' Marler drawled, 'we have heard about that business down on the *quai*. A topic banned for the moment,' he added as Tweed frowned at him. 'We have been prowling around Montreux. You know the Vice-President has reappeared?'

'No, I didn't.' Tweed was surprised and disturbed. 'Where has he been, then? How do you know this?'

'I'm observant,' Marler said with a smile. 'He was driving his own Mercedes all by himself and slipped back into the hotel very early this morning. Well before dawn. You know I'm an early riser. Went straight up to his suite, wherever that is in this palatial hunk of masonry. He was carrying a large suitcase.'

'So he'd been off somewhere?'

'Can you think of any other reason why he would be carrying the suitcase?'

'When he's campaigning he's everywhere. But on his own he's like a man who moves in the shadows. Normal and abnormal.'

Paula glanced up quickly when she heard the last three words. Tweed gazed back at her with a warm smile. He switched his gaze to a large table nearby, the Arbogast table. Roman was smiling a lot and Tweed's sharp ears heard him congratulating Sophie on her great achievement in Vevey. He was tactfully not mentioning the mysterious locked room. Sophie sat up straighter, modestly concealing her pleasure. Marienetta, next to her, gave her a kiss. Black Jack was tucking into his large breakfast as though there was no tomorrow. Unusually for him he was not saying a word. Tweed thought he looked tired, as though he'd had an exhausting night.

185

Tweed told his guests of the invitation to join the party going by train up to Rochers de Naye and said he'd like everyone to come. Newman frowned. He was wondering what Tweed's reason was for taking them all up the mountain.

Paula had just finished joking with Pete Nield when a tall athletic man appeared, walked over to their table. She was stunned. It was Ed Danvers, the FBI man attached to the London Embassy who had visited them at Park Crescent.

'Am I interrupting you guys?' he said pleasantly. 'If so I'll vanish in the proverbial cloud of smoke. It's quite a trick.'

'Of course not,' Paula piped up. 'There's space for you next to me. The waiter overheard and he's bringing a chair.'

Danvers sat down between Paula and Tweed. Dressed in an American sports jacket and jeans, he smiled briefly. He looked healthy and athletic but then his expression became one of acute exasperation. He accepted coffee, drank some.

'You're the last person on earth I expected to see here,' remarked Paula.

'It happened quickly. I was ordered to accompany the Vice-President everywhere he went,' he explained, speaking very quietly. 'Two days ago we fly to Geneva, travel in the waiting limo to this place. Straub goes up to his suite, tells me to enjoy myself. I protest and he shuts the door in my face. I haven't seen him since until he rolls back here early this morning. I've spent two days patrolling Montreux, looking for him. He's nowhere to be seen. When I check with the concierge his key is on the hook, which means he's no longer here. Until he gets back this morning. Why am I telling you this? Because your pal Cord Dillon, Mr Tweed, is my pal. He gave you both a glowing testimonial. So I trust you when I need someone to groan to.'

'Why does Straub behave like this?' Tweed asked softly.

'Damned if I know. Says he's on a confidential diplomatic mission. Let slip – or pretended to – that he visited Paris. So why didn't we fly there first? Don't ask me. I'm just the messenger boy. With no messages.'

'We're going up to Rochers de Naye after breakfast,' Paula told him.

'So is Straub. Maybe Roman Arbogast asked him. I wouldn't know. I wish I were back at Grosvenor Square.'

'Roman is waving to us,' Tweed reported. 'I think the trip is about to start.'

'Well, nothing can happen on top of a mountain,' Danvers said.

Limos, organized by Roman, took the large party to the station, although they could have walked there. The station for Rochers de Naye was across from the main-line station and separate from it. The train was a surprise. Streamlined, it was like a toy version of France's TGV, very modern and like a bullet. Locals, carrying shopping, piled into the front coach, leaving the rear coach empty for Arbogast's party.

There was plenty of room. Tweed and Newman occupied a seat at the rear while Paula sat by herself opposite and across the aisle. Newman nudged Tweed, nodded towards the front seat some distance away. Russell Straub had appeared out of nowhere and had parked a bag next to him. This had compelled Danvers to sit behind him.

The Arbogast party was scattered in different seats. As the doors closed automatically and the train glided forward Paula whispered to Tweed.

'Black Jack must have run himself into the ground last night. He's already fallen asleep.'

'Trawling the bars.' Tweed paused. 'Or something.'

'I wonder how Dr Seale found his way to Montreux.'

'We may never know.'

'Why is the Arbogast family tree so important? You were very intense when talking to Monica.'

'Just a hunch.'

They were starting to climb. Montreux faded behind them. Paula, who had come across to converse with Tweed, went back to her seat. The view out of the window was more interesting. Small Swiss villages stood just beyond platforms where the train stopped. From the front coach women carrying shopping alighted. Newman realized they used the train to commute down into Montreux to buy necessities. Paula admired the neatness of the houses, the creepers trained over white walls. They stopped at many villages, then the incline of the track began to go up steeply. The villages, the frequent stops were left behind. Rocky, less fertile ground appeared as the slowing train climbed and climbed at an ever steeper angle. Ahead through the windows Paula could see the line swinging round an endless succession of hairpin bends, like two metal snakes. She felt they were heading for the roof of the world.

Tweed leaned close to Newman, spoke clearly even though his voice was little more than a whisper.

'This is a direct order. When we alight at the top you will stay with Paula every second. Whatever happens.'

'Understood.'

'Bob,' Paula called across the aisle, 'do you mind changing places with me? I'm being selfish but the view now on your side is much more dramatic.'

'Be my guest . . .'

Tweed gave her his window seat. As they swung round another sharp bend, still climbing, an immense peak appeared higher up. A huge menacing knob of rock. Tweed pointed to it.

'That is the ultimate summit of Rochers de Naye. You can't get on top of that. Only an expert mountain climber would attempt it.'

'It's another world,' she said.

'And I'm wondering why Roman Arbogast organized this trip. It's out of character.'

He said nothing more and Paula watched as dense clouds of mist shrouded the peak. It simply disappeared. Near the front of the coach Black Jack had woken up, rubbed his hands through his thick dark hair, stretched his arms as though limbering up for some difficult physical task. Behind him Roman Arbogast, sitting by himself, sat up straighter. The last station was close.

'With that mist it will be cold,' Tweed remarked. Taking off his light waterproof topcoat, he wrapped it round Paula's shoulders like a long cloak. 'That will keep you warm.'

He stood up before she could protest. As she stood up as well Arbogast glanced round, his right eye twitching. Tweed was now convinced the twitching indicated he was under tension. Why? What was bothering him now? Or was he steeling himself for something?

The train glided into the final station, the doors opened automatically, the passengers were piling out onto the small platform. Tweed tried to see who was going where but it was hopeless. Paula had tucked her long hair under a peaked baseball cap. Newman took her arm as she alighted.

'I need company,' he said. 'Don't like heights. Let's stick together.'

'I never knew you suffered from vertigo.'

'It's six thousand feet up here. That's a lot of feet.'

Tweed walked by himself up the rocky slope leading towards the edge. In places he could see clearly several yards ahead. Then the mist would roll in and he sensed the right direction by instinct. The rest of the party had vanished as he plodded on and upwards. He was moving slowly through the dense mist, then speeding up when a clear patch appeared. He stopped once or twice to

189

listen. The silence was complete, almost ominous. He was confident he knew the way to the edge. Years before he had been here on a clear sunlit day, had stood at the edge. He was determined to repeat the experience. He took off the heavy coat which was hampering him, threw it over his shoulders like a cloak.

He was moving more slowly now, not sure of where he was. The mist ahead of him cleared suddenly. He had paused and through the wide 'window' provided by the sunlight he saw he was a dozen yards or so from the edge. Beyond the sun glittered on the lake far below, on a fantastic panorama of the Vallée, way down, as seen from a plane. He walked to within a few feet of the brink and stared down the immense abyss, as he had done once before long ago. The abyss was dropping vertically, sheer, falling, falling, falling.

Suddenly the mist rolled round him, blotting out the view. He was encircled by cloud, could see nothing of the view, the drop. He was beginning to get confused about direction. Stand perfectly still until the mist clears again, he told himself. Then he felt the knuckled hand in his back, perfectly positioned in the centre of his spine. Perfectly positioned to give one shove and he'd go over, down and down the abyss. He had only a millisecond to react. He spun round to his left, backing away from the precipice. His left hand clenched in a fist and he struck out with all his force. The thrust sailed into mist, hit nothing solid. He backed slowly down the slope, away from eternity. The mist cleared and a corridor of clarity revealed the station well down the slope. His hands were clammy, and not from the mist.

19

The mist continued to disperse. As he trudged down the slope Tweed observed where everyone was. Over to his right Roman Arbogast was padding down slowly. To his left, a long way down, Black Jack was jogging at a deliberate pace. Nearer, also to his left, Marienetta was strolling down alongside Sophie. He saw her clasp Sophie's hand. Sophie snatched her hand free, walked briskly, her head raised, her brown hair tied back in a ponytail. Her attitude expressed both frustration and anger.

Lower down still Newman walked next to Paula, carrying out Tweed's command. Tweed sucked in his breath, glanced down at the overcoat thrown over his shoulders like a cape. Its colour was very similar to the raincoat he had given Paula and which she still wore over her shoulders. Like a cape.

Oh, my God, he thought. I wasn't the target at the brink of the precipice. Seen as a blurred shape in the mist my back view would look like Paula's. *She* was the target. Shall I tell her? She's gone through so much. The horror at Bray, the second horror in Maine, her experience down on the *quai* when she recognized Abraham Seale. Her nightmares. I'll talk it over with Newman first.

Then he saw someone he could hardly believe he was seeing. Sam Snyder striding down the slope. He hadn't seen him on the train, but the coach had been crammed. And Snyder could have been hunched down in his seat.

191

Coming closer to the platform he saw Pete Nield standing at one end of the train, Harry Butler at the other end. They had stayed behind to make sure the train wasn't sabotaged. They rarely missed a trick.

'Didn't know you were with the party, Sam,' he said, catching up with Snyder.

'I'm everywhere.' The hawklike faced creased into its peculiar grin. 'That's my job. I've got some good shots looking down that fearsome drop.' He patted the compact camera slung by his side. 'And one earlier which is worth a packet if syndicated.'

'Which one is that?'

'A perfect shot of Professor Seale, headless in the body bag. Just before a policeman shot out that TV light. It really is a beaut.'

'Charming.'

'We're occupying the front coach going down,' Arbogast called out in his throaty voice. 'It's cost enough to get up here. Any shopping women who come aboard can use the rear coach.'

'In that case,' said Paula as Tweed caught up with them, 'I'm grabbing the front seat. Straub may be Vice-President but he can't hog the best seat every time.'

She dived into the front coach the moment the doors opened. As she did so Russell Straub came off the mountain. On the platform Ed Danvers stood, hands on his hips, not pleased. Tweed and Newman were close when Danvers voiced his complaint.

'Goddamnit, sir, I lost you in the mist. Couldn't see you anywhere.'

'Ed,' Straub gave his famous facing-the-audience smile, 'I had better remind you. The cabin boy doesn't hang on to the skipper's tail night and day. And someone's in my seat.'

'Choose another one,' Danvers snapped, apparently extremely annoyed.

With everyone aboard, the train started its slow descent. Paula was delighted to see beyond the driver's window an uninterrupted view of the spiralling line ahead as the train driver kept down its speed. Tweed had guided Newman into a seat with no one behind or in front of them. He quietly told him what had happened, the similarity between what he had been wearing and Paula's garb.

'Tell her,' Newman said firmly when Tweed had finished.

'I'm not so sure . . .'

'Tell her. She's become very tough. It's your duty to warn her.'

'I'm not sure. If you say so.'

'I do say so.'

As Tweed and Newman got out of the limo outside Le Montreux Palace a figure grabbed Tweed by the arm led him along the promenade away from the emerging crowd. Arthur Beck, Chief of Police.

'Heard where you'd gone. Waited for you to get back. We've searched Abraham Seale's room at the Eurotel. Inside a case we found this collection of cartridge papers. As you'll see they're perforated near the top.'

Tweed recognized the paper Seale had been working on as he had sat on the steps leading up to the ACTIL building in London. They had been leaving when Tweed had spotted Seale, had stopped to have a word with him. He told Beck about the incident. *A dangerous place to indulge in such an activity*.

He quoted Seale's words to Beck, said that Seale had explained his hobby was genealogy, the creation of family trees. Beck handed him the sheaf of cartridge papers for him to examine. Tweed held up the sheaf, looked closely at the top sheet. The sun was shining brilliantly even though it was a cold morning.

'I can see a complex diagram of straight lines,' he mused. 'Seale would have pressed hard to draw the diagram of the Arbogast family tree he was creating. But someone has torn off the top sheet which would have the names. You can see the rough edge. Pity we can't see the names.'

'I noticed that,' Beck agreed. 'The Arbogast family? So it looks as though a member of that family is involved. Abraham Seale is now in an ambulance, should soon reach Zürich for the autopsy. You tell me Seale used the word "dangerous". Now he is headless. He used the right word.'

'Yes, he did,' Tweed said, handing the sheaf back. 'And you might like to know that Black Jack Diamond is a cousin of the Arbogasts.'

Tweed went inside the hotel and straight up to Paula's suite. When he knocked on the door it was opened by Newman who winked at him. He was taking Tweed's order to guard Paula very seriously.

'I'm on my way,' Newman said and left.

Paula was standing in front of a mirror, brushing her hair. She gave him a big smile as she put down the brush and turned round. She gestured towards a chair but Tweed preferred to remain standing as he took off the overcoat from his shoulders.

'I have something to tell you that happened up at Rochers de Naye.'

'Oh, what was that?' she asked as she sat in a hard-backed chair.

He told her everything, starting with his searching for the brink of the precipice. She frowned, stood up as he completed his story. Her reaction took him completely off guard. She rushed at him.

'You bloody fool! Taking such a risk. Standing at the edge of that precipice! Why? Just because that's what you did years ago. A bloody repeat performance. I know your theory that it could have been me. But for God's sake, it could have been *you*! After what happened to Foley, to Holgate. And now to Seale. You could now be a battered hunk of smashed bones six thousand feet down. How could you?'

She was thumping him on the chest with her clenched fist. Then she burst into tears, sobbing nonstop. He put his arms round her. She buried her head in his chest, sobbing her heart out. He stroked her hair, used soothing words. She had her hands round his neck. He had a large handkerchief ready when she suddenly recovered. She took it, mouthed, 'Thanks,' began wiping her eyes, her face.

Then she stood back, glanced in a wall mirror. She dabbed her face again with the handkerchief. She managed a smile. From a carafe he poured her a glass of water. She drank the lot. He refilled the glass and she sat down. She managed another smile, a more normal one.

'I wish you'd sit down,' she said. 'You're standing there like a sentry. I'll be back in a minute.'

She went into the bathroom to wash her face. Tweed sat down. He was upset because he had so upset her. He felt guilty. It had not been a good idea. But he'd had to tell her, to warn her. When she came back she was wearing a blouse and skirt.

'Those trousers were too hot in here,' she explained. 'I'd turned down the heating but it takes a while to work.' She went to the drinks cupboard, took out a balloon glass, poured brandy, took it to him. 'You look so miserable. Drink this. It will buck you up.'

She sat in an armchair close to him as he took a sip, then another one. She was right. She was always right. He began to feel better. Her voice was calm, normal, when she spoke.

'I'm so sorry I broke down. I've never done that before. Not like that anyway. I'm OK now. You were right to tell me I was the target. Absolutely right. I'm very grateful to you. We can always trust each other.'

'True.' He hoped his voice was normal. Talk about something else. 'Beck grabbed me as I got out of the car. On his way to Zürich now.'

He told her about what Beck had found at the Eurotel. She nodded as he explained in detail his conversation with the police chief. She crossed her very good legs, perched one elbow on them, placed a finger at the side of her face, not saying a word until he had finished.

'Maybe there'll be information from Monica at the police station in Zürich. You did ask Monica to leave a message with Beck.'

'I know. I think the next thing we do is we all travel by train to Zürich.'

'I'd say that was the best idea.'

'Just remind me,' he suggested, 'how many people we know have travelled to America. We have heard a bit of that data here and there.'

He was so relieved they were talking normally again. He also realized how very fond of Paula he was. What surprised him was that the affection seemed to be reciprocated. She used her fingers to count off who had travelled to America.

'In no particular order, Marienetta, now and again. Sophie flies out more frequently. Roman has been there. Aboard the Gulfstream, the one they keep hidden away at Heathrow, I imagine. Black Jack darts off there, probably when the whim strikes him. You can visualize him lighting up New York – or Boston. We know Sam Snyder goes there. Poor Abraham Seale went there a lot on lecture tours. Russell Straub, of course, is over there most of the time. Now he's over here, has been for days. No one seems to know why.'

'And he evades his bodyguard, Ed Danvers, a lot. Why, I wonder?'

196

'No idea.' She frowned. 'Could Danvers travel back to the States every now and again?'

'No idea.'

'Did you know Broden, Roman's security chief, was on the mountain?'

'I most certainly didn't. Are you sure?'

'Certain. He travelled somewhere on the train wearing a heavy fur coat, a fur hat and huge dark glasses. He was the last one to come down. I saw him emerge from the mist. Recognized him because of the way he walked. Body language. That awful phrase.'

'Was he anywhere near Roman?'

'No. Broden came down a long time after Roman was near the station. So he wasn't acting as bodyguard to his boss. Just like Ed Danvers wasn't. Are we getting anywhere?'

'I'm waiting for a signal, maybe an observation, which will pinpoint someone. As we go along we learn more and more.'

'Well, no more murders, I hope.'

'Don't count on it.'

20

Zürich, the powerhouse of Switzerland. They would soon be landing. In Montreux Tweed had changed his mind about using the train, which involved changing expresses. Checking an air timetable he calculated they could be driven back to Geneva by hotel limos, have time for lunch at Cointrin Airport, then take an internal Swissair flight to Zürich. Marler was in the seat next to him while Paula and Newman occupied the seats behind them. At one stage aboard the plane she had tapped Tweed on the shoulder.

'Look out of the window. I thought I saw Rochers de Naye.'

'No, you wouldn't,' Tweed replied, staring out of his window.

To the south reared the majestic range of the highest mountains in Europe, the Bernese Oberland. Their crests were snow-tipped at high altitude. He saw the Jungfrau, pointed it out to Paula. The Bernese Oberland loomed like a giant mountain wall, which is what it was. The sun sparkled on the snow. Paula thought it one of the most awesome sights she had ever seen.

'Rochers de Naye,' Tweed explained over his shoulder, 'is a southern projection of that massive range. And in any case not high enough to be seen from here.'

'Thank God there wasn't snow on Rochers de Naye,' Paula said under her breath, thinking of Tweed perched on the edge.

They lost more and more height. As the machine canted to the left prior to landing he had a clear view of Kloten Airport. He leaned over Marler and stared. Paula gripped his shoulder, kept her voice down.

'What is it?'

'At an isolated spot near the outside of the airport I saw a big Gulfstream plane. It could be Arbogast's. If so, what is he doing here?'

'Will Beck have arrived yet?' she wondered.

'He will,' Marler replied. 'He took off in a chopper to get here. I saw something curious while you were way up on the mountain. A photograph taken by Newman's pal, Sam Snyder.'

'No pal of mine,' Newman growled from behind.

'You don't know how to handle Snyder,' Marler told him. 'With me Snyder knows I'll stand no nonsense, so he doesn't try it on.'

'What was the photograph?' Paula asked.

Marler took a stiffened envelope from his coat pocket, handed it back. Paula opened it, took out a cellophane envelope and the photograph inside it. She gazed at it in astonishment.

'Where was this taken? Looks like somewhere near the *quai* in Montreux.'

'It is. Let Tweed see it.'

Tweed took the photo, was if anything more taken aback than Paula had been. He studied the picture of the woman who was smiling grimly, as though she'd had the satisfaction of being proved right. The picture of Mrs Elena Brucan.

It was a colour print and she was wearing the same pale green overcoat, the same green fut hat that she had when she visited Tweed in his office at Park Crescent. Marler had been in the room at the time, he recalled.

'Why do you think Snyder took this picture?' Tweed wondered. 'I get the impression she was in a crowd, looking down at the body of Abraham Seale.'

'She was,' Marler confirmed. 'Snyder was struck by her unusual appearance, thought it made a good shot, which it does. He introduced himself and she said she was Elena Brucan. She said she was following a murderer. He thought she was batty. You all went back to the Montreux Palace and I brought up the rear. Ahead of me – I hadn't seen the photo then – and as you went to your rooms, I saw someone ahead of me, entering the hotel. Mrs Elena Brucan.'

'She was staying at the hotel then?' Tweed asked.

'No.'

'Marler,' Paula said impatiently, 'you're talking far more than you usually do. I get the feeling something else happened. Do get on with it.'

'Patience, my dear. I was curious. I lingered in the hall, pretended to be looking at a brochure. The receptionist was holding two air tickets. He called out to one of the staff to take these tickets from Geneva to Zürich to Mlle Sophie Arbogast's room. If she wasn't in take them to M. Diamond's room. And it was very urgent.'

'So they were flying together to Zürich, just as they flew out here together,' said Tweed thoughtfully.

'There's more,' Marler continued. 'While this was going on Mrs Brucan was pretending to study a picture on the wall. She was actually eavesdropping. When the chap with the air tickets had gone she turned round, saw me. I went over to her and she recognized me, so I introduced myself, said maybe we could go for a walk. She was pleased, said she was on her way back to her hotel. It was the Eurotel.'

'Where Abraham Seale was staying,' Tweed recalled.

'Is there a connection?' Paula speculated.

'Time will tell.'

'Haven't finished yet,' Marler drawled. 'In the reception

hall I offered her coffee. She pointed out where I should go, then hovered by reception. I left her, stayed just inside the entrance to the lounge. I heard her ask the receptionist to book her on the next flight from Geneva to Zürich. She then dashed up to her room, ditching me.'

'She was in a rush to pack and get to Geneva,' Paula said.

'I'm sure she was,' Marler agreed.

'Food for deep thought,' Tweed mused. '*She was following a murderer.* Her exact words to Snyder.'

'So,' Newman decided, 'it looks to be either Sophie or Black Jack.'

'Maybe yes. Maybe no,' Tweed replied. 'Perhaps she was tracking the Arbogast clan.'

The plane touched down, an exceptionally smooth landing. As they waited for the lights Butler and Nield, who had sat well behind them, came up the aisle. Tweed looked up at them, spoke in a clear whisper.

'First, we get cabs from the airport straight to Beck at his police headquarters here. After that, on to the Baur au Lac – I booked rooms for all of us before we left Montreux.'

Paula loved Zürich. She gazed out of the window as they were driven into the ancient city, across the bridge over the River Limmat which divided the city. Large modern blue one-decker trams trundled past, traffic sped when it could.

Nield and Butler preferred to wait outside the large stone building which is police headquarters. Beck was waiting for them in his usual office with its windows looking out across the river to the massive University building on the opposite bank.

'Welcome,' he said with a warm smile and again hugged Paula. 'My favourite Englishwoman. Anna,' he said to a uniformed girl, 'coffee for everyone. Cream for Robert Newman here.'

'I left Nield and Butler outside,' Tweed remarked.

'I'll see them afterwards,' Anna responded, smiling seductively at Tweed.

'Anna likes you,' Beck said when she had gone. 'I think she is after you. Now to work. Sit down, please. Saafeld has reacted quickly. A courier arrived from him this morning.' He handed a thick envelope to Tweed. 'Addressed to you. Feels as though it's stuffed with films and photos.'

Beck had a new table. Oblong and large, its surface was covered with a sheet of glass hinged in the middle. The edges were rounded so no one could get hurt. As Tweed carefully opened the well-wrapped package, Beck, seated, tapped the table top with the palm of one hand.

'This cost a fortune. I can lift half of it and place it on the other half. Easy to place material under the glass. The accountant in Berne nearly went mad when he had the invoice. I should care.'

Tweed had extracted latex gloves from his pocket, put them on before he took out films and photos. Saafeld had sent films and photos not only of Adam Holgate – he had also included the material sent to him by his medical examiner friend in Boston, the films and photos of Hank Foley, late caretaker at the asylum in Pinedale. Beck added photos, X-rays from Zeitzler's autopsy.

Marler had also produced latex gloves, was wearing them as he extracted from a pocket a jeweller's glass which had been wrapped in velvet. Beck was most approving.

'Ah! We have a professional!'

Swiftly Marler selected photos and films of the necks of the three murdered men. Pressing the glass into his eye he examined them closely one by one. He grunted, removed the glass from his eye.

'It's the same killer,' he announced. 'The notch in the axe used is apparent in all three cases. We are hunting a serial murderer.'

'But *not* a random killer, I'm convinced,' Tweed said firmly. 'There is a link between all three victims.'

'All the way from Maine to London to Switzerland?' Beck queried.

'Yes,' Tweed repeated in the same firm tone. 'All we have to do is to trace the link. It's buried somewhere.'

They were driven to the Hotel Baur au Lac in two unmarked police cars. The drivers were in plain clothes. In the front vehicle Paula sat next to Tweed in the rear compartment, while Marler, perched on a flat seat, faced them. Newman was travelling in the car behind them with Butler and Nield.

Paula was fascinated because most of the journey took them down Bahnhofstrasse, the most famous, the richest street in the world. Banks alternated with expensive shops and the legend was the street was paved with gold. Actually the bank vaults where the gold was stored were beneath Bahnhofstrasse. Smart elegant women strolled along the pavements.

'So now we know the same killer murdered Foley in Maine, Holgate at Bray and Seale in Montreux,' Paula pondered aloud. 'It's a frightening thought.'

'Very frightening,' Tweed agreed.

'Why did you choose the Baur au Lac?'

'Because if the Arbogast family is coming to Zürich that is the type of hotel they're likely to use. To say nothing of the other players in this hideous drama. Like Black Jack.'

'He is an Arbogast,' she reminded him. 'A cousin.'

Ahead of them in the near distance they could see light reflections on the Zürichsee, Lake Zürich. They had now moved from French-speaking Switzerland to the large German-speaking area in the north. Their car turned right off Bahnhofstrasse, crossed another street and passed through the wide entrance to the ultra-luxurious

Baur au Lac. They got out, entered, leaving the driver to hand their luggage to a flock of impeccably dressed waiting porters. Paula nudged Tweed before they turned right to reception. They had a view into a spacious lounge.

'You were right,' she said.

Seated well back by himself in the lounge was Roman Arbogast, a drink on the table before him. He was staring straight at them.

'Looks like a good place to start,' Tweed agreed.

He had just spoken when, from the direction of the lift, Marienetta appeared. She was wearing a green two-piece suit and her golden hair was loose. She came to them with a warm smile, tall, her movements elegant. She's like a goddess, Paula thought.

'Welcome to Zürich now,' Marienetta greeted them. When Tweed kissed her on both cheeks he caught a faint whiff of perfume as she squeezed his arm. Turning to Paula she kissed her. 'I'm so bored with the people here. Thank Heaven you have arrived. You will join me for tea in the lounge, Paula. I won't take no for an answer.'

'I could do with some refreshment. Let me go up to my room and I'll join you.'

'I'll grab a quiet table.'

'The pace is beginning to accelerate,' Tweed commented as they headed for registration. 'There always comes a stage when this happens.'

'Don't understand you.'

As Tweed was registering the young man behind the counter started chatting.

'We have another honoured guest, Mr Tweed. Mr Russell Straub, Vice-President of the United States, is staying with us.'

'Really? When did he arrive?'

'At lunchtime. It is really rather funny. He has a bodyguard with him. A Mr Danvers. Mr Straub refuses to allow him to accompany him. He has been out all afternoon on his own.'

'Have you been here long?' Tweed enquired with a smile. It was unheard of for staff here to be so indiscreet, giving out information about another guest.

'No, sir. I'm only temporary. I shall be leaving within a week. I've obtained a post at a hotel in Geneva.'

Both Paula and Tweed found they had good rooms overlooking the entrance where a Rolls-Royce was parked. Tweed had just opened his case when the phone rang. It was the police driver who had brought them there.

'I'm sorry to disturb you, sir. My employer, with whom you were talking recently, would like to see you again urgently. Provided it is convenient. I could drive you back when you are available.'

'I'm available now.'

The driver had been the soul of discretion. No names mentioned. It must be important for Beck to want to see him so soon again, Tweed knew. He tapped on Paula's door. She opened it with a towel wrapped round her.

'Beck wants to see me again. Back at police head-quarters. No idea why. In any case you'll be having Marienetta for company.'

When he had gone Paula, who moved quickly, had had a wash and was removing crushable items from her case. She changed into her blue two-piece suit and wondered what Beck wanted to see Tweed about. Sounded like an emergency.

As she walked into the uncrowded lounge she saw Roman Arbogast get up from his table, padding off somewhere. At another table a good distance from where Marienetta sat Sophie was having tea by herself. Odd, she thought.

'I have ordered tea for you,' Marienetta said as Paula sat facing her. 'I do like that suit.'

'And I like yours. Very chic.'

206

'Oh dear!' Marienetta chuckled. 'We're turning into a mutual admiration society. This might be a good opportunity to compare notes. We did agree to collaborate.'

'A good idea.'

A man walked into the lounge. Russell Straub, wearing a different suit, smart, biscuit-coloured. His tie was cinnamon, a perfect choice over a freshly starched white shirt. The Vice-President had good dress sense. He walked with a purposeful stride, about to pass close to their table, staring straight ahead.

'Hi, cousin,' Marienetta called out to him.

He stopped, stood stock-still for several seconds. Glancing at Marienetta he glared at her, his intense dark eyes vicious. The same look he had given Tweed during their brief confrontation at Sophie's birthday dinner in London. Then, without a word, he walked on, disappeared.

'So, what did I say?' Marienetta said to Paula. 'Brits do refer to our American cousins. I have a friend at the Foreign Office who often uses the phrase.'

'I think he must have a volatile temperament,' Paula replied.

'Weird. At Sophie's birthday party I chatted to him over drinks before we started dinner. He must have had a disappointing afternoon. Now, these terrible murders. Have you come to some conclusion about the killer's identity?'

'After you. I'm concentrating on food. Ravenous. But I can listen.'

'Well, first there's that strange reporter, Sam Snyder. I remember when he first came to see Roman. He showed him a critical article he'd written on ACTIL as a global giant. Roman didn't like it at all. He offered Snyder the use of our Gulfstream to travel to the States when it was available. On condition he toned the article down.

The article never appeared. Roman is wily,' Marienetta chuckled.

'So did Snyder use your Gulfstream to fly back and forth to the States? I mean, the other way round.'

'Yes, he did. It was a dream offer. If something big happened in the States, Snyder could beat his British rivals, get there first. I find it intriguing that his profession is that of crime reporter.'

'I see what you mean. Incidentally, why is Sophie having tea so very much on her own?'

'She's avoiding me.' Marienetta smiled wrily. 'We have these spats – or rather she does. Occasionally, especially when my sculpture isn't going well, I have dinner with Black Jack. Don't trust him but he's lively. I try to make sure Sophie never knows. But if she finds out she goes wild with rage. She could kill me.'

'You're speaking rhetorically?'

Marienetta paused. 'Of course I am,' she said after a few moments. 'She just gets these moods. Sometimes she decides she's going to marry Jack. Then, thank Heaven, she goes off him. It's a muddled relationship. But I digress. I wondered about Abraham Seale. Such a strange character. But now the poor man has fallen victim to the deadly blade. So I'm not getting far yet. What about you?'

Her cat's eyes gazed straight at Paula. Was she hoping her collaborator had better luck?

'I do think a lot about it starting in Maine. When did you first meet Russell Straub?'

'In New York. At a party. He was all over me then, wanted me to fly to California with him. I didn't.'

'Is Straub married? I should know but I don't.'

'He was but his wife divorced him. It was kept quiet.'

'Why did she take that decision?'

'She told me she was fed up with the Potomac running through her living room. She meant politics. Said he was a fanatic, that he'd do anything to become President. Which

208

is going to happen. He has key figures and groups lined up behind him.'

'Fanatic?' Paula repeated.

'That was the word his wife used.'

They talked some more and then Paula saw Tweed returning, heading for the lift. She thanked Marienetta for the tea and they agreed to meet later.

Paula was going to collect the coat she had left with the concierge – she had thought Marienetta might suggest a walk after tea. Pausing, she saw Roman, wearing a heavy black overcoat, leaving the hotel.

Grabbing her coat she put it on as she left the hotel. It was dark outside now. Night falls early at this time of the year. Hurrying along the wide drive and out of the entrance she was just in time to see Arbogast turn left up Bahnhofstrasse. He was carrying a large executive case which looked weighty.

Reaching Bahnhofstrasse she saw his heavily built figure padding rapidly up the main street. She walked after him, aware that the street was otherwise deserted. She was thankful for the powerful street lights at intervals. Behind her she heard rapid footsteps. She glanced back as Newman caught up with her.

'What the devil do you think you're doing? Going out in the dark by yourself?'

'I'm following someone. That's Roman Arbogast in front of us. Please don't tell Tweed.'

'I'll think about it.'

Suddenly Roman disappeared. He had turned down the first side street to the left. Where on earth could he be going to? At this time of night? Newman gripped her arm, swung her round.

'Back to the hotel. There's no one about . . .'

Inside the hotel Newman left her as she entered the lift.

She dashed to her room, took off her coat, hung it in the wardrobe, went back to Tweed's room. She tapped on the door. His expression was grim when he opened it.

'What's the matter?' she asked, sitting down in a chair.

'Beck called me back because Monica had called him, wanted to speak to me urgently on a safe phone. I got through to her immediately.'

'And why was she calling you?'

'Monica, I'm sure, hasn't slept for over twenty-four hours. She has been calling the world to build up the Arbogast family tree. She hasn't completed it yet by any manner of means, but she has given me invaluable data.'

'Can I get a big pad? I want to make notes. There, ready.'

'The Arbogasts originated in Italy. Their real name was Arbogastini. Three generations back there were two brothers – Benito and Vicenzo. They were born in Rome. When they grew up they moved to Milan. They probably couldn't make it there, so Benito moved to London while Vicenzo moved to New York. They had children. Vicenzo changed the family name to Arbogast – to avoid sounding like Mafia. He became a key figure in a Democrat political machine in Memphis, Tennessee, controlled by Boss Crump. I've heard of him by reading American history.'

'We're coming close to this generation,' she said.

'We are. Vicenzo had also changed his Christian name, to Vincent. This is where the political element came in. Vincent's eldest son changed the name again – to Straub so there was no possible hint of Mafia. His Christian name he changed to Russell. He was brought up in a highly political atmosphere.'

'So in America we have reached the present?'

'As you know Russell Straub is staying in this hotel. But Vincent had other children. Names as yet unknown. Meanwhile Benito in London became Alfred Arbogast. Then we come to the second generation. The eldest son was Roman. I suppose there was a desire not to sever all links with Italy. This branch of the family never entered politics. They moved from one trade to another. It was Roman who had the idea of building the ACTIL empire, a global system. He succeeded, had a daughter, Sophie. Both in the States and here there were other brothers who produced families. So far we know nothing about them.' Tweed stood up, began pacing. 'At long last a vague pattern is emerging. I have a theory but nothing to base it on. When I have I'll tell you. Of one thing I'm now convinced. These horrific murders concern power, *power*, POWER . . .'

'I'm not sure I've grasped this,' Paula said, staring at the scribbles on her pad.

'Simplify it. Work it backwards. Today we have the older generation, represented by Roman Arbogast. Roman has a daughter, Sophie. He also has a niece, Marienetta – who must be the offspring of a brother of his who also came to Britain. We haven't traced the brother yet.'

'I'm quite clear now on the sequence.'

'In the States Russell, the son of Vincent Arbogast, changed his name to Straub. His father was involved in Boss Crump's political machine in Memphis. Which is why Russell became a politician and ultimately Vice-President.'

'Soon to be President once the present occupant of the Oval Office retires. And the existing President is backing Russell to be his successor.'

'You've got the picture. A significant factor I suspect in these horrible murders. Hence my emphasis on power. I do believe Russell Straub would go to almost any lengths to make sure nothing blocked his ambition.'

'You're making me think,' Paula told him.

'That was my purpose. To make your realize what

we are investigating has the world's future security at stake.'

'Then we could be up against colossal forces,' she said.

'We are. This explains the intervention of Nathan Morgan and Special Branch. They are doing everything they can to stop our investigation. I'm sure the President has asked our Prime Minister for a favour. The PM wants to keep in the good graces of Washington. Hence the pressure we are facing. I must not discover the great secret.'

'You think the PM knows what it is?'

'I don't think for a moment he does. I also doubt whether the President knows what it is.'

'So,' she suggested, 'you find it strange that Russell Straub keeps turning up?'

'Very strange.'

'I haven't told you about my conversation with Marienetta over tea.'

Tweed had been pacing as he explained what he had learnt from Monica. Now he sat down, facing Paula, his expression alert, preparing to concentrate.

'Oh, before I start, it did strike me as possibly significant that all the victims so far have been men.'

'I had pondered that. Now, it sounds as though you found out something interesting from Marienetta.'

'I did . . .'

She stopped speaking as someone hammered urgently on the door of the suite. Tweed jumped up, opened the door on the chain, then released it. Beck walked in.

'There's been another murder. Close to this hotel.'

21

It was very chilly in the night as Tweed and Paula were led by Beck out of the main entrance where he immediately turned left up the street runnning parallel to Bahnhofstrasse. Two plainclothes detectives, escorting their chief, kept their distance.

'Have you identified the victim?' Paula asked quietly.

'Not yet. I'm waiting for Dr Zeitzler to arrive. He insists nothing is touched until he's made a quick examination. He's right, of course. Ah, there is his car . . .'

They turned left again and Paula realized they were walking along an extension of the street she had seen Roman Arbogast disappear down from Bahnhofstrasse. That seemed ages ago now.

'At the end of this street is the River Sihl,' Beck explained. 'It's an offshoot from the Limmat and not far down from here it enters the lake.'

The street was narrow and a tunnel of darkness apart from the occasional street lamp. As they drew closer to where it ended Paula saw the glow of police lights perched on tripods, a lot of police cars parked, a police tape across the end of the street.

'Does Roman Arbogast have an office around here?' she asked.

'There.' Beck pointed to a building they were about to pass on the opposite side of the street. On the second floor a light glowed behind a closed blind. 'That is his headquarters for running his plants in Switzerland and certain surrounding countries. It has a big staff.'

'And we're now approaching this little river, the Sihl?' she enquired.

'You'll see it any moment now. Boat owners moor their craft here for winter. Some very expensive.' He stopped suddenly, turned to Paula and Tweed. 'This is pretty grim. I'm not sure Paula should see it. I don't doubt her courage but this is pretty eerie and horrific.'

'I have seen worse things,' she snapped obstinately.

Beck raise both hands in a gesture of resignation. As they came to the corner she saw the narrow River Sihl, almost black in the darkness except where the police lights reflected off it. Dr Zeitzler suddenly appeared. When he saw her he took her arm, spoke in English, no longer abrupt in manner. His tone was gentle and sympathetic.

'Fraulein Grey, I beg of you not to proceed one step further. This is an escalation – I trust that is the right word – in horror.'

'I appreciate your sentiments, Dr Zeitzler. But I have seen beheaded bodies before. Please do not stand in my way.'

Zeitzler looked at Beck. He made a gesture. *I have done as much as I can.*

She walked round the corner. Boats covered with green canvas to protect them against the winter were moored at intervals. Policemen who had been chattering went quiet when they saw her. A ghastly silence descended on the promenade running along the side of the Sihl. One powerful police light was focused on a boat where the green canvas had been rolled back. At the stern there was a seat with a canopy and it was occupied.

A woman sat in the seat, propped up by the back rest. Her green fur cap was tilted to one side. Her eyes were open. Paula stopped, stood quite still, unable to take her gaze away from the occupant.

'Oh God, no!' she gasped, muffling her outburst with her hand which she clamped to her mouth. She stiffened her legs, steeled herself. 'Oh, dear God, no,' she said behind her hand.

The figure sitting so still in the boat was that of Elena Brucan. Apart from her extreme immobility she appeared normal, as if taking a rest. Throwing off Zeitzler's hand, which had again grasped her arm, Paula advanced slowly along the narrow walk. Tweed was now beside her, Newman, who had rushed from the hotel, behind her.

'At least it didn't decapitate her,' she said in a steady tone of voice.

She was walking closer to the boat as she spoke. Behind her back Zeitzler glanced at Beck with an alarmed expression. The police chief made a gesture of resignation. No point in stopping her now. She'd just have to see it.

The first thing Paula noticed with puzzlement and then a shock of growing presentiment was a large brownish pool on the walkway alongside the boat. In the middle was a clear area, an area shaped like the oblong she had seen imprinted into the grass near the asylum at Pinedale. The site of an execution block. She went closer to the still figure of Elena Brucan, propped against the headrest at the stern. A few inches below the chin a brownish rim of encrusted blood encircled the neck.

'She has been beheaded,' she said in a low voice. 'That is why her hat is tilted at the wrong angle.'

'And then,' Tweed said, 'it lifted the head by the hair from where it had fallen and perched it back on the severed neck.'

'*It's obscene!*' she shouted. '*I'm going to locate it and when I do I'm going to kill it . . .*'

She was shaking as Tweed, gripping her by the arm, led her back to the hotel. Both he and Newman thought it

215

was the appalling shock of what she had seen which was making her tremble. They were wrong. She was shaking with fury.

'She was such a nice lady,' she said eventually as they approached the entrance to the hotel. Her voice was trembling now with sorrow. 'She meant no harm to anyone. Why?'

'Probably because she spoke to the wrong person,' Tweed told her. 'It realized Elena suspected it.'

'Can we pause here for a moment?' Paula asked.

They waited while she took in deep breaths of the ice-cold air. Her figure stiffened and she turned to Tweed and spoke.

'I'm OK now. I've got control of the anger. Let's not say anything to anyone we meet.'

As they walked into the hotel Marienetta rushed out of the lift. She stared at Paula, came forward with an expression of concern.

'You've lost all your colour. Are you all right?'

'I'm fine. I tripped up as we were coming back from a walk. Sprawled full length. Knocked the breath out of me.'

'You'd better go upstairs and lie down.'

Paula was looking past her into the lounge. In a chair near to the entrance Sophie, wearing an overcoat, was gazing at her. She had the most peculiar look on her face, a strange smile as though she had just achieved something which delighted her.

'Not feeling so good, Paula,' she called out.

'I was wondering why you're looking so pleased with yourself.'

'She gets like that sometimes,' Marienetta remarked.

'Marienetta thinks she's *so* clever,' Sophie sneered.

'That's enough of that,' Marienetta rapped back.

'She thinks she's the Queen of ACTIL,' Sophie sneered again, standing up. 'She should have been an actress,' she ploughed on. 'She tried to be once in the provinces and the producer threw her out, told her to get a job as a typist.'

Marienetta swung round. Her manner was calm as she walked to Sophie. Her right hand swung up and gave Sophie a ferocious slap on the side of her face, a slap which caused her to sway and almost fall.

'Nearly took her head off her shoulders,' Newman whispered. 'Sorry, just realized what I said. Let's get upstairs. We can do without this.'

He had just spoken when Black Jack, clad in an overcoat, came in from outside. He was carrying a large leather bag. Paula thought he was drunk as he grinned at everyone, buoyantly shouted at the top of his voice.

'I'll take the first lift. Damned well freezing out there. A hot shower is next on the programme for me. Sure you won't mind.'

Newman had never seen him in such a joyous mood. A man who was so pleased with an achievement he had pulled off. He blocked Black Jack taking another step. He was in a mood to knock him down.

'The lift is booked for us. And there's no room for you. It's warm enough in here.'

'Don't like your tone of voice, old man.'

'I've never been over the moon about yours.'

Tweed was escorting Paula to the lift, waiting with its doors open. Behind them Newman and Black Jack glared at each other face to face. It was Black Jack who backed down. He called across to Marienetta still standing close to Sophie.

'I don't think either of you should have anything to do with that thug. He's only a cheap reporter.'

'I rather like him—' said Sophie.

They didn't hear the rest of her sentence because the lift doors had closed and it was ascending.

★   ★   ★

'A small brandy for you, Paula,' Newman said once they were inside Tweed's suite.

'Not brandy,' Tweed said sharply. 'A glass of water. Then maybe another.'

'Yes, please.'

Paula had collapsed into an armchair after throwing off her coat. She swallowed the water in the glass Tweed handed her, gave it back to him for a refill. She sat with her knees close together, her hands on the arms of the chair. Staring into the distance she said nothing for a few minutes. Tweed put a finger to his lips, warning Newman not to speak. She had three glasses of water before she relaxed and spoke.

'That was quite something to come back to downstairs. Sophie and Marienetta at each other's throats.'

'Sophie asked for it,' Newman commented, sitting opposite to her.

'Then the strange arrival of Black Jack who seems so anxious to get away from us.'

'The Arbogast family in action,' Tweed remarked. 'Except for Roman.'

'I saw Roman leaving the building – I was with Bob – well over half an hour ago. I think he was in his headquarters near the Sihl where it happened. There was a light in one window on the second floor, the blind drawn.' She frowned. 'That doesn't mean there was anyone in the room. Whoever had gone up there could have drawn the blind, switched on the light – and left.'

'Your brain's whirling round,' Tweed said.

'It could be staying at this hotel,' she went on as though her mind were far away. 'It. Whoever committed that foul atrocity. The indignity of it. Why didn't it take the head away as it did with the others?'

There was a knock on the door. Newman opened it and Arthur Beck walked in. His expression was grimmer than Tweed had ever seen it. Paula looked up, stared at him.

218

'Why didn't it take the head away this time?'

'I think . . .' Beck paused and studied Paula to assess what state she was in. He was surprised by her normality. 'I have thought about that,' he started again. 'My theory is that as it took place in the middle of a big city, whoever is responsible thought it would be too risky to take away the head. At Montreux no one would be on the front for several hours – it was still night. I presume similar isolated conditions prevailed at Bray in Britain, at Pinedale in Maine.'

'They did,' Tweed confirmed.

'Now all hell is going to break loose in Switzerland,' Beck's tone was grim. 'Two Europeans beheaded within days. The press will go mad. The horror of the way they were killed will add to the panic. Zeitzler is working through the night on this, his second autopsy. Results will be ready in the morning. We have the data – films and photos – of the murders abroad for comparison. I'll let you know, Tweed. Now I must dash.'

As Beck left the suite Marler slipped into the room and took off his raincoat. Tweed stared at it.

'You've been outside, prowling around?'

'To some profit.' Marler stood against a wall, produced a cigarette, lit it. 'Did any of you know Sam Snyder is here in Zürich?'

'No, we didn't,' Tweed replied.

'Odd how he keeps popping up whenever there's one of these beastly murders,' Paula said quietly.

'Snyder,' Marler continued, 'is staying just up Bahnhofstrasse. At the Baur en Ville. I strolled into their bar, which you can enter directly from the street, and there he was, having a drink.'

'You asked him why he was here?' Newman demanded. 'What the devil he was doing?'

'Not quite in those terms,' Marler drawled. 'He'd have closed up like the proverbial clam. Had a drink with him.

219

Listened. He's pursuing the Arbogast family. Tracked Sophie and Black Jack to Zürich, slipped aboard the same plane. The way he traced them from Heathrow.'

'He'd have loved,' Paula began, 'to get a picture of poor Mrs Elena Brucan in that boat.' He voice was tinged with rage.

'How was Snyder dressed when you found him in the bar?' Tweed asked Marler.

'Wearing a fur-lined coat as though he'd just come in from outside. Under the table was a leather camera case.'

'So maybe he did get pictures,' Newman commented. 'He could have walked down the narrow promenade alongside the Sihl from the other direction. That would be the quick route from the Baur en Ville.'

'If that leather case was for the purpose of transporting his camera,' Paula observed.

'Now,' said Tweed, anxious to change the subject, 'I think Paula is ready for a small brandy – if you'd do the honours, Bob. And you were going to tell me, Paula, about your chat with Marienetta over tea.'

With her perfect memory Paula recalled every word of her conversation. What she had said, what Marienetta had said. She also remembered to describe the brief confrontation Marienetta had with Russell Straub when the Vice-President entered the lounge. Tweed listened, his eyes never leaving her, recording every detail in his memory. She took a sip of brandy, spread a hand.

'That's it. Don't think I've left out anything.'

'And,' Tweed checked, 'Straub looked furious when she called him cousin.'

'Looked as though he could have killed her.'

'And Marienetta quoted Straub's ex-wife as calling him a fanatic? That was the exact word used?'

'It was. She confirmed it twice.'

'A wife should know, even if she was on the verge of throwing him overboard. Gives us an interesting view of Russell Straub.'

'I could have told you that anyway,' Newman said dismissively. 'Any politician with a load of money and party-machine support is not going to be too fussy about how he gets to be President.'

'I'm rather intrigued by the word "fanatic",' Marler said.

'Then there's the axe,' Paula said vehemently. 'The killing weapon. We haven't thought enough about that. If – and it looks pretty definite – the same axe was used across the Atlantic in Maine how was it transported over here?'

'It could have been taken over from Europe in a case wrapped in fibreglass,' Newman suggested. 'The case travels in the cargo hold.'

'So how was it brought back for committing three more hideous murders?' Paula wanted to know. 'Heathrow Customs can order anyone to open a case. The killer would never take that risk.'

'Then I don't know the answer,' Newman admitted.

'Paula, list those people who we know have travelled to America,' Tweed requested.

'Here we go again. Marienetta, Sophie, Roman Arbogast, Black Jack Diamond . . .'

'And why does he fly out there?' Tweed persisted.

'From what we've heard to enjoy himself, tour the clubs, I'd imagine, look for girl friends. It's his style.'

'And who else do we know has gone?'

'Sam Snyder, who from his arrangement with Roman, has the use of the Gulfstream when it's available. I'm running out of names.'

'You're forgetting someone because they're so obvious,' Marler interjected. 'The Vice-President, Russell Straub. A man like that can move anywhere without interrogation.'

'There is one more,' Newman added. 'Broden, security chief for ACTIL. He's in this hotel, presumably watching over Roman. With his authority he could move anywhere he liked.'

Tweed had been sitting in a hard-backed chair. He was leaning forward, hands clasped in front of his lap. They were suddenly aware he hadn't spoken for a while. He was looking into space. He spoke now very deliberately.

'I could narrow that list down. A big piece is missing from the picture slowly forming in my mind. Paula, how are you feeling?'

'Normal,' she replied immediately, 'as poor Abraham Seale used to say. Ready for anything.'

'Then could you go downstairs and see if Sophie is still in the lounge? She was when we came in, and had a coat on. I'd like you to talk to her on her own. Providing Marienetta is not there. Most people will be having dinner. We'll have ours after you've talked with her. It's important.'

Paula found Sophie, her coat on another chair, sitting by herself in an otherwise empty lounge. A waiter had just served her with glass of Scotch. Not the first, I suspect, Paula thought as she walked up to her.

'Hello, Sophie, mind if I join you for a drink?'

'Another double Scotch,' Sophie shouted before the waiter had disappeared. 'Sit down, Paula. I'm feeling neglected.'

'That's entirely my fault,' Paula replied as she eased herself into a chair facing Sophie.

She quickly studied Roman's only daughter. Sophie was goodlooking. Not in the glamorous manner of Marienetta, but in a more comfortable way. She had good features, grey eyes which looked frankly at Paula. Her nose was snub but well shaped and her chin suggested determination. Her brown hair, still tied back in a ponytail, suited her. She wore a blue evening dress, long-sleeved and with a high collar. When Paula's drink was brought they clinked glasses. Sophie smiled and looked round to make sure they were alone, then pulled her chair closer to Paula's.

'I'm sure any impression you have of me has come from Marienetta. We don't get on too well. Maybe my fault. I get periods of fatigue, then I'm full of energy and ready to push the whole world over. I've always been like that. I was once lured into seeing a psychiatrist – thought he was just a doctor. He said I was wired. Funny word, but he told me not to worry about it. A question of temperament.'

'Who "lured" you, as you put it, into seeing this medical man?'

'Marienetta. She thought my moods were dangerous. I heard her say that to my father. I had the feeling she was disappointed when the shrink said I was just wired.'

'Was this consultation in London?'

'No, when I was in the States.'

'Whereabouts were you? This must have been disturbing.'

'In Boston.' Sophie drank more Scotch without any apparent effect. 'My father has a plant there manufacturing explosives. I visit it now and again. This time Marienetta jumped on the plane at the last moment. Which made me suspicious.'

She giggled like a schoolgirl. This unexpected change in her personality startled Paula. She had been so mature and logical earlier.

'It's the Scotch,' Sophie explained, her normal self again. 'Makes me see the funny side of life. I thought Marienetta such a joke – boarding the Gulfstream at the last moment. Then she started talking about this doctor who wasn't a doctor.'

'Been anywhere else in the States?' Paula asked casually.

'New York. Went there with Black Jack. Something strange about him. Talk about my moods. You should see his.'

'What's he like when he's in a mood?' Paula wondered.

'Crazy. Capable of doing anything in public. Once we were in a New York club and he jumped onto an empty table, started dancing madly. An attractive woman stopped to watch. Reaching down he hauled her up, snapping one of her shoulder straps. He had a good grip on her and to start with she looked annoyed, then she began to take to him. He started singing at the top of his voice "America the Beautiful". He has a good voice. He'd have been thrown out but everyone started joining in the singing. The manager joined in. He has this extraordinary personality.'

'Sounds as though he has.' Paula checked her watch. 'I have enjoyed our conversation but I must get up now and change for dinner.'

She turned as she was leaving the lounge. Sophie was giggling, waving her empty glass for another refill.

Vigliano's bar is in a side street off Bahnhofstrasse, not far from the Baur au Lac. In the Altstadt – the Old Town – it has several rooms separated from each other. All with stone walls, the ceiling shaped in stone arches. The phone booth is near the entrance, opposite the bar.

The phone call was made from this booth late in the evening. The call was answered by a certain Luigi Morati, not a man you would want to have a drink with. Picking up the phone, Luigi reacted cautiously.

'*Si?*'

'Am I speaking to Luigi Morati?'

The voice was strange. Couldn't tell whether it was a man or a woman. Luigi caught on immediately. The caller was using a voice distorter.

'You might be,' he answered in English. 'What is it?'

'It is about a hundred thousand dollars.'

That caught his attention. But he still proceeded cautiously. In his 'profession' he had to if he was to survive.

'Who gave you my name?'

'I am not allowed to tell you. Are you interested or not?'

The voice had sharpened, sounded impatient, as though the caller was prepared to slam down the phone. Luigi took a deep breath.

'What do I do to earn one hundred thousand dollars?'

'Kill someone. Within the next twenty-four hours.'

'Give me the details. I need a description, where they can be found, their—'

'Shut up! Name of the woman is Paula Grey. Staying at the Baur au Lac. I have just stuffed an envelope behind this phone at Vigliano's Bar. How long for you to get here?'

'Five minutes.'

'Inside the envelope is a photo of Paula Grey. Inside the same envelope is one hundred thousand dollars in used notes. If you take the money and do not do the job you will be dead.'

'Don't talk to me like that. I am reliable. My reputation is my living. I am leaving now.'

22

It was late and Zürich was very quiet as Broden, wearing a cap and with his overcoat buttoned up to the neck, walked down Bahnhofstrasse. He could have been anybody. The cap concealed his *en brosse* haircut, the coat collar concealed the lower part of his face. He carried a suitcase.

He turned off Bahnhofstrasse down the side street leading to ACTIL's headquarters. At the far end he could see police tape closing it off, lights from police cars. Taking out a key, he unlocked the door, went inside without turning on the light, re-locked the door.

Climbing the stairs he reached Roman's office, door closed, a light on behind it. He knocked. No reply. He opened the door quietly. Roman was sitting at his desk in front of the window with the blind pulled down, poring over a file.

'It's me,' Broden said softly.

'Why the hell don't you knock?' Roman demanded.

He glared at his security chief. His right eye twitched several times. Which meant he was under pressure. Broden took off cap and coat – it was damned Siberian outside. The office was warm.

'I did knock. You didn't hear me. Something wrong?'

'Yes, money is missing. I've checked and double-checked. It's Dorf. Sack him in the morning.'

'We could prosecute . . .'

'We do *not* want the police creeping around us. What's in that suitcase?'

'Warmer clothes. Earlier I found one shop just closing. I don't know whether you've heard. There's been another murder.'

'What!'

Roman swivelled round in his chair. The eye started twitching again. Broden waited for him to say something but his employer remained silent. He slipped the file into a large briefcase. Standing up, he put on his heavy overcoat. He picked up the briefcase.

When they left the building Roman never glanced to his right where police tape fenced off the street. Carrying his bulging briefcase, he turned left, his head bowed. Broden was not surprised. He knew his chief's remarkable brain was always concentrated on building up ACTIL, on sweeping out of his way anything that might interfere with expansion. Or anyone.

They were approaching the entrance to the Baur au Lac when Roman spoke. Looking at Broden his eye was twitching again.

'That would be the fourth murder. Anyone we know?'

'Yes.'

Entering the hall after an excellent dinner, Tweed, Newman and Paula found Marler waiting. He wore a raincoat and carried a suitcase. He shook his head. He didn't want any conversation in public. Only when they were all inside Tweed's suite, with the door locked, did he speak. First he placed his case on a luggage rack, opened it.

'I've visited someone I know in Zürich. Spent a lot of money. This is for you.'

He handed Paula a .32 Browning automatic and several magazines. She immediately checked that the weapon was unloaded, then slid a magazine into the butt. The

228

Browning was then slipped inside the special pocket in her shoulder bag.

'Thank you, Marler, I've felt naked without this.'

Marler produced a .38 Smith & Wesson revolver, handed it to Newman. He then gave him a bag containing ammo. Next he brought out a Walther 7.65mm automatic which he handed to Tweed. Most of his life Tweed refused to carry a weapon but this time he accepted it. He was convinced that when he confronted the killer he'd have to shoot it. After the crimes it had committed that would be the best solution. Marler took out another Walther.

He was holding the automatic in his hand when Newman let into the suite Butler and Nield. Walking forward to Marler, Nield held out his hand.

'Gimme.'

'Sorry. My supplier would only give me four hand weapons. I had to coax him to get the ones I've dished out to Paula, Tweed and Bob. It's the two murders here in Zürich. The supplier is worried they'll provoke the police into visiting him.'

'Not to worry,' said Butler. 'Wherever you are there's always something you can use as a weapon.'

'Where have you two been all this time?' Tweed asked.

'Trawling Zürich,' Nield replied. 'It's a complex city. In an emergency we need to know it like the backs of our hands. I took the Altstadt on the other side of the Limmat, Harry explored this side.'

'On a motorbike,' Harry said. 'Bought a second-hand Yamaha. Goes like the wind. Blindfold me, drop me anywhere this side of the Limmat, remove the blindfold. I'll know exactly where I am.'

Newman checked his watch. 'It's getting late. I'm feeling sleepy. Time to go to bed. Who knows what tomorrow will bring?'

'Lord knows. Off you go.'

Paula waited as they were leaving. She came up to

Tweed and whispered. Newman, last to leave, turned at the door, looked at Paula.

'See you in the morning.'

'That's what I want to talk to you about,' Paula said when she and Tweed were alone.

The phone rang. Tweed answered and it was Monica. She spoke in coded language, realizing the call was going through a switchboard. Tweed listened, thanked her, looked at Paula as he put down the phone.

'That was Monica. She's traced two brothers who emigrated from Italy about the same time as Roman moved to London, and Vicenzo – Vincent – emigrated to the States. A Silvio went to London, got married. A Mario went to the States, he also married. This means there are probably more offspring in Britain and the States. She hasn't any names yet.'

'It's a step forward.' Paula paused, staring hard at Tweed. 'You look worried. I can tell. That's very rare for you.'

'Well, we move from A to B to C. Our arrivals are punctuated by more murders. I think I can see *it*, but I can't put a face to the killer.'

'It's frustrating,' she sympathized. 'You know I'm good at sensing what people are really like behind the masks they wear in public. Earlier today when I was out with Newman I went into a bookshop. In the window there was a book by Abraham Seale. Titled *Normal and Abnormal*. The bits I've read so far are fascinating. I want you to let me go out on my own and talk to all the people we've met – including Sam Snyder. Without Newman tagging along. I know he's protecting me – and I'm grateful. But he'd get in the way. Please.'

'Well . . .'

'And I've got my Browning now,' she pressed.

'Perhaps you're right. Do it.'

'Thanks.'

230

She kissed him on both cheeks before she left the suite. Once on his own Tweed immediately called Nield. He worded his request carefully.

'Pete, Paula wants to mooch around on her own – without Newman. Tomorrow morning. Can you discreetly follow her without her knowing? You'll have to be clever.'

'Easy. I'll be the Invisible Man.'

Inside the stone-walled flat he occupied in the Altstadt, on the far side of the Limmat, Luigi Morati oiled his Glock pistol, a deadly weapon. Earlier he had collected the envelope his mysterious caller had left in the telephone booth in Vigliano's Bar.

Inside the envelope he had found a hundred thousand dollars in used notes, a photo of Paula Grey. As he checked the weapon he kept glancing at the photo pinned to the table he worked at. A handsome-looking woman. In different circumstances he wouldn't have minded getting to know her.

He looked at his face in the mirror on the wall. Greasy black hair, cold eyes, a crooked nose broken in a fight long ago, a fight which had ended in his opponent ending up with a broken skull smashed against a wall. *Finito*.

He had considered using a silencer, had rejected the notion. A silencer could jam a handgun. So the vital decision was his escape route. He had long ago been taught to think of this first, by an experienced hitman during his days in Rome.

The solution came to him as he continued maintaining the gun with loving care. His motorcycle, now chained up inside an alley near the entrance to the old building where he lived. His flat was not so far from police headquarters on the opposite bank, an irony which amused him.

Satisfied with the state of the Glock, he stood up, aimed the unloaded weapon at the photo. He pulled the trigger.

Small, but wiry and strong, able to kill with one blow from his hand. If Paula Grey came out of the Baur au Lac tomorrow she was dead meat. He had never failed yet.

23

Without a warning forecast, the following morning the temperature had dropped ten degrees Fahrenheit. As Paula walked out through the entrance she was clad in a leather outfit. She was by herself and it was early as she entered Bahnhofstrasse, turned left up the street. She had already decided on her first objective.

A municipal cleaner was sweeping the gutters. His hands were only protected by half-gloves, the tips of his fingers exposed. They were blue with the intense cold. Men and women hurrying to their jobs were huddled up. Shop windows were coated with ice. A short distance further up the street a police car was parked with two uniformed officers inside.

In the rather scruffy park facing the entrance to the Baur au Lac, Luigi Morati recognized her immediately and cursed. The presence of the police car meant action at the moment was impossible. He wheeled his motorcycle into the street, began pushing it.

Pete Nield, who had shopped earlier, stood on the far side of the street. He wore an overcoat she had never seen and a hat he had purchased. Nield never wore a hat. Hidden inside an alcove leading to a shop he watched her proceeding past the police car. A motorcyclist, smartly dressed in leather and with a crash helmet on his head, pushed his machine past him.

The sun was shining brilliantly but without warmth.

Paula realized the pavement had to be watched. There were patches of ice. She wasn't worried. She was wearing rubber-soled knee-length boots. A blue tram rumbled past, sounding like a tank going in to attack.

She crossed Bahnhofstrasse just before Parade-platz, a zone where trams changed direction. Several were stopped behind each other as passengers flooded off while others waited to board. The Swiss went to work early and Zurich was alive with activity.

The entrance to the bar of the Baur en Ville is separate from the main reception area of the hotel. Semi-circular steps lead up to tall glass doors which open automatically. As soon as she entered Paula realized she was lucky.

As she had hoped, Sam Snyder was seated at a table by himself on the lower level, eating breakfast. He waved to her with his fork, used the other hand to beckon for her to join him. She was concentrating on him as she sat down, so she didn't notice a man in a camel-hair coat and a Swiss hat walk slowly past, hunched up, and climb the stairs at the back to the upper level. Nield now wore tinted glasses and settled himself in at a table at the back. It gave him a good view, looking down, of Paula.

'What an unexpected pleasure.' The hawk-faced reporter greeted her with a warm smile. 'I do like company when I'm having a meal.'

A waitress appeared immediately. 'I needed coffee to warm me up,' Paula explained after ordering.

'I like the cold. But I don't expect everyone to agree with me.'

'Who did it, Sam?'

She threw the question at him without warning. He helped himself to the rest of his omelette before replying. She could hear the wheels churning round.

'Who did what?' he eventually enquired.

234

'Oh, come off it. You investigated the murder of Hank Foley at Pinedale in Maine. Then Adam Holgate at Bray. You were in Montreux when another hideous murder took place. Here, Elena Brucan.'

'She was a nice lady.'

'You knew her?'

'She approached a lot of people. Had the type of personality to do that. She trapped me down on the *quai* at Montreux when I'd taken pics of the late Dr Abraham Seale. Asked me if I'd known him.'

'Had you?'

'No.'

Paula caught the hesitation before he replied. He drank more coffee and his dark eyes bored into hers. He hadn't liked the question. His mouth twisted into a sneer. Friendship time was over. She persisted.

'Get some good pics of Elena Brucan?'

'Who sent you to interrogate me? Tweed? Newman?'

He was leaning back, openly assessing her. Hostile now. She had extracted all she'd get. His suggestion irked her. She slammed her cup down.

'No one sent me, as you so politely put it. I came here all on my own. I'm not manipulated at the end of a string. Get that into your thick skull.'

'My, the lady has spirit. I like that. Why don't you come up to my room? We could continue the conversation in peace and quiet.'

He was smiling. But the twist still existed. He didn't earn top marks for self-control. She gestured to the waitress, paid her bill.

'You're not walking out on me, are you? Women don't do that to me.'

She was staring straight at him, studying his expression. So she didn't notice the man in the camel-hair coat descend slowly from the steps to the upper level, dragging his feet as though walking was a problem. Nield paused

235

by the door, adjusting his coat collar, making sure she was leaving.

'Maybe your choice of women isn't very sophisticated,' she rapped back.

The smile vanished. He leaned towards her, his right hand clenching and unclenching. His eyes seemed darker than ever. *Normal and Abnormal*. The latter was disturbing. Get out of here, she said to herself. Your time wasn't wasted.

She was standing up when he reached over, clasped her right arm. His grip was surprisingly strong. His hawk-face was inches from hers. She spoke calmly.

'If you don't take your hand off me I'm going to call the manager.'

'If I have offended you I apologize.' His expression was normal and his smile seemed genuine. He sat down as though to reassure her. 'To prove I am not your enemy let me warm you. On the grapevine I have heard you are in great danger. You have been targeted.'

'Really? Who by?'

'A top-flight professional. Identity unknown.'

'That seems unlikely.'

She walked to the automatic doors which opened for her. She slowly descended the steps, cautious about the ice. Now she was safe.

Luigi Morati had positioned himself in the middle of the Parade-platz. He was hidden amid the endless convoys of trams which arrived and left endlessly. He was smoking a cigarette, leaning against his motorbike. Dropping the cigarette, he watched her coming down the steps. He moved his machine, dipped his hand into the pannier for the Glock. One swift shot at this range and the job was done.

The police car which had been parked further down

Bahnhofstrasse cruised slowly towards Parade-platz, then parked by the kerb again, much closer. Luigi swore. They could not have spotted him.

Once he had broken into a police station in Berne when all the police had rushed off to answer an emergency call. It had taken him no time to find Records, to extract his file. He had been given the codename *Bull*. Presumably short for Bullet. Which amused him. No name for him in the file, no description of him, no data about his nationality. Merely a list of assassinations credited to *Bull*. Three correct, the other five nothing to do with him.

He began wheeling his motorbike back down Bahnhof-strasse in the direction Paula was taking. It was quiet now in the area.

The extremely low temperature had kept even the winter-hardened Swiss off the streets. The elegant lady shoppers had stayed at home. The workers were inside their offices. An ideal situation for Luigi. Then it went wrong.

Paula, who always reacted to her instinct, had the feeling she was being followed. She had seen nothing suspicious, but the instinct was strong. Her original destination had been ACTIL headquarters. She hoped to find Roman working there.

Now she paused on the kerb, looked to her right, then her left. Wrong way round, idiot. You're on the Continent. She crossed the empty street, began walking back the way she had come. Luigi just had time to change direction, to start wheeling his machine back to Parade-platz. So she didn't notice him.

Harry Butler, who had been more cautious, remained where he was. Seated on his motorcycle he was out of sight amid the muddle of trams converging on Parapade-platz, most of them empty. Patiently he waited to see where Paula had decided to go next.

Pete Nield had been alerted by her standing on the

237

kerb, looking the wrong way. He'd pull her leg about that mistake later. He had dodged into the large entrance to a shop, was studying the goods on display when she walked past.

Paula had her right hand inside her shoulder bag now, gripping the Browning. She couldn't see anything to disturb her. Opposite Parade-platz she turned right, as though returning to the bar. Walking past it, she continued down a side street where a strange triangular-shaped church stood to one side. Passing it, she knew she was entering the Altstadt with its maze of streets.

Luigi grinned to himself. The perfect killing ground. No one would be about down there in this weather. He wheeled his machine across the street. Too early to rev up. Walking quickly, revelling in the stimulus of the biting cold, Paula reached an open space. Behind she heard a motorcycle's engine starting up. She looked back swiftly. Something about the rider worried her. Luigi had already grabbed the Glock pistol out of the pannier, shoved it down the inside of his belt. A large truck, driving slowly from a street to the right, was about to close off her exit.

The truck driver stopped, doffed his cap to the attractive lady, waved her on. She gave him a warm smile, a brief wave, started to cross the wide open space. The truck driver began moving forward, completely blocking the exit.

Luigi swore. This would have been the perfect place. Across the bridge over the river beyond the open space was his flat. He waited impatiently, hoping he'd see which route his target had taken. He was so absorbed he hardly heard the motorcyclist approaching behind him. Harry was suspicious. When Pete Nield appeared on the narrow pavement beside him he fingered the machine ahead.

As the truck turned across the open space to cross the bridge Luigi saw Paula disappearing up the Schlussel-Gasse, a narrow cobbled street leading into the heart of the Altstadt. Perfect! He knew the area so well. She was walking into a death-trap.

Paula knew the Schlussel-Gasse, had explored this area on an earlier trip to Zürich. From here on the surface was cobbled. She was glad she'd worn her rubber-soled boots. She was well inside the narrow alley when she heard the machine coming at speed. Ahead of her the alley became a steep slope fit for goats. At the top on the right she saw the Vetliner Keller, one of the best restaurants in the city and where Tweed had said they would eat tonight. She looked back, saw the rider crazily holding the handlebars with one hand, something in the other. A gun. She dived inside the entrance to a small shop. A bullet whistled past. She had her Browning in both hands.

The assassin on the motorbike roared past. He'd heard Harry coming behind him like a thunderbolt. Paula had no chance to use the Browning. The machine had flashed past like a rocket. Now Luigi's motorcycle was wobbling madly as he increased speed, ascending the cobbled slope. At the top he entered a large square. He tried to turn with the Glock aimed at his pursuer. Couldn't do it and keep control of his machine. Harry was too close, gaining on him every second.

He began racing round the square, enclosed by ancient houses, one dated 1673, and a church on the far side. It became a gladiatorial contest, both machines circling the cobbled square, swaying, bumping up and down. Harry was very close when Luigi changed direction. Near a wall, he paused and turned his machine broadside on to use the Glock. Mistake. Harry's machine hammered into Luigi's, the front wheel slammed into it. The assassin's machine was hurled back against the wall. Luigi, very nimble, jumped off, ran just in time to avoid being killed by his own machine. He scrambled over the wall, dropped out of sight.

Paula appeared, Browning in her hand. Harry had come

off his machine, was lying on the cobbles. She knew who it was – she'd recognized his crouched figure as he'd flashed by the shop where she had sheltered. Breathless from rushing up the slope, Paula forced herself to run to the prone Harry as Pete Nield arrived.

Harry had streaks of blood running down his face from a cut on his forehead. She bent over him, hauling out the small first aid kit she always carried. Harry opened his eyes, spoke.

'He . . . went over that wall . . . Get him . . .'

Paula handed the first-aid kit to Pete, knowing he was without a weapon. She darted over to the wall, was careful not to poke her head over. He might be waiting for that down below. When she peeked over she was surprised at the extent of the drop. She was more surprised to see no body. Only an empty alley. She ran back to Harry.

'I think he's just dazed,' Pete told her.

He had already applied a plaster to the cut and was wiping the last of the blood off Harry's face. Harry was blinking regularly. Paula was worried that he was seriously injured. She bent over him, spoke softly.

'How are you feeling, Harry? Pretty bruised?'

'Help me up.'

'I don't think that's a good idea,' she warned. 'Not until a doctor's seen you.'

'Hate doctors . . .'

He pressed both hands on the ground, began to lift himself up. Paula grabbed one arm, Pete the other as Harry continued to heave himself up until he was standing. He took one step forward, then another, pulling himself away from them. He walked normally, swinging his arms, bending his elbows, taking off his motoring gloves, stretching his fingers.

'I'm OK. Would you recognize him again, Paula? See him at the bottom of the wall?'

'No. He'd gone. And I wouldn't recognize him again.'

'Neither would I.'

He hauled his machine upright, sat in the saddle, pressed the button. The engine ticked over normally. He shut it down, turned round and grinned. The colour was coming back into his round full face. He walked to the assassin's machine, grinned again.

'The swine won't be riding this any more. Shot at you, didn't he, Paula. Bastard.'

He looked down with satisfaction at the machine lying against the wall. The handlebars were twisted at an unnatural angle. The front wheel was torn loose, the saddle lay on the ground. Before they could stop him he'd lifted his own machine off its strut, was wheeling it towards the slope.

'Funny that no one has come out to see what had happened,' Paula commented, staring round the deserted square. 'I did see a net curtain twitch.'

'The Swiss believe in keeping out of harm's way,' Pete replied. 'Sensible people.'

'I could do with a drink,' Harry remarked.

'Water first,' Pete said firmly. 'Then maybe a beer. We can go to that bar where Snyder was first spotted.'

'Beer first,' Harry retorted, 'then water – for you to drink.'

Both Paula and Pete were ready to grab Harry's arms but he wheeled his machine down the bumpy slope confidently. At the bottom, in the open space, she gave them the slip, walking down another street. She had deliberately not asked what they had been doing so close to her. She was off to interview her next 'client'. Roman Arbogast.

241

24

One contract Luigi had carried out had involved leaving
the apartment of his target by a rope attached to a fifth-
floor window. Knowing this, he had practised in advance
over and again. He had first dropped from a height of
fifteen feet from the ground, letting go of the rope. After
several successful trials he had next dropped from twenty
feet, then thirty feet. He had immensely strong and supple
legs. They had served him well when he had gone over the
wall in the Altstadt in Zürich.

Now, by a devious route, he had returned to his apartment overlooking the Limmat. He was confident that when
he made his final attempt to kill Paula Grey he wouldn't
be recognized. During his first attempt he had worn his
crash helmet. Now he was making a radical change to his
appearance.

With coloured lotion he changed his red hair to black.
He was very thorough. Then he unlocked a wardrobe, the
contents of which would have surprised the very few people
who knew him in Italy.

He changed his underclothes, which no one would see,
but it made him feel more the part, wearing silk. He
put on an expensive starched white shirt, a black suit,
black socks, black shoes. A modest but expensive grey tie
looked right.

Picking up a pair of gold-rimmed spectacles – the lenses
of plain glass – he stood back and studied the impression

in a cheval glass. He was now Aldo Moldano, a Swiss banker. He could walk into the Baur au Lac and no one would think him out of place.

Finally, to complete the transformation, he picked up the executive case all bankers carried with them. Inside it would be the Glock. The only other item he lacked was an expensive limousine. He would hire that, dressed as he was now.

Paula had a twinge of trepidation as she walked down the side street to ACTIL's headquarters – disturbed by the police tape fencing off the end of the street. She was still appalled by the murders of Hank Foley, Adam Holgate and Abraham Seale. But what was driving her on, the controlled fury she felt, was the brutal killing of Elena Brucan, the obscene, callous touch of placing the severed head back on the corpse's shoulders.

Arriving at the entrance to the building she paused. The heavy front door was not quite closed. Her right hand whipped into her shoulder bag, gripped the Browning. She pushed the door open slowly, soundlessly. Hinges well oiled. Immediately inside was a large rubber mat. She carefully stepped over it onto the stone floor beyond. Not much light.

Slowly she began to mount the old wooden staircase beyond the door. The fifth tread creaked. Reaching the second-floor landing, she headed for the door which had to open into the front room where she had seen a light the night before. Listening, she heard nothing. It was too quiet.

Using her gloved left hand – she had slipped the glove off her right gripping the gun inside the special pocket – she took hold of the door handle. She turned it slowly, pushed gently. Daylight. She would sooner have had the Browning aimed and ready but if Roman was inside he wouldn't

244

have liked it. Not the best way to start a conversation. The door opened wider and she could see inside. Roman wasn't there.

Instead, sitting at Roman's desk, files spread out before him on the desk, was Broden. He sat very still, staring at her, a Mauser Military Model 7.63mm pistol in his hand, the long barrel aimed point-blank at her.

'Do come in, Miss Grey,' he said in a neutral tone. 'You avoided the pressure pad by the front door, but the fifth tread on the stairs creaks.'

'Yes, it does,' she said in an uncertain voice.

'Take your hand out of your shoulder bag, slowly. I hope it has nothing in it.' The same neutral tone.

She obeyed his command. He smiled, laid the Mauser on the desk. Always before he'd looked grim and dangerous. Now, wearing a suede jacket, zipped up at the front, with his wide smile and *en brosse* hair, he reminded her of a teddy bear. He offered her coffee and she refused. Wrapping his huge hands behind his thick neck he was still smiling. She wished he'd put the Mauser away in a drawer. Designed long ago its engineering quality was superb. She knew the magazine could take ten rounds.

'You're tough,' Broden remarked. 'You've looked at some very grisly sights but I can tell you're still in control.'

Paula wasn't going to fall for that approach. She held his hard eyes as she made the remark.

'I think your security is lousy. Anyone can walk in here.'

'I agree. But I'm under orders. Roman is coming. Hates to waste time fiddling with the two locks. I rely on the pressure pad.' He grinned. 'With people like you the fifth tread warns me.'

'I came to see Roman. Now I'm here maybe we could talk.'

'My pleasure.'

245

'Have you met Russell Straub, the Vice-President?'

It threw him. She knew this by the crinkle of his bushy eyebrows. He made a performance of taking out a pack of cigarettes, offering her one, which she again refused. He lit it, stared at the ceiling while he took a puff.

'I have been briefly introduced to him by Roman. Where does he come into the picture?'

'Anyone who was in the area when all the murders were committed is a suspect.'

'Well, I wasn't in Pinedale when Hank Foley got his.'

'You could have been.' She was building up a head of steam. Don't pander to this tough nut. He'll despise panderers.

'I could?'

'By flying first to Boston on the Grumman Gulfstream which, I'm sure, is at your disposal.'

'You are tough.' With a forefinger he twirled the Mauser so at one moment the muzzle was aimed at her. He continued twirling until the muzzle pointed at the wall. 'No one knows you're here, I'm sure. You take chances.'

'Know any hitmen?' She was really wound up.

'Once. One. Hired to hit my Colonel. Colonel played poker, lost a bundle, refused to pay up.'

'Some Colonel.'

'Rank doesn't mean you're honest. I learned that in the SIB.'

'SIB?' She knew what it was but she had him on the defensive, talking about himself. She doubted he did that often.

'Special Investigation Branch. The army's SIS, up to a point. Investigates crime in the army.'

'What happened to the hit man?'

'I broke his arm, the one with the gun in it. He's still serving time for attempted murder.'

'What made you leave the army?' she pressed.

'Term of service was up. Roman had somehow heard

of me. He interviewed me. He's good at that. Hired me as security chief for ACTIL. I answered him back. It impressed him. Not many people do that to Roman.'

'What sort of a boss is he?'

'All right. So long as you don't ever grovel. He admires you, takes quite an interest in you. You must have stood up to him. Now, if you don't mind, I think—'

'I think I should go,' she forestalled him. 'You're not quite what I thought you were,' she said standing up.

'What did you think I was, then?' he said smiling, standing up.

'You don't want to know.'

Leaving, she stepped over the fifth step, to amuse Broden. On the ground floor she stepped over the pressure pad. She had just reached the pavement when a tall heavily built figure well muffled with scarf and overcoat gently took hold of her arm. Roman Arbogast.

'What have you been up to?' he growled.

'I've been up to your office hoping to see you. Instead I saw Broden.'

'Couldn't have been much fun, talking to the stone face from Easter Island.'

'Actually, I'd come to see you, but Broden was interesting.'

'Interesting? We can't be talking about the same man. Can you come back and see me at, say, three this afternoon? Don't be late. I value punctuality.'

'That must be the one thing we have in common. 3 p.m. then.'

She left him before he could reply. She was dying for some coffee. Sprüngli, the most famous cake and coffee shop in Zürich, was just up the street. Absorbed, her mind playing back the confrontation with Broden – because that was what it had been despite his constant amiability – she entered Bahnhofstrasse, turned left. A hand grasped her left arm.

Her right hand dived inside her shoulder bag. She was swinging round, the weapon half out of its pocket, when a familiar voice spoke.

'It's me. Not going to shoot, are you?' Newman joked.

'What did you crawl out of?'

'News travels fast,' he went on, walking alongside her as she hustled up Bahnhofstrasse. 'Pete Nield phoned Tweed about the attempt to kill you in the Altstadt. Sent me out to find you PDQ. I should have been with you. I am now.'

'Look, Bob, I'm going to Sprüngli's. I'd like to be on my own. Nothing personal. I've a job to do and you'll get in the way. Nothing personal. Tweed OK'd it.'

'After what happened in the Altstadt, Tweed says I have to stick to you like glue.'

'Bob, I can't do my job with you hanging on to my coat-tails. I won't even try. But I *am* going to do my job.'

They were moving fast up the street because Paula, furious, was walking so quickly. Tweed had no right to countermand his previous agreement. And she'd tell him when she saw him.

'Could we compromise?' Newman suggested.

'I don't think so. You're too well known. What had you in mind?' Maybe she was being too rigid. Bob had saved her life in the past.

'You're going into Sprüngli's,' he began quietly. 'Suppose I stay outside. Out of sight?'

'We could try it, I suppose . . .'

They had arrived opposite Sprüngli's entrance. She darted inside. Newman walked on a short distance, put on dark glasses. He wouldn't look conspicuous. The sun shone as a brilliant glare now.

*   *   *

Paula thought the only drawback to Sprüngli's was the staircase you had to mount to reach the first floor. The ground floor was devoted to their shop. The staircase curved dangerously, on one side the treads were narrow at the middle curve. She wondered how women with high heels managed. Of course, they went up on their toes.

At the top she paused, the cash desk on her left. Not many customers this morning. The bitter weather. She was about to walk to an empty table when she stiffened. A shock. She couldn't move for a moment. Seated at a table with her back to Paula was a woman with a fur hat. Same colour, same type as the one Elena Brucan had worn. Same coat. Same size.

Her legs felt leaden as she walked to the table. She stood on the opposite side behind an empty chair, stared. The woman was well over eighty, thin-lipped, haggard lines barely masked with makeup. Her fierce eyes glared at Paula. She spoke in German, a language Paula understood.

'This is *my* table. I am expecting a friend. Plenty of empty tables,' she snapped.

'From the back you looked like someone I know.'

Paula didn't apologize. The woman's manner, her words, had been downright aggressive. One of the *grandes dames* who came here daily to chatter with her friend. She chose a table well away from her. A waitress appeared immediately and she ordered coffee. A strong hand rested on her shoulder from behind. Paula had had enough of people grasping her. She swung round, her expression bleak. It was Marienetta.

'Oh, hello there,' she managed.

Marienetta had a sable coat over her arm. She was holding two plates, each with a creamy cake. Putting one in front of Paula she sat down facing her, ordered coffee when the waitress reappeared. She spoke softly.

249

'You had a shock, like me, when you arrived. You thought that woman was Elena Brucan, didn't you?'

'Yes, for a moment.' Paula noticed Marienetta had a folded newspaper under her arm. This was too opportune not to exploit. 'How did you come to think it was her?' she asked. Marienetta had not appeared while she was viewing the body and police were keeping people well away from the horror.

'Simple.' Marienetta smiled, opened the newspaper. The front page of the *Neue Zürcher Zeitung*. Today's edition. A huge slamming headline, easy to translate.

SECOND HEADLESS BODY FOUND – IN ZÜRICH

A lot of text below. The story by Sam Snyder. He'd even included the fact that the head – after severing – had been perched back on the neck. There was a large, accurate drawing of Elena Brucan's head, the fur cap now straightened up. Paula looked up at her companion.

'That's how I knew,' Marienetta explained. 'Like you, I saw her from the back when I arrived just before you. And back in London she came to see Roman. At the Cone. Said she had vital information for him. He only saw her for a short time, then thought she was weird, called me to take her away. She was wearing the same clothes as that woman we both saw when we arrived.'

A very pat explanation, Paula thought. But she had learned something from Marienetta chatting. The links Tweed was desperately seeking were beginning to come together.

'Did you go and look at her?' Paula asked.

'Yes, then saw it was someone else.'

'Which tells me why she was so ratty with me. She was fed up with people trying to occupy the reserved chair. What was the vital information Elena had for Roman?'

250

'Damned if I know. Don't you like the look of your cake? I can go and get another one.'

'Sorry. The newspaper story distracted me. I see it even gives details of the tragedy at Montreux. I think this cake looks delicious.' She used her fork to taste it. 'The cake *is* delicious. I think I'll take one back to the Baur au Lac.'

'Sit still. Don't move,' Marienetta commanded.

She jumped up and went back to the counter where a great variety of cakes were displayed. You chose what you wanted, paid one of the spry women beyond the glass counter. Soon Marienetta was back with another cake inside a carton which she pushed across the table.

'I must pay for this one,' Paula said firmly.

'Don't be silly. It's only a few marks. What are you up to this morning? You're always up to something. Making any progress with your investigation?'

'Sometimes I get lucky,' a cheerful voice boomed out as a hand squeezed Paula's shoulder. Here we go again, she thought.

She looked up. Black Jack Diamond stood behind her. Clad in full riding kit. Spotless jodhpurs tucked into gleaming boots. His right hand held a whip. She glowered up at him.

'Kindly remove your sweaty hand.'

'Sweaty?' He took his hand away. 'Had a wash five minutes ago.'

'Have another.'

He hauled a free chair from another table, sat down on it between them. His healthy face was flushed with the cold. He snapped his fingers for the waitress. Paula was to remember that snapping of the fingers. The waitress appeared with a blank expression.

'Coffee for the customer, darlin'. I'm the customer.'

'This is Sprüngli's – not some cheap bar,' Paula told him.

'Got results, didn't it?' He grinned. 'I've been riding in

251

the fresh air. At a riding school outside the city. Feel like a million dollars.'

'You don't act like it,' Paula rapped back.

'You ladies looked so serious when I came in.' He reached for the newspaper. 'You don't want to dwell on the seamier side of life.'

'I'll take that,' said Paula, easing the paper out of his grip. 'After what happened yesterday this is no time for exuberance.'

'Oh, come on! Life is for the living.'

'Ever seen a few dead bodies?' Paula enquired.

'Not since yesterday.'

Paula stood up. Behind the bravado she had sensed a touch of menace. He'd presumably intended it to be a joke but his tone of voice had been odd. She looked at Marienetta, picking up the carton with the cake.

'Let's meet under pleasanter circumstances. I must go now.'

'We'll do that,' he called out after her. 'Dinner tonight suit you?'

He stood up and behind her she heard the crash of a chair falling over. Glancing back she saw him stooping to pick it up. His movements were wobbly and while at the table she'd caught a whiff of alcohol. What had caused him to drink so early in the day?

Leaving Sprüngli's with the newspaper folded under her arm, she paused, looking round for Newman. He materialized out of nowhere. She handed him the paper.

'You can read German,' she said. 'I'm going over to that bar Sam Snyder frequents. I could do with the heavy mob on this trip.'

'I'm the heavy mob. Wait a minute.' He scanned the news on the front page. 'I think we have to ask Mr Snyder a few serious questions. Beck will be appalled at

252

the detail. Sam has no respect for anyone if he can get a scoop . . .'

'And after that back to Tweed. I've done rather well. Caught more than one of the people involved off guard.'

They entered the bar and Sam Snyder was sitting at the same table, the newspaper spread out before him and a glass of beer next to it. Paula started out slowly after Snyder had greeted them with apparent delight. They sat opposite to him.

'You've seen my story?'

'We have. Read every word. Makes interesting reading. So quick.'

'Thank you, dear lady. What are you drinking?'

'Nothing. I'm curious, even disturbed. Zürich will be in a panic after reading that.'

'Ace reporters,' he began with a smile, 'do just that. They create stories that create panics.' He leered at Newman who was staring at him with a blank expression. 'Stories all so-called respectable citizens just *have* to read. Why? Because it gives them a secret satisfaction they still have their heads on their shoulders.'

'You had to use a drawing of Elena,' Paula observed, still quietly.

'Couldn't use the camera. The flash would have alerted the police to my presence. I always carry a small sketch block. I did another sketch when Zeitzler – that's his name, isn't it? – lifted the head off the shoulders to show it was severed from the neck. Hoped they'd use that one but they funked it.' He reached towards his back pocket. 'I'm sure you'd like to see it.'

'Keep it in your underpants – where it belongs,' Paula snapped.

'Don't think the lady has a high opinion of me.'

'She thinks you're a louse,' Newman burst out. 'And so do I.'

'Keep it cool, Bob,' Paula advised. 'Now, Mr Snyder,

how were you able to get this material? I was there and didn't see you anywhere. Obviously, neither did the police.'

'Ah!' Snyder placed a thick index finger by his nose. 'A trade secret. But since she's asked me so nicely – Newman, you ought to study her technique – I'll tell you. On the opposite bank of the Sihl there's a shadowed walk. That's where I stood, keeping very still. I could even hear what was being said – the Sihl's pretty narrow. Had to be careful not to move much while I was making the sketches. The editor of the paper was away – some temporary guy in his place. Which was lucky. I could tell he wanted to make his name before he moved on. Think I saw the killer when I first arrived before the police rolled in.'

'What did it look like?' Paula asked, lighting one of her rare cigarettes.

'Tall, wore a black coat, very long. And a funny hat. It walked stiffly. Mind you I only had a glimpse so don't take that description as accurate. Vanished in the direction of the Baur en Ville, where we are now.'

'You didn't include that in your article,' Paula remarked.

'No.' Snyder grinned. 'If I had, Beck would have locked me up for hours while he interrogated me. That I could do without.'

'Ever seen anyone like that figure before?' she asked.

'Can't say I have.'

'Sure?'

Snyder lifted his glass, drank quite a lot of beer, smacked his lips as he put down the glass. He was so pleased with himself Newman could have smashed his fist into his face. But he was leaving the floor to Paula, who was doing so well.

'Mr Snyder,' she said, still quietly, 'was the figure carrying something?'

'Could have been holding a very large briefcase, something like that.' He waved a large hand. 'Can't be sure.'

254

'And this was before the body was discovered – and before you'd noticed it?'

Snyder took out a small cigar. He spent his time lighting it. Then he took several puffs, gazing round the bar. It was spacious, a luxuriously furnished room with mahogany walls, a crescent-shaped counter way over to the right with black leather stools where several customers sat. In the middle of the room was a large black piano and illumination came from stud lights embedded in the ceiling.

'You haven't answered my question,' Paula prodded.

'You know what?' Snyder took another puff at the cigar. 'I reckon I've answered more than enough of your questions.'

'Thank you for your support, Bob,' Paula said as they headed back to the Baur au Lac.

'I didn't say anything – except for one brief outburst.'

'That's what I meant by your support.'

She glanced at Newman and he had pursed his lips. Not best pleased with her attitude. She didn't care – she'd done the job.

'What did you think of his vague description of someone he suggested could have been the killer?' she asked.

'Vague is the word.'

'I'm developing a new theory from the way he dragged that in when he needn't have done. Sam Snyder was in the right place at the right moment. Earlier he could have walked down the promenade on the opposite bank from where he made his sketches. He could be it – the killer we're tracking.'

25

'Hello,' said Tweed, answering the phone in his suite.

'Ed Danvers here.' Voice abrupt. 'Mr Straub wishes to see you. We're in suite . . .'

'And I'm in suite . . .'

'We know where you are. The Vice-President wishes to see you immediately.'

'Then he will be very welcome to come down and see me. I will be waiting for him.'

Tweed broke the connection. He went over to the well-stocked drinks cupboard. Yes, he had whiskey, what the Americans preferred to drink. If anyone came down to see him. They did. A heavy hammering on the door, nonstop. Tweed opened the door and Straub pushed his way in.

He now wore a white two-piece suit, a pink shirt, a tie with the emblems of the American flag. The colours clashed horribly but you couldn't miss him. Refusing Tweed's offer to sit down he stormed round the suite. The expression he wore did not go with his clothes – his long lean face was twisted into fury.

'I *am* the Vice-President, in case you'd forgotten. People come to see me when summoned.'

'I'm not people.'

'You won't hold your job for long when I return to Washington.'

'So when are you going home?' Tweed enquired in the same calm tone.

'Not yet.' He suddenly calmed down, saw the whiskey bottle. 'I'll have some of that,' he snapped, sitting in an armchair.

'My pleasure. You are a very worried man, Mr Straub,' Tweed observed as he poured whiskey into two glasses. Then he sat down facing his guest, raised his glass. 'Cheers!'

'What makes you think I'm worried?' Straub asked.

'You are noted for never stopping smiling. You face any audience and answer the most hostile questions amiably. Yet you came in here as though your ship was going down. Is it?'

'A strange simile.' Straub stared hard at Tweed. 'These serial murders are hitting the headlines in the States. And over here. They always mention my presence.'

'Because you always happen to be in the vicinity when it hits again? And I must disagree with you. The words "serial murders" suggest random killings. I believe they are all linked.'

'Linked?' Straub's normally ruddy face paled. A pause before he responded. 'What on earth do you damned well mean?'

'I mean that when we identify it we'll find a personal motive behind these atrocities.'

'That's so implausible as to be ludicrous,' Straub said savagely.

'Your reaction suggests this is what is worrying you. Were you in Pinedale, staying at your mansion near the asylum when it was burned to the ground?'

'I did *not* come here to be interrogated.'

'No, you came here to discover how far my investigation has progressed. Well, I will tell you. Since arriving here in Zürich I'm beginning to link up the elements in the chain. The appearance, once more, of the Arbogast family is very significant. I believe you know them.'

'You believe wrongly. And I could do with another drink.'

Tweed did the honours. He watched as Straub lifted his glass again. His hand was shaking. He steadied it by pressing the glass against his lips, swallowing half the contents of the stiff one Tweed had poured.

'If you were in court, and I was a barrister, I would next ask you about your visit to Roman Arbogast at the Cone in London. I would produce evidence to back up my question.'

Tweed, his voice still calm, was bearing down hard on his guest. He produced an envelope he'd slipped down the side of a cushion before Straub had arrived. He selected a photo showing Straub mounting the steps to the entrance to the Cone. He placed it on the table in front of the Vice-President.

Straub stared down at the picture which also included the limo by the kerb which had brought him there. He spent too long gazing at the picture before looking up at Tweed.

'Naturally I have a distant acquaintance with Roman Arbogast. He has a plant employing several thousand workers in Boston.' He attempted a smile. 'Politicians have to think of voters.'

Straub, like some Americans, spoke very rapidly. Watching him on TV, addressing an American audience, Tweed had sometimes found it difficult to catch what he'd said.

'And Pinedale?' Tweed said quietly.

'I never knew Hank Foley—'

He stopped suddenly. It was obvious he regretted replying so quickly. He drank the rest of his whiskey, gripping the glass tightly.

'I'm surprised,' Tweed observed, 'that you remember the name of a caretaker. And that photo was taken by Elena Brucan, whose body was discovered yesterday evening close to this hotel.' He was speaking slowly and very deliberately. 'I refer to poor Elena Brucan, whose head

259

was severed from her body and then – a really foul touch – placed back on the severed neck.'

'Never heard of her.'

Again he stopped. Again he had regretted reacting to the name so fast.

'As a politician don't you read the newspapers?'

'Of course I do. But I don't understand German.'

'I don't remember saying that the newspaper report was in German.'

Straub had slipped up again. For an experienced politician to make so many mistakes so quickly told Tweed he had underestimated the pressure Straub was under.

The Vice-President settled back in his chair in a clear attempt to relax. To regain complete control. He used the technique he always fell back on when faced with a dangerous opponent. He attacked.

'Tweed, I came here to suggest you dropped this investigation. It is crazy. Why not go home and leave it to the Swiss?'

'Because I am cooperating with the Swiss. Two of these awful murders – so similar to the ones in Britain and the States – have taken place on Swiss territory.'

'You mean you won't go along with my suggestion?'

'No. I will not.'

Straub jumped up from his chair. He strode to the door, opened it, then turned before he left. His usual bland expression was transformed into a glare of pure hatred, reminding Tweed of the painting of Roman shown to him by Marienetta when Roman was 'in a bad temper'. Straub's voice was a snarl.

'*Sonofabitch.*'

He slammed the door shut behind him.

26

The reception hall was crowded when Paula entered with Newman. Several guests were waiting to consult the concierge. Three more heading towards registration. Behind the counter the temporary clerk was in a flap. He caught sight of Paula, waved to her holding a fat envelope. Puzzled, she took it and then the clerk was immersed in guests. With Newman she took it over to a couch facing the entrance to the lounge. She assumed it was something Tweed had ordered. The flap was tucked inside, not sealed.

With Newman seated beside her she took out a large sheaf of rail tickets. First class. Dated the next day. Departure time of express 13.07. Zürich HB Lugano. Smoking compartments. Four tickets. She frowned, looked at the front of the envelope. It was addressed to Herr Roman Arbogast. The idiot clerk had given her Roman's envelope. She looked at Newman who had watched as she checked the tickets.

'Now we know,' he whispered. He raised his voice to catch a waiter. 'What are you drinking, Paula?'

'Coffee and a bottle of still mineral water. I must get rid of this . . .'

The clerk was having a rough time with a guest who was complaining about his bill. Two other guests stood impatiently waiting for the dispute to be settled. Paula eased her way to one side, dropped the envelope on the counter.

'This isn't for me. Look at the front of the envelope.'

The clerk pushed the envelope to one side. He continued his conversation with the guest who was not in a good temper. She walked back and sat by Newman. Refreshments had arrived. Newman's drink was a double Scotch. As she sipped her water she looked into the lounge.

Seated by himself at a table near the entrance was a typical banker type. The usual black suit, white shirt, executive case, a number of A4 sheets in his hand. Youngish, he had been gazing at her through his gold-rimmed spectacles. He looked away immediately. Damned sauce, she thought, he can see I'm with someone.

'Four tickets,' Newman whispered. 'Roman, Marienetta, Sophie and Broden.'

'Or Black Jack. As soon as you've finished your drink we'll go up and let Tweed know what we've found out. No hurry.'

'Zürich to Lugano tomorrow,' Newman remarked. 'The 13.07 express from the Hauptbahnhof. So—'

He stopped speaking suddenly. Paula glanced at him. What had disturbed him? He finished his drink quickly. They made their way to the lift, which was waiting, empty. Once the doors had closed and it began ascending Newman spoke.

'Did you notice that banker type sitting by himself?'

'Yes, he seemed interested in me. Probably my imagination.'

'He can lip-read. He probably digested the data I spoke of.'

'Does it matter?' she said dismissively as they stepped out.

She knew Newman had been on a course at the Surrey mansion which had included spotting a lip-reader. Their eyes widened. They stared at their target with a certain intensity. Now she thought it was Newman's imagination. Tweed opened the door, ushered them into his suite.

Marler stood against a wall, smoking one of his long cigarettes. He gave them a little salute.

'You've been out a long time,' Tweed said to Paula, 'but I'm glad Newman found you.'

'He's been very good, keeping out of my way. I have a lot to tell you.'

'Including,' Marler interjected with a smile, 'your visit to ACTIL's headquarters. Funny the door wasn't locked. You just walked straight in.'

'So I'm being spied on from all sides,' she snapped.

'Be grateful,' Marler drawled. 'They tried to kill you in the Altstadt. Wouldn't you expect Tweed to take measures to protect you? And you never saw me.'

She had taken off her coat and scarf and gloves. Sinking into an armchair she gratefully accepted the glass of water Tweed handed her.

'Sorry,' she said. 'I shouldn't have said what I just did. I know we work as a team. I'm grateful for the protection. I've had a busy morning. What's annoying me is I'm feeling jittery again – and I can't pinpoint what's caused it.'

There was a tap on the door. When Newman opened it Butler and Nield walked in. Butler still wore the bandage on his forehead. Nield looked round.

'Maybe we should leave you alone?'

'No,' said Tweed. 'Paula has been out seeking information. I suspect she's done rather well. So sit, listen, remember.'

'I want to keep my interviews with various people in sequence,' Paula began. 'Before the Altstadt fracas I had a talk with Sam Snyder at that bar . . .'

There was silence while she recalled her first conversation with the reporter. As she repeated both sides of what had been said Tweed brought out water glasses, filled them up, handed them out. Butler frowned, pointed to the bar. Tweed nodded, fetched a bottle of beer. He was reflecting that Paula would have made a top-flight barrister with her skill at interrogation. Also he liked the way she took risks, stating something as though it were a fact.

'That's him,' she said after a while.

'So,' Tweed summed up, 'Snyder didn't deny he'd been to Pinedale, had investigated the other murders. Significant.'

'Unless he committed the murders,' Newman suggested.

'Now we also know that he was acquainted with Elena Brucan. Strikes me he knows a few too many people in this tragic drama. And finally, he warned you that you were targeted. *Before* the Altstadt attack.'

'That's possible,' Marler interjected. 'Like Bob, like me, he'll have plenty of underworld contacts. He mentioned the word "grapevine".'

'Unless he'd arranged the contract on Paula, was covering himself in advance,' Newman speculated.

Paula gave him a look. *Do please shut up.* Then she switched to her visit to interview Roman. 'When the phantom Marler saw me,' she said, giving him a quirky smile. She described her shock when she found Broden seated in Roman's office. Vividly she told them of what had been said between them so they almost felt they had been there with her. She concluded by reporting her meeting with Roman, that she had an appointment to go and see him at 3 p.m.

'Broden is a tough guy,' Newman remarked. 'SIB? Special Investigation Branch. I knew someone who had that job. They can be very rough, often like their work.'

'And,' Tweed observed, 'Broden practically admitted he'd flown more than once to Maine. Significant.'

Paula asked for more water. Talking nonstop dried up her throat. She drank the whole glass Tweed fetched her, then resumed her analysis.

She then described her experience inside Sprüngli's.

Again the listeners felt they were witnesses to the scene she described. The woman she'd thought was Elena Brucan, the arrival of Marienetta, their conversation, the arrival of Black Jack Diamond.

Tweed was now sitting in a hard-backed chair, his eyes never leaving her. She had the feeling he had spotted something she had missed, something important. What could it be? She ended with a sigh.

'So,' Tweed commented, 'Marienetta knew Elena Brucan in London.'

'So I gathered,' Paula agreed. 'Lord! I forgot the cake.' She opened her capacious shoulder bag, carefully lifted out the carton, gave it to Newman. 'Bob, this is for you. Heaven knows what state it's in.'

'It's cold weather.' Newman opened the carton, lifted out the cake, which was intact, munched it. 'This is great. I was hungry.'

'Well, you can say thank you by telling everyone about my confrontation with Snyder during my second trip to see him. You were there and my voice is giving out . . .'

Tweed again listened without interruption to Newman's account of the meeting with Sam Snyder. Newman did not conjure up what had taken place anything like as vividly as Paula. But he recalled their conversation accurately.

'Then we walked out and left the weasel,' he concluded.

'You discovered that Snyder knew Elena before he flew here. In London, in fact. That could be important.' Tweed paused, looked round at everyone. 'You may be confused by the avalanche of information you've just heard. I can simplify it.'

'Wish you would,' said Nield.

'Paula has accomplished more in a day than most people could have managed in a week. She saw Broden – and that interview I find interesting. I regard Broden as a mystery man – and doubt he told Paula everything about himself.

We must not forget Broden. Elena Brucan is a key figure. Now we know she knew them all, so which one became so anxious about her that she was murdered?'

'Could have been any of them,' Nield commented.

'Maybe. While all this was taking place I had a confrontation with Mr Russell Straub, Vice-President.' He described what had happened. 'I find it interesting that Straub has been present at the scenes of all four murders. And he is a very worried man. Why? I'm reporting my duel with Straub to Beck. I think Beck may want to see him. Now I suggest we separate and have a late lunch.'

'And I have to rush off,' Paula said, after checking her watch. 'I'm not hungry and I have this appointment at three with Roman Arbogast.'

Luigi Morati, now posing as Gianni Vorano, banker, had used his forged passport to reserve a room at the Baur au Lac. He was still sitting in the lounge when he saw Paula hurrying to the lift. Shoving his papers into his large executive case the left the lounge, checked the floor number above the lift carrying Paula up to her room.

Luigi ran up the stairs, paused at the top, saw Paula emerge from the lift, walk away briskly. He followed her with caution. Peering round one corner he saw her insert her key card, disappear inside the room.

He walked along the same corridor, made a mental note of the room number. The key card, which was supposed to be safe – its combination was changed as soon as a guest departed – posed no problem. He had an American device which would enable him to open her door in less than a minute. He walked back to his own room.

Luigi had long ago realized that the most important trait a professional hitman should possess was patience. He had failed badly in the debacle in the Altstadt. This taught him that to attempt to kill her in the streets of Zürich was a bad tactic. It would be so much safer to eliminate her inside her room. During the early hours of the morning. The escape route? The fire door at the end of the corridor. He would check that later.

When booking his room for a month he had paid in advance in cash. He had explained to the cashier he might have to suddenly go to Germany on a business trip. He would be away for the night but wanted to feel sure he'd have a room to return to.

This was a wise precaution. In Switzerland one of the most heinous crimes is to leave a hotel without paying the bill. He decided he would have lunch outside – probably at the Baur en Ville bar.

Paula had rushed to her room to tidy herself up before her meeting with Roman. As she unlocked her door she thought she saw out of the corner of her eye a shadow in the corridor where she had turned to reach her room. When she glanced quickly in that direction she saw no shadow, nobody. Get a grip on yourself, she thought.

Reaching the ground floor on her way out she saw Newman talking to the concierge. He was ordering six first-class rail tickets on the express to Lugano for the following day.

Before leaving his suite Paula had heard Tweed telling Newman to book the tickets. This was his reaction to Paula telling him about the tickets she had seen inside the envelope addressed to Arbogast.

'It's just a precaution,' Tweed had added. 'I think we have reached the stage where the unknown enemy is using deception operations to throw us off the track.'

Leaving the hotel she hurried up Bahnhofstrasse. At this time of the day it was deserted. And the temperature had dropped even more. The air was positively Siberian. Overhead loomed a solid ceiling of dark cloud.

She paused before turning down the street leading to ACTIL's building. It was totally deserted and almost as dark as night. She could see the police tape across the far end of the street but no police car, no sign of any police, no sign of anyone. She found it unwelcoming.

Walking down the side of the street opposite to the building, she looked up. No light in Roman's office. No lights anywhere in the building. Strange. She checked her watch. It was exactly 3 p.m.

Gritting her teeth, she crossed the street quickly. The door was closed. She pressed the bell several times. No response. Slowly she took hold of the door handle, turned it, pushed. It was locked.

She was puzzled, faintly disturbed. She recalled Roman's remark about his insistence on punctuality. It seemed to be getting even darker. She decided it was not wise to linger in this isolated street. She walked back towards Bahnhofstrasse. She never saw Nield slip inside a doorway. He had followed her from the hotel.

What had happened to Roman? She worried over it as she entered the hotel. She noticed the idiot of a staff member was no longer at the cashier's counter. Another man she had never seen before was in his place. She approached the concierge.

'Could you please phone Mr Arbogast's room? He wants to see me.'

'He's not there.' The concierge glanced at the key board. 'He's out somewhere.'

'I see you have a new man at the cash desk,' she remarked.

'Yes.' The concierge paused, pursed his lips briefly, then smiled. 'The other man was only temporary and has left to take up another post.'

They realized he was no good, she thought as the lift ascended. Tweed was in his suite and so was the rest of his team. She told him about her abortive trip to meet Roman as Nield joined them.

'That's very strange,' Tweed commented. 'Roman struck me as a man who is always punctual. What can have happened to him?'

'Anything,' Newman replied grimly. 'Considering what has already happened to different people.'

Paula took off her coat, settled herself in an armchair so she could see everyone. Her expression was serious and she felt this was a good opportunity to share her thoughts on certain key factors, bearing in mind what they had experienced so far.

'The axe,' she began, 'used to behead four victims. It has to be transported by *it*, whoever it may be, so how is it done? Brought all the way from Maine to Britain and then here . . .'

'Let me quickly tell you something,' Tweed interjected. 'I have just heard from Beck that his pathologist, Zeitzler, has confirmed he believes the same weapon was used to murder Elena Brucan. He has compared his own films of her with the material sent to Beck from the Boston pathologist. So you are right. In some way what must be a cumbersome weapon has been successfully transported from location to location.'

'I find this frightening,' Paula continued, 'but also it is a possible clue. And also the execution block is being transported in the same container. I found its imprint in the ground near the asylum at Pinedale, then again in the grass near Abbey Grange at Bray where Holgate was murdered. And I saw the same shape in the blood on the promenade alongside the River Sihl where Elena Brucan was slaughtered.'

'What could this container be?' Nield asked.

'Maybe a reinforced suitcase or large executive case.'

Paula leaned forward to emphasize what she was saying. 'It – the killer – must be carrying around something which looks innocent. Something not out of the ordinary. Then there are the missing heads.'

Silence descended on the room as everyone considered the grisly prospect Paula had conjured up. Tweed, who remained standing, clasped his hands as he asked his question, looking at Paula.

'You seem to have thought this out ingeniously. What is your suggestion about the heads? Why are they taken? What happens to them?'

'Don't think me crazy,' she replied, 'but I suspect the heads are transported inside the same container. As to why, I have no idea.'

'That reminds me,' Tweed told her, 'Zeitzler wants someone to visit his morgue to positively identify Elena's head. I know you saw the horror on the banks of the Sihl but Zeitzler is very precise. He says he must have an identification which cannot be challenged.'

'Then I'll go to the morgue,' Paula said calmly.

'Not on your own,' Newman said firmly.

'I'll go with Paula,' Tweed replied. 'We have both had conversations with Elena face to face. Or Newman could go with me instead.'

'I'm going,' Paula said stubbornly. 'I owe it to her.'

Beck himself drove them to the morgue. He apologized for submitting them to the ordeal as he pulled up outside the building. Tweed dismissed his apologies with a wave of his hand. Beck then made a similar remark to Paula, suggesting once again, as he had earlier, that her presence was not essential.

'It's part of my job,' she told him severely. 'I am a fully paid-up member of the team. Let's get on with it.'

It was dark, which did not help the atmosphere. Zeitzler

was waiting as a member of his staff opened the door, led them into a stone-floored hall. Zeitzler took over, leading the way to another door, beyond which a flight of stone steps descended so far that Paula felt she was going down into the bowels of the earth.

Through another door into a room brightly illuminated by overhead fluorescent tubes. Here everything was modern – metal-topped tables scrubbed hygienically clean, cameras suspended above them with telescopic tubes which could be adjusted to any angle, any height.

It was here Paula had to take off her coat, as did Tweed, and a lean-faced Swiss gave them their special clothes: white overalls which buttoned to the neck, latex gloves, rubber bootees which had to be pulled on over their shoes, face masks with breathing apparatus and eye-holes.

Paula took a deep breath as Zeitzler unlocked a heavy door. She adjusted her face mask and a familiar odour penetrated her nostrils – familiar because she recalled it from entering Professor Saafeld's spacious mortuary at Holland Park. The unmistakable odour of formalin, used for preserving body parts.

She held her head high as Zeitzler ushered her into a smaller room. The walls were lined with large closed drawers which, she knew, contained bodies. She walked straight in after Zeitzler. Perched on a table was something concealed with a heavy white cloth. Something about a foot wide and deeper. Zeitzler looked at her.

'Ready? If you need the toilet it is just beyond that door.'

He was expecting her to be sick. Wanted her to rush to the toilet if that should be necessary. She looked at him and nodded. He took hold of the cloth at the top, removed it swiftly. Inside her latex gloves her fingers clenched.

She was looking at the head of Elena Brucan, sliced off just below the chin. Elena's glazed eyes gazed back at her through the formalin which covered her head inside a large round glass jar with a glass lid topped by a glass knob. She stared fixedly at the grim relic. Gazed direct at Elena's eyes, which seemed to be trying to convey a message. Pure imagination. She pointed one latex-covered finger.

'That is what we would call a laboratory jar in Britain.'

'Yes, it is,' Zeitzler answered, his voice muzzled by the mask.

'That's it,' she said to Tweed, her finger steady as it pointed.

'That's what?' Tweed asked.

'What it uses to transport the heads.'

27

'You wouldn't find anything by looking through Elena's clothes,' Tweed remarked. Beck had dropped them at the hotel entrance but they were strolling in the hotel's park opposite where they had been driven in. Tweed was in a ruminative mood. 'In any case Beck's men – as well as Zeitzler – will have examined them thoroughly.'

Just before they had left the morgue Paula had asked to see the clothes. Tweed had humoured her, knowing it was a waste of time. He pulled up his coat collar as the night chill had become raw.

'I didn't find anything,' Paula agreed. 'But I did,' she added.

'Don't talk to me in riddles.'

'You're always doing it.'

'So what do you mean?' he asked irritably.

'I found something wasn't there. You remember the embroidered scarf she always wore? Well, it was missing.'

'Could have been taken off before . . .' Tweed phrased his sentence carefully: 'Before the killer did its evil work. It would have got in the way, if you see what I mean.'

'Then what happened to it?'

'Probably thrown into the River Sihl.'

'I don't think so. I asked Beck if they had checked the river for the missing head.'

'The head wasn't missing.'

'Sorry, I'm feeling rather tired. I asked him if they had

273

checked the river for clues. They had. Even sent down divers to explore it. So the scarf wasn't in the river.'

'When you come to think of it,' he remarked, 'the killer has a liking for water. Way off in Maine the murder was committed close to the Atlantic. The body was even found in a crevasse just above the storm level. At Bray Holgate's body was found dumped in a creek off the Thames. Then, in Montreux, Seale's body floated in from the lake. Too many coincidences for me to swallow.'

'And,' Paula mused, 'Elena's body was in a boat on the edge of the River Sihl. What does it mean? Do we know someone who likes sailing?'

'Not so far.'

'I've had a feeling for some while that an important remark was made by one of the people we know. I just can't recall who it was or what was said. Or when it was said. It was a little while ago.'

'Stop trying to remember it. Empty your mind and it may fly back out of your subconscious.'

'I'm convinced it is very important,' she insisted. 'One of those chance remarks. And I'm wondering now if whoever made it has realized their mistake. Hence that attack on me in the Altstadt. Why me? Because I know too much – but I don't know what it is.'

'Put it out of your mind.'

As Tweed was talking he kept searching the shadows in the park beyond the hotel. He was sure he had seen movement. He had his hand inside his coat and jacket, gripping the Walther. They had better get inside quickly.

'We're going straight back into the hotel. Now . . .'

Luigi had been walking in the park, checking the grounds, when he saw Tweed enter the approach to the doors with Paula by his side. For a short time he wondered whether this was the moment to act as he took out his Glock. Then he saw Tweed looking towards where he hid in the shadows. No, it would be too risky. Wait until the middle of the night and do the job inside the woman's bedroom while she slept. Then leave the hotel via the fire escape with his single bag.

He would leave Zürich driving the car he had hired in another name, heading for Austria. With luck he would be across the border before the body was discovered.

He would stay in Austria for several weeks, growing a beard which would completely change his appearance. Luigi was a good forward planner. It was the key to why he was still alive.

'The one person I haven't had the chance to interview,' Paula remarked as they entered the hotel, 'is Sophie.'

'Can't imagine she's involved,' Tweed commented.

'And how many cases have you dealt with where the last person anyone would suspect was the criminal?'

'Quite a few,' he admitted.

'I'm going to leave you,' she said suddenly. 'There is Sophie. Sitting by herself in the lounge. The place is a bit crowded.'

As she walked into the lounge Sophie was raising her glass to drink. An almost empty bottle of gin sat on her table. Was she tipsy? Sophie saw her, raised the glass to her instead of drinking.

'I feel like some company,' Paula began as she took off her coat. 'Or would you sooner be on your own?'

'So do I.' Sophie glanced round the lounge. 'We can't have a proper talk in here. Let's go up to my room.'

They were silent inside the lift as it took them up to the second floor. Sophie had a room at the front overlooking the entrance. Entering the room Paula glanced round in astonishment. There were suitcases everywhere, some very large. Two, on luggage stands, were open. Inside the contents were neatly packed, which again surprised Paula. Her previous impression of Sophie had been that she was careless and disorganized.

'Take your coat,' Sophie said.

She opened a wardrobe. Inside there were coats suspended from a dozen hangers. Sophie liked clothes, Paula decided as she sat in an armchair. She also noticed how nimbly Sophie moved despite the amount of alcohol she must have consumed. Tall, all her movements were athletic.

'I'm having a drink,' she said as though it were her first of the day. 'What's your tipple?'

'A glass of Chardonnay unless that's a problem.'

'Problem? There isn't one in the world I can't handle.'

She disappeared into the bathroom. When she reappeared she had two cut glasses tucked under her arm. In one hand she carried an unopened bottle of Chardonnay, in the other one of Scotch. She poured the drinks, settled herself into an armchair facing Paula. She raised her glass, clinked with Paula's.

'Here's to murder.'

'I think I'd sooner drink to the solution of the murders we have witnessed in the past week or two.'

'I brought you up here so Marienetta wouldn't barge in on us. Not that it's likely. She's disappeared.'

'Really? So, it seems, has your father.'

'Let's hope it's permanent. If I never see either again that would be too soon.' She giggled, drank half her glass.

'Do you mean that?' asked Paula.

'Sure do.' Her mimicry of an American accent was perfect.

Sophie was different from how Paula had seen her

276

before. Her voice was soft, her words without a trace of malice. Almost indifferent. She wore a black velvet dress with slim straps over her strong well-shaped shoulders.

Her brown hair was no longer tied in a ponytail. Now it flowed down to the tips of her shoulder blades in silken waves. Sophie was a well-built attractive lady. As they chattered on Paula felt drawn to her eyes: grey, at times they were animated and then they would glaze over. Paula had the weird feeling they were hypnotic, that she was falling under their spell. She looked away and blinked, gazing round the room.

'You do have a ton of luggage.'

'I like clothes. You should see Marienetta's collection. Big brutes. Yet she can carry a couple as though she's holding paper bags. She's tough and wiry.'

'Do you quarrel much?' Paula asked, recalling when Marienetta had given Sophie a tremendous slap. 'What about when you were young?'

'Fought like cat and dog. She was older "sister", I was superfluous baggage. Until one day I got fed up, nearly broke her jaw.'

'How did you do that?'

'Pinched a knuckleduster off my boy friend. Wore gloves, one hiding the knuckleduster. When I hit her she went over backwards.' She giggled. 'She was in hospital a week. After that she left me alone.' She giggled again. Her eyes glazed over and once again Paula had the feeling she was being drawn into the depths. The sensation disturbed her.

As she sipped at her Chardonnay, Sophie refilled her glass with another slug of Scotch. She had been sitting forward, elbows on her knees. Now she sank back into her chair, her head resting on its back, staring at the ceiling. Was the drink taking effect?

'Who do you think committed these terrible murders?' Paula threw at her.

277

'Maybe George Karazov. I read a book once. *Copycats*. It was about Karazov. Used to cut up his victims as though they were slices of meat. Seemed unnecessary. Once he slipped into a morgue where one of his achievements was lying on a slab. Took a lot of photos, slipped away. Sent the photos to the FBI with a typed note. *From me. You'll never catch me*. They never did. Maybe he's resurfaced.'

Paula knew all about the Karazov case. She was curious to see how Sophie reacted to it. She was beginning to feel uncomfortable but she persisted, firing another question.

'You used the phrase "seemed unnecessary". What did you mean?'

'He had a knife. Why didn't he just stick it in their throats and be done with it?'

'And you also used the word "achievements". I didn't understand what you meant there.'

'Well, I guess he enjoyed his work.' Sophie abruptly sat up straight in her chair. Her eyes gazed at Paula's. 'Who do you think is the guy?'

'Hard to say at this stage.'

'But you must have evidence by now. So which direction is it pointing in?' Sophie asked vehemently.

'Nothing specific. We have to wait. It will make a mistake.'

'Hasn't done so far, has it?'

'I'm not sure. We have to wait,' she repeated.

'If it is Karazov come to life again you'll wait a lifetime. He's too clever. He's had too much experience.'

'True.' Paula paused. 'Except I don't think it is Karazov. Now, I must get back or they'll wonder what's happened to me. I've enjoyed our conversation,' she lied.

Normal? Or abnormal? She wondered as she made her way back to report to Tweed. She had very little doubt what the answer was.

*   *   *

In the night the Mercedes was one of the few cars on the road outside Zürich. Driven by Ed Danvers, it was now parked facing the lake, a still sheet like a black mirror. In front of them there was nothing but a wide flat wall dropping sheer to the water on the far side. In the passenger seat Russell Straub sat very erect, tense.

'Tweed is becoming a problem,' he said grimly. 'He has to be stopped from pursuing this investigation.'

'Why, sir?' The FBI man liked information.

'Because if he locates the killer the case will blossom into a worldwide sensation. I can do without that.'

'Are you thinking of the Hank Foley murder?'

Straub turned his head away, stared out of the window, which was tinted and covered with frost. No risk of anyone seeing who was inside. He puffed at the cigar held between his thick strong fingers.

'Don't forget I never smoke in public. A lot of votes in the anti-smoking lobby.'

'Are you concerned about the Hank Foley murder?' Danvers persisted. 'That you happen to have a house close to where it occurred in Pinedale isn't going to appear if the press does create a sensation.' His instincts as an FBI agent told him this wasn't the real reason for Straub's anxiety.

'Shows you know damn-all about the press. The *Washington Post* doesn't like me.'

'If there's another reason why Tweed worries you I'd better know what it is. Otherwise I'm operating in a fog.'

'There's no goddamn other reason,' Straub snapped. 'And do not forget that when I become President I'm throwing out Cord Dillon as Deputy Director. I could slip you into his place as easy as I lit this cigar. On the other hand . . .' His tone became menacing. 'I could leave you to rot in London for the rest of your career.'

'You're not suggesting I hire some thugs to put Tweed out of the way?'

'Would I take a chance like that, Ed?' He turned to the agent and smirked. His tone had been unconvincing.

'With my experience,' Danvers said slowly, 'I might be able to exert diplomatic pressure on the Swiss. To get Tweed removed from Switzerland.'

A figure in a trench coat and a trilby hat pulled down over the face strolled along the top of the wall. As it slowly passed the front of the car it glanced in through the windscreen which was clear – Danvers had defrosted it. The figure disappeared.

'Who the hell was that?' Straub snarled. 'He looked straight at me.'

'Just a Swiss guy out for a walk. Want me to get back to the hotel?'

'Do that. And don't forget we've so far had a long association which has worked well. So far,' he repeated as he turned to Danvers and smirked.

The man in the trench coat continued his leisurely stroll until the Mercedes had gone. Marler then turned back and headed for his motorcycle, which he had purchased in Zürich. He had been outside the hotel entrance when Danvers had driven the Mercedes into the wide parking area. Immediately the Vice-President had dashed out, jumped into the front passenger seat.

Intrigued, Marler had got onto his motorcycle parked outside. He had followed the Mercedes at a discreet distance until it pulled in by the lake. Now he would report his observation to Tweed.

Paula was in Tweed's suite when the phone rang. It was Monica. After talking to Tweed briefly she put him on to Howard, the Director. This conversation was longer and Paula gathered it was not good news. Earlier she had told him about her experience with Sophie. Tweed put the phone down.

'Trouble?' Paula enquired.

'Some people would call it that.' Prior to the phone call she had thought Tweed seemed worried. Now he was almost jaunty. He took her by the arm, sat her down in an armchair, then sat facing her.

'Monica has surpassed herself. In her efforts to build up the Arbogast family tree she has discovered that Vicenzo, the uncle of Roman, who settled in the States, had three children. Two boys, one girl. Another brother, Mario, who also emigrated from Rome to the States, also married and had a son and a daughter – the latter born in Britain. No names for the children, though. The family tree I'm creating is filling up. Then Howard told me he'd been summoned to see the PM twice. Nathan Morgan, the new chief of Special Branch, is on his way here to escort me home.'

'Will you go?'

'Of course not, but the pressure on us is increasing. What I like is that they are giving themselves away. It proves power is a vital factor in our investigation. Again I say, what is the great secret they are trying to hide? Truly enormous power is involved in what, apparently, the PM called the Holgate case. You notice how they try to isolate a whole series of brutal murders to one.'

'You do sound buoyant.'

'Then Monica's data begins to fit in with what I have started to suspect. We are moving.'

'I'm not supposed to ask yet what you now suspect,' she said wrily.

'Too early.'

'And what do you think about my strange conversation with Sophie?'

'Illuminating. Interesting that usually she appears to be

281

so quiet we're inclined to forget about her.'

'And Abraham Seale said that unbalanced people often seem so normal most of the time. Something like that.'

'We are getting there. You look a little tired.'

'I'm nearly dropping. I think I'll go straight to my room and sleep the sleep of the dead. Oh! Unfortunate phrase.'

As she was walking along the corridor to her room Marienetta appeared. She was carrying a fur-lined raincoat and the speed with which her long legs moved made Paula feel even more tired.

'We thought you'd got lost,' Paula said.

'I've been on the pub crawl to end all pub crawls. Playing detective, as we agreed. Lots to tell you.' She grasped Paula by the arm. 'Not a step further. Here is my room, so join me for a drink. No arguments. So much to tell you.'

Paula suppressed a yawn. Maybe she should listen to what had happened. Marienetta seemed so triumphant. Inside the large room she glanced round. Not much different from Sophie's. Large suitcases everywhere, some piled on top of each other.

'Chardonnay for you,' Marienetta said gaily. 'Scotch for me. I'd better stick with it after the rampage. Guess who I've been with. He talked his head off. Black Jack. Said too much.'

Pouring the drinks, Marienetta perched herself on a couch facing Paula, who had sunk into another couch. They touched glasses, Marienetta drank a long gulp, half-emptying her glass. She wore a gold dress which matched the colour of her long hair. Round her slim waist was a green belt fastened with a jewel. She crossed her legs.

'We've patronized six bars. Black Jack was in top form. My guess is he's now sprawled out on his bed without taking off his clothes. Although he wanted me to take off mine, which is when I said good night after I'd opened his door for him.'

'He must have been half-seas over. Not able to use his key.'

'He doesn't fool me. His capacity for liquor is bottomless. But after a lot he says things he wouldn't normally say.'

'Do get to the point.'

'The subject of the death penalty cropped up. Jack said he was in favour of it. Then he said there were people the world was better off without. That a number had been dealt with already.'

'You're sure he said that?'

'Quoting his exact words. He said he had a list of people who wouldn't be walking around much longer. I asked him who was on the list. He went coy on me, said that would be telling, that the last thing we wanted was publicity. I said what did he mean by "we"?'

'Go on.'

'He said the world in general, which didn't make much sense. Need a refill. What about you?'

Paula shook her head. While Marienetta poured another large slug of Scotch she was working out what to say next. When Marienetta sat down again she gazed at her. The cat's eyes were glowing.

'Tell me,' Paula said slowly, 'did he actually confess to killing one of the people who have been murdered?'

'I've told you what he said. And I have a good memory for dialogue.'

'Then he didn't actually confess to having murdered someone specific?'

'Interpret what he said any way you like.' Marienetta shrugged. 'All this was hours after a lot of other conversation.

At one point he went on and on about how much he liked sailing, that he'd take me out on Lake Zürich. I said some other time. Well, what do you think of me as a detective, as a collaborator with you?'

'I think you've done very well.'

'And you will report all this to Tweed? He should know. It could be a breakthrough. Jack travels a lot. He's flown to Boston on the Gulfstream, courtesy of my uncle.'

'Oh, where is Roman? He seems to have disappeared.'

'No idea. He's a law unto himself. Very secretive about his movements.'

'And are you thinking of going somewhere?' Paula asked, looking at the pile of suitcases.

'Oh, those. I like to be ready to take off at any moment. I have to be when Roman is about.'

'I think, if you don't mind, I'm going to bed. I've had rather a busy day,' Paula said, standing up.

'You've left half your bloody drink.' There was an edge to her voice now. 'And I was going to hear how you've got on with your investigation.'

'In the morning, if you don't mind.' She was walking towards the door. 'And I've had enough to drink, but thank you for the hospitality.'

Marienetta stood up. Her cat's eyes seemed to be glowing like glow-worms. She marched forward as Paula took hold of the door handle.

'I give you what I've found out and you give me nothing.'

'In the morning. Good night, Marienetta . . .'

She walked quickly to her suite, anxious lest Marienetta should follow her. She didn't. She forced herself to take a quick shower. She still felt exhausted but it did not prevent her doing what she had to do.

*   *   *

284

At precisely 3 a.m. Luigi, dressed in his 'banker's' outfit, left his room. He checked the fire door to make sure it worked. Then, carrying his large executive case with the Glock inside it, he made his way along the deserted corridors to Paula's room.

28

In the morning Paula woke up from the first deep night's sleep she had enjoyed for a while. Slipping on her dressing gown over her pyjamas, she stared at the door. Prior to getting into bed she had taken two precautions.

First she had tilted the rear of a hard-backed chair, tucked it under the handle. Second she had taken out of her suitcase the thick rubber wedge she always carried, had jammed the thin end under the door, pushing it in tight.

The door was now open two inches. The tilted chair's back was bent but it had held. What had really saved her was the wedge. Whoever had tried to force their way into her room had pushed hard. The harder he had pushed the tighter the wedge had jammed under the door.

Fetching her Browning from under her pillow, she approached the door, peered through the gap, listened. She removed the chair carefully then threw her weight against the door. It was released from the wedge and slammed shut. She heaved a sigh of relief.

After taking a shower, she dressed quickly in a woollen jumper, woollen skirt and a comfortable pair of shoes. Looping her bag over her shoulder, the Browning concealed in its pocket, she walked to Tweed's suite. Company had arrived just before her.

When Tweed had opened the door he was confronted with Nathan Morgan, wearing a bearskin coat and a fur hat. These clothes made him look fatter and ridiculous.

Tweed ushered him inside. He did not suggest that Nathan sat down.

'To what do I owe this pleasure?' he asked with a wry smile.

That was the moment when Paula tapped on the door and Tweed let her in. She glanced at Nathan, then settled herself in an armchair. Tweed repeated his earlier words.

'This mission,' Nathan said in his most pompous manner, 'is secret.' He glanced at Paula. 'We have to be alone.'

'I thought by now you'd have realized Miss Grey is my personal assistant, who has worked closely with me for years. And she is on the verge of establishing the identity of the brutal mass-murderer who travels from continent to continent.'

Am I? Paula thought to herself.

'What!' Nathan exploded.

'I don't want to keep repeating everything I say,' Tweed replied at his most suave.

'It is bitterly cold here,' Nathan said. 'Worse than it is back home.'

His slab face was beginning to perspire. He would dearly have loved to take off his heavy coat but so far no one had offered to take it. He breathed heavily and began again.

'I have just come straight from the airport. My mission is to escort you back to Britain at once.' He produced from inside his coat an envelope which he handed to Tweed. After reading the typed sheet inside Tweed casually dropped it on the table but it missed and floated onto the floor.

'That is my authorization,' Nathan continued assertively.

There was a knock on the door, then an urgent rapping. As Tweed opened the door Beck hurried into the suite. He glanced at Nathan, his expression still grim.

'Let me introduce you,' Tweed continued in the same amiable manner. 'This is Nathan Morgan, who is . . .'

'Director of Special Branch,' Nathan emphasized.

'Temporary Director of Special Branch. It is a trial appointment. He says he has come here to escort me back to Britain. Oh, this is Arthur Beck, Chief of Federal Police.'

'Just the man I need,' Nathan said eagerly. He held out his ugly hand but Beck ignored it. 'You can help me with my mission,' Nathan went on quickly, 'by providing an escort while I accompany Tweed to the airport to catch the next plane back to Britain.'

'The only problem,' Tweed remarked, 'is that I have no intention of returning home with this gentleman.' He looked at Nathan. 'I can see I have to explain to you the structure of our security services. The SIS comes under the direct control of the PM. The Special Branch answers to the police commissioner. On the floor,' he went on, turning to Beck, 'is a silly letter from the Home Secretary which Nathan alleges is his authorization. It is not worth the paper it is typed on.'

'I protest!' Nathan was now sweating profusely. The suite was many degrees above the world outside due to the central heating. 'Mr Beck, I demand your cooperation in this matter.'

'You don't seem to hold a lot of authorization in Britain,' Beck told him bleakly. 'In Switzerland you hold none whatsoever. If Mr Tweed agrees I suggest you go home by yourself.'

'This is outrageous!'

'Your coming here is certainly that,' Tweed remarked mildly.

Nathan, gloves tucked under his arm, had produced a handkerchief. He used it to wipe his forehead and face. Before he had completed the exercise the handkerchief was sodden. Paula had stood up, poured a glass of water, which she handed to him.

'Drink this before you leave. Or you'll be dehydrated.'

'Thank you,' Nathan managed to splutter.

Paula went to the door and opened it for him. Nathan stared round, now bewildered. He had drunk the whole glass. It was probably the heat which decided him. He walked to the open door, turned just before he left, glaring at Tweed.

'You may rest assured I shall compile a full report on this incident.'

'Do that,' Tweed agreed.

Paula closed and locked the door when their guest had departed. Tweed relieved Beck of his overcoat and the police chief sat in an armchair. He accepted a glass of water from Paula, drank it, then ran his long fingers round the glass.

'I rushed over here to see you, Tweed, because a problem cropped up concerning your presence in Switzerland. Don't worry.' He raised a finger. 'I have sorted it out. Just possibly that stupid man who has left could be a part of it, although I doubt it. I had a long phone call from the Minister in Berne suggesting you kept a lower profile in your investigation into the murders.'

'Excuse me,' said Paula, 'but how would he know Tweed was here in Zürich?'

'I'll come to that. I let him maunder on, then I exploded. I said Tweed was our best hope of solving the murders because it was international – starting in Maine, where you had visited. The next murder took place in Britain – and you had investigated that. Now we have two more here in Switzerland and autopsies strongly suggest the same murderer is responsible. Then I let fly. I asked him how many tourists would come this year if an international killer was on the loose, beheading his victims. Or didn't he value the money the tourist industry brought in to the country? He backed down quickly when I again said that in my opinion you were our best hope of solving the case. He ended up by wishing you luck!'

'You've had a tough but successful day already,' Tweed told him.

'Now,' Beck continued, 'Paula asked how he knew you were in Zürich. The answer is Roman Arbogast. He has visited Berne.'

'So that's where he went missing,' Paula commented.

'Roman has just returned here. He, also, while there, asked the Minister to cool off your investigation. Why, I cannot imagine.'

'I can,' said Paula. 'Don't press me at the moment.'

'Again,' Beck explained, 'he backed off after I exploded, saying the same reasons applied which I had given.'

'Power,' said Tweed emphatically. 'That is the driving force behind this whole case. Power – emanating from Washington.'

'That's rather frightening,' Beck replied. 'It has to be something very big.'

There was silence in the suite for a short time. Everyone was contemplating what had just been said. Paula broke the quiet by telling them what had happened to her bedroom door during the night. Tweed and Beck listened to her with serious expressions until she had finished. She added one thing.

'It convinces me I know something I shouldn't know. Wish to Heaven I could recall what it was . . .'

Tweed then explained to Beck how during some conversation with someone she couldn't recall, a significant remark had been made. Nor could she recall what had been said.

'I know what you mean,' Beck said to Paula. 'I once had a serious case which hinged on what someone had said to me. And for a long time I couldn't remember what it was. When I did I knew who the criminal was.'

'I've asked Newman to book us first-class tickets to

Lugano,' Tweed told Beck, 'today.' He told Beck that the Arbogasts were going there – and how Paula had found this out by accident. 'Does Lugano mean anything to you?'

'Only that Roman Arbogast has another of his headquarters there. It's close to our border with Italy. Roman makes a lot of money exporting explosives. It worries us. This is really why he went to see the Minister with documents detailing the latest cargo. It is already on its way south by freight train.'

'Explosives? That department is handled by Sophie,' Paula remarked. 'Why the worry?'

'Because we don't know their ultimate destination. They travel by freight train across the border – after examination – to Genoa. They are transferred at that port aboard a ship. We have quietly checked the route. The consignment is supposed to be oxygen cylinders. The ship this time is the *Saturn*, registered in Liberia. Roman deals with a very respectable Italian middleman. The trail ends there.'

'So what is the worry?' Paula repeated.

'Supposing some of those cylinders contain armaments?'

'ACTIL,' Paula said. '"A" is for armaments.'

'Exactly. And if this is the case what is their destination? Once aboard the *Saturn* they could be taken anywhere. Who at ACTIL *controls* explosives, any type of armaments?'

'Sophie,' Paula almost whispered.

29

'Mannix,' said Tweed. 'A Mr Mannix is staying at this hotel.'

'What!' Paula exclaimed. 'There was a phantom Mannix at the hotel in Montreux. We checked his room. Found nothing.'

'I mention it while you are with us,' Tweed said to Beck. 'I thought maybe you could persuade the manager to let us take a look inside his room.'

'I can do that.' Beck jumped agilely to his feet. 'Now would be best . . .'

Five minutes later, with Beck's authority and mention of his investigation into the murder near the hotel, the assistant manager, after knocking on the door, opened it with his master key. The room was large, overlooking the entrance to the hotel. The manager summoned a maid who reported the bed had not been slept in.

Paula began opening wardrobes. It was a repetition of what she had seen in Montreux. A long black overcoat hung from a hanger. Next to it was a black suit which Beck estimated was for a man six feet or so tall.

In the bathroom history repeated itself again. There was an expensive shaving brush on a shelf over the basins, unused, plus a stick of shaving soap and a razor, which looked brand new. Hotel soap was still inside a paper wrapper. A hairbrush, also brand new, and without a trace of hairs.

She searched everywhere but there was no sign of a hat or any gloves. There was an atmosphere in the room she detected, an atmosphere suggesting no one had lived here. It was creepy. Putting on a pair of latex gloves she opened a large black suitcase. It was empty.

'Mr Mannix booked the room for a week two days ago,' the manager told them. 'He paid in advance. With cash.'

'Any description?' Beck asked.

'Apparently he arrived with several other guests. So the man on duty who booked him in is vague about a description. He thinks he remembers a tall man in a black overcoat, wearing a large brimmed hat which, pulled down, concealed most of his face. The porter who brought up his bag is even vaguer. Said the guest never spoke a word. Merely handed him a fifty-franc note, didn't answer when the porter asked if that would be all.'

'A phantom,' said Paula. 'Like Montreux. What is going on?'

'If he comes back call me at once,' said Beck, handing the manager a card. 'If you could leave us for a moment, we'll be sure to close the door . . .'

When they were alone Beck said, 'I have something else to tell you. It might shock you. In a pocket of Elena Brucan's coat we found a large packet of cocaine. Could she have been a courier?'

'No,' replied Tweed emphatically. 'And don't bother to check this room for fingerprints. There won't be any. Paula used the word phantom. Shrewdly. It is very clever. All this is distraction – to divert us from our investigation. Mr Mannix doesn't exist – except he is the killer. Same with that packet of cocaine. Another move to divert us, to send us on a wild-goose chase. To make us think of a drug-runner. We are up against a truly diabolical mind.'

*   *   *

They accompanied Beck downstairs to see him off. Paula was ahead of them and saw Sophie sitting in a chair in the lobby, surrounded by suitcases. She jumped up and hugged Paula.

'We're off to Lugano later in the morning. I like to have everything ready in real good time. We'll be staying at the Splendide Royal. It's another lovely hotel, I gather, and overlooks Lake Lugano surrounded with super mountains. Why don't you come with us? We're catching the 13.07 express from the Hauptbahnhof. You'll have time to pack. For a change my father is in a jolly mood. Do come! Then I'll have someone to talk to.'

Sophie was in full flood, the words tumbling over each other. Paula stared straight at her. The eyes seemed normal and full of life. Which was the real Sophie? The schoolgirl who giggled or the mature adult who ran two key divisions at ACTIL?

'Let me think about it,' Paula replied with a smile. 'We may have business to attend to in Zürich.'

'Oh! I like Zürich. But I've seen it now. I want somewhere new. They say the Ticino – that's the Italian-speaking canton of Switzerland – is all palm trees and fun and different food. I can't wait to get there. Marienetta took it all in her stride even though she's never been there before. I'm so excited. The train is a marvel, they say. Whizzes along. You will come, won't you?'

'If I can, yes.'

She turned to say goodbye to Beck and realized he had gone. Tweed was talking quietly to Newman, who was wearing a coat as though about to go out. Which he did as Paula was walking over to them.

'I wanted to say goodbye to Beck, but I think I've missed him,' she said.

'You have,' Tweed told her. 'But he sends you his love and thinks you're a natural detective. Now, let's go upstairs.'

At that moment Black Jack appeared, flashily dressed in a yellow suit with a purple tie and white hand-made shoes. He was carrying two very large cases, which he parked with Sophie's.

'My dear Paula,' he greeted her with an inviting smile. 'It seems years since we met. Let's have a drink in the lounge. I won't take no for an answer.'

'Just one as I'm short of time.'

As they walked into the lounge Paula turned to wave at Sophie. She had a shock. Sophie had completely changed. Her face was like a thundercloud, distorted almost beyond recognition. She tossed her head and looked away. Her moods seemed to change more rapidly than the weather. What had enraged her now? Could it be seeing Black Jack walking off with her?

As she sat down with Black Jack at a table in a corner her mind was revolving. The cocaine packet in poor Elena's pocket. The confrontation with Nathan Morgan. Had he really left Zürich? The Mannix phantom. Was he really a phantom? In the room she had noticed – but had had no time to point out – a large rug by the bed which was all ruffled. Almost as though someone had slept on it.

In his banker's outfit, complete with gold-rimmed glasses, Luigi had emerged from the lounge in time to hear Sophie giving the details about their trip to Lugano, including the details of the train they would be travelling on.

He had slipped past behind Paula and out into the court-yard beyond. In his right hand he carried the executive case with the pistol concealed among clothes. In the middle of the night he had experienced great frustration.

Opening the lock on Paula's door had been no problem for a man of his experience. When he slowly pushed it open he had a shock. It wouldn't shift. Being careful to keep quiet he had persisted, pushing at it fraction by fraction.

He had soon realized it was blocked. He had used all his considerable strength to try and overcome what was holding it. It had come to a point when he realized it was jammed tight. Cursing to himself, he had returned to his room. Luckily he had booked – and paid – for one week.

He was accustomed to the unexpected, to setbacks. He had stayed on in the hotel. Now all he had to do was to hire a car, park it near the entrance. Then he decided it would be wise to order a first-class ticket aboard the 13.07 leaving for Lugano. He called the Hauptbahnhof from his room, ordered the ticket, said they should have it ready and he'd pay for it in cash before the express departed. His target had sounded as though it was not certain she would be aboard. He'd wait in the car which, if all went well, he could leave at the station and later phone the company to tell them where they could pick it up.

Tweed was alone in his suite when the phone rang. It was Beck calling him. The normally calm police chief sounded tense.

'I want you to leave the hotel, go out and find a phone box, then call me back. OK?'

'I'm leaving now . . .'

Tweed was curious as he threw on his coat and went down to the lobby. This had to be a very serious development. Beck did not trust talking to him on a line which went through the hotel's switchboard. He was walking briskly out of the exit when, appearing from nowhere, Harry Butler joined him.

'Don't mind if I keep you company?' Harry suggested.

'Of course not. But why?'

'We've all heard about how someone tried to break into Paula's room in the middle of the night. Probably

297

the second attempt to kill her. Don't forget I was there when someone fired a shot at her in the Altstadt. You could equally be at risk.'

'I appreciate your concern. I'm just going to make a call from a phone booth. A personal call.'

'So I'll stay outside while you make it.'

'Yesterday evening Marler followed a car driven by Ed Danvers with Russell Straub as his passenger beside him. They parked outside Zürich, talked for a while. I'm curious because the meeting was obviously pretty secret. I shouldn't be long.'

The sun was a brilliant glare but the cold was intense. As he entered the booth Tweed glanced back. Ripples of water on Lake Zürich at the end of the street glittered like mercury. It looked so cheerful but the few pedestrians about were muffled up and walked huddled up. He called Beck's number, using coins he'd obtained from the concierge.

'It's me,' he said when the police chief answered.

'You haven't wasted much time, thank Heaven. I had bad news. The Minister has called me again from Berne. He's anxious you leave Zürich today. I argued but he was stubborn.'

'Any idea what has changed his mind? Yesterday you indicated you'd quietened him down.'

'Russell Straub, the Vice-President, has been in touch with him since. He's complained you're harassing him, ruining his visit. The people in Berne want to keep in America's good books – for trade reasons. I gather Straub blew his top, threatened to get in touch with Washington. I had to be forceful to extract this information.'

'Thanks for the warning.'

'I hope you're off to Lugano today. Then if the Minister calls me again I can say you've vanished from Zürich, maybe left the country.'

'We're all going if the Arbogasts go on that express. I

298

think they will. I saw Sophie sitting in the lobby with a pile of luggage. As I told you, Newman has booked seats for us.'

'Did he order them from the concierge?'

'No. I thought we'd just disappear. Newman went to a travel agent to get the tickets.'

'Good. I'm relieved.'

'Why?'

'The situation is getting so white-hot the Minister might send some of his officers to Zürich to see if you're still there.'

'Doesn't sound like Switzerland.'

'Well.' Beck sighed. 'I've never known Berne react in this way before. It's damnable, but this time I may not be able to hold them off. Oh, which hotel are you staying at?'

'Same one as the Arbogasts, although they don't know this yet. The Splendide Royal.'

'Thank you. I may fly down there myself in a chopper. Lugano has an airport. Watch your back . . .'

Entering the hotel again, Tweed saw Paula at a table in the lounge. She was chatting to Black Jack Diamond. She never stops gathering information, Tweed thought. She's remarkable.

'My dear Tweed, how good to see you again,' an American voice greeted him.

Looking to his left Tweed saw Russell Straub, smiling from ear to ear. His campaign smile when he was grabbing for votes. Tweed stopped and Harry stood back a short distance.

'You look pleased,' Tweed replied. 'As though you've just scored a victory.'

'Oh, when I'm after something sooner or later I always end up victorious. Stamina, determination, will-power.'

'With the emphasis on power,' Tweed shot back, his expression: blank.

'That does come into it,' Straub replied, completely unfazed. 'But the key to success in politics is personality.'

'And a completely unblemished past.'

Straub's whole attitude changed. His smile was wiped away, he looked as though he could kill someone, his eyes dark as night, his mouth a vicious twist. He recovered quickly, anxious to cover up what his loss of control had revealed.

'I could not agree more.' He lowered his voice after glancing round. 'They tell me you are the cleverest detective in the whole of Europe.'

'They, whoever they are, exaggerate. Please excuse me. I have a day's work waiting for me . . .'

'I wouldn't trust that skunk to take a child across a road,' Harry commented when they were inside the lift. 'Seen him on TV. Never stops smirking.'

'What you heard, Harry,' Tweed said, 'was the very ultimate in treachery.'

Seated at the table in the lounge Paula was getting sick of listening to Black Jack. Clad in a new polo outfit he was so pleased with himself. So far she had heard nothing worth reporting. She decided it was time to needle him.

'I gather you are a fervent advocate of the death penalty.'

Up to this point he had been very relaxed, lolling back in his chair, legs crossed as he regaled her with his exploits. She might have touched him with the burning end of a cigarette. He jerked upright, uncrossed his legs, the self-satisfied smile vanished. His face became hard, his eyes flashed with rage.

'I suppose you've been talking to Marienetta. That bitch

just loves sticking the knife in. Under her undoubted glamour she's a fiend.'

'Strong language, Jack. And one of our people happened to be in the same bar when you two were talking last night.'

'Oh.' He patted her on the knee, which she did not enjoy. 'My outburst was completely unjustified, then. I had a huge breakfast and get a touch of indigestion stabbing me now and again. The Scotch is quietening it down.'

'Better have another, then.' She was still sipping from the glass of Chardonnay she had ordered when they sat down.

'Think I will. Jolly good idea. Waiter!' He snapped his fingers. 'Over here. Another double Scotch.' He turned to Paula, who shook her head.

'It didn't shock me when I heard what you had said,' she assured him. 'There are some beastly people in this world. For example, the thing that has been decapitating people here in Europe. And in Maine.'

'You think they deserved it?' he asked quietly.

'No, I don't. I was referring to the inhuman thing which has committed these crimes. I wonder if we'll ever catch it?'

'Any ideas as to the thing's identity?' he asked casually.

'It has to be someone with easy and near invisible access to fly to America,' she said, staring at him.

'Lots of businessmen flit over there,' he said after a pause. 'Some fly there, do what they have to, then fly back the same day. What do you think?'

She sipped her drink as though considering what he had suggested. 'They wouldn't be very invisible, would they,' she replied eventually. 'And then there's the weapon used to carry out these brutal assaults. The pathologists say it's some kind of axe.'

'Do they.' He drank half the fresh glass the waiter had

301

served. 'Anything to declare, sir! Only a large axe.' He laughed but not his usual joyous burst.

'I'm being very serious,' she told him.

'Of course you are, my dear.' Again her knee was patted. 'I did realize that. I was just trying to lighten the atmosphere. My mistake.'

'Do you often make them?'

'Make what?' he asked.

'Mistakes.'

'So far . . .' He was running his fingers round his glass. 'I've avoided making any major mistakes. After all, I did manage to buy out Templeton's, my gambling place in Mayfair. That really was a coup.'

'Which must provide you with an adequate income.'

'Adequate!' He gave a great burst of laughter. 'I suppose you could use that word. Amazing the way so-called intelligent men throw away a fortune in one evening. We have to be careful they can afford to lose such sums.'

'How you do you ensure that?'

'I have a very good grapevine. We know who is who, how much they can afford to lose. Rather like your outfit, the SIS, I imagine. You must have sources.'

'I must go. I've a phone call to make. And I want a word with Marienetta. Haven't seen her this morning.'

'Not surprising. She caught an early train.'

'Really. Where is she gallivanting off to now?'

'You'd better ask her. And you haven't answered my question. You must have sources?'

'I thought that was a statement. We all know people who love gossiping.'

'You still haven't answered my question. And are you going anywhere with that long-drawn out investigation?'

'Don't suppose for a moment she is,' a sneaky voice remarked. Sam Snyder had crept up on them. Dressed in a military-style trench coat, the reporter stared at Black Jack with a cynical smile as he rattled on. 'Extracting

302

information from Paula Grey is like getting the proverbial ship out of the proverbial bottle. And where are you all off to? I passed the delightful Sophie in the lobby, surrounded with enough suitcases for a trip to Mauritius.'

'Which is where we're going,' Black Jack answered, his face ugly as he stared up at Snyder. 'Mauritius.'

'So you're off too. Interesting. Maybe the whole Arbogast clan is on the move.'

'Oh, shove-off, Snoop,' Black Jack snarled, furious with himself for his slip in revealing he was going too.

'My job. To snoop,' the reporter rapped back with a grin.

Maybe it was the grin, more likely his slip of the tongue, but Black Jack erupted. Jumping to his feet, he slammed his fist into Snyder's jaw. At least, that was his intention. Snyder realized what was coming, agilely leapt back so the heaving fist hit air, throwing Black Jack off balance.

'While you two continue your ballet dance I'm off,' Paula informed them and made for the lift. She had more news now to report to Tweed, some of it important.

30

Entering Tweed's suite, Paula was surprised to find the whole team assembled, Marler leaning against a wall, armchairs arranged in a large semicircle. Seated in them were Newman, Butler and Nield, so she occupied an empty one next to Newman. Tweed stood well back, standing with his hands gripping the top of a hard-backed chair, his expression very serious.

'You've arrived just in time,' Tweed told her. 'Anything to say?'

'I've found out that Black Jack is also going to Lugano. And now Sam Snyder knows this . . .'

She tersely reported her experience in the lounge. Newman grinned when she described the abortive fight.

'Pity Black Jack didn't break Snyder's jaw. But that chap has a habit of turning up when he can pick up information.'

'Now,' Tweed began, his voice harsh, compelling, 'I want you all to know the situation, which is bad. People with great power in London and Washington are going all out to stop our investigation into the murders. We leave here to board the express for Lugano only when I've seen the Arbogasts leave. And, to add to the pressure, Beck phoned me a few minutes ago to tell me a detachment of no less than four FBI agents has just flown in to Zürich. Probably in the hope of following us, maybe attempting intimidation.'

'Or something worse,' Newman suggested.

'Unlikely, but not impossible,' Tweed agreed. 'This whole business started at the asylum in Pinedale, Maine. The key is probably the mysterious tall figure in black who left the place in a limo – and then returned. Identity completely unknown.'

'Which is where the murders started,' Paula interjected.

'Precisely,' Tweed agreed. 'And several people have recently asked how our investigation is proceeding, whether we have uncovered any evidence. Someone is nervous, which may increase the danger. I am thinking of one person in particular who, from now on, must be discreetly but efficiently guarded night and day. I refer to Paula,' he said, looking at her.

'I can't operate like that,' she protested. 'Not with loads of guards by my side everywhere.'

'I did say discreetly,' Tweed reminded her.

'And,' Nield interjected, 'you didn't see me when I followed you to the Altstadt and later when you went to visit Roman and he wasn't there.'

'I am grateful to you,' she emphasized.

'What I'm driving home,' Tweed continued in the same compelling manner, 'is that Paula is the next target. Someone tried to break into her room while she was asleep. I suspect that the attacker in both cases was a hired hitman. He's failed twice, so—'

'You think,' Paula interjected again, 'that the killer who beheaded people will come after me, whoever it may be.'

'I do,' Tweed agreed. 'And it has a terrible track record of success. So, Paula, you will obey my orders.' He paused. 'The situation is the worst we have ever faced, certainly the most dangerous. All the pressure from London and Washington, which is intensifying almost by the hour. Even the hitherto invincible Beck has admitted he may have trouble holding the dam before it bursts. He is relieved we should be leaving for Lugano.'

'Never known him to be like that before,' commented Marler.

'Which,' Tweed continued, 'is an indicator of the degree of pressure being exerted. Incidentally, I'm convinced that both Abraham Seale and Elena Brucan sensed who the killer is, maybe asked the wrong question, which betrayed what they knew.'

'So the killer is very clever, diabolically so,' Newman remarked.

'I'm intrigued by the execution block it uses,' Paula said. 'It must be very heavy, very difficult to transport from place to place. Yet I found the same imprint of the same shape and size in the grass at Pinedale, in the ground near Abbey Grange, Roman's mansion at Bray, and also on the promenade by the Sihl, not ten minutes' walk from here. Then there is the axe.'

Tweed suddenly walked over to the window. For a short time he looked down, then returned to his original position.

'I have just seen Roman Arbogast and Sophie getting into a limousine. Tons of luggage is being loaded. So now we know. They are leaving for Lugano.'

'Time we moved,' Paula said, starting to get up, but Tweed waved her back into her seat.

'I have one final deadly thing to say,' he said. 'The real reason why I am so worried. You should all know what we are dealing with. The true nature of it.'

'What is that?' Marler asked.

'Insanity.'

31

Like most Swiss trains, the 13.07 express, the Cisalpino, glided out of Zürich station exactly at the hour and the minute shown in the timetable. A long streamlined express, shaped like a huge bullet, it rapidly picked up speed and soon Zürich was far behind.

The weather was dark, almost doomladen, the sky smothered in a pall of low black clouds. Aboard, in a coach near the front, seats were occupied by the Arbogast family. Roman sat in a front seat by himself, clutching a leather case on the seat by his side. The seat opposite also had only one passenger. Broden. Further back sat Sophie, a long stretch of luggage rack above her stacked with her cases. On the seat opposite her sat Black Jack who had made several futile attempts to engage her in a conversation across the aisle. Sophie had ignored him, her expression sullen as she gazed out of the window.

In a middle first-class coach separated into individual compartments Paula sat facing Tweed, the corridor to her right. Paula was very quiet, also staring out of the window. *Insanity.* The word spoken by Tweed in his suite had shaken her. Through her mind flitted pictures of all the people involved. How did you spot insanity? She remembered Seale had made some remark about such people appearing normal most of the time. She was deeply troubled.

Tweed was studying the timetable which showed the few places the express stopped at before, eventually, they arrived in Lugano.

'We stop only at Zug, which is coming up soon,' he told her. 'After that a nowhere place, but quite large, called Arth-Goldau. Then we roar through Göschenen at the entrance to the famous Gotthard tunnel. Takes us ten minutes to travel through it under the Bernese Oberland range. Place called Airolo is just beyond the exit, which we don't stop at. From there we enter a different world and it's straight through to Lugano.'

'How long does that take?' Paula asked.

'Quite a while before we get to Lugano.'

Newman opened the door, entered from the corridor, closed the door and sat down next to Paula. He grinned at Tweed.

'A worthwhile journey. I've checked the whole train. The Arbogasts are near the front. Roman, Sophie – and Black Jack, who can't seem to leave them alone. I wonder why.'

'What about Marienetta?' Tweed enquired.

'Oh!' said Paula. 'I completely forgot to tell you. Marienetta caught an early train. By herself, I gather.' She smiled. 'My guess is she didn't want to travel with Sophie. They've never got on well, I heard.'

'Surprise,' Newman went on. 'At the very rear of the train there's someone in a compartment with the corridor blinds drawn down. Guess who? Russell Straub, the Vice-President. Ed Danvers was standing outside so I joked with him. "Still looking after the next President of the United States, are we?" He said his Lordship – my words – didn't want to be disturbed.'

'So why is he following the Arbogasts?' Tweed mused.

'Because I'm sure we'll find his destination is Lugano.'

'And probably with a suite at the Splendide Royal,' Paula said grimly.

'I also,' Newman continued, 'collected tickets for lunch for us in the dining car. Which is thataway.'

'You don't seem to have missed anything,' Tweed commented.

In saying this he could not have been more wrong.

From the Baur au Lac, Luigi had followed Tweed's team as it travelled in two taxis to the station. Parking his hired car he followed them across the spacious concourse, saw them turn on to a platform. The board above gave him the express's destinations. *Lugano, Milano*.

He rushed to the ticket office, bought a first-class return ticket to Milan, in case they travelled all the way. Carrying the case which contained the loaded Glock, he boarded the express at the rear, only three minutes before departure.

A well-built youngish man stood outside a compartment with all the blinds closed. When he spoke as Luigi approached him it was obvious he was American.

'This compartment is reserved,' he said aggressively.

'I am proceeding further up,' Luigi told him as the American squeezed against the shielded windows to let him past.

He went on into the next coach. Now he was walking slowly, glancing into each compartment. He chose one where inside two *grande dame* type of ladies sat opposite each other, talking. He had noticed their luggage on the rack had Heathrow labels. English probably, and he was right.

'Excuse me,' he said politely, 'I hope you don't mind my sitting here.' He was careful to choose a corner seat as far away from them as possible. 'The train is rather crowded.'

'Of course not.' The stately white-haired lady he had spoken to had checked his smart clothes, his good manners. 'We are going all the way to Lugano.'

'My own destination.'

311

He sat down, opened his case carefully, took out the papers he'd pretended to be checking in the lounge at the Baur au Lac. However, in a few minutes he was engaged in a warm conversation with them, opening by explaining he was a bank director, which he knew would reassure them.

So when, later, Newman glanced into this compartment he saw a typical Swiss banker type with gold-rimmed spectacles in animated conversation with two ladies. He walked on towards the rear of the express.

Newman, settled in the seat next to Paula, looked happy with what he had achieved, the information he had passed on. The express had already stopped at Zug for two minutes, was now hurtling south. Paula glanced at Newman, saw his expression.

'You look smug, Bob.'

'I have a final bit of news to report. You're never going to believe this.'

'Try us,' Tweed snapped.

'There's one more person aboard. In a compartment by himself. Located about halfway between us and the rear of the train. Sam Snyder.'

'We could do without him,' Paula commented.

'Did he see you?' Tweed wanted to know.

'He did. He looked up as I glanced in. He turned his head away, went on scribbling notes in the book on his lap.'

'Where are Butler and Nield?' Tweed asked.

'Strategically situated. Harry is in the corridor, gazing out of the window, near the rear. Pete is doing the same thing, standing near the front of the train. I spoke with both. At intervals they'll be strolling along the complete length of the train. When they glance in here they won't acknowledge us.'

'Then we've done everything we can,' Tweed decided. 'It's in the hands of fate now.'

'You sound as though you're expecting an attack,' Paula replied.

'Maybe. And isn't it time we went to the dining car so we can pick out seats.'

The dining car was almost empty. The Arbogasts were sitting at the far end, so Tweed chose a table as soon as they entered. Roman, who was facing them with Sophie by his side, was drinking wine. He saw them over the rim of his glass, gave no indication he had ever known them. Sophie stared, her expression sullen, looked away. Opposite her sat Black Jack, who had caught on that she had seen someone. He swivelled in his chair, smiled broadly, gave them a cheerful wave. Paula responded.

'Someone at least pretends to like us,' she said.

'Roman,' Tweed began, 'is not happy with our presence. I do wonder why. He's shrewd and my guess is he's decided we also are heading for Lugano.'

'He'll have a fit when he finds out we're staying at the same hotel,' she said with satisfaction. 'Why is he so worried? Is he trying to hide something?'

'A number of people are trying to hide something,' Tweed told her. 'Ah, here is our waiter . . .'

At Tweed's suggestion they ordered a light lunch they could eat quickly. He was anxious to return to their compartment before they entered the Gotthard tunnel. They had stopped for two minutes at Arth-Goldau, a large town. Newman had left them briefly to peer out of the open automatic door near the dining car entrance. He came back to report no one had left the express, no one had boarded it.

Their meal, which was excellent, was served quickly. They wasted no time eating it and drank water, refusing

313

wine. As she ate, Paula kept looking out of the window. The beautiful valleys of Switzerland, way below them, flashed past. She liked the sturdy Swiss houses with sloping roofs and first-floor balconies decorated with window boxes. They had the look of homes of wood and stone which had stood there for generations. The weather had cleared. Cobalt-blue skies, the sun reflecting off a large lake on the opposite side stretching away into the distance where a mountain peak topped with snow speared high upwards.

'That's Lake Luzern,' Tweed told her, 'and I think that superb peak at the far end is Pilatus.'

'It's all so peaceful, so wonderfully scenic,' she said.

Tweed had paid the bill and they were leaving the dining car when Black Jack ran down the aisle after them. They were walking back along the corridor, Tweed in the lead with Paula behind him and Newman bringing up the rear, when Black Jack caught up with them. He called out to Paula over Newman's shoulder.

'Great to see you again, Paula. What a coincidence that you're on the same train. We're staying in Lugano at the Hotel Splendide Royal, which I can recommend. It really would be marvellous if your destination is Lugano!' His voice was bubbling with enthusiasm.

'Time will tell,' Paula called back.

'Well, I do hope I'm right. Safe journey . . .'

On that note he returned to the dining car, where the Arbogasts were still eating. Newman snorted as they reached their compartment.

'I suppose he was sent to spy out the land by Roman. To find out where we're going.'

'I don't think so,' Paula replied. 'Roman wouldn't want to show he minded. In any case, Black Jack is not the type to act as messenger boy.'

They had just resettled in the same seats when Pete Nield passed their compartment, walking slowly along the

314

corridor. He glanced in, gave no sign that he knew them as he went on towards the dining car.

'We'll soon flash past the small station of Göschenen, then we enter the Gotthard tunnel,' Tweed remarked. 'If you're on a stopper and get off at Göschenen you can cross the line to a tiny rack-and-pinion train which ascends up through the rock to Andermatt, a skiing centre.'

Paula was only half-listening. She had her face pressed to the window, staring up. The immense vertical rock walls of the Bernese Oberland range were so close she felt she could reach out and touch them. Soon she couldn't see the snow-crested summits – they were so far above they were out of sight.

'Göschenen's coming up,' Tweed warned.

They flashed past the tiny station so fast she hardly saw it and then they plunged inside the Gotthard tunnel.

Feeble lights had been switched on but Paula was very aware of the black tunnel outside. Her sensitive imagination began working overtime and she was nervous – she hated tunnels. She was thinking of what was above them: the immense massif of the highest mountain range in Europe. She imagined the incredible pressure of billions of tons of rock settling on top of the tunnel. She did her best to conceal her nervousness, asked the question casually.

'How long does it take to get through the tunnel?'

'Only ten minutes,' Tweed assured her. 'We shall be through it in what seems like a flash.' He had observed her clenched hands, kept talking. 'When we emerge from the far end in no time we pass through the little town of Airolo and enter a different world.'

In no time? To Paula they seemed trapped inside the tunnel forever. Had there ever been an accident? she wondered, but was careful not to ask. Someone came along the corridor from the rear end, paused outside their compartment, slid the door open. A slim man with black hair, wearing a black suit, a crisp white shirt, a dark tie. He wore gold-rimmed spectacles and was carrying a large executive case. A typical Swiss banker, Newman thought.

'Excuse me,' the intruder said, 'I look for dining car.'

'That way.' Newman indicated forward with his thumb.

'My most grateful thanks.'

The banker type carefully slid the door closed and walked in the direction Newman had indicated. Luigi now knew that when the time came the door opened easily. Paula frowned. She was aware that during this brief incident Tweed had moved. He had his right hand tucked inside his jacket and kept it there.

'I think I've seen that man somewhere before,' she said.

'A dozen times his replica,' Newman said dismissively. 'At eight in the morning. Bankers hustling to their offices.'

She stared across at Tweed. He still had his right hand tucked inside his jacket. She managed a smile as she teased him.

'Sitting like that you look just like Napoleon.'

'To do that,' he replied, 'I'd have to have one of those funny hats worn sideways.'

She looked out again at the blackness of the tunnel wall flashing past. When on earth were they going to emerge from this tomblike situation? She wished she'd checked her watch when Tweed had said ten minutes. Paula never suffered from vertigo but claustrophobia was her great weakness, her fear. This is more like ten hours, she thought.

Then they were out in the open. The express had lost speed as it began an endless descent. No sunlight. The sky a sea of clouds. Not at all what she had expected. Where were the palm trees, the cypresses, the exotic plants with their brilliant hues? Not here.

'We'll soon pass the little town of Airolo,' Tweed told her.

Since the express had slowed down to negotiate the steep descent she was able to see everything more clearly. She felt she was looking out on a desert. Rocky barren ground sloped down from the previous heights of the Bernese Oberland. It was a landscape without people, without habitation. Then the express passed through Airolo, a town of narrow streets and alleys between stone and wooden buildings. No sign of life. Then Paula stared fixedly.

Half a mile or so behind the town where the ground sloped reared two tall large watch-towers with a wall between linking them. A pale grey mist was creeping down from the heights. She felt uneasy as she continued to gaze at the towers, which had a menacing feel. A wide track led from the town up towards them. A much narrower track climbed south, away from the towers, then vanished behind a crag. It seemed to begin at the end of one of the alleys. She still gazed, transfixed, at the two tall towers. The mist had crept below them but seemed reluctant to envelop them as though they might vaporize it. Why did the towers so disturb her?

'Behind Airolo,' Tweed said, 'ages ago they mined a special ore or rock. They had underground railways to transport the ore. When the ore ran out they sealed off the railways.'

The express continued its descent and she closed her eyes and rested her head on the seat. Even with her eyes closed she could still see the outlines of the twin towers. Tweed said something she didn't catch. He patted her knee with his hand.

'Feeling all right?'

'Yes.' She opened her eyes, gave him a warm smile. 'I think the tunnel made me feel sleepy,' she fibbed.

'Well, we *are* in a different world now. The Mediterranean. The Latin world as opposed to the Nordic we have visited

317

for a while. Here, in this unique canton, the furthest south in Switzerland, they speak Italian. No longer *gasthof*. Now it's *ristorante*. We are in the Ticino canton.'

'I expected more. It's so bleak, so rocky, so barren.'

'Wait until we're lower down. You'll see a transformation in Lugano. A semi-tropical paradise, although it will be out of season, so rather quiet.'

'I can't wait.'

She had just spoken when Newman's mobile buzzed. He answered briefly, then handed it to Tweed, who pressed it to his ear as Newman called across.

'It's Beck.'

'Hello, Tweed. I've landed by Sikorsky chopper up at Airolo. Couldn't call you earlier. This thing wouldn't have worked with the mountains in the way . . .'

'I don't trust security on these gadgets, gizmos, whatever. Let's communicate discreetly.'

'Couldn't agree more.' Beck was secretly proud of his command of colloquial English. 'Soon as this call is over I'm flying to Lugano, which has an airfield. I'll be there before you. I've arranged for a car to be waiting to drive me to Bellinzona and that's where I'll meet you.'

'Our compartment is very close to the exit nearest the front. In the coach three behind the dining car.'

'Got it. Take care.'

Tweed handed the mobile back to Newman. He didn't want any more to do with it. He told them what Beck had decided to do.

'Bellinzona?' said Paula, reaching for the timetable.

'It's the last and only stop before Lugano,' Tweed told her. 'About twenty minutes before Lugano itself.'

'Why is he bothering to drive to Bellinzona?' Paula wondered. 'He could have met us at Lugano.'

'My guess would be because he's worried about something. You should find Bellinzona interesting, even with a two-minute stop. It's encircled with castles.'

Paula rested her head and fell into a deep sleep. The tunnel had in fact exhausted her. She was woken by Tweed squeezing her knee. She woke up suddenly, stared round.

'Are we there?'

'We'll be calling at Bellinzona in ten minutes. I do want you to see it.'

She looked out of the window. Everything had changed now they were at a much lower level. Fields stretched out on both sides, the soil ploughed up. Here and there she saw an evergreen. The express, now on the level, was moving fast again. Tweed had several times taken his right hand out from inside his jacket and rubbed his hand on his knee. He did this again, returned the hand inside his jacket.

'Is there something wrong with your hand?' she asked anxiously.

'No.' He smiled. 'I just rather like mimicking Napoleon,' he joked.

The train was slowing down. She peered out of the window the way they were going. Huge castles loomed everywhere, perched above the town. She had never seen anywhere with a more fortress-like atmosphere. She prepared to stand up.

'I'll go and see if I can spot Beck,' she suggested.

'Everyone will stay in exactly the position they occupy now.'

Tweed's tone was grim, commanding. Paula couldn't understand his sudden change of mood. He was sitting very upright, his gaze fixed on the door leading to the corridor. An atmosphere of extreme tension had pervaded the compartment. Paula didn't dare reach into her shoulder bag for her Browning. Tweed's order had forbidden any movement. It happened very suddenly.

The train had just stopped. Paula heard the automatic doors opening just down the corridor. The door to their compartment slid open about a foot. In the gap stood the banker type. He was holding the Glock aimed at Paula.

The mouth of the muzzle looked like a cannon. Two shots were fired. The man in the black suit sagged to the floor, half of his face gone. Blood and brains scattered over the corridor. Tweed replaced his Walther in its holster. Newman turned to Paula.

'Are you all right?'

'Better him than me. And here's Beck.'

32

They concealed themselves in the waiting room, keeping out of sight until the Arbogast party and then the Vice-President with Ed Danvers had gone. Beck opened the door half an hour later, spoke briskly.

'You can go to your hotel now. The Arbogast lot and the Vice-President have been picked up by limos. I can get a statement from you later, Tweed. Fortunately I was a witness, saw the hitman aiming his pistol into your compartment. Keep your automatic carefully for the moment. You were damned quick. But the serial killer is still out there somewhere. I'll call on you later.'

As they made their way to the two taxis Beck had waiting for them Tweed didn't think it necessary to explain he'd been holding on to the Walther for most of the journey. Ever since Luigi had opened their door in the tunnel asking the way to the dining car. Occasionally he had taken out his hand and spread it on his knee. To dry his hand and stretch his fingers.

Paula rode in the same taxi as Tweed, Marler and Newman. Butler and Nield travelled in the second taxi. She looked out of the window with interest to muffle the shock. This is more like it, she thought.

The sun shone out of a clear blue sky as the road descended and curved through Lugano. Between buildings she caught glimpses of a sparkling duck-egg-blue lake. On the opposite shore, not far away, majestic mountains climbed to their peaks. There were palm trees, cypresses and blood-red plants in window boxes. This *was* the Mediterranean.

Swinging round a curve at the bottom of the descent they were at lake level, driving along a road curving round Lake Lugano. Distant white triangles, very small, were yachts cruising slowly since there was no wind. The taxi swung off the lakeside road abruptly, up a steep drive. They had arrived at the luxurious Splendide Royal.

Paula was escorted by a porter carrying her bag in the lift to the first floor, shown into a vast room with a double bed. The porter took her to the far end of the room, slid back two large plate-glass windows. She stepped out onto a balcony and the panorama spread out before her. Below was the lake and now she saw there were two peaked mountains, each like a huge triangle with the apex the peak. The porter pointed at the gap between them.

'Italy there. Behind the mountains.'

'Thank you.'

She gave him a generous tip and felt glad to be alone when he had gone. She needed time to herself. She gazed at the spectacular view, then jerked herself into action. After unlocking her case and lifting the lid to reduce the pressure, she explored the different wardrobes and drawers. Storage was spacious. Swiftly she unpacked, carried toiletries into the magnificent bathroom.

Concentrating on what she was doing, she could not banish from her mind the brief, very violent episode on the train. Newman had reached for his Smith & Wesson, but he would have been too late. The Walther had appeared in Tweed's hand like magic. He seemed to have fired two shots with the same movement. The assassin's face had disappeared, along with a section of his forehead. Then Beck had appeared, his automatic in his hand, a weapon he'd never had to use. He, also, would have been too late, having boarded at the Bellinzona stop.

She had just completed unpacking when there was a tapping on her door. When she opened it Tweed was standing there with a smile. Behind him stood a waiter with an ice bucket, the neck of a champagne bottle protruding.

'Do come in . . .'

The waiter opened the bottle, poured two glasses, then opened a litre bottle of still water and poured two more glasses. As soon as he had gone Paula rushed to Tweed and hugged him. She burst into tears as he wrapped reassuring arms round her. Eventually she backed away, taking out a handkerchief to dry her eyes.

'I'm sorry,' she quavered. 'It's not like me to break down.'

'Delayed shock. Inevitable reaction after what happened. I suggest you drink water before we sample the champagne.'

'I've already drunk two pints from a bottle they left in the bedroom. You must see my balcony.'

Taking him by the arm, her other hand holding her champagne glass, she led him out, shivered. 'It's colder here than it was in Zürich. Don't understand that.'

'It was like that when I was last here. Night is coming on and the temperature can nosedive, even when the sun shines as it's doing now.'

They clinked glasses. Paula took an exploratory sip, then a long drink. The champagne seeped into her like liquid fire. She began to relax. She was still holding on to Tweed's arm and he felt the tension receding. Tweed was wearing a suit and she excused herself for a moment, leaving her glass on a table on the balcony. Whipping off her jacket, she put on a warmer version, ran back onto the balcony. Tweed was seated at the table, nursing his glass. He heard the swift tapping of her shoes and knew she was recovering speedily. She sat down close to him.

'Over there,' he began, pointing to the left-hand peak, 'is Monte Bré, which has a funicular to take you to the top. It is a bit of a swizz. When you buy your ticket at the bottom they don't explain it's a double funicular. You travel halfway up in a spacious car, then get out and you're expected to transfer to another one no bigger than a large box. I was so annoyed I ignored the box and returned to base when the lower one descended.'

'What's the peak to the right?'

'Don't know what it's called. But round the corner from us to the right is Monte San Salvatore. That one does take you right up by funicular. The view down the lake curving round the corner south from here is breathtaking.'

'I must remember we're not here on holiday. I'm still puzzled as to why it takes the heads – all except poor Elena's.'

'As Beck explained, she was murdered in the middle of a big city – and in midafternoon. It's a quiet area by the Sihl but the killer could never have been sure someone wouldn't appear.' He nearly added 'so it would have to be a quick job' but he wanted to lead the conversation away from horrors.

'And I simply can't recall that vital remark someone made to me which I'm sure is very important. Can't even recall who it was.'

'As I told you earlier, don't struggle to remember. Fancy a drop more?'

'Just a drop. You're spoiling me. I saw the bottle. We are drinking Krug.'

'Only the best is good enough,' he said, refilling her glass.

'Beck was good to us,' she mused. 'He's taken the whole thing on his shoulders. And when we left the waiting room I noticed the train had gone.'

324

'He organized that well. I had a brief chat with him after you were inside the taxi. He waited until all passengers had disembarked and the platform was empty. They stopped passengers from Lugano from entering the station with some cock-and-bull story. Then the ambulance he'd called arrived. Medics and a local pathologist boarded the train, removed the assassin on a stretcher, took him away. The pathologist was hardly another Zeitzler. He didn't even take photographs. Would you fancy some tea downstairs yet?'

She had drunk her second glass of champagne and was surprised how light-headed she felt. She took another look at the view. The colour was changing, a pink and violet haze shrouding the mountains. The temperature had dropped again.

'I like the idea,' she decided. 'Give me five minutes to change. No need to leave – I'll do that in the bathroom. A shower will have to wait. I had a good wash before you arrived.' She chuckled, looked at him. His grey-blue eyes were looking at her. 'I wonder who we may meet downstairs? Should be interesting.'

When they left her room Newman appeared and joined them in the lift. He'd put on a smart new suit patterned with small grey checks. Tweed glanced at it, wondered if he also should have changed.

'I gave you two lovebirds plenty of time,' he chaffed.

'I beg your pardon,' Paula said with mock severity. 'What did you say?'

'Gone out of my head.' Newman stared fixedly at the roof of the elevator.

Tweed led the way to the spacious lounge, paused at the entrance. Paula peered over his shoulder to see what had stopped him. In a large armchair facing them sat

Roman Arbogast, about to consume a cream cake. The cake remained halfway to his thick lips. His eye began to twitch. He put down the cake, lumbered up out of his chair as Tweed advanced.

'My dear Tweed, what a startling and pleasant surprise. You are the last man I expected to see here.' He paused, smiled but it was a grimace. 'A cynic would wonder whether you are following us.'

'I'm a cynic.'

The reply baffled Roman. He was searching for a reply when someone touched Tweed's sleeve. He turned and Marienetta was smiling with pleasure. She threw her arms round him, kissed him on both cheeks, long lingering kisses.

'Now I can start enjoying myself,' she said. Her cat's eyes stared into his, full of suggestiveness. He felt compelled to return her warm embrace. 'Let's go somewhere alone,' she whispered. 'When we can. As soon as we can.'

'A tempting idea I'd find hard to resist.'

Paula heard every word. She stood with a composed expression and then Marienetta swung round to face her. Roman's niece was wearing a very stylish green and form-fitting dress, her slim arms bare, the dress held up by thin shoulder straps. She grasped Paula in both arms, hugged her tightly.

'I think I'm getting somewhere with my investigation,' she said in her soft voice so no one else clould hear. 'For Heaven's sake let us get together on our own as soon as we can lose these bores.'

'Great idea,' Paula responded as she was released.

Tweed led Newman and Paula with Marler to a side table by the wall. As she sat down Paula realized why he had chosen this one: from their table they had a complete view of the Arbogast family some distance away. Also, Tweed was now angled so he faced Roman sitting sideways on. Without turning round in his chair Roman couldn't see Tweed.

At Roman's table sat Marienetta and Sophie. All conversation had ceased and there was a tense attitude in the lounge. As Paula lifted the cup when their tea and cake had been served she saw Sophie staring straight at her. To Paula's surprise Sophie gave her a beaming smile, her whole face lit up with warmth. She was wearing her long brown hair in a ponytail.

Nield and Butler walked in, paused, then sat down at a table near the entrance where they could watch everyone. Nield's glance passed over Tweed's table as though they were strangers.

'I feel we've spoilt their tea at the Arbogast table,' Paula whispered.

'Which is my intention,' he replied in a grim voice. 'The moment has come to apply pressure from our side. We are short of time.'

'Why?'

'Because in my room I had a call from Beck. He's heard our friend Nathan has not left Zürich. When governments are frightened they will resort to any method. Nathan is waiting at Kloten Airport. Beck thinks he's expecting reinforcements.'

'They can't know we're here.'

'They can – if Roman has told them. Now I think you're going to have interesting company.'

Black Jack, wearing his polo outfit and carrying his whip, had just entered. He looked round quickly and walked over to Paula. He bent down to speak very quietly.

'When you have finished could you join me in the lobby? I've discovered something you should know about.'

'I've finished now. I can join you in a minute,' she replied.

Black Jack's expression was anything but his normal

jocularity. He looked very serious, had spoken urgently. As he left the lounge he waved to the Arbogasts. No one waved back.

'One thing you should remember,' Tweed said, his manner still grim. 'The occasion back at the Baur au Lac in the lounge when you were talking to Marienetta. She called the Vice-President "cousin". And you said he looked as though he could have killed her. When you get up look at the very back of the lounge in the left-hand corner.'

She got up slowly, made a performance of adjusting her shoulder bag, glancing at the left-hand corner at the far end. Sitting at a table with Ed Danvers was Russell Straub. He was gazing straight at her. His dark expression reminded her of what Tweed had just recalled. Straub looked as though he'd like to kill her.

She swept her gaze slowly round everyone in the lounge. My God! she thought. *It* is probably staying in this hotel. In the lobby Black Jack came straight over to her.

'It will be very cold outside.'

'Then excuse me for a moment. I'll just dash up and fetch my coat.'

Opening the door to her room she found an envelope which had been pushed under her door. Locking herself in, she took a slip of paper in Nield's handwriting. *Have hired cars for all of us. Yours is a red Peugeot.* The plate number followed and an ignition key was taped to the paper. She quickly removed the key, put it inside her shoulder bag.

Before putting on her warm coat she took her .32 Browning out of the special pocket in her bag. She checked it very thoroughly, loaded it, returned it to its pocket, put on her coat, was careful to loop her shoulder bag over the coat so she could reach inside quickly. Then she returned to the lobby.

Black Jack, the sole occupant, was studying a gilt-framed oil painting hung on the wall. It was a picture of a large and ancient house perched on the edge of the lake. Two-storeyed, it had evil-looking dormer windows protruding from its sloping roof. It had been painted by moonlight and something about it disturbed her. Black Jack pointed to it.

'It's very strange but after I arrived someone told me Roman owns that place. They explained how to reach it. I've drawn a map.' He produced a folded sheet of paper, gave it to her, leaned over her, their shoulders touching as he explained. 'Going out of here down the drive you turn right. You continue along the lakeside road until you see a signpost pointing to Finero, a small village apparently. Then you're up on the mountain. You drive through Finero and keep a lookout for a narrow road on your left which descends to the house. If you continue on after Finero and reach another village called Intragna you've missed the turn-off.'

It struck her that he was describing the route as though at some time he had driven to this sinister house. She looked at the painting again and didn't feel any happier about the propect of visiting it.

'You're coming with me?' she asked in a neutral tone.

'Wish I could. But Roman would notice my absence and that could be dangerous. If I go back into the lounge he'll think you've just gone to your room. Weird that this painting must have been produced ages ago. You do have a car?'

'Yes.'

'Thought so. I saw Nield outside talking to drivers who had delivered a fleet of cars.'

You damned well don't miss much, she thought. Someone had left the lounge and disappeared out of the front entrance. She had been so absorbed studying the map she didn't see who it was. Black Jack left her, vanished back into the lounge. She was still uncertain about this strange journey. Then Newman strolled out, picked up some brochures, looked at her. She nodded, went outside, looking for the Peugeot.

Despite her warm coat the intense cold hit her. As she got into her Peugeot another car, an Audi, started up. Whoever was driving it had a thick scarf like a cowl pulled over their head. She couldn't even see whether it was a man or a woman. In her rear-view mirror she saw Newman striding out, unlocking and getting behind the wheel of another Audi. That decided her. She had protection.

As she started down the steep drive she saw the Audi with the cowled driver had turned right – in the direction she was going. The only lights to cheer up the pitch black of night were the promenade street lamps, and her own headlights. She was still following the Audi, proceeding at a civilized pace. She kept distance between them, glancing in her rear-view mirror for sight of Newman's headlights. Nothing.

Back outside the front entrance Newman was desperately trying to fire up the engine. It refused to come to life. He tried again and again. The battery had to be flat. He got out, rushed back into the hotel to get the key to another car from Nield.

He slowed to a casual pace as he entered the lounge. He was holding an unlit cigarette. He dropped it close to Butler's chair. He was on his own. As he bent to pick up the cigarette he whispered to Butler.

'Harry, where is Pete.'

'In the bathroom.'

Newman cursed inwardly. By now he had probably lost the Peugeot. And he had no idea where Paula was going. He began to feel frustrated – and frightened for Paula.

* * *

Paula was driving at a sedate pace past the promenade lined with trees on her left. She was keeping pace with the Audi ahead of her. She was not sure why her instinct was to behave like this but she was accustomed to following her instinct.

There was very little trafffic. What there was was driving into Lugano. She was conscious she was driving away from the town. The moon had been out when she'd left the hotel. Now it was gone. Glancing over to the promenade she saw a dense pale mist creeping across the lake, reaching the promenade, which was now a blur. Just what I needed she thought.

She had checked each turn-off to her right but so far no signpost pointed to Finero. Then she saw the red lights of the Audi ahead of her disappear. The Audi had turned off to the right. She slowed. On an ancient wooden signpost she could just read the letters engraved in it. *Finero*. She swung her wheel after one last glance in her rear-view mirror. Still no sign of Newman.

The turn-off was narrow but well surfaced. It also immediately climbed steeply, curving frequently. She was going up the mountain. At intervals she spotted the red lights of the Audi and now it was travelling much faster, spinning round steep tricky curves, climbing higher and higher. No sign of houses, no sign of people. On either side the ground was rocky. And the mist was drifting over the road.

Sometimes she had a clear view. At others she was driving into fog. After a particularly steep ascent the road levelled out. Ahead she saw an ancient village but the red lights had vanished. It must have really rammed its foot down she decided. Then realized she had used the word 'it'.

She drove slowly along the village street. Not a light

in a house anywhere. She soon saw why. Single-storey houses on either side. Some with broken windows. Tiles sliding off the sloping rooves. Damn it! No one lives here any more. It's an abandoned village. Very reassuring.

With the road ahead mist-free she pressed her foot down in the vague hope of catching up the red lights. There was nowhere the Audi could have turned off. She gritted her teeth as the village seemed to go on for ever. Was she walking into a trap? She left the village behind with a sense of relief. The way this whole trip had started began to worry her. Why had Black Jack not come with her? Was he acting on orders from Roman?

She was so glad to leave Finero behind she nearly missed the track. Finero? *Finito?* Now you're getting morbid, she admonished herself. She braked suddenly. To her left in the headlights she saw a wide track paved with stone, swung left and down. The change of surface, the steep drop made her drive slowly. She frowned. In places the track narrowed and she saw large wheel tracks on the rocky surface, oil marks. She had the impression large trucks travelled this way. But why? And where to?

The descent became incredibly steep. Which was probably why, long before she expected, she had reached the bottom, her headlights shining on the lake. She followed the track slowly to her right, alongside the lake. The moon reappeared. She stopped. Just ahead was the large ancient house of the painting. Crouched like an animal at the edge, more weird even than in the painting.

She studied it for any sign of life before getting out of the car. No lights anywhere. It seemed more sinister because of its aged mansard roof. She opened her window and listened, the silence was so unsettling she almost hoped she would hear something. Then the mist crept back and everything vanished.

*   *   *

332

She glanced at the seat beside her. Leaving the hotel she had snatched up a large umbrella with a spiked end from a stand by the exit. She never knew what had urged her to do this. Now at least she had something to shield her from the damp creepy mist. Time to explore the house of darkness.

She took the umbrella and her torch before locking the car. The mist crawled over her face before she opened the umbrella, a sensation she disliked. The paved road continued to the entrance to the house, a flight of wide wooden steps with rails on either side. The wood looked very old.

She was nearly at the top of the tall flight when a tread gave way, collapsed, fell to the ground below. She had one hand on the rail which held fast. Was this a good idea? No one had any idea where she was, no friends anyway. Something odd about this place. She refused to give up. Beyond the veranda at the top a solid wooden door barred her way. Her torch showed a large modern lock. She'd probably never get into the place. Quietly, she reached out, took hold of the handle, turned it, pushed. The door opened inward.

Again, not reassuring. Was there someone inside? Only one way to find out. She tucked her powerful torch under one arm, closed the umbrella, extracted her Browning. She pushed the heavy door wide open, flat back against the wall – in case anyone was hiding behind it. Her free hand felt along the side of the wall opposite the hinge. She found the switch, pressed it. Light flooded a spacious hall which was completely empty. The floor was wooden planks and to her left an open doorway led into another room. She switched off the light, not wishing to advertise her presence to anyone outside.

She had become mistrustful of the structure since the tread fell from the steps outside. She listened. The heavy silence was almost a sound in itself. Cautiously she moved forward towards the open door on the left.

Before she took a step she used the sharp end of the umbrella to go first, tapping the planks. In this dogtrot manner, the torch under her arm illuminating the way for her, she made her way out of the musty hall into the next room. Often she stopped to listen.

At times she heard creaks, decided it was the age of the house. She was startled when the whole place seemed to move like a ship in a quiet sea. She continued walking along the middle of the room, eerily dark beyond the beam of her torch. She tapped hard with the ferrule of the umbrella and under its prod the floor gave way. She stopped, shone the torch down.

A large piece of the floor where she would have stepped had vanished, leaving a large square gaping hole. Like a trapdoor. She sucked in her breath. Then she directed the beam downwards. It illuminated the stone walls of a large cellar a long way down. Two red diamonds were reflected in the beam. Then another pair. She widened the beam and looked down on two of the largest rats she had ever seen. The 'diamonds' were their eyes, staring up. Their tails were hideously long. If she had gone down there . . .

To finish off someone like me exploring, she thought. What was there to hide? The rats scuttered round as though they smelt fresh meat. She made her way round the trap, tapping ahead of her feet. She didn't like this place one bit.

Pausing, she heard rocks slipping outside. A sound like the crunch of feet crossing the rocks. Without hurrying, she made her way back to the front door, keeping the beam of the torch steady to show her the way. She also continued to tap the floor ahead of her with the ferrule. Her experience – gazing down that dreadful drop, the huge rats looking up at her. The drop into the cellar's stone floor must have been at least twenty feet. At the very least she'd have been knocked unconscious, if not killed. She imagined those hungry-looking rats feeding on her.

She was close to the front door, which she had left wide open, when she saw the moon was out again. She switched off her torch, peered out, stiffened. Below and beyond the veranda she could see wraiths of mist drifting round her parked Peugeot. Something was moving in the mist near the car, the vague silhouette of a tall figure. She couldn't see how it was dressed. It was a phantom outline in the mist.

Paula had had enough. She raised her Browning, took careful aim above the almost invisible figure, fired one shot. The figure vanished. Tucking the umbrella under her arm freed both hands. Her left held the torch, ready to switch it on, her right hand gripped the Browning.

There was the same dreadful silence as she made her way slowly down the rickety steps, avoiding the gap where the tread had collapsed. At the bottom she paused again, listening. The brooding silence was shattered by the sound of a car's engine starting up, revving madly. She never saw it as the car roared away, driving at high speed up the sloping road she had driven down.

Then briefly she saw red tail-lights as it plunged up the dangerous near vertical spiral, spinning out of sight as it negotiated a bend. The sound of its mad ascent vanished in no time as she approached her Peugeot, climbed in after shining her torch inside. Locking the doors, she inserted her ignition key, turned it. Nothing. She tried again. More nothing. The engine was dead. She was marooned in this desolate spot and outside it was bitterly cold.

Unlocking the door, she climbed out, thankful the moon was still shining. She had pulled the lever which released the bonnet. Lifting it, she peered inside, checking with

335

her torch. She swore. Someone had jerked a wire loose from a plug. It took her several minutes to insert the wire back into its correct position. Returning, she saw a notepad on the grass, picked it up. She climbed back behind the wheel.

She was reaching forward to insert the ignition key when her cold hands dropped the keys. Oh God! With the doors locked it took her almost half an hour to locate them. They had slipped down the inner side of her seat. Her relief was total when she turned the key and the engine started. She tucked the Browning down the inside of her skirt, uncertain what she might meet as she began ascending the diabolical road slowly.

The moon had disappeared, dense mist was rolling round her when she eventually turned onto the road to Finero. She still drove slowly through the dark depressing village, all the time waiting for an ambush. Her mood only became less tense when she was driving back along the lakeside road towards Lugano.

'I'm going to get Tweed to grill Black Jack until his teeth rattle,' she said to herself. The louse *had* sent her into a trap. She was in a grim mood when she reached the drive leading up to the hotel. So much so she only vaguely wondered why there were police cars parked below the entrance, their red lights flashing.

More police cars parked outside the hotel made it difficult to find a parking spot. As she got out, locked the car, a uniformed policeman stopped her, said something in Italian. She waved her hands to show she did not understand.

'I'm English.'

'You cannot park here. The hotel is closed.'

'Don't be so damned silly,' she fumed. 'I'm staying here. Paula Grey is the name.'

'Let her in,' a familiar voice called out. Beck, wearing a trench coat, appeared.

'Tweed is in the hall,' he said, coming up to her, his expression grim. 'Very worried about you. And there's been another murder.'

33

All her frustration and tension had burst out when the policeman tried to stop her at the door, but the moment she entered the lobby she saw Tweed. His expression was a mixture of anger and relief. She knew he'd been worried out of his mind by her absence.

'Where *have* you been?' he demanded. 'I've had Butler, Nield and Newman driving round looking for you . . .'

'I didn't leave on my own,' she rapped back. 'Newman was going to follow me but never appeared. I've got a lot to tell you when you've quietened down.'

Her mind was so full of her recent experience that what Beck had said to her hadn't sunk in. He took her by the arm, led her into the empty lift. It was ascending when she started again.

'And one thing I do want you to do is to grill Black Jack until his teeth rattle. He led me into the most awful trap.'

He said nothing as she found her key, opened the door to her room and they walked inside. On a table were three new bottles – Scotch, water and Chardonnay. She calmed down as she realized Tweed had ordered them sent up for when she returned.

'A drop of Scotch might help,' Tweed suggested. 'I'm not sure. Maybe water and then Chardonnay?'

'Water, then Chardonnay,' she gasped, sinking into a chair.

He waited until she'd drunk two glasses of water, then

sipped some Chardonnay. He sat down facing her, his expression serious.

'I'm so relieved to see you back safely. Sorry for my bad temper. And I do know Newman was supposed to escort you. Trouble was his car wouldn't start. He phoned up the car-hire firm and gave them hell. They've replaced it already.'

'I want Black Jack grilled to the limit,' she repeated. She then gave him a full account of her nightmare drive up the mountain, following the Audi. She continued with her experience at the horror of a house by the lake, mentioned there was a painting of the beastly place on the wall down in the lobby. She produced the map Black Jack had drawn for her. Tweed took it, glanced at it, placed it on the table.

'I have grim news.'

'Oh, my God!' Her mind had clicked back to the present. 'Beck told me there has been another murder.'

'Yes, there has. And I won't be able to grill Black Jack – his body has been discovered at the foot of the Monte San Salvatore funicular, which is closed at night and just round the corner. Are you feeling better?' She nodded, smiled. '*It* has been at work again,' he continued quietly. 'The body was headless.'

'That's terrible,' she said after she had absorbed the shock. 'He was such a mixture. Sometimes I liked him – he was so lively. At other times he irked me. How long ago did it happen?'

'So far as we can tell at this at age, roughly half an hour ago. I've just got back from seeing it.'

'Then it could have been the phantom figure which sabotaged my car outside that strange old house by the lake.' Her mind was working overtime now. 'After I'd fixed my car it took me ages to come back – whereas the saboteur drove off like a racer at Le Mans.'

'Any idea at all what this figure in the mist looked like?'

'No, I haven't. It was like seeing a ghost – and then only for seconds. Is there an Audi parked outside now? I should have looked, felt the engine.'

'Wouldn't have told you anything. In this intense cold an engine would lose any warmth quickly.'

'But at least we can find out who it belongs to.'

'I know. It belongs to Sophie. And she's tall.'

Paula stared at Tweed in sheer disbelief. She reached in her jacket pocket for a handkerchief and pulled out a small writing pad. It was the type of pad to be found all over their hotel, had the name printed on it. She pursed her lips, wondering if she was losing her mind. She handed it to Tweed.

'I'd forgotten this in my rush to get away from that old house. I found it on the grass just outside the driver's door when I dived in and found the car wouldn't start. The saboteur must have dropped it, maybe when I fired a shot over its head. I'd have thought we have confirmation that *it* is staying at this hotel.'

Tweed studied the top sheet. On it was written *CH* – – – – –. He showed it to Paula, asked her what she thought it meant.

'Well, CH is the beginning of all car number plates in this country. Stands for Confederation Helvetica. What the dashes mean I've no idea.'

Tweed took back the pad, wearing latex gloves in case there were fingerprints. Lifting up the sheet he stared at the one underneath. At the top of the pad was the remains of another sheet which had been torn out. He held it under the table lamp. He swivelled it this way and that.

'Something else was written on the sheet below which has been torn out. I can just make out the faintest imprint

341

of another word written on the missing sheet – on the page below. Darned if I can make out what it was. But you're right – it does confirm that *it* is staying at this hotel, which narrows the field a lot.'

'Couldn't we check on who has left the hotel while I was trying not to get myself eaten by outsize rats?'

'Beck has already attempted to do that after Black Jack was found. He didn't get anywhere. A lot of people were out. Those who were in said they'd been in their rooms ever since tea.'

'Then I think we ought to go and tackle Sophie. It *was* her car that was used.'

Tweed knew which was Sophie's room. On the same floor as Paula's, it would also have a view of the lake. And, Paula was thinking, it would look down on the car park beyond the hotel's entrance. Tweed tapped on the door, waited, then tapped louder. A muffled voice called out behind the closed door.

'Who is it?'

'It's me,' Paula called back. 'With Tweed. Could we have a word?'

The door was unlocked but the safety chain was still in place when Sophie, clad in a dressing gown, peered out. Then she removed the chain and they walked in. Sophie replaced the chain, locked the door. She had obviously washed her hair and only half-dried it. She waved the hand with the brush towards chairs.

'I'm a bit of a mess,' she remarked. 'Just out of the shower. Have to take me as I am.'

'You look fine,' said Paula.

'Don't feel it. Not after the dreadful news about Black Jack.'

'I realize you were fond of him,' Paula said sympathetically.

'Didn't like the man at all,' Sophie said as she sat down

in an armchair facing the couch her guests occupied. 'Couldn't trust him an inch.'

The reaction struck Paula as surprisingly callous. Sophie had made up her face and looked anything but upset. What kind of woman was this? She looked anxious, as though she wished they had not invaded her room.

'Makes you wonder who is going to be next,' she went on.

'I can understand that reaction,' Tweed said amiably. 'We'd like to ask you some questions. Just to clear up certain aspects which puzzle us.'

'What aspects?' Sophie snapped, her eyes narrowing.

'Your car is an Audi. Have you used it to drive anywhere since we arrived here?'

'How the hell could I?' she shouted at him, her full cheeks colouring with rage, her eyes blazing. 'When someone pinched my keys!' She was working herself up. 'Just tell me that.' She turned to Paula and sneered. 'Marienetta tells me you're a great detective. So you solve the problem.'

Paula was considering this outburst when Sophie reached for a bottle on a nearby table. She poured herself a generous slug of gin, swallowed half of it, hammered the glass back on the table. Paula spoke very quietly.

'Help us to understand. When did someone pinch your car keys? This could be important.'

'In the blasted lounge at tea time. I liked the cake. Maybe ate too much. I have to watch my figure. It was the best cake I've tasted in ages. I gorged.' A smile of satisfaction crossed her face. 'You have to let yourself go some time. I need some fun in my life. So much is expected of me at ACTIL. I do most of the work, Marienetta gets most of the credit.'

'That's tough,' Paula went on quietly, trying to haul her back to what they needed to know. 'So how did the keys vanish?'

'Off the table in the lounge. Your very close friend –' she said the words with insinuation – 'Bob Newman handed me the keys when we were starting tea. I put them on the table, which was crowded. When I stood up to go they were gone.'

'So when did you leave the lounge after finishing your tea?' Paula persisted in a persuasive tone. 'It must have been a shock.'

'When I'd finished all the cake.'

Sophie's personality seemed to undergo a sudden change. Now she was like a little girl, her full lips pouting.

'Who was still in the lounge when you left it?'

'No one. I was the last to leave. I'd had a spat with Marienetta much earlier.' She sat up very erect. 'I do *not* like her.'

'Possibly Russell Straub and his aide, who sat at the very back, were still there?'

'Paula!' Sophie flared up again. 'I've just told you no one was in the lounge when I realized the keys had gone. People sometimes think I'm stupid. I'm a lot cleverer than most people realize.' She looked cunning now. 'Maybe you think I am stupid? You could get a surprise.'

'So,' Paula continued, exercising all her patience, 'no one was in the lounge. I suppose you searched for the keys, as I would have done.'

'Searched the whole damned place. Got down on my hands and knees, moved furniture.' She leaned forward. '*Paula*, the keys weren't there any more. Somebody whipped them.'

'I believe you.'

'Really?' Sophie stared at Tweed, eyes still blazing. 'You heard that? Now she believes me. A miracle.'

Tweed stood up, and with his hands in his trouser pockets he walked over to the double windows looking out onto the balcony. Sophie also got up, followed him slowly as he gazed out and down.

'Marvellous view,' he remarked to her. 'Even at night with the lights over on Monte Bré. You see that chain climbing the mountain?'

'Yes, I suppose there must be a road up,' she said with a smile. Her mood had changed again. 'There'll be another marvellous view over there, I imagine – looking back here.'

'There is,' he agreed. 'And I'm pretty sure that chain of lights is illuminating the track of the funicular which takes you up to the summit.' He looked down below the balcony. 'I assume that Audi parked down there is for you.'

'Yes, it is. And I've had *no* chance to drive the perishing thing.'

'Your missing keys may turn up, Sophie. If they don't I'll get Newman to phone the car-hire people in the morning to send over a duplicate set for you.'

'Thank you. Actually I could get Black Jack to collect them for me. Oh, no, I can't,' she went on in her indifferent tone, 'he's not around any more.'

She looked at Tweed. His expression was stunned, as though he couldn't believe he'd heard what she had said. She tugged at his arm impatiently.

'I'm a scientist. We look at life in a different way. We even count up how long someone is likely to live, how many times we'll see them again before we complete any undertaking they may have given us.'

'I think we ought to go,' he said, standing stiffly. 'There are so many things we have to attend to.'

'Well, we can talk more over dinner . . .'

'What a cold-blooded little devil she is,' Paula said, her voice strained as they walked slowly along the corridor when she had closed the door on them. 'And she had an on-and-off thing going with him. If she tries to join us at

345

dinner, find a way of stopping her. I don't think I could say a word to her.'

'I must admit,' Tweed said slowly, 'for a moment she took my breath away. The off-hand way she said it.'

'The Arbogasts are a very strange family,' Paula mused.

'And they're in the thick of this business somehow. After what you told me I'm convinced *it* was in that Audi you followed to that old house by the lake. I further suspect it had lured Black Jack into feeding you that story which took you there. Then it had to get back here fast to eliminate Black Jack so he couldn't reveal who had asked him to give you that map.'

'Well, even a lot of money wouldn't have persuaded him.'

They had reached her room. She was unlocking the door when the lift opened and Beck stepped out. He looked grim, but pleased to see them. He joined them as they entered her room.

'I hate to bother you,' Beck began, 'but I have some photos to show you. Not pleasant.'

'Do you need me to go and identify the body?' Tweed suggested.

'Thank you, but that has already been done – earlier I bumped into Marienetta downstairs and she volunteered. I went with her. She was shaken but she held up well. She made the identification, then wanted to leave the funicular immediately.'

'How could she be sure?' Paula asked. 'If the body was headless?'

'The clothes he wore, a signet ring on his right hand. There was no way of checking by anything in his pockets – they'd been emptied. I'm upsetting the local pathologist by insisting on flying the body back to Zürich. There's no one like Zeitzler. Now, if you're ready? Maybe we could sit round that table.'

He produced a large envelope from the briefcase he'd

been carrying. As they sat down he spread out a series of prints of the body, many of the severed neck. Paula fetched a magnifying glass, studied them slowly, then looked up.

'It has used the same vicious method – and with the weapon used before. The axe with the notch. I'm sure I can see a small ragged area, despite the incredibly neat slice of the blade just below the chin.'

'I agree,' said Tweed. 'And in a minute I'll show you proof Paula found which confirms the killer is staying at this hotel.'

'One thing I noticed,' Paula interjected, 'when we were with Sophie. Every room has a pad with the hotel's name on it by the phone. There was no pad in Sophie's room.'

'Circumstantial but interesting,' Tweed replied.

There was a knock on the door. Beck hastily slipped the photos back in their envelope. Tweed opened the door and found himself facing Sam Snyder, wearing an expensive business suit and smiling his crooked smile.

'I've got pics I took of the victim – the latest – at the funicular round the corner. Thought you'd like to see them.'

'Do ask him in,' Beck called out.

Tweed, about to send Snyder packing, ushered him into the room. He entered clutching a folder, glanced round the room, smiled again as he addressed Paula.

'Ah, the most attractive lady in Switzerland is with us. A bonus.'

'Just don't come near me,' she told him. 'I don't want to catch anything infectious.'

There was another knock on the door. This time Newman walked in. His expression froze when he saw Snyder. He sat down next to Paula.

'Maybe we could see these pictures,' Beck suggested quietly.

'That's why I'm here,' Snyder rapped back. 'Nice that

it's a party.' His grin became cheeky. 'We could have a drink afterwards to celebrate my coup.'

Nobody reacted as he opened his folder while Tweed sat again at the table. With a flourish Snyder produced picture after picture, dropping them on the table. Beck leant forward with Paula. They were not close-ups, like the photos Beck had shown them, but they were horrifically dramatic, clearly showing Black Jack's decapitated body.

'How were you able to take these?' Beck enquired in the same level tone. 'The police should have stopped you.'

'Ah! The local ghouls were out, a small crowd. I stood at the back of them, used a non-flash camera.'

'Very clever of you,' Beck commented. 'I'm impounding all these pictures as evidence. I'll even give you a receipt.'

'Thought this might happen.' Snyder opened his mouth and let out a braying laugh. 'So I have copies made at a local shop. They're on their way now by express to *The New York Times*, *Time* magazine, *Le Monde* in Paris, *Der Spiegel* in Germany and other top publications. Together with the article I typed on my laptop.' His grin became more obnoxious. 'Want to hear the headline? "Three More Headless Corpses in Switzerland."' He let out another braying laugh. 'And that should do your tourist industry a power of good. I'm asking them all to bid. I'll make a fortune.'

'Which I hope you spend on drink,' Newman snapped. 'And that it chokes you.'

'I may get a warrant to deport you,' Beck remarked, though he knew he had little chance of this.

'Freedom of the press!' Snyder bawled.

'I think it's time for you to go,' Tweed suggested, standing up.

Newman also stood up, his right fist clenched. He began walking slowly towards Snyder. Beck called out, ordering Newman to sit down, then turned to Snyder who had hurried towards the door where Tweed waited.

'Mr Snyder,' Beck asked, his manner still controlled, 'may I ask you where you were when the murder was committed?'

'In my room – before I heard about the fresh murder. The news is all over the hotel. The staff are gabbling about it.'

'But you didn't ask when the murder was committed,' Beck continued. 'You could have been anywhere. By the funicular, for example. You have a witness as to your whereabouts at the vital time?'

Snyder had lost his normal arrogant manner. Tweed still stood by the locked door, the key in his pocket. For a long moment there was silence as everyone else in the room stared at the reporter. Perspiration drops appeared on his forehead.

'I was in my room,' he repeated nervously, 'until I heard what had happened. I imagine so were a lot of guests – also on their own.'

'Don't leave the country without informing me of your intention,' Beck concluded.

Tweed unlocked the door, opened it and Snyder rushed out of sight.

'I've never really considered Snyder as the murderer,' Paula remarked. 'He's such an unlikely suspect.'

'And how many times has the most unlikely suspect turned out to be the villain?' Newman pointed out.

'I suppose,' she went on, developing a new theory, 'since he is a chief crime reporter he may have toyed with the idea of committing a series of crimes – really hideous ones – then reporting them and making a fortune. He did say he was going to do just that – make a fortune.'

'You're forgetting,' Newman reminded her, 'the patient who was treated at the asylum in Pinedale. Hardly likely that was Snyder.'

'Unless he is insane,' Paula persisted. 'If so he wouldn't want the records of his stay there to be found. Hence the burning down of that asylum. Later he realizes Abraham Seale has detected what he really is, so he has to be eliminated. The same reason later still for decapitating Elena Brucan.'

'So what about Adam Holgate murdered at Bray? Where did he fit in?'

'Snyder was investigating ACTIL, we know he was inside the building from the photos Elena took. Holgate could have caught him checking their records. Snyder decides he's going to be exposed. One thing leads to another.'

'It's bizarre,' Newman said forcefully.

'There have been a number of bizarre murders,' Beck chipped in. 'We are investigating a classically bizarre series of murders carried out in a bizarre way.'

Tweed had stood up during the conversation. He was pacing between their table and the balcony. He was seriously considering what Paula was saying.

'And we do know,' he recalled, 'that Snyder has visited the States secretly aboard Roman's Gulfstream. But there are other people.' He turned to look down at Beck. 'Any idea where Russell Straub was when Black Jack was killed?'

'I have interviewed him,' Beck replied. 'Not an easy man to interrogate. Threatened to report me to my Minister. I told him to go ahead. He'd told me he'd been alone in his suite all afternoon. The place was littered with sheets with names of contributors to his campaign. He'd answered all my earlier questions with one word. No.'

'He's involved in some way,' Tweed asserted. 'And Paula had a frightening experience earlier today. Tell Arthur about it . . .'

She described what had happened when she'd followed the Audi. She was terse, but left out no detail. Beck was

350

watching her as he listened. When she had finished he asked about the timing when she found her car had been sabotaged.

'There would have been ample time for whoever it was to get back here and murder Black Jack. I was worried it was waiting for me so I drove back very slowly . . .'

'It?' Beck queried.

'That's what I call the killer. Because it can't be human – normal – after the dreadful things it has done.'

'I see. One development you should know about. The Arbogasts are travelling south tomorrow. A plainclothes man I planted in the ticket office at Lugano station informed me. In the late afternoon.'

'To Chiasso,' Tweed suggested.

'Yes.' Beck was startled. 'How did you guess?'

Tweed produced the hotel pad Paula had found on the ground near the house by the lake. 'CH – – – – –.' He showed the pad to Beck. 'I had thought CH was for the letters which precede any car's plate number in this country. Then out of the blue it struck me. *Chiasso*.'

'It's on the border between Switzerland and Italy,' Beck explained. 'We have heard this strong rumour that Roman's consignment of oxygen cylinders is bound for the Middle East – and they contain poison gas, not oxygen. Roman knows we're checking them and said he'd like to be present. Dramatic events may take place on the border tomorrow. Now I must leave – I want to escort the ambulance taking Black Jack's body to the airport. What are you two going to do now? Paula, you must go nowhere without a trusted escort. That is an order. For some reason you are the killer's next target.'

'I know what I'm going to do next,' Paula said when they were alone. 'I'm going to miss dinner, take a shower and then sleep and sleep and sleep.'

'No more dreams,' Tweed warned.

34

Nightmare.

Before getting into bed Paula made a mental effort to banish from her mind her unnerving experience at the old house, the hole into the cellar inhabited by huge rats. As she switched out the bedside light she knew she had succeeded. She fell fast asleep. Her mind began working on her.

First she was alone on a deserted slope. The mist appeared from nowhere, insidious coils slowly encircling her. Her feet leaden, dragging, she toiled up the slope. It was dark. She had no idea where she was, which worried her.

Then the grey mist wrapping itself round her throat changed colour. It became pink, a rose colour. Dawn was approaching. Her hands were so cold that when she reached up to push away the mist from her neck it was like touching ice.

It was dead silent. Too silent. She couldn't hear her booted feet stepping on the rocky slope. Then she heard a strange rumbling sound, like massive giants coming slowly down the slope towards her. She tried to turn back, to go down the slope. Her feet were motionless, too heavy to lift.

Paula, you must go nowhere without a trusted escort. She heard Beck's order echoing inside her head. Where was Newman? Why had he let her climb this desolate slope by herself? The rumble of enormous giants was coming closer and closer. Now she was able to move her feet a little, but they were taking her towards the giants coming down to meet her.

Ahead of her and higher up the mist was thinning, becoming more a spectrum of many colours. For God's sake, why didn't dawn break so she could see the danger? The mist above her was retreating, she could just make out massive silhouettes which were still, like gods guarding their Olympus which no mortals must disturb.

Her heart was in her mouth as her feet took on a life of their own, taking her up where she didn't want to go. She tried to force them to stop. They wouldn't respond. They were transporting her towards the huge silhouettes. Behind them the sun had not yet appeared but its multicoloured glow was growing stronger.

'I don't want to go up there,' the voice inside her head protested fearfully.

Her feet continued their remorseless tread, climbing. She had lost all control. The sound of moving giants had faded. The dreadful silence returned. She opened her mouth to scream and nothing emerged. The silence was so ominous, so full of menace. Was she going mad?

Then the pre-dawn light, so brilliant, grew stronger. The mist continued to retreat, as though drawing her upwards. She thought now she could hear the slow muffled booming of a church bell, a sound she had disliked from childhood. The intervals between the booms were long and she thought they had ceased. Which was the moment when she heard the faint booming repeated.

The glow of pink and orange and green and rose was now a band of light. Suddenly the silhouettes she had seen earlier came into view clearly. Her feet were moving more quickly upwards. She stared, hypnotized, in disbelief.

Perched on a ridge were two tall, wide towers of stone, linked together by a wall halfway below their summits. She

354

had seen these before. She knew where she was. How had she got here from faraway Lugano? These were the two ancient towers she had seen from the express when it had shot out of the Gotthard tunnel. Behind Airolo.

Then she woke up, both hands clutching a tumble of sheets.

Tweed was still up, working at the desk in his pyjamas with a carafe of water close by. It was a delicate task he was struggling with. Before him was the hotel pad Paula had found during her experience at the old house – the pad on the ground at the foot of her car.

He had folded back the first sheet which contained in square block letters – the kind used by an intelligent child – CH – – – – –, which he was sure was short for Chiasso, the border crossing. He had also folded back the second sheet where someone had thoroughly scrawled over what had originally been written. He was working on the third sheet, where he had detected the faintest imprint which had come through when the deleted word on the second sheet was written.

Using a pencil he slowly scrawled across the imprint, hoping to bring up the original word. He manipulated the pencil with a very light touch and something began to come. He refused to hurry, to press harder in his eagerness to locate the word.

At 4 a.m. he put down the pencil, staring at the word he had conjured up out of the imprint. Didn't make sense. He lit one of his rare cigarettes, tried to link it up with all the events which had taken place. He gazed down at the word, trying to penetrate its secret.

Airolo.

35

Paula left her room at 7 a.m. She was anxious to tell Tweed about her nightmare. She was walking down the corridor when a door opened as she passed. Marienetta appeared. She clutched Paula in a firm grip by the arm and almost dragged her inside.

'You and I have a date for a talk. To compare notes, see how much progress we're making. If any.'

'Just for a few minutes, then. Something I have to deal with.'

'Coffee? I'm having some. You do look as though you didn't sleep well. I like that outfit. Powder blue suits you. Do sit down. I expect you've heard I was the one who identified poor Black Jack. Beck asked me. He'd heard we knew each other fairly well. I managed but I can't say it was the most enjoyable experience of my life.' She handed Paula a cup of coffee after suggesting she sat down. 'The killer has a hideous mind. Black Jack was lying there with that whip still in his hand. It must have been put there after what happened.'

'Typical of the deranged mind we're up against. And you look all dressed up for a trip.'

'I am. We're all catching the 5 p.m. train to Chiasso. Doesn't take half an hour to get there. Roman has some big export order the Customs are questioning. Being Roman, he has to be there to make sure everything is properly repacked. They tell me it's a claustrophobic place. Vertigo

I can handle. That road over the Alps has one spot where you look down a horrendous drop. Now, to our investigation. Have you come up with anything interesting?'

'You first. I'm just waking up.'

'Well . . .' Marienetta paused, although earlier her words had flowed like a river in flood. Such vitality, Paula thought. 'I had begun to wonder whether the killer was Black Jack. The poor devil is bankrupt, you know. Or was. So now my main suspect is out of the picture.' Her voice trembled. 'He was such a nice guy. I hoped I was wrong – and I was. But, oh God, what a hellish way to realize that.'

She opened a bottle of mineral water. The neck was rattling against the side of the glass as she poured. Paula desisted from helping – she had weighed up Marienetta as someone who, under her extrovert personality, was a solitary and preferred to do everything for herself. A very strong woman.

'That's better,' she said as she put down the empty glass. She patted the couch she had sunk onto. 'Come and join me so we can talk.'

'It astonishes me,' Paula began, 'to hear Black Jack was a bankrupt. He owned Templeton's, the very profitable gambling house in Mayfair.'

'The trouble was he invested huge sums in those dotcom companies when they were shooting up to heaven. He even took out a huge mortgage on Templeton's to invest more. Came the huge crash and he was broke. Two banks were going to repossess Templeton's. He had nothing.'

'He kept it very quiet.'

'He was proud of his reputation as the man who turned to gold everything he touched. I have one more suspect.'

'Who is?'

'Broden. He's tall and big and very ruthless. He has this rocklike personality but underneath I've detected this suppressed rage. He was running a successful private

358

detective agency before Roman hired him. So he had qualifications for becoming chief of security.'

'Detective agency?' Paula was mystified. 'He told me he'd been in the army's SIB, their Special Investigation Branch.'

'And you believed him?' Marienetta put a hand on Paula's arm, turning towards her with a peculiar smile. 'Broden changes his story about his earlier life according to who he's talking to, even on a whim. A strange man.'

'I really think I've got to go,' Paula said, checking her watch.

'Not before you've told me what you've discovered. Fair's fair.'

'The more I find out – about things like family relationships for example – the more confusing it gets. I'm concentrating on who could have a motive.'

'Motive? You don't think they are random killings, then?'

'No, we don't. The trouble is to link up the victims. Not easy to do. But random? No. And that's about as far as we've got. We'll suddenly hit on something. Luck plays a great part in solving murder. Now, I really must go, if you'll excuse me.'

'Of course. Just take care of yourself.' She gazed at Paula with her cat's eyes. 'Sophie is the one least affected. She thinks of nothing but business. I don't know how many times she's visited Boston where our plant is. And she's doing a wonderful job. She even coaxed a general in the Pentagon to place a huge order with us.'

'Good for Sophie,' Paula commented as she got up to leave.

She was hurrying to Tweed's suite when a tall burly figure wearing a woollen pullover and slacks blocked her way as he opened the door to his room.

'A word with you, please,' said Broden.

Paula hesitated but decided she hadn't talked enough to him since their chat in the ACTIL office in Zurich. His normally bleak expression was smiling as he escorted her to a chair, asked her what she would like to drink.

'Coffee would do nicely, thank you.'

'This pot was delivered only minutes ago. Cream and sugar?'

'No, just black.'

'Black as sin, the lady prefers,' he said as he poured, handed her the cup. 'God knows there's enough sin about. The murder of Black Jack has surprised me.' He sat down in a chair close to hers. 'Now Abraham Seale and the Brucan lady, both of whom came to see Roman, were the sort of weird characters who could end up dead. I was present when they met Roman – at his request because he didn't want them staying too long. But Black Jack, he was the type I'd have expected to live to a ripe old age. A nice guy if you answered him back, which I did.'

'What about Hank Foley in Pinedale?'

'Probably never solve that one. Mind if I smoke?' He took out a small cigar from a box on a nearby table.

'Go ahead.'

While he was lighting up she studied him. His weather-beaten face suggested a man who had spent a lot of time outdoors. His eyes were like glass, never revealing what he was really thinking. They were heavy-lidded and at times closed down like shutters. He had the nose, lips and jaw of an ex-boxer.

'Why do you think they'll never find who murdered Hank Foley?' she asked.

'That policeman, Parrish, who I shared a few beers with, is so thick if you held a clue under his nose he'd never see it. As for the FBI, a friend of mine in Boston told me they have filed the case as pending. Never-never land.'

'Have you any idea as to the identity of the murderer?' she asked, standing up to go.

'Someone in this hotel.'

'No, we can't go down for breakfast yet,' she told Tweed when she was inside his suite. 'I've so much to tell you . . .'

He sat down, and never said a word as she recalled her conversation with Marienetta, then her encounter with Broden. His only comment was when she had concluded telling him about her unexpected meeting with the security chief.

'You know, I don't think we've paid enough attention to Mr Broden.'

'I did have a horrible nightmare,' she continued. 'It was so vivid and terrifying . . .'

Again he listened to her without saying a word. He watched her face all the time. She conjured up what she had experienced so well he felt he had been involved in the nightmare. Her hands, normally so still, were intertwined in her lap, fingers twisting round each other. On several occasions she closed her eyes, recalling the experience. She gave a sigh as she completed her narrative.

'I'm sorry you went through that,' Tweed commented, 'but on more than one occasion you've mentioned those twin towers haunting you in flashes.'

'I'm probably being silly about them,' she decided.

'We are going to Chiasso late this afternoon. I'm going to hang on to the tails of this strange Arbogast family until we've broken the case. And you should know that some of the things you've heard this morning have filled in the picture I'm building up. I sense we are approaching the climax.'

'I'm pleased what I've told you has helped. It was all by chance I had those conversations.'

She got up, went over to the open windows and stepped

out onto the balcony. The sun was shining as Tweed joined her. Beyond the promenade below them the two triangular peaks on the far side of the lake glittered in the sunlight. The lake was a magnificent cobalt blue.

'It's so beautiful and peaceful,' Paula remarked. 'Not a place for horrific events to take place.'

'The district where Black Jack was found is called Paradiso.'

'What a diabolical irony.'

There was a tap on the door and Newman entered. He wore a cheerful check suit and greeted them with a grin as he joined them on the balcony. He took a deep breath as he stared at the view.

'It really is glorious,' he enthused. He glanced at Paula's solemn expression. 'Relax and enjoy. It's paradise.'

'I've just told her that,' Tweed said grimly.

He took her by the arm, led her back into the suite. Then he sat her down in an armchair. She looked up gratefully. Her voice was shaky when she spoke.

'I'm feeling jittery again. Lord knows why.'

'The dream . . .'

'Forget about it. We won't refer to it again. I'm sure I was just hallucinating.'

'Maybe not. I sat up in the night working on the imprint of the word which had been crossed out. On the third sheet. By persistence and patience I brought it up clearly.' He took out the pad, turned to the third sheet, showed it to her. She stared down at it, hardly able to believe her eyes.

Airolo.

36

They were having a late lunch at Sayonara, a bar with a good restaurant. Tweed had chosen the place carefully – in the middle of Lugano it was close to the funicular which transported passengers up to the rail station. Newman had already bought four return tickets to Chiasso.

'The service and food are excellent here,' Tweed remarked as he rapidly consumed paella, clearing his plate before anyone else.

Paula sat next to Tweed, who faced Newman and Marler. At this late hour the restaurant was quiet. Tweed had planned their departure from the Splendide Royal carefully. First, Newman had taken a taxi by himself into Lugano, where he had hired a people carrier. Driving it back along the lakeside road he had parked it in the nearby street not far from where Black Jack's body had been found at the foot of the funicular. Police tape still cordoned off the area, uniformed police were taking more photographs. He walked back to the hotel.

'The people carrier is parked,' he informed Tweed in his suite.

'People carrier, my foot,' Tweed had protested. 'What you have hired is a minibus. People carrier is a stupid phrase. All cars, small, medium and large, carry people . . .'

In midafternoon they had left the hotel one by one on foot, strolling along the promenade until they arrived in

Lugano. None of the four had encountered any Arbogasts when leaving the hotel.

They had plenty of time to eat their meal. Paula, feeling tense, was the last to finish. She drank some more of her single glass of Chardonnay, spoke softly even though no one was near them.

'What do you think is going to happen at Chiasso?' she mused.

'No idea,' Tweed replied. 'Going into breakfast, as you know, I bumped into Roman. He seemed relaxed and confident.'

'Would he be like that if there is poison gas in the oxygen cylinders? And if there is where would they be going to?'

'Middle East. To Muslim fundamentalists. They'd pay a huge fortune to get their hands on poison gas. I imagine after leaving Chiasso they'd travel in freight cars to Milan, then on to the port of Genoa. There they could be put aboard a ship.'

'Roman,' Newman commented, 'would be relaxed and confident if you pointed a gun at him. One very tough guy.'

'But would he take the risk?' Tweed pondered. 'He's built up ACTIL into a world conglomerate without anyone accusing him of unsavoury dealing. We'll soon know. Beck told me he will be there with a team of specialists to check every cylinder. Meantime, if we can, I don't want Roman to know we'll be travelling aboard the same train . . .'

It all happened quickly. Tweed checked his watch, said it was time to leave. Turning right when they walked out of the bar they entered a large empty square surrounded with old well-preserved buildings, the 'Mayfair' of Lugano. The ground was *pavé*, the Italian version of cobbles but much smoother to walk on. It was dark now but the square was illuminated by lanterns suspended from wall brackets.

The small funicular had just arrived after its descent

364

from the station a distance above them. As they entered a car the automatic doors closed and the funicular began moving up its steep climb, passing through a short tunnel. Newman was wearing an old well-used overcoat, had put on tinted glasses and a beret.

The moment she left the restaurant Paula was aware of the penetrating icy chill. In the funicular she sat down, still clutching her fur coat round her neck. Again it had all been planned in advance by Tweed. The funicular jerked gently to a halt, the doors opened and Newman stepped out, disappeared. Paula waited until Tweed, followed slowly by Marler, had left the car before she alighted and climbed the steps up to the platform. At that moment a limo arrived, pulled up close to where Newman had parked their minibus.

Roman stepped out, muffled in a fur coat and wearing a Russian-style fur hat. He was followed by Sophie and then Broden. No Marienetta. From her hiding place behind an iron pillar Paula decided Marienetta had thought it was a boring exercise – or was disassociating herself from some lethal discovery.

The train glided in. The three Arbogasts entered the front first-class coach. Newman appeared, hardly recognizable. He beckoned for them to board the second coach. Paula sat in a window seat when the train moved on. It was a two-minute stop. Tweed sat in the window seat facing her while Marler, in his usual way, occupied a seat at the rear as Newman sat in a seat on the opposite side of the aisle to Paula. The upper regions of Lugano passed swiftly and they were in the wilds.

'Until we get close to Chiasso,' Tweed said, his manner relaxed, 'this is a scenic trip by daylight – and even by night. If you go and sit by Bob you'll soon see the summit of Monte San Salvatore.'

She was studying a map of the area picked up in the hotel. She looked across at Tweed.

'Lake Lugano is like an octopus with tentacles spreading out in all directions.'

'A good simile,' he agreed.

Staring out of the window she saw, as the train swung round a curve, the lights of Lugano, chains of lights as bright as diamonds coiling high up what she imagined must be Monte Bré. She crossed over to sit in the seat opposite Newman, who was pointing upwards. An immense limestone crag was soaring up, reminding her of the approach to the Gotthard tunnel, but here she could see the summit, a red beacon light flashing on and off to warn aircraft. Tweed called out for her to come back to her original seat.

She moved back, fascinated by the moon glowing on the surface of the lake which was the colour of mercury. She felt she could almost reach out and touch it. She sighed with pleasure. It seemed unreal, like a beautiful dream.

'It's so romantic,' she commented.

'From this point on for a while,' Tweed explained, 'the rail track runs alongside the lake.' He checked his watch. 'And soon we cross the lake over a large road-and-rail bridge. When we do look up the lake. In the distance you'll see Monte Bré again.'

He had just spoken when the train swung left onto the long bridge. She looked straight up the lake and saw a long way off the glittering lights of Monte Bré sprawling up towards its summit. She was entranced. And she had slipped off her coat, savouring the warmth inside the train. Too soon for her the train swung right off the bridge onto the mainland and the view was gone.

'From here on,' Tweed warned, 'it gets rather dull. And don't expect much – if anything – from Chiasso. It's just a rail junction, a big one.'

She did have a view of the lake through the windows on Newman's side for a while. Then it was gone. As if it had come out for their benefit, the moonlight vanished, blotted out by clouds. She settled back in her seat, calling out to Tweed.

'If there's trouble, at Chiasso, I imagine Beck can handle it.'

'Told me apart from the specialists he had half the local police force sent there. Better put on your coat. We'll be pulling in shortly. Train's slowing down.'

She stared out of the window as it slowed to a halt. The station sign announced CHIASSO. She thought she had never seen such a dreary deserted platform. She wondered why she had, after her heaven-like experience, suddenly felt nervous.

37

Wandering along the platform, which seemed to go on for ever, Paula thought she had never seen a more dreary and depressing station. Even the roof above her was a dirty grey and she soon realized the vast junction was hunched inside a gulley. On either side beyond the station, boring low hills rose up, their slopes a tangle of miserable undergrowth and small stunted trees. A short distance behind her Newman strolled, taking in everything.

She had not seen a single uniformed railwayman until the platform curved for quite a distance. Now she saw cylinders laid out, men in white coats, wearing masks, bending over the cylinders. One held what looked like a glass pipette which he held in one hand while with the other he turned a tap. There was a hissing noise as the contents were released into the pipette he had inserted. He quickly turned off the tap, held up the pipette to check its contents.

Roman, in his fur coat, hands inside his pockets, looked on. She expected him to be furious since the huge number of cylinders piled in crates showed they were checking every one. Instead Roman sounded amused.

'Again clear as crystal,' he remarked. He turned and smiled at Paula. 'If the contents changed colour that would indicate something else.'

'Poison gas,' snapped Broden, who stood near him. 'Anyone with sense would stop fooling around now, let the consignment proceed.'

'The Swiss are very precise,' Roman replied as Beck appeared out of nowhere. 'Very precise,' he repeated, staring at Beck. 'Which is why they take so long to make a cuckoo clock.'

'We check all suspect goods,' Beck answered.

'So why are these oxygen cylinders suspect?' Roman enquired with a note of sarcasm. 'Because of a rumour spread by one of my competitors. Haven't you worked that out yet? Another rumour tells me you are the Chief of Federal Police.'

'Which I happen to be. These oxygen cylinders are supposed to be en route to Cairo.'

'*Supposed* to be?' Roman flew into a rage, moved closer to Beck. 'Now listen to me, because obviously you are plain ignorant when it comes to international trade. The Egyptians need these for their hospitals. The stuff they manufacture is not pure. Typical of Arabs, but they have now seen the light of day. So you understand now, Mr Chief of Federal Police?'

His tirade over, Roman stepped back, as though close contact with Beck was obnoxious. He pushed up his coat sleeve to check his watch. Then he started again.

'With your Swiss precision, Mr Beck, is it possible to calculate how much longer this farce will take?'

'About half an hour, maybe a few minutes longer.'

Beck's expression was blank as he stared back at Roman. He'd shown no reaction to Roman's insults, to his bullying manner. While this was going on the specialists had checked another three cylinders, which were then carried by staff and placed very carefully in the waiting crate, which was almost stacked full. Between each cylinder, which they had wrapped in some kind of paper which looked like polystyrene, they packed a large quantity of straw.

It seemed to Paula the Swiss team was proceeding very efficiently. Beyond the roof it had started to rain, not the first shower recently to judge by the gleaming metal of various goods wagons parked on another line. At least half an hour, she thought, in this dump. She began to walk further along the curving platform, leaving the checking exercise behind. Then she spotted Sophie huddled on the only seat in sight. Stacked at the end of the seat were three large suitcases.

'Hello, Sophie,' she said, easing herself onto the damp seat. 'Might just as well be outside in the rain.'

'The roof leaks but this is the only seat,' Sophie grumbled.

She was dressed to repel the wet in a heavy rainproof coat. On her head she wore a large rainproof hat with a wide brim. She showed no pleasure at Paula's arrival. In one of her moods, Paula decided. She nudged her and tried to cheer her up.

'At least you're dressed for this weather, which is more than I am.'

'Don't touch me. I don't like people touching me. And no one asked you to sit here.'

'You did say this was the only seat . . .'

'No, I didn't. I suppose because you can't see another one you think this is the only seat. It is,' she added maliciously and giggled.

'Why did you bother to come here? Roman is watching them.'

'Because I am a scientist. I supervised the filling of those cylinders in London – after checking the quality. When I got off the train I could see immediately they were checking properly. Father thinks that by standing over them they will get on with the job. Good luck to him.'

'I haven't seen Marienetta.'

'Hardly surprising. She said she wasn't coming and went up to her room. Which probably means she'll turn up on the next train. She's such a liar. Can't believe one word she says.'

371

A drop of water fell on the brim of Sophie's unusual hat. By now Paula had wrapped a scarf over her own head. Sophie stood up, took off the hat, shook it so water splashed on Paula. Sophie's ponytail was tucked well down inside the collar of her raincoat. She put on the hat, sat down again heavily.

'You two seem to love each other,' Paula remarked with a hint of amusement.

'We don't. We never have. Never will.'

Paula heard an engine trundling on the line behind them. It continued a short distance and then there was a loud *clang* which made her jump. She looked in that direction but the angle of the curve now hid the engine from view.

'What on earth was that?' she asked.

'They're shunting freight cars behind us, forming a convoy.'

'Wish they'd blow a whistle first.'

'You get used to it. This really is fun,' she grouched.

Paula was inclined to agree with her. More light rain was falling, like a watery veil. It was very quiet where they sat together – apart from the *clang* she had just heard. I think this is one of the loneliest places in the world, Paula was deciding. And to think Lugano and the lake with the lights on Monte Bré was only thirty minutes north of them.

She glanced to her right and a dozen yards away saw Newman standing by one of the ugly iron pillars supporting the roof. He had just finished a cigarette, stubbed it, placed it in a litter basket. He gave her the thumb's-up sign.

'The stupid Swiss,' Sophie began to rave. 'Do they really think we'd export poison gas to the Middle East? The oxygen is costing them a fortune. I negotiated the deal with a real haggle over the phone. I ended up by telling him that if he wouldn't accept our price he could buy inferior material elsewhere, then slammed down the phone. He was back on the line within ten minutes, accepting my price. I made the thug wire the money in advance.'

This was a side to Sophie Paula hadn't seen before. She was an expert and tough negotiator. She decided to risk asking a dangerous question.

'If Roman retires I suppose one of you – either yourself or Marienetta – will take over running the whole of ACTIL.'

'It is between the two of us,' Sophie said promptly. 'So Marienetta flatters him which, I think, is a mistake. I just do my job.'

She took off the glove of her right hand to adjust the collar of her raincoat. Paula noticed on the third finger of her right hand she wore a ring with a large ruby. Don't think I've seen that before, she said to herself. She stood up, feeling she'd had enough of Sophie. Where she had sat in the middle of the seat there was a dry patch.

'I'm going for a stroll,' she said. 'Sitting too long makes me restless.'

'I'm bored stiff,' Sophie said, yawned. 'I'm going to have a nap.'

A strong breeze was blowing up from the north as Sophie shut her eyes, huddled deeper inside her heavy raincoat. Paula pulled up her own collar as she crossed over the platform, which swept round in a wide curve. Ahead of her a familiar figure was mooching along, his back to her. Russell Straub.

What on earth was he doing in Chiasso? It was as though he couldn't stay away from the Arbogasts. What was the link? A candidate for the next President of the USA and a powerful and successful businessman based in London? Didn't make sense.

In the distance behind her she caught the faint sound of the shunting engine returning with another large goods wagon. There must be a loop line the engine could turn on to so it would be behind the next wagon. How mind-killing it must be for the staff who worked here. Some maybe posted here for all their working lives.

She shivered. The fresh breeze was bitter, penetrating her coat. She waved her arms, slapped her hands round her body. Didn't seem to make any difference. At least it was better than sitting still on that seat with miserable Sophie.

However, she had learned something. If Roman retired one day control of the giant conglomerate would pass to Marienetta or Sophie. Which one would he choose? Paula had no idea. She also doubted whether Roman had any intention of retiring for years. If ever.

As she approached the convoy of wagons she saw they were linked together. Obviously at some stage, when a fresh wagon had been shunted to join the convoy, a member of staff must come along and link the latest arrival. Nearing the end of the convoy she folded her arms to try and keep in the warmth still left in her body. She stopped a distance away, standing near the edge of the platform. It was something to watch.

The knuckles with a hard end pressed against the middle of her spine, shoved with great force. She flew forward, unfolding her arms to have the use of her gloved hands. Then she landed on the track in the most awkward position, legs and knees perched on the platform, the rest of her body over the drop below her thighs. Her gloved hands had hammered down on stones between rails which stunned her. She tried to heave herself back but her hands felt like blocks of ice, wouldn't give her the leverage she so desperately needed. The upper part of her body seemed anchored to the platform, she couldn't move it. Her head was spinning with shock.

She made herself look towards her right, saw with horror what was coming. The shunted wagon was moving steadily towards her. She realized her neck was lying across the inner rail nearest the platform. She saw the huge nearside wheel of the oncoming coach rotating as it advanced closer and closer to her neck. Oh God! It was going to decapitate her. The revolving wheel gleamed with wetness. She could even see a tiny defect in the rim of the relentlessly advancing wheel. She made a supreme effort to lift herself with her hands. No strength at all left. Her arms ached. She had never before felt so paralysed with fear as the remorseless wheel rolled forwards within yards of her.

38

Strong hands grasped her round the chest, heaved her up and swung her in the same motion to the left – to avoid the projection of the front of the wagon. Newman was kneeling on the brink of the platform, the only way he could have reached her. She came up like a cork out of a bottle as he stood, hauled her back against himself. There was a deafening *clang* as the buffers of the newly arrived wagon slammed into the waiting convoy.

Newman lifted her off her feet, carried her towards the only seat on the platform. As he conducted this manoeuvre an American voice began bawling at the top of its bellow.

'*Emergency! Emergency! Emergency . . .!*'

Paula had her eyes open, saw Russell Straub standing a mere few feet from where the wagons had collided. He had his hands cupped round his mouth as he repeated his frantic call.

'Do shut up!' Newman growled.

As they neared the seat Paula saw Sophie open her eyes and blink. She also saw a dry patch of seat as though Sophie had moved her position. While asleep? Newman's request to Sophie was not polite.

'Get off that damned seat. It's needed for Paula. So shift, damn you.'

It worked. Sophie was so indignant she jumped up and walked off, her face like thunder. Newman lowered Paula gently onto the seat. He looked appalled and so guilty.

377

Resting her back against the seat Paula stretched out her legs one at a time. They worked normally. She performed the same exercise with both arms. Same thankful result.

'Are you OK?' Newman asked hoarsely.

'I'll survive,' she said softly. Her throat was so dry.

'God, I'm so sorry,' Newman gasped out. 'I was having trouble lighting a cigarette. The wind. Had my back turned towards you. Supposed to guard you, protect you. What a lousy job I made of that. I am *so* sorry.'

'Don't be silly,' she croaked. 'You did the job. Somebody pushed me over the edge.'

'*Who?*' His expression changed to overpowering rage. If she had been able to give him a name she felt he would without a second thought have killed them.

'No idea. I'm terribly thirsty. Makes it difficult to talk.'

By now a flock of uniformed officials had rushed down to the seat, some with white coats, holding masks in their hands. A guard, who had heard her, reached into his back pocket and produced a flask.

'What's in that?' Newman snapped. 'She needs water.'

'This is water.' The guard had a kindly face, had taken out a folded clean handkerchief, used it to carefully wipe the neck of the flask, handed it to Newman.

'Now sip,' Newman urged her. 'Go on sipping. Otherwise you may choke.'

Further back along the platform, a few minutes earlier, an express from Lugano, bound for Milan, had pulled up alongside the opposite side. Tweed, who had not heard Straub's shouts, was standing by the open door of the long train. A few passengers left the express and then Marienetta stepped out.

'Welcome to Chiasso,' Tweed greeted her ironically.

'It's good to see you.' She threw both arms round him and hugged tightly. 'I wasn't coming, then I changed my

378

mind. Thought I'd better make sure Roman was doing his job properly.' She was smiling warmly as she released him. 'How much poison gas have they discovered?'

'None. Absolutely none.'

'Stupid Swiss. Oh dear!' She covered her mouth as Beck ran up to them.

'Come with me,' he said urgently. 'Paula's nearly had a most terrible accident. She's quite all right,' he added quickly as he saw Tweed's expression.

They hurried down the platform, past where the specialists had just finished their check, were taking off their white coats. Other railway men were carrying crates of cylinders to forklift trucks. They hurried on with Tweed in the lead, legs moving like pistons. Newman was waving people away from the seat to stop them crowding in. Paula was on her feet with Newman by her side. She was walking up and down, testing her legs, swinging her arms.

'I've had enough now,' she said and sat down on the seat as Tweed arrived.

'Are you all right?' he asked, bending down, anxiety written all over his face. 'I heard you had an accident.'

'Accident be damned!' she flared up. She had drunk all the water from the guard's flask and her voice was normal. 'I was standing on the edge of the platform watching the shunting over there. Somebody came up behind me and shoved me over the edge. Not far up the line a wagon was being shunted. I couldn't move. The wagon's wheel would have sliced me in two across the neck. Bob rescued me just in time.'

'Show me the exact spot,' Beck commanded.

Paula started to get up but Newman pressed her down again, his hand on her shoulder. He told Beck he would show him. When he had looked, Beck returned, striding like a general marshalling his troops. He held his identification under the guard's nose.

'No one leaves aboard that express until I've walked through it and checked every passenger.'

The guard rushed off and Beck noticed Russell Straub standing a short distance away. He walked up to him.

'Where were you when this murder attempt happened?'

'You know who I am,' Straub said stiffly.

'And you know who I am,' Beck retorted, holding his identification under the Vice-President's nose. 'So where were you?'

'Guess I was quite a way down this curving platform!'

'On your own? Usually Ed Danvers is with you. Body-guard.'

'Sure, on my own,' Straub said breezily. 'Thinking out the next move in my campaign back in the States.'

'That's right,' the voice of Danvers called out. He stood behind several railway officials. 'Likes to be by himself when he's working politics. Before you ask me, I was up by the platform where the express came in.'

'If it's all right by Mr Beck, you can both just go away,' said Newman.

As they departed Marienetta sat on the seat next to Paula. One hand was clutching the collar of her fur coat closer to her neck. The other hand gently took hold of Paula's and she lowered her voice.

'Are we really feeling a bit better after your ghastly ordeal?'

'Much better, thank you.'

'Do you know where Sophie was when this happened?'

Paula thought the question very strange. She looked round at Marienetta, whose expression was serious. Why be so concerned about Sophie?

'When I got up from here I left her on this seat. She said she was going to have a nap.'

'I see.'

'Time we left this dump,' Roman's voice growled. 'This has been a farce. And there's a train just come in from

Lugano. Going back there soon. We should be aboard it.' He was standing behind Ed Danvers. He tapped Marienetta on the shoulder. 'Come on. Let's get going.'

Tweed, with Paula and Newman, boarded the same train. Seeing the Arbogasts again choose the front coach they entered the second coach to be on their own. Paula was relieved as she sank into a window seat with Newman by her side. She had had enough of the Arbogasts, more than enough of Chiasso which she never wanted to see again.

When the train crossed the bridge over the lake she stared at the empty seat opposite. The glitter of Lugano no longer had any appeal to her. Sitting across the aisle, Tweed noticed, understood her lack of interest. At that moment the connecting door from the front coach opened and Marienetta appeared. Newman shook his head at her. She nodded, smiled, disappeared.

'I can't imagine who tried to shove me under that wheel,' Paula said suddenly.

'There's a limited cast of suspects,' Newman told her. 'You want some dinner when we get back?'

'I just want bottles of mineral water and bed.'

'Then that's what the lady will get.'

'Sorry if I've been unsociable since we left Chiasso. I do feel like talking now.'

'In that case,' Tweed called across, 'maybe you can tell me exactly where you found that hotel pad with Chiasso and Airolo written in it.'

'It was just in the open, near the driver's door of my car. I saw it easily after I'd fired one shot at the ghost in the mist, whoever it was. Why?'

'Because it strikes me now you were intended to see it and to pick it up. *It* is a very good planner. Which gives me food for thought.'

'What thought is that?' she enquired.

'Still turning it over in my mind.'

'Cryptic devil,' she chaffed him. Which made Tweed realize she was recovering from her state of shock. He was relieved. He looked across the aisle a few minutes later and Paula's head was resting on Newman's shoulder, eyes closed. She had fallen fast asleep.

Arriving in Lugano, Newman had to wake her. They left the coach cautiously, with Tweed the first one out, standing on the platform. He gestured for them to follow him. It was pitch dark in the car park but in the distance they could see Roman climbing inside a chauffeur-driven stretch limo. Sophie followed him, carrying all her suitcases herself, then Marienetta.

'Sophie must be very strong,' Paula observed. 'And independent.'

They watched as Russell Straub, followed by Danvers, entered the limo. Its red lights were disappearing down the hill towards the hotel when Tweed made his remark.

'I find it very curious the way Straub always travels with the Arbogasts. Maybe that's the key.'

Paula was too tired to ask him what he meant as they boarded their parked minibus. She again told Tweed that when they got to the hotel she wanted to go straight up to bed with plenty of bottles of mineral water.

When they arrived and Tweed, with Newman, escorted her to her room she was very relieved when he made his suggestion.

'If you don't mind I'm going to draw up a roster so there's always one of us sleeping on that couch through the night.'

'I'd welcome it. That way I'm sure to get a good long sleep.'

Pete Nield, who wasn't hungry, volunteered to act as guard for the first few hours. He waited on the balcony while she took a quick shower, put on her pyjamas and dived under the sheets. She was only half-asleep for a while. In her mind faces flitted vividly. Roman, looking like the ferocious picture Marienetta had painted of him in London; Sophie, on the seat at Chiasso, the seat which had a dry patch when she returned from her ordeal; Marienetta, cat's eyes glowing as she took hold of Paula's hand on the same seat; Straub, who had said he had been walking further down the platform; Danvers, grim and distant as he stood behind the guard. Normal? Abnormal? They all looked abnormal. Her mind closed down. She fell into a very deep sleep.

After dinner Tweed assembled his team in his suite. He told Harry Butler to tell Nield later what he had said when Newman took over the duty of guarding Paula.

'Who is going to tell Paula?' Marler enquired.

'No one. That's an order.' He looked round at Newman, Butler and Marler. 'Before I asked you to come here I slipped out to phone Monica from a public box I'd noticed. She gave me some interesting information which just about completes the family tree of the Arbogasts she's been building up so very assiduously. Not an easy task. She's had to rely on the network of contacts she's built up over the years. But it still required a lot of persuasion. The data is supposed to be unavailable except to family members.'

'Good for Monica,' said Butler. 'She's a treasure.'

'We know,' Tweed continued, 'that Roman's father had a brother, Vicenzo, who emigrated to the States, changed his name to Vincent. We also know there was another brother, Mario, who also emigrated to America, got married, produced a family. His son, Aldo, later also produced a family – a son and a daughter. We have now reached Sophie's generation. Monica hopes soon to have their names. I find this development highly significant.'

'Why?' asked Marler.

'Because we are tracking a *monster*. A very clever one. But we must always be on our guard. I have puzzled greatly over the motive for these ghastly murders. I think I have it now. This grim business is all about power. Enormous *power*. So ponder what I have said.'

'Why not tell all this to Paula?' Marler insisted.

'First, because she has suffered terrible ordeals. Second, because I believe she now knows the truth. Which is why we are all going to Airolo tomorrow.'

'Airolo?' Marler sounded taken aback. 'That's way back from here – almost at the Gotthard.'

'When we arrived back this evening I went to the night clerk to ask him something. As you know, I read documents upside down. Lying on the counter, which he removed but not before I'd scanned it, was a large bill for the Arbogasts, including breakfast tomorrow. They are slipping away secretly.'

'Secretly?' queried Marler. 'They've probably bought their train tickets.'

'They haven't. I called Beck, who still has his man at the ticket office at Lugano station. No such tickets have been bought.'

'Maybe Roman's leaving it until the morning,' Marler persisted.

'No, he wouldn't. He's a first-rate organizer. He'd have done so by now if they were travelling by express train.'

'Then how are they leaving?'

'When I returned from making my phone call to Beck after dinner I saw in the drive that stretch limo still parked. Mechanics were checking it. This time they will drive a long distance, so we will do the same in the minibus.'

'Where the hell do you think they're going to?' Marler asked.

'To Airolo.'

'You know that?'

'I am relying on Paula's instincts, which have proved so

384

accurate in the past. She has been haunted by those two twin towers on the mountain behind Airolo. Then there is the pad she found when she was leaving that weird old house by the lake. Which, I am sure, was left for her to find. The pad marked with Chiasso, where she was nearly killed. Then a crude effort to cross out a word the killer knew I would decipher. Airolo, gentlemen.'

'What could be there in that dump?' Butler wondered.

'The key to everything. The reason why two of the most powerful men in the world have looked more and more worried.'

'Roman Arbogast and Russell Straub?' Marler suggested.

'Exactly. So tomorrow we'll use the same devious method we used today to leave the hotel one by one. I'll get Newman to park the minibus, fully tanked up, in the same place where he parked it before.'

'Thanks a lot,' said Newman, who had remained silent up to now. 'The police are probably still prowling round where Black Jack's body was found at the foot of the funicular. I dodged them before. It could be more tricky this time.'

'You'll manage,' Tweed assured him.

'Again, thanks a lot. What time do you think the Arbogasts are moving off?'

'Midafternoon, I'd guess. I've just remembered. Tomorrow's lunch was on that Arbogast bill.'

'You do realize,' Newman said grimly, 'this could be yet another trap. Like Chiasso?'

'I do. And I sense we are approaching the final climax. It is time the trap sprang back in their faces.'

39

It was morning. Tweed had taken over the last phase of guarding Paula. He stretched, aching from lying on the couch. He realized Paula was still fast asleep. He checked his watch. 9.30 a.m. She had slept solidly through the night.

He stood up and light percolated through the drawn curtains. Enough light for him to see someone had silently slipped an envelope under the door. He hadn't even heard them doing it. A hotel envelope with the flap tucked in. He opened it and stared at the sheet of hotel paper inside. One word had been written on the sheet. *Airolo*.

He tucked the sheet back inside the envelope and the envelope inside the pocket of his jacket neatly folded on a chair. So it was a trap. Newman had been right. Putting on his shoes, he donned the jacket, looked at himself in a mirror while he buttoned up his shirt collar, used a comb to tidy up his hair.

'Time to wake up,' he said quietly as he shook her shoulder.

'What time is it?' She had woken instantly. He told her. She covered a yawn with her hand. 'Is that all right? I've had the most marvellous sleep. Hand me that dressing gown.'

She had a quick shower, dressed in the bathroom, came running back into the room. Her normal colour, her briskness, was back. She drank more water while he explained the plan. Her reaction was positive, almost eager.

'Airolo! Thank heavens. I've felt we should go there for some time. It fits in somewhere. I know it does. Good job we brought the minimum of luggage. I've only one case to smuggle out to where Bob's parking the minibus. What about the bill? The Swiss regard it as a major crime not to pay a hotel bill.'

'I booked all the rooms for a week,' Tweed told her. 'I'll wait my chance to pay what we've eaten so far when the desk is quiet. I'll tell the clerk we'll be coming back to use the rooms for the rest of the time we've paid for them. You looked excited.'

'I am. I want to lay the ghost of Airolo which has been nagging at me. Lord, that was a wonderful sleep. I'm hungry.'

They met Newman in the deserted hall. He was dressed to go out and looked cheerful at the prospect of action.

'I'm on my way to fill up the tank,' he told Tweed. 'Marler's also had a huge breakfast and will join me shortly. He has volunteered to stay at the hotel so he can warn me on his mobile when the Arbogasts leave. I'll bring the minibus back, park it round the corner, ready to take the rest of you to the Sayonara for lunch.'

'I'd love to have time to look at the shops in the Piazza Cioccaro at the foot of the station funicular,' Paula pleaded.

'No,' Newman said. He gave her a look. 'I mean it. From now on you stay with the team. Enjoy your breakfast . . .'

Later, they had another leisurely meal in the restaurant in the centre of Lugano. The sun was shining, Paula enjoyed her lunch, but now she couldn't wait to get out of Lugano. It was midafternoon when Marler called to say *they* had left, that he was on his way to join them.

Marler arrived on a motorcycle. Tweed, standing outside, raised an eyebrow. It was a powerful machine and he watched as Newman helped Marler to put it aboard the minibus, storing it at the back.

'What's the idea?' he asked Marler.

'May come in useful. It's rough country outside Airolo. You have the same model back in London, don't you?'

'Yes. Now let's get moving.'

Tweed only used his motorcycle in London when he left his flat very early – and returned late in the evening, to avoid the gridlock traffic. He sat at the front next to Newman who took the wheel. Behind Newman sat Paula with Marler alongside her. Butler and Nield were in the back. They moved north out of Lugano quickly. Paula, with a map on her lap, was navigator.

Travelling on the motorway, they bypassed castle-encircled Bellinzona. It wasn't long before the great ascent towards the Bernese Oberland began. Looking out of the window Paula saw the barren slopes on either side which reminded her of a wilderness. No more palm trees, no exotic lake. She wasn't sorry to leave it all behind. What lay ahead was what counted. She suddenly recalled the faces she'd seen floating in her mind before she'd fallen asleep. One had been missing.

Sam Snyder.

It was getting dark now, which caused the wilderness to seem even grimmer, desert-like. They climbed higher and higher as night fell. The only illumination was Newman's headlights. She called out to Tweed.

'I expect you've booked rooms at a hotel for us?'

'I have not. Airolo has only two hotels, the Supremazia and the Grandezza. We don't know which one the Arbogasts will stay at and I want to be in the other one.'

'Sounds five-starrish. Supremazia means Supremacy, Grandezza is Grandeur.'

'I wouldn't expect much in Airolo,' Tweed warned her.

'You seem so confident the Arbogasts are heading for Airolo,' Marler remarked.

'I am.' Tweed took out the sheet of paper which had been slipped under Paula's bedroom door in the night. 'Written in the same block letters as those two places on the hotel pad you picked up when you were having fun in the old dark house.'

'What does it mean?' Paula asked.

'It means the killer wants us to go there. So be it.'

His words created a silence inside the minibus which lasted a long time. Now the road was really climbing. They came to a point where the motorway suddenly started to descend round a diabolical hairpin bend. From the top they could look down on the road immediately below. That was when Newman told them.

'Red lights ahead. A very big black stretch limo. Somebody hand me a pair of night glasses. Give Paula the second pair. When we come to another twister I'll stop. Then we should be able to look down on the limo, see who's inside . . .'

Newman had slowed down to avoid catching up with the vehicle ahead of them. Tweed rested binoculars in his lap, gave the other pair to Paula. It wasn't long before they came to another twister. Newman stopped, picked up the binoculars at the same time as Paula pressed them to her eyes. The hairpin was so dangerous the limo was moving slowly. Through their lenses they both scanned the interior of the crawling limo.

'You were right,' Newman told Tweed. 'Your gamble paid off. Marienetta is driving with Roman next to her. Behind them Sophie is sitting next to Snyder, staring away from him – typical. They probably haven't exchanged a word.'

'And in the back,' Paula called out, 'are Russell Straub with Ed Danvers next to him. I saw them clearly.'

'Slow down,' Tweed ordered. 'We don't want to catch them up. But don't lose them.'

'Catch-22,' said Newman. 'I lose either way.'

'When we reach Airolo,' Tweed continued, 'I want to see which hotel they choose – without them seeing us.'

'Piece of cake,' Newman replied sarcastically. 'Maybe you would like to take over the wheel?'

'How high up is Airolo?' Paula asked to stop an argument.

'Eleven hundred plus metres,' Tweed replied. 'Over three thousand feet.'

'It's getting cold,' she commented.

'So I turn up the heater,' Newman replied. 'And from now on maybe everyone will keep damned quiet.'

The moon had come out, a luminous glow over desolate Airolo. The Arbogasts had chosen to stay at the Supremazia, a hotel a short distance up the main street from the Grandezza. To Paula's amazement several shops were still open, one next to their hotel with motor scooters for sale parked on the pavement. Fascinated, she walked up to them with Marler, sat on one. Marler showed her how to start it, how to control its speed. The owner, small and swarthy, came out and smiled. He told her the price for hiring, for one day, for one week – plus the deposit. She said she'd think about it.

'There are rooms for all of us,' Tweed said as she walked in with Nield. Marler was still inspecting scooters.

'Place is empty,' Tweed went on. 'Out of season.'

'Is there ever one here?' Nield whispered.

The corridors were narrow, the furniture wood which had seen better days. But the proprietor, who looked like the brother of the man who sold scooters, assured them dinner was available when they were hungry. Outside

Paula heard the motorcycle start up briefly, then the engine was cut.

'Took the machine out of the minibus to check it,' Marler said as he entered. 'I've parked it on the cobbles behind the transport. Couldn't be bothered to struggle lifting it inside again. Not much gets stolen here, I'm sure. No one about.'

'*I* am hungry,' Paula informed the proprietor, 'but if I could first see my room?'

She carried her case herself, refusing his offer. She felt she needed exercise. He led her up a narrow twisting staircase, unlocked a door, waved his hand for her to enter. She smiled, said it would do fine and he left. She explored.

Hoisting open the blind, she stared in disbelief. Below, on the opposite side of the dark street, an alley led down at a steep angle, ending in a narrow track leading up onto the mountain slope. It was the same track she had seen, from the train. She sucked in her breath, looking beyond. Higher up the mountain slope she gazed at the massive twin towers linked by a wall. The towers which had haunted her ever since she had first seen them. She shivered. They had the same air of menace, of a threat of doom.

40

Paula woke as pre-dawn light filtered in. Before going to bed she had showered in tepid water and had not closed the shaky blind over her window. Someone had just rattled the handle of her door. She jumped out of bed, still wearing the clothes she had donned after her shower. It was almost as cold inside the room as outside.

It had not been possible for anyone to stay in her tiny room to guard her. Instead she had resorted to her previous tactic, ramming her wedge under the door, tilting a chair under the handle.

Another envelope had been inserted under her door. The envelope was the same type as the Splendide Royal. She tore it open. A blank sheet of the Lugano hotel's writing paper was inside. Nothing on either side. What the devil was going on?

Then she heard the distant sound of a powerful engine fading. Running to the window she saw the minibus climbing the mountain slope towards the twin towers. It had a long way to go before it arrived. She snatched up the binoculars she had brought up to the room, focused them. Four men in the vehicle. She could make out Butler and Nield in the middle row, Newman and Marler in front, Newman behind the wheel. What the devil is going on? she thought again.

*   *   *

It was Tweed who had taken the decision after she had gone to bed, had instructed the four men assembled in his room.

'Paula seems very worried about those two towers half-way up the mountain. In the morning very early, before dawn, I want all of you to go up to them in the minibus. There may just be something there we should know about.'

'Can't see that it's necessary,' Newman had objected.

'It's necessary to set Paula's mind at ease once and for all. She's gone through hell on this trip. Do it.'

Puzzled, Paula sat on her bed. For something to do she took out her .32 Browning, checked the mechanism, then fully loaded it. She had just completed this operation when she heard the powerful *put-put* of a scooter's motor starting up, then speeding off.

Could that be Tweed deciding to join his team? In that case she was left alone in this one-horse town. Well, if it came to it, she'd cope. She walked back to the window, stared out, froze for a moment.

The scooter was already two-thirds of the way down the alley leading to the track up the mountain. The rider was tall, wore a long black coat tucked around the tops of black boots, with a wide-brimmed hat pulled well down over the head.

She returned the Browning to the special pocket, slung her bag over her shoulder, ran to unlock the door. She ran down the tricky staircase. The proprietor, greeting her with a smile, stood behind the reception counter. She waved the envelope in his face.

'Know anything about this?'

'Yes, signorina. Man comes, asks for your room number so he deliver that. I tell him I deliver, write Room 11 on outside. Tall man in black coat, strange hat . . .'

She ran out of the hotel to the shop next door. The shop

was open. Already scooters were standing outside on the pavement. She had a large Swiss banknote in her hand, more than enough to cover a week's hire plus the deposit. She shoved it at him.

'Too much—'

She was already settling herself on the saddle of a scooter, thankful Marler had refreshed her memory as to how to operate it. 'The Italians make the best scooters in the world,' she remembered he had said.

She felt comfortable in the saddle as she started the engine. In her mind she was back in her early teens when she had owned a scooter. She turned down the steep alley surfaced with *pavé*. She sped down the steep descent and it was a bit bumpy but she held her balance. On either side ancient two-storey stone houses hemmed her in. The shop's proprietor must get up early, she was thinking, probably went to bed very early to save electricity. They'd watch the pennies here.

At the opposite end of the alley the track began between two houses. She drove up it and turned right, where it entered a small gully. Looking up she saw no sign of *it*. Must be miles higher up by now. She stopped briefly to shout at the distant minibus.

'Wrong way! You're going the wrong way!'

Her cry echoed back across the mountain slope. The minibus went on climbing, becoming smaller and smaller. No chance they'd ever hear her. She began riding up the gully. Up and up.

She had recalled how to adjust her balance, which was necessary. The track's surface was covered with stone chippings. But it was more than wide enough to manoeuvre a little. She had grabbed her motoring gloves before she fled from her room but it was still bitterly cold. She passed the limestone crag she had seen from the train and rode on to a plateau before the track entered another stretch of gully. She paused, looked back and up.

Dawn was now glowing with the two towers silhouetted against a fantastic variety of colours. Wild pink, rose, orange and red. Just as she had seen the massive towers in her dream.

'Keep moving,' she told herself, 'otherwise you'll lose *it*.'

She roared across the plateau, reduced speed as she entered the second section of gully, which was much steeper. Now she really had to watch her pace. Her scooter bumped and at intervals wiggled. She held her balance. Despite her gloves her hands were aching with gripping the handles so tightly. Where the hell are you? she asked herself. I'm not losing you this time, you fiend.

Back at the hotel Tweed had watched the minibus start out on its long climb. Satisfied, he sat down in his pyjamas and warm dressing gown, drinking coffee from the flask he'd obtained from the proprietor before going up to his room and issuing his instructions.

At that moment he heard a scooter starting up. Rushing to the window he was just in time to see a figure wearing a long black coat and wide-brimmed hat disappearing behind a crag high up along the track up the mountain. Then he saw Paula's scooter, racing down the alley, heading for the entrance to the track.

Cursing because he had put on night clothes, he stripped them off, pulled on clothes without attention to appearance. Before donning his overcoat he checked his 7.65mm Walther, which was already loaded, something he would have chastised a member of his team for taking risks. Slipping it into his hip holster, he pulled on the coat, unlocked the door, scrambled down the stairs.

The proprietor said something to him but Tweed dashed past him outside into the street. To his relief he saw Marler's motorcycle was still standing on its strut. He swung onto the saddle, pressed the starter button, then he was racing down the narrow side alley, turning at the far end onto the track inside the gulch. It was just wide enough to accommodate his machine. He began speeding up the track – knowing Paula must be a long way off by now.

Will I never reach the top? Paula asked herself. Is there a top? She had been ascending the gulch for what seemed for ever. No hint, no view as to where it was leading, but she knew she was high up. The cold was penetrating her gloves, which meant she had to grip the handles more tightly.

When I meet *it* will I have the strength to fight? she worried. She crouched forward as the road surface became bumpier. She had to struggle to keep it balanced upright. Then she blinked. The track was leading up onto a wide shallow dome-shaped plateau. She slowed down, switched off her engine as she observed the signs.

Smooth rock, a scooter thrown carelessly down on its side. No sign of anyone. Then she saw the manhole cover, what it had uncovered when removed. She parked her scooter on its strut, listened, stretched her aching legs several times to bring back strength, mobility. She had the Browning in her hand as she walked to the edge of the large dome, looked down a sheer drop, saw Airolo far to the north like a toy town. She swung round quickly, raising her automatic. She wasn't going to be shoved off the edge – as she had been in Chiasso.

In the far distance she saw the twin towers bathed in sunlight, looking much smaller. Then she heard something she didn't like. The slow moaning boom of a large bell echoing across the mountain slopes. She walked to the manhole cover, bent down to lift it by the handle. God, it was a weight.

Taking cautious steps, she walked to the large hole it had

covered. She risked using her small powerful torch to shine down into the blackness. A wide old iron ladder led down. The treads were rusty and there was only one handrail, on the left. Now she remembered what Tweed had said about long ago mining for ore, a rail system to transport the ore. She listened again. Only a horrific silence.

'Get on with it, girl,' she said to herself.

It was awkward descending backwards. She shoved the torch, the illumination still shining, under her belt. In one hand she gripped the Browning, used the other to grasp the rail. As she descended deeper, away from sunlight, she detected an odour she had smelt before. In Saafeld's morgue in Holland Park back home. In Zeitzler's morgue in Zurich. The odour of formalin. Used to preserve body parts.

41

Before starting her nerve-racking descent she had taken the glove off her right hand, so now she had a firm grip on her Browning. The torch was not a lot of help: she had to use a foot to feel down for the next tread on the ladder. Then, casting a brief glimpse down, the torch illuminated the base of what she realized was a tunnel, with ancient rails closer together than with a modern system. Her foot trod on rock unexpectedly. She had reached the bottom.

She slowly moved the beam of her torch round and up. Yes, it was an old railway tunnel, carved out of rock with an arched roof. To her right the rails ended at a concrete wall covered with mould. It had been sealed off. To her left the rails vanished round a bend. She'd go that way.

It was further to the bend than she had thought. She tried to walk without making a sound but loose stones between the rails rattled. She stepped to the side of the rails, near the rock wall. The odour of formalin was becoming stronger. She raised the angle of the torch and nearly dropped it.

By its beam she was saw on the opposite wall a level shelf of rock, about five feet above the floor. She was looking at a large round glass laboratory jar with a lid and a round knob to lift it. The jar was occupied. Inside she gazed at the head of someone she had never seen, covered with transparent liquid to well above the crown. The head was of a man probably in his fifties, the cheeks sunken and gaunt, the open eyes glazed. Hank Foley, caretaker from Pinedale, Maine, she guessed.

She swivelled the beam to the laboratory jar perched next to it and nearly choked. She knew this one – Adam Holgate, blurred eyes half-closed as though asleep. Clenching her teeth, she moved the beam to the next jar, nearly let out a cry of misery. Abraham Seale's owl-like nose so clear, the open eyes staring at her as though trying to convey a message. Like the previous ones his head had been severed just below the pointed chin.

Knowing what she was going to see in the next jar she again clenched her teeth. Her torch shone straight on Elena Brucan's scarf. It had been missing from her decapitated body perched in the boat by the River Sihl. Then she saw something which was a vile obscenity. Elena's embroidered scarf was neatly coiled below where the head would have rested. How inhuman.

She was moving by reflex now. Her whole body was stiff with revulsion that anyone could do all this. The next jar contained Black Jack's head. His lower lip had slipped open. He looked as though he were leering. She found this almost worse than what she had seen before.

After tucking the Browning inside her belt she took off the glove from her right hand. It was damp with perspiration. She wiped it quickly on her trousers, then grabbed hold of the weapon. That was when she sensed movement behind her. Someone had hidden in one of the alcoves she had passed. She dipped her head to the right – Saafeld had said it was the left side Holgate had been struck a hammerblow. Even so, the blunt end of the axe grazed her head, she stumbled, twisted round, fell backwards. Her right hand had hit the rail and she lost her grip on the automatic.

The torch had also left her grip but hadn't broken. By its illumination she saw the tall figure clad in a black coat, the wide-brimmed hat pulled well down so the face was hidden. Dazed, she still realized her neck was raised up, resting on something smooth. She glanced both sides. She saw a white curved surface enclosing her. She had fallen on to an execution block. The tall black-coated figure stood above her, raised the axe in its right hand. By the illumination of the torch she saw the razor-sharp edge of the blade, poised to slice down on her. It began its downward sweep.

She rolled her whole body over to the left, completed a circle as her body thudded into the tunnel's wall. Her right hand fell on something. The Browning. She grabbed it, aimed, fired point-blank as cold-blooded fury seized her. She was going to kill, kill, *kill*. She kept on pulling the trigger, fired nine times.

Two more shots were fired. Tweed, awkwardly clinging to the ladder, had fired twice. The tall figure in its long black coat stood still as a statue, then collapsed backwards, lay still.

Paula was hauling herself to her feet as Tweed reached the base of the ladder, came to her. He bent over the black-coated figure, checked the carotid pulse, looked up.

'Dead as the dodo.'

'But who is it?'

She could hear the faint sound of a helicopter landing, then feet climbing down the ladder. A man shouted out a command at the top of his voice.

'No one moves or I'll shoot.'

Beck's unmistakable voice. Tweed, still crouched over the prone body, shouted back. Repeated what he said twice.

'You won't be shooting anyone. I'm here with Paula. Shut up.'

Paula picked up the torch, shone it on the corpse Tweed was bent over. He reached out a hand, carefully lifted off the strange hat. The light shone on the face.

Marienetta. Cat's eyes still open. Staring up at Paula with what seemed to be hatred.

Epilogue

STRAUB ANNOUNCES HE WON'T RUN FOR PRESIDENT
'For Health Reasons'
COUSIN MARIENETTA MASS MURDERESS

The screaming headlines in the *Daily Nation* stared up from Tweed's desk. Below was a long story about the headless murders. The by-line was Robert Newman's. In his office at Park Crescent Tweed sat in his swivel chair, looked at all the members of his team. They had flown back from Zürich four days after leaving Airolo.

It was evening and outside in the London streets rain sluiced down. Paula, seated behind her desk, was the first to speak.

'Congratulations, Tweed. You got there in the end, as you always do.'

'That was the most difficult case I've ever tackled,' he admitted. 'But the congratulations are yours – despite truly terrible ordeals *you* solved the case.'

He waited as everyone cheered, gave her an ovation. She looked embarrassed, stared down at her desk top. She spoke softly, feeling she had to say something.

'It was so close – down in that old mining tunnel. The absurd thing is I knew it was her before you pulled back the hat. I'd remembered – rather late in the day – the words I couldn't recall, or who said them. *I like creating museums*. We couldn't understand why the heads were missing. Marienetta had the idea of creating a museum of the dead. It was even worse than that, even madder. Remember, Tweed, before we left the mining tunnel I walked further in, found her workshop with a complete set of sculpture materials. She was going to use the heads in the jars as models for sculpting their heads.'

'Beck also explained to me,' Tweed told them, 'the secret of the execution blocks. He visited the plastics plant at Vevey. Marienetta had a duplicate key to Sophie's private room where Sophie invented the new, very flexible, strong and lightweight plastic. Hidden away he found a metal cast, size of the plastic block in the mining tunnel. Sophie had left instructions. Marienetta mixed the plastic, poured it into the cast, heated it. Bingo, she had an execution block, very strong but easy to carry. He had found two more in the mining tunnel at Airolo.'

'How the devil did she transport the heads?' Nield wondered.

'Beck,' Tweed continued, 'found a Bloomingdales carrier in the tunnel, its interior reinforced with leather. Large enough to take a laboratory jar – with a head inside it and the axe. New clothes were also inside to cover the real contents. He found another similar carrier inside the tunnel.'

'Marienetta must have been the villain who shoved me down onto the line at Chiasso,' Paula puzzled. 'Yet she arrived on that express later.'

'She played the old trick,' Tweed explained. 'At the Splendide Royal she said she wasn't coming, went up to her room. Then she caught a much earlier train, was waiting for you. After she tries to kill you she runs back, boards the express when the doors are opened, walks through several coaches, emerges into my arms as though she's just arrived. Days earlier she plays the same trick – leaving Zürich very early on a train stopping at Airolo.

She's carrying the trophy heads, gets off at Airolo and takes them to start her lovely museum. Catches another stopping train to Lugano.'

'And,' Paula suggested, looking at the newspaper, 'Bob must have had evidence establishing she *was* Straub's cousin.'

'Arriving back in Zürich,' Tweed told her, 'I phoned Roy Buchanan. Armed with a search warrant and a large team, he entered ACTIL's London HQ. Breaking into a steel cabinet, they found Marienetta's birth certificate. Born in America, her father was a brother of Straub's father Vito, her mother English. That made her Russell Straub's first cousin. So that's it. I said power was the motive. So Newman's story makes that point, destroying Straub's ambition for ever. Who would elect to the Oval Office someone with insanity in the family?'

'You think Straub knew what she was doing?'

'I now know he did. Marienetta was the mysterious patient held in the locked room in the Pinedale asylum. The Bryans, who ran the asylum, have surfaced in Ohio, worried when more murders were committed. They've admitted to the FBI that Straub paid the huge bill. While waiting to come home from Zürich I phoned my old friend, Cord Dillon of the CIA. He told me.'

'So that's why Straub was following the Arbogasts round like a lap dog. He was becoming frantic about Marienetta as murder followed murder. He knew his career was on the line. And it was – he's finished politically now. And who was Mannix?'

'Marienetta,' said Tweed. 'Diabolically clever. It was a diversion she hoped would put me on the wrong track. Mannix was nonexistent – created by Marienetta.'

'Why kill Adam Holgate?' asked Butler, who had known him.

'We know Holgate had been caught snooping in the files ACTIL kept. I think Marienetta thought he'd seen her birth certificate which might have blown the case wide open. So she lures him out to Bray and *whop*! She has another head for her museum.'

'It's quite horrible,' Paula exclaimed. 'And she asked me to join her in playing detective.'

'Because she feared you, had to know how close to the truth you were getting.'

'That leaves Seale, Brucan and Black Jack,' Nield remarked.

'Seale was a criminologist. Probably made the mistake of letting slip he suspected her sanity. Same reason for Brucan, so sensitive to the presence of evil. As for Black Jack, she had chosen him to give Paula the map showing the way to the old house by the lake. When Paula evaded the hole into the rats' cellar Marienetta hurried back to eliminate Black Jack, who could have told Paula what had happened. She must have bribed bankrupt Jack.'

'And Hank Foley, the caretaker back in Maine?'

'Like Holgate he was a snoop. We heard that from Millie, the asylum's cleaner. There would be a record with Marienetta's name and treatment for an outbreak of madness. Marienetta couldn't risk him knowing about her, so when she left the asylum – *whop*!'

'I do wish you wouldn't keep using that word,' Paula protested. 'It's so descriptive. My last query is: how did she transport all the heads to Airolo?'

'Don't you remember? She caught an early train, a stopper, I'm sure. She gets off, deposits her treasures in the museum, catches a later train to Lugano which gets there after we've arrived. It all fits.'

'What doesn't fit is that Sam Snyder was sending an earlier account to papers all over the place. Yet it hasn't appeared.'

'That was me.' Newman chuckled. 'Snyder had played so many dirty tricks in the past I thought it was my turn. I wired all the papers and magazines warning them they were about to receive a sensationalist report before the case was solved. Which it wasn't. Their lawyers would order editors to hold off. They were later quite happy with my report.'

'Now I know why I kept feeling jittery,' Paula said. 'It was always after spending time with Marienetta. My subconscious was screaming warning signals. I think I'd better get off home.'

'No, you don't,' Tweed rapped out. 'I've booked a large table at Santorini's on their platform projecting out over the Thames. They assured me they have plenty of champagne. So everyone here on your feet. Including you, Monica. You did build up that vital family tree of the Arbogasts.'

**POCKET
BOOKS**
Rhinoceros
Colin Forbes

'NO ONE IS WHAT THEY SEEM TO BE . . .'

Who is Lisa Trent, mysterious redhead who warns
Tweed of impending catastrophe? Aides to top
statesmen in Washington, London, Paris, Berlin are
murdered by the invisible Mr Blue.

Tweed, Paula and Newman race to East Sussex to
view the second victim, then back to London which,
mercifully, they reach alive. Tweed meets slippery
Gavin Thunder, flamboyant Oskar Vernon, the
devious Mrs France, murderous Delgado. Lisa –
fleeing for her life – keeps reappearing.

Pursuing the secret Elite Club, Tweed and his team
fly to Hamburg, meet a key informant – just before
he too is murdered. The frenetic pursuit leads to
ancient Flensburg on the Danish border, the team
always under attack.

But who is Rhinoceros? Could it be urbane Victor
Rondel, partner in the world's richest bank? The
startling climax erupts without warning on Berg
island – in the Baltic.

ISBN 0 7434 1522 1
PRICE £6.99

POCKET
BOOKS

This book and other **Pocket** titles are available from your book shop or can be ordered direct from the publisher.

0 743 41522 1   **Rhinoceros**   £6.99

Don't miss the new Colin Forbes novel coming out in January 2003!

Please send cheque or postal order for the value of the book, free postage and packing within the UK; OVERSEAS including Republic of Ireland £1 per book.

OR: Please debit this amount from my

VISA/ACCESS/MASTERCARD _____
CARD NO: _____
EXPIRY DATE _____
AMOUNT £ _____
NAME _____
ADDRESS _____
_____
SIGNATURE _____

Send orders to: SIMON & SCHUSTER CASH SALES
PO Box 29, Douglas, Isle of Man, IM99 1BQ
Tel: 01624 836 000, Fax: 01624 670923
www.bookpost.co.uk
Please allow 14 days for delivery. Prices and availability subject to change without notice